I0639747

INFLAME

TOXIC DESIRE
BOOK 1

VICTORIA DAWSON

PAPER HEART PUBLISHING LLC

Copyright © 2023 by Victoria Dawson

Inflame

All rights reserved.

This book contains material protected under International and Federal Copyright Laws. Any unauthorized reprint or use of this material is prohibited. No part of this book may be reproduced or transmitted in any form or by any means, electronic or mechanical, including photocopying, recording, or by an information retrieval system without express written permission from the author.

All characters and storylines are the property of the author. This book is a work of fiction. Names, characters, businesses, places, events and incidents are either the product of the author's imagination or used in a fictitious manner. Any resemblance to actual events or people living or dead is purely coincidental. Any trademarks, product names or named features are assumed to be the property of their respective owners and are used for reference only.

Publisher: Paper Heart Publishing LLC

Cover Designer: K. B. Barrett Designs

Editing: Happily Editing Anns

ISBN (Paperback): 978-1-959364-07-8

ISBN (e-book): 978-1-959364-06-1

AUTHOR NOTE

Inflame is the first book in the *Toxic Desire Duet* that follows the same two main characters throughout both books. It is advised to read the books in order.

If you enjoy a longer story, feel free to start with the *Entice Trilogy* (*Spark of Obsession*, *Rush of Jealousy*, and *Taste of Addiction*), as story elements are present in those three books that assist in character development and world building in this series.

Trigger Warning: This book portrays what it means to be in a toxic relationship. The physical, emotional, and psychological abuse featured in this book may be triggering and not meant for anyone under the age of eighteen.

To those struggling to fit in…
Stop trying.

It is way more fun being the rebel.

1

CLAIRE

I jog up the street, trying not to be any later than I already am. I shift my vision board under my arm to keep from dropping it. I finished an invigorating workout class that I led down by the river with just enough time to get back to the apartment, clean up, and grab my visual.

Springtime in Portland is my favorite time of the year, and this one has been particularly warm for being the end of March. Everything smells fresh again, and the new budding life sprouting from the trees gives me hope in possibilities.

My hair is in pigtail braids, still damp from the shower. My outfit is a simple pastel plaid wrap dress, paired with overpriced flip-flops. From the way they are making my toes hurt, I really don't see the appeal.

I push open the cafe door and find my fellow party planner, Nic Hoffman, watching me from the corner table. I use his job title loosely. He has basically done nothing to help thus far, unless you count the blatant ignoring of my emails or vetoing of my ideas. I actually think he thrives on being difficult.

For the past three months—since Angie and Graham appointed us as maid of honor and best man—I've been doing all of the work. Granted, it has mostly been from a socially safe distance from each other. But I can no longer avoid the roadblock that is Nic Hoffman. I mean, I should have seen it coming. His brother lives by his own set of rules. It must run in the family.

Nic's fingers tap the smooth surface, while his eyes study my every movement. His other hand is curled around a mug of coffee, forgoing the handle completely. My gaze lands on his gold ring. I guess when your brother is running the top jewelry company on the entire West Coast, you get special privileges of custom pieces meant only for you. But something tells me there is more to this ring than simply the family connection. Nic doesn't seem like the man to be random about his style selections, and he definitely isn't the type to follow a fashion trend either.

I hate how he is looking at me. It is borderline rude. Or perhaps it is just my own salty projection of my feelings toward him.

"You're late," he says flatly.

I guess I expected more indifference from him than directness. I want to reply with some snide remark, and normally I would without hesitation. But I still subconsciously think of Nic as my boss, since my name is still floating around the Entice database. My boyfriend, Ethan, insisted on me keeping my employment status as a high-class escort inactive instead of quitting entirely. He rattled off a bunch of stuff about insurance and benefits-package perks that I honestly wasn't really following. When it comes to money and healthy financial decisions, I am clueless. College was paid for by my parents who I think were happy I switched coasts just to alleviate some of the face-to-face guilt they were experiencing when I was in their presence.

"My Zumba at the River class ran over, and I needed to go back to the apartment to shower," I explain, watching him rise from the table.

The gray military-style fabric belt adjusts to allow his jeans to hang low on his hips, but tight enough to keep the sag away from his legs. He has on a solid black T-shirt that I know did not come from one of those three-packs at the department store. His outfit is casual, yet completely put together. He looks amazing.

His blue eyes catch mine and in this instant, I wonder if he knew I was checking him out. I shake my head as if my thoughts will clear from the movement. I need to stay focused on our job that we both agreed to do—together.

"I brought my—"

His hand moves up to halt my words. "What would you like to eat and drink?"

"I, um," I stutter, not really planning on consuming a meal right now. I turn back and glance at the menu that is written on a whiteboard with washable markers. It only takes me a few seconds to realize that there is nothing here for me. I am in the middle of a five-day cleanse that I need to complete prior to the trip. I turn back and look at Nic. Despite his hair being shorter and lighter in color, he looks alarmingly like his brother, Graham.

"My treat," he says, reaching for his wallet.

"Oh, I'm good actually," I answer quickly. I dig out my lip gloss and reapply it.

Nic's eyes narrow. "Not even a drink?"

I look toward the list of beverages and frown. There just isn't anything here for me other than water. "Maybe just a bottled water."

With a single nod, Nic vacates our corner table and goes to wait in line. I sit down opposite of his coffee mug and spread out my trifold board. It bumps into his mug, and I gasp as the liquid sloshes up the interior sides. Why am I so nervous? Nic returns and hands me my drink. He also places a muffin wrapped in plastic wrap onto the table in front of me.

"In case you change your mind," he says simply.

I smile. "Thank you."

"You've been busy," he says, pointing toward my picture board and itinerary planner. I designed, printed, and laminated all of the things we need to get accomplished on the long weekend to Vegas. On the backs of each slip, I glued Velcro so we can discuss the plans and the overview of the trip—while being able to easily rearrange any events to allow for flexibility. Nic glances at his watch. "You know this place closes at ten at night, right?"

"Okay, great, that gives us roughly eleven hours to hash this out," I say blankly. I can't tell whether or not he is trying to be annoying or cute. Either approach unnerves me. I'm here to get the job done, not make jokes. Giving my bestie the best bachelorette trip of her life is my goal. Surely, her future brother-in-law and I can meet in the middle in regard to planning this thing.

Nic takes a sip from his mug and leans back into his

chair as if he doesn't have a care in the world. Must be nice to have such freedom from the mental clutter that I typically have to sift through on a daily basis.

"We could have avoided this meetup if you would have just answered my email, you know?"

"And miss out on this…"—he points to my board and snickers—"special display of resource over-usage." His eyes focus in on my perfectly crafted details. "What is it exactly?"

My eyes narrow. "It's a vision board."

"A vision board," he echoes, looking at it as if he is suddenly interested in everything I have been working on this past month.

"So I took your one suggestion, and—"

"Completely ignored it." He slides into the seat beside me, so neither of us have to look upside down.

I glance over to his look of indifference. I cannot get a read on this man. He lacks the ability to have real conversations—whether it be through text, phone call, or in person. Trust me, I tried. He seriously needs to brush up on his social skills before he dismantles every last thread of patience I have reserved for him. I am being very kind and flexible, since he is my bestie's fiancé's brother.

I take a deep cleansing breath. "You suggested us 'winging it' and I counter-negotiated that we could—"

"A negotiation implies an agreement on *both* sides. I never agreed," he says flatly.

I lift my butt and pivot my chair so I can read his body language better. It feels like we have beaten around some proverbial bush to the point where there no longer is a point.

My eyes narrow, while his remain laser focused on my

every twitch and fidget. No one gets under my skin like this. He is treating me like I am a spectator sport. While I'm not inexperienced when it comes to competitions, it feels like we are knocking heads despite needing to achieve the same goal. If I could do this on my own, I easily would. However, it was made clear when I decided to be the maid of honor that I would be willing to work with the best man on some of the planning.

So, unfortunately, our paths are going to cross a lot since I have my hand in every aspect of this wedding planning extravaganza. Avoidance is not going to be a valid strategy for coping with his mood. Angie lost her mom when she was twelve and then her only sibling when they were eighteen. I'm the closest thing she has to a sister. The least I can do is suck it up and learn to block out his—

I don't even know.

Sure, we have hung out on a few occasions when I roomed with Angie, but this just seems different. It's like he is staring into my soul, without my permission granted. It is borderline violating to feel this stripped down.

Nic is just so different from most men I have encountered, and I have dealt with a lot of different types. Hell, I either am making myself sound super slutty or super old, and I'm not sure which is better.

I need to get this meeting back on track before he railroads me further off course. "Where were we," I mumble, looking over my vision board.

"I think we were about to discuss how you took my suggestion to keep our schedule loose and less rigid," he says, sipping his drink but never removing his eyes from me.

I frown down at my ideas. I have spent a lot of time researching the attractions and events that Las Vegas has to offer to give Angie and Graham the best joint bachelor and bachelorette party that they deserve. Neither of us has ever been there, so naturally I wanted to plan enough touristy activities, while still hitting up a couple off-the-strip places. What has Nic done? Tried to veto nearly everything I proposed to him via email, to the point that I stopped sending him any information. That brings us to this very moment, where I'm still met with a roadblock.

"We are planning this trip together, Nic. Please work with me. Your brother is an extreme control freak, and I promised Angie that all she will need to do is pack her bags and show up at the airport. I would have everything—"

"We," he interrupts.

"Excuse me?"

He motions with his finger between us. "I'm just pointing out that *we* would have everything handled. As in you and me."

"That's what I'm trying to say." I throw my hands up, knocking over my sealed water bottle, sending it rolling off the table.

Nic leans over, catching it midfall. "Can you just calm down?"

I exhale so strongly that the air expelling from my lungs cause the flaps on my board to flutter wildly, some strips barely hanging on. I count to ten, forward and backward. I twirl the loose hair that hangs from the end of my braid around my finger. Does he not realize how aggravating it is for a man to tell a woman to calm down—especially when she is not acting hyper or crazed? How does he not know that he is supposed to save that question in his arsenal and only use it when absolutely necessary? Now is not necessary. He has a sister and a mother who are both lovely. How did he not learn anything from them?

"Let's just verify that we have all of the checklist items marked off our list," I suggest, trying to start over with this meeting. "Did you book the hotel and plane tickets?"

"Yes."

"How are we handling the cost of these big-ticket items? Each pay half?"

"No."

"Divide it four ways?" I counter.

"No."

"Can you share your idea without the use of a monosyllabic word?"

"Yes."

"Do it then!" My words come out harsher than I mean them to and much louder than I intend. I tilt my head down, trying to avoid looking around the cafe to see if anyone has noticed my outburst. The smile on Nic's lips is unmistakable. I don't need to look at him to know it is beaming across his chiseled face. He is enjoying my frustration. Maybe he wants me to look crazy, so that he in return looks normal.

"I have it covered."

"That doesn't seem fair."

Nic shrugs. "Life isn't fair."

I frown over his nonchalant words. They are riddled with a bitter aftertaste. "This is true. So, I looked up a list of the top fifty restaurants in a ten-mile radius from the strip.

Would you like to pick out some of the places we plan to eat at?"

"No."

"No?" I want to toss my hands up toward the ceiling or bang my head against the wall, but I resist. Why turn my headache into a migraine? Instead, I lean back and close my eyes to squeeze in a quick moment of meditation. I take a few deep, calming breaths. Once I'm back to my equilibrium state, I open my eyes to find the sea of blues in his eyes sparkling with amusement.

"No," Nic reiterates.

I take out my top fifty list anyway, then dig through my bag for my twenty-four pack of multicolored pens. I remove the green, yellow, and red, setting the rest of the package off to the side of the table.

"Oh yes, I love arts and crafts," Nic deadpans. "Did you just growl?"

"Probably," I grumble, unable to look at him. I roll back my shoulders. *You can do this, Claire.* "So, I thought we could look at each name of the restaurant and the type of food served there, and then circle the favorites in green. Maybes can be marked in yellow, while reds can be—"

I stop my sentence as Nic takes the list from in front of me and the red pen. Then he strikes through one after the other, moving down the list.

"No, no, no," he says, as he crosses each one out.

I rip the paper from his hand, tucking it under my vision board. "What is wrong with you?" I snap. "Seriously? Why are you being so difficult?"

Nic rubs his fingers against the scruff on his chin. "Where did you hide Spontaneous Claire? She seems to be way more impulsive than the Claire I'm witnessing today. Bring her back. I miss her."

Nic has seen me run wild with my costume ideas and quest for a *good time*. We even spent last Christmas together at his parents' house and participated in family games. According to both him and his brother, I'm trouble when it comes to Angie's and my excursions. However, this task of helping with a wedding and being the maid of honor has sobered up my fun. I feel the pressure and take my job very seriously.

"I just want everything to be perfect for Angie and Graham. They deserve a nice party and celebration week-end, stress free." It's just the four of us going. If we jack this up, it falls on us.

"And they'll get it. But why do we have to map out every hour of our days? Leave some room for organic moments. If you plan for us to have Italian one night but Angie really wants Chinese food, how are you going to handle the veering off the path? What if one of us needs to use the bathroom off schedule?"

I bite my bottom lip with my top teeth, hating to admit that Nic has a point. "Fine."

He spins his ring on his finger but doesn't take his eyes off me. "Fine?"

"I'll narrow down the list of restaurants by half, categorize them based on type of cuisine, and then group them according to location. I can even assign a number to each and plot them on the tourist map I sent away for from the travel website. I will not make any reservations and just assume that wherever we decide to eat will have an opening for us."

"They'll have an opening."

I take a sip of my water and then look at Nic with confusion. "How can you just assume that?"

"Because most places will accommodate anyone that is willing to pay extra for a stellar experience," he says casually.

I shake my head at him. "Can you sound any more entitled?"

He shrugs. "Can you stop pretending you don't like the perks that money offers?"

"You are exasperating."

"You are cute when you're frustrated."

What? What did he just say? I could not have possibly heard that correctly. I sit farther back in my seat and cross my arms over my chest. He is making literally everything I have planned burn up in smoke. I sit in silence for several moments, using my phone as a distraction. I can feel Nic's gaze bore into me, noticing my every twitch. I would give anything for him to stop staring at me. I can feel him judging me, and I hate myself for letting a man like him get under my skin.

"I, um…" I trail off, playing with the cap on my bottle.

Taking my restaurant list, he rips it in half and then into fourths. "I'm boycotting all lists. They are offensive."

I glare. "Offensive?"

"Yes."

"Can you get the hotel you booked to do something special in Graham and Angie's room? Maybe flowers, gift basket, and bottle of champagne? Oh, I bet Angie would love chocolate-dipped fruit upon arrival. Maybe matching robes and an in-house massage certificate? Or get the cleaning staff to make towel animals like they do on cruise ships? She would probably—"

"I miss Quiet Claire," he says seriously, but the corner of his lip is elevated, giving him a lopsided smile. "I enjoyed her for the three minutes I knew her."

"I. Am. Done."

I have had enough of his sabotage and little comments. I slap the folds of my vision board down onto the center panel and snatch it up against my chest. Nic does not appreciate all of the things I have done to try to make this trip special. Everything is going to go to shit because we have basically confirmed zero plans. I have no idea where we are staying. Who knows, maybe we don't even have a place to stay yet. I am beyond my breaking point, and I'm done swallowing my own feelings for the sake of not crossing some arbitrary line drawn between family and friendship.

I storm out of the cafe and stomp my way to my car. I reach into my—

Shit.

I left my purse inside and it has my keys. There goes my dramatic exit scene, meant to prove a point that Nic will most likely miss. I reluctantly turn around and make my way back into the cafe, finding him right where I left him. He has my purse in the palm of his hands, extending it like it's an offering.

"Thank you," I mutter. "See you at the airport."

"Looking forward to it. Oh, and Claire?"

I stop and turn back around to look at him. "What?"

"Don't worry, I'm pretty fond of Disorganized Claire too."

"Shut up, you clown."

2

NIC

I lean back in my chair and rub at the tense muscles at the back of my neck. I can still smell the lingering scent of Claire's cupcake lip gloss. How can someone so extroverted look so innocent wearing pastels and pigtails? She isn't fooling me. I know better.

The bigger question is, how am I going to survive an entire trip to Vegas with her? Claire is so different from any woman I have met before. Since Tara shattered my view of the female population by cheating on me while we were engaged, I have kept my heart from further damage by only engaging with a certain type of woman. It is easier that way. Besides, what guy with a working dick doesn't love a bad girl?

Most women flirt and are overly sexual when it comes to getting my attention. While I know firsthand that Claire is the wild one in comparison to her best friend, Angie, both women have caused my brother a ton of stress—and by default me too. Graham recruited me with my cyber privacy and security skills to plant trackers on them and their cars. With Claire's spontaneous behavior and wild ideas, paired with Angie's lack of real self-preservation instincts, it was one hundred percent necessary. Soon my big bro will be tying the knot with the love of his life, and I'm doubtful his possessive and jealous tendencies will diminish. If anything, they are going to increase exponentially.

Graham and I used to run a secret company that specialized in catching cheaters. It was extremely lucrative and involved some less-than-legal evidence gathering techniques. Now, Graham's jewelry company, ironically named Jealousy, houses a division meant for securing trackers inside necklaces, watches, and bracelets. Being able to do this legally requires some creativity in the contracts we secure with clients. On the personal level, the ability to locate those we care about is a luxury from a security standpoint. With Angie and Claire, I have to make sure my tracking capabilities are not thwarted by a piece of jewelry that can be easily removed or only used for special occasions.

I tell myself that I'm essentially doing something good and productive with my nefarious skillset—and most of the time I am. However, it is in the dark moments of my mind that I want to slip back into my shady ways, where I would track others for entertainment or for the sake of testing out a product. Treating this whole thing like a sport lumps me in the same category as criminals, and despite acting like I don't give a rat's ass about anyone's opinion, I still have to sleep with myself.

If it weren't for all of the trackers Graham and I had on her, Angie would have been dead after getting herself involved in a drug ring takedown that I was an FBI informant for back around Christmas. Having that amount of valuable information about a person's exact location is hard to part with, even if the danger no longer exists. Old habits are hard to break, and my brother's stubbornness and control tendencies definitely just add to the addiction.

I get up from my seat at the corner table and refresh my coffee. I then open up my laptop and log in to my VPN to keep myself as anonymous as possible. If Claire knew what I do for shits and giggles, she would lose it on me. Her sassy attitude doesn't scare me; it excites me. I wait for the map to load and then lean back in my chair as the little red dot moves steadily down the streets of Portland. I expect her to head back to her apartment that she shares with her boyfriend, Ethan Maxwell, a day trader and former real estate broker. Instead, I find her at the ATM beside Hank's Market. She doesn't linger there long and is back in her car. I stare at my screen as if I'm watching the most entertaining show. Claire enters the Portland Financial Bank and stays there for twenty minutes, followed by a trip to the Japanese Garden. It is easy to lose track of time watching all the sites she frequents, wondering what her motive is for visiting them in the first place.

I log out of the VPN, pack up my belongings, and then place my empty mug in the dirty dish bin on the top of the trashcan. A moment of guilt flashes over me, but I tell myself—as I usually do—that my tactics are for the benefit of others. Although Graham and I reassure his fiancée that all of the danger that followed her last year is over, neither of us is stupid enough to not keep tabs on his woman and the best friend she spends most of her time with. You don't get to be as influential and as powerful as we are by sitting back and waiting for danger to arrive at our doorsteps before making a move. Being proactive—rather than reactive—is key.

It is difficult giving up access when it is so easy to achieve. Even though my cheaters network days are over, those close to me often have me check out their loved ones. With wealth and standing comes insecurity and paranoia. Being in love is putting yourself in a vulnerable position to get hurt. I will be fine in this lifetime just quenching my thirst on women willing to cut the strings that would typically be attached. I do not need another Tara fiasco. She ruined me for every woman who is stupid enough to try to get close to me.

I exit the cafe and walk the three blocks to Hoffman Headquarters, my brother's pride and joy. He started his jewelry company from the ground up and has recently acquired the family hotel. His escort agency, Entice, is a company I run and pretty much own. We co-own and manage so many different projects and business ventures that it is sometimes difficult to remember who holds the majority for deciding votes, if we don't check our cheat sheet. Entice just isn't something that excites me anymore. It is dangerous for a person like me to grow bored. Thus, I am yearning for a bigger project or job to focus my energy toward.

I need to nurture my talents better and work at erasing the ingrained mindset I developed while working for the FBI. I no longer need to seclude myself from others for the sake of protecting them from the collateral damage that could erupt from someone discovering I was working undercover. While I'm thankful I never had to testify or go to trial being an informant, I would have loved the chance to pass the fuckers who tried to bring me and my family down, and punch them in the face when those guarding them turned their backs. It would be worth a visit to prison to release some pent-up aggression. Just for closure purposes, of course.

I badge into HH, wave to the three security guards on the main entrance patrol, and make my way over to the elevator banks. Graham isn't expecting me, but he should be used to me just popping into his office by now, since he knows I keep tabs on his schedule. It is a hobby of mine knowing what is going on around me. Plus it annoys the fuck out of him that I can still infiltrate his fleet of security —from the inside out—just in my spare time.

I make it up to his floor and wave at Kylie, who looks about as used to me being here as the rest of the staff.

"Go on back, he's expecting you," she says with a smile. I halt in my tracks and turn back to try to read her expression for truth. My face must portray my confusion, because she quickly elaborates. "Miss McFee was just on the phone with him."

"Okay…"

"She wasn't happy either," she says with wide eyes.

I nod and walk down the hall. I imagine Graham has his hands full with Angie and her temper. He met his match when he set eyes on her. They haven't even been dating a year, but it is easy to see that they are destined to be together. Even my jaded soul can see that. Knocking twice, I open the door without waiting for permission. Graham is at his desk, feet on top, leaning back in his leather chair.

"Was hoping you would pop in," he says, placing his hands behind his head, as he examines me.

"Oh really?"

"Just got an earful from my stressed-out fiancée after her best friend called her in an uproar over the planning committee that you two are heading."

"We are the only two members," I point out.

"Then it should be even easier to learn to be civil," he counters. "You just have one person to work with. Surely you can do that, baby bro. Claire cannot be that difficult to manage."

I chuckle under my breath and take the chair in front of his desk to relax into. So she called Angie to vent about me. I must be getting to her, and the thought of getting under her skin makes me smirk. I kick up my legs and my feet join his on his polished surface. "You know how crazy Claire can get with her ideas," I explain, as if her bad mood toward me is her own fault.

"Tame her."

"You know I can't do that."

"You choose not to."

I shrug. "Fair enough."

"You know she's taken, right?"

"Had no idea," I deadpan. He only brings it up at least once a week since this whole engagement thing started. With the whole wedding planning underway for a spring wedding at the mansion, the venue we use for hosting Entice mixer events, there is no escaping Claire and her...

Ideas? Spirit? Tight ass?

Simply put, she intrigues me. How could she not? I can't stop thinking about her dream board—or whatever it is called—with the little perfectly cut out magazine pictures. And let's not forget the color coding. Is she in middle school? Who even reads magazines anymore in print and does crafts? She had them impeccably arranged and added Velcro. Velcro! Who does that? No one who is in their early twenties. I may not be an expert, but that much I know is a fact.

If she shows up in Vegas with her twenty count of pens, I may have to say something. I laugh to myself as I remember the look on her face when she watched me cross out each restaurant name, one by one. I'm honestly surprised she didn't hit me. I think I may have deserved it.

"Play nice with her," Graham warns. "For Angie's sake. You know how much she has been through in her life. Don't piss around with her best friend. Because if you do and Angie comes charging after me, then I'll have to get involved."

"What does that mean, Graham? You going to fight me?"

"If I have to."

"Just like old times?" I ask, remembering the many times we sparred during our high school wrestling days. I have an inch or two on him despite being younger by a couple of years, but we think alike and are challenging opponents.

Graham's smile is genuine. He has been sporting a shitty grin ever since he met his girl. I sure hope it lasts. "Seems much longer than a decade ago. So much has happened between then and now. When are you going to start taking your dating life seriously again?"

"Never." I hate talking about myself—especially my sex

life—and need to change the subject before big bro starts in with the L-word topic.

"Don't let one bitch derail your entire life."

"Too late."

He sighs and brushes hair off his forehead. "Going to get lonely."

"My dick is never lonely."

"Okay, that's my cue to change topics," he says, tilting his head toward the ceiling and exhaling.

Good, any talk of my genitalia usually sets him straight. He needs to stick to his own lane when it comes to his love life and quit trying to persuade me out of the darkness that surrounds mine.

"Your security is very lax," I comment.

Graham removes his feet from his desk and sits up straight in his chair, obviously interested in my opinion. "How so?"

I smirk. "I was just able to walk in without a fuss."

He sighs in frustration. "You are impossible. Just like Mom always said."

"She always liked you better," I tease. It is a crock of shit. That woman is a saint and loves all three of her children. I just like to play that card whenever I need to deflect.

"Not even going to address that with a comment," Graham mumbles to himself. "Have you heard from Penny?"

"I went up and visited her last weekend. Seems to be doing remarkably well and moving toward a discussion on being released from the program."

"That's what Dad was saying too. I'm glad the therapy is working, but I wish Seattle was closer so I could keep a better eye on her. Maybe everything is looking up though."

"Just in time for your nuptials too."

"Are we all set for Vegas?" he asks, his tone serious. "You know how I hate relinquishing control on these types of plans. Makes me feel edgy, like I'm walking with a blindfold on."

I nod. "Yeah, I get it. I think everything is set. You sure you don't want me to charter a private jet? It's not too late. There is a risk of a delay flying commercial."

"Angie is obsessed with the whole airport and flight experience. You should have seen her when I took her to Florida for her Christmas gift. Couldn't tell what she was the most excited about. Kept talking about how cute the snacks were with the little airplane emblems. Walked on the moveable platforms just to 'experience it.' Was very excited when her carry-on was flagged and had to get a separate search with the 'cute metal wand.' Those are her words not mine."

"Joined the Mile High Club," I interject.

Graham shakes his head. "Too cliché."

I nod. "Anyway, you aren't supposed to be part of the planning of this trip. I have it all handled. Just relax."

"Security?"

"I set up the monitoring. To be clear, you're not wanting to be intrusive, correct?"

"Correct."

"Then I did what I could do without violating every law in this state—and the state of Nevada. But if your fiancée finds out—"

"She knows I have some form of eyes on her. She also

requested that she doesn't know any further information about how I keep tabs and wants to live her life as if she is oblivious. So, in my defense, I'm not going behind her back."

I nod. That does make me feel better. I had liked Angie as soon as Claire brought her into my office for an interview to join the escort agency. I knew both girls were trouble, each in their own way. With time, they have proven me right on my initial analysis. It's a mystery as to how my brother is not completely gray. They both test my patience, even on a good day.

"Another favor," Graham starts. "I need you to stop the hacking of my meeting slides and editing them to insert inappropriate emoji. I cannot review every document an hour before a scheduled conference."

I throw my head back and burst out laughing. "You really need to add more firewalls and three forms of authorization on your access points. You make it so easy to infiltrate your network."

"Dude, get a hobby," he chuckles.

"Fine. But I need a favor too."

Graham clears his throat. I rarely ask him for anything, so he knows this is going to be worth hearing.

"I need Collins to dig around and retrieve information for me." He's been Graham's bodyguard for years and essentially the backbone to his entire business. If anyone can find the information, it'll be Collins. "I can only see so much virtually and need more concrete documents and information that I cannot easily gather on Ethan Maxwell."

"Should I be worried?"

"Not yet."

"Remember what I said about upsetting Angela."

His voice is deep and gruff, most likely meant to add emphasis to his warning. While I may have more cyber connections and experience in the privacy sector, Graham has built an empire of wealth that buys him power. Even if we are family, it is best not to piss him off. I may act recklessly with my heart, but with my brain? I know better than to be stupid.

"I am aware."

"Pretty sure Mom will lose her mind if something prevents this wedding from happening. You know that woman sends me a threatening text at least once a week. Follows up on it with a phone call to Angie just to make sure she is happy."

I laugh because I can totally see Mom doing something like that. "How does it feel to be ending your days of being a player?"

He clears his throat. "Amazing. Except it is a lot of responsibility to make sure Angie continues to be content and that I stay diligent on giving her a good life."

Pangs of envy stab at my heart. Seeing my oldest sibling deliriously happy does make me wish for that feeling too but only briefly. Tara broke something inside me that I doubt will ever be healed. And while I have no problem filling my bed with women, my heart will never be filled again with anything but the memory of what could have been.

3

CLAIRE

"I cannot believe we are about to leave for Vegas tomorrow evening!" I announce, pumping my fists into the air like we are at some sporting arena. Granted, neither of us are into organized team events. Pretty sure I don't even own a jersey or a hat to support any of the local teams, which is weird because in high school I was all about those things. It's almost like I'm a completely new person—cynicism and all. "This is going to be the best bachelor and bachelorette party that ever existed. I have a whole itinerary planned from morning to—"

Angie sits up from her reclining position on the L-shaped sofa. "Hold up, hot mama."

I stow away my cheering fists and look up at her with confusion. We are relaxing at the apartment I share with Ethan. Although it became official after the townhouse lease ended with graduation, I had taken up residence here back in the winter and have considered this my new home ever since. "What's the problem?"

"The morning part," she whines. Her bottom lip pops out, making her look a decade younger than her current age. "You know I'm not a fan of mornings."

"But if we are going to see everything Vegas has to offer, we cannot waste any time."

"We don't need to see everything it has to offer, Claire. That's what postcards are for."

"I'm choosing to ignore that." I shake my head at her. She doesn't know what she's saying—obviously. "Besides, doing things in the morning is the way to go to avoid all the rambunctious tourists."

"Aren't we those type of tourists?"

"We are not rambunctious. We are tasteful."

"Claire…"

I sit up and curl my feet under my butt so I can see her face better. "Angie, trust me on this." Why is everyone meeting me with resistance? How can I execute my job if I'm met with so many roadblocks? I hate blindly navigating something so monumental. "I just want everything to be perfect."

"You know Graham couldn't care less about seeing anything outside the master bedroom."

I make a face. "Ew. Really, Angie? Gross."

"Just sayin'."

"I know exactly what you're saying, but you guys need to save some of your stamina for the actual honeymoon."

Angie looks off into the other part of the room, almost as if she is in a different place. "Oh, he sure can go all—"

I block my ears. "La, la, la, la…" Ouch! I rub at my sore arm. "Why did you hit me?"

She shrugs, no longer looking innocent. "It feels like a

weird personality reversal is happening, and it is unsettling. When have you gotten all shy about sex?"

Since I've been having less and less of it these days. Hell, maybe my vagina has resealed itself. She's a needy bitch. I brush off Angie's question, trying not to let it bother me. This is not about me right now. "It's very difficult to fulfill my role as maid of honor with Graham's best man judging all of my suggestions—"

"Also called demands?" She puts her hands up in defense. "*His* words, not mine."

I growl. "His words?"

Angie closes her eyes and covers her hands over her face. "Oops."

I dart up from the sofa and toss my hands flippantly into the air. "That man! He is impossible to work with, you know that?" I can feel my pulse quicken, as I think back to how Nic just stared at me. I'm not even that interesting, and yet, he couldn't stop…

Analyzing me? Like I was the most fascinating—and not in a good way—person in the world.

And his smirk.

It was subtle but still fucking annoying. Everything about him is annoying. Why does he have to be so freaking attractive? The universe is cruel.

I pace along the dingy area rug that could use a good power wash. I never really noticed before now. It's actually kind of gross. Yuck.

"Claire?"

"Hmm?"

"Seems like I lost you for a minute."

I turn to look at her. "I thought Nic would be way more

laid-back about this trip. Nope. The complete opposite. If he jacks everything up, I just want you to know that I tried. Believe me, I tried."

"You're putting way too much pressure on yourself. You know I'll be happy with anything."

Which is precisely why Angie deserves *everything*. She is always thinking about everyone else. Celebrating her is a joy. If only my co-planner thought similarly.

I detour into the kitchen in search of a bottle of our favorite wine. I crack open the fridge and push the few items out of the way to retrieve the bottle I have been saving. I will need to hit up the grocery store after the trip and restock some of the essential items. My cleanse ended, so I am back to enjoying alcohol in moderation. Talking about Nic warrants a drink—if just to settle my nerves. "I can't help it if all my ideas are better. It really is a curse," I call out so she can still hear me.

"How so?"

"Well, for one," I say, uncorking the bottle, "I struggle to sleep when my mind is on overdrive planning you the best damn weekend that has ever existed." I pour two glasses and meander back into the living room. I really need to decorate and add some life into this place. Angie is the fanciest thing in the room—and she is just wearing lounge clothes. "And when I do finally fall asleep, I still end up seeing my ideas pop into my dreams."

"Have you ignored everything I just said?"

I give her a sheepish look. "Probably. What did you say again?"

"Claire, you don't need to do this. All the fuss. It's not necessary." She takes her first sip and smiles over the taste.

Who doesn't enjoy a glass of Moscato at noon? "We'll all be happy hanging at a pool, getting drinks, seeing a show, and maybe hitting the slots."

"You can't go to Vegas and not see strippers," I blurt out. It was a last-minute addition to the itinerary I'm still planning without Nic's approval. His opinion no longer matters to me. It's not even like he has any better ideas. He has no ideas at all—except to sabotage all of mine.

"Strippers." It's not a question.

"Don't act surprised. I was able to score tickets based on a lottery system and am shocked my number was pulled. It is fate. And you know it gives us all bad juju to go against fate. Do you want karma to bite you in the ass?"

"None of that stuff you just spewed is actually a thing. Plus, you know Graham will blow a gasket if I'm surrounded by a bunch of dicks."

I take a sip of my drink and sigh over the delicious flavor. It feels good to be drinking something fun again. The toxin cleanse was intense. "Don't worry."

She groans. "That's what you said last time. And we both know how that turned out."

"I cannot take full responsibility for that." If she reminds me one more time about the online dating profile I set up for her, along with a surprise blind date, I may lose it. She is going to have to release some of her animosity toward that whole situation. It totally worked out in her favor anyway, so why the grudge holding? "I promise to keep it classy. Very dignified. I'm all about that shit."

She shakes her head at me and then laughs at my best pouty face. Works every time. "Fine. But I need to sign a waiver that relinquishes me from Graham's wrath. You know how that man gets when he is territorial."

"When is he not territorial, Angie?"

"Good point. See? He's going to really hate this idea."

"Pretty sure this entire engagement has brought him to another level of overprotectiveness."

She lets out an audible exhale. "Hundred percent, yes."

"Good luck with that."

"You mentioned Nic's judging of you, but are you two at least getting along after I raged at Graham over your cafe meetup?"

"If by getting along, you mean ignoring each other, then yes, yes we are."

She narrows her eyes at me. "What's the holdup with you two? Something is obviously going on."

"Nothing is going on, Angie. It's just that he is some sort of emo-alpha man who barely has any words to say, but whenever I present anything to him, he just makes these weird hums or facial tics—but not the kind where you think it is a neurological problem. They're the kind where you think he is about to say something profound—maybe even give me a positive remark—then nothing. Silence. Oh," I say, swinging my wine glass into the air as I talk animatedly, "and then when he does grace me with some verbal communication, it's snarky. He's driving me mad. But I'm your best friend and surely I can suck this up until you get the wedding of your dreams."

Angie listens intently as I rattle off about Nic. I'm all over the place with my emotions, and for as long as she has known me, I've never been this frazzled over a guy I'm not even dating. Maybe I just have a case of mischanneled passion.

"Sorry Nic's getting under your skin. I can talk to him directly and stop using Graham as the middleman. Nic usually caves when it comes to me. This past year was very eye-opening for me and what I want out of this life. I need you to be happy too. My happiness does not trump yours. Okay?"

"No, it's fine. I'm sorry I dumped all of this on you. Things will be fine."

"You sure you're going to be able to endure the four of us hanging out for the entire duration of the trip?"

"Yeah, and Ethan will be joining us toward the end, so that should be fun."

"Well, just know that I'm here if you ever need me. Always."

I give her a big hug. "You are the bestest best friend."

She squeezes me back. "I feel the same way about you. Off topic and less glamorous to talk about, but have you had any luck finding a job in your field?"

I release my hold on her and frown over her question. I turned down my dream job in Los Angeles back in January to avoid having a long-distance relationship with Ethan, who has a son here in Portland from a previous marriage. "I put my résumé into fourteen different places around the city that are hiring a health coach or nutritionist. I went on five interviews and had two places offer second interviews."

"Okay," she says slowly, knowing there's a catch.

"When I looked at the starting salary for someone with zero real experience, I would be making barely above minimum wage. That's less than I make working at the gym part-time."

"Wow, that sucks. Can you pick up more hours at the gym?"

"I can try to compete for more, but with warmer weather approaching, new gym memberships decrease in volume because people want to be outside to exercise. That's why I am advocating for outdoor classes and pioneering a few on a trial-run basis. I actually taught a Zumba at the River class, and everyone seemed to really enjoy it. I have a yoga class this evening that I'm leading, as well." I'm just trying to stay busy to keep myself from thinking of all the things I wish I had.

"That's wonderful. I want to attend a class like those. Sounds fun."

I nod. "But my degree is not in physical fitness."

"Claire, I spent over four years of my life striving to be an investigative journalist and now, what am I? I am a stay-at-home fiancée without kids. I feel useless most days."

"Oh, Angie, don't say that. You are just taking a couple of months to try to find your stride. You just finished up your rehab program and are on maintenance mode. This is a huge accomplishment. It's not like you *need* to work either."

"I want to feel like I'm contributing to the relationship and to society."

"I just want to not have to rely on my monthly allowance to get by," I groan. "Funds get depleted fast."

"Hold up," she says, readjusting herself on the sofa. "Go back to this allowance thing. Tell me more."

I shrug. "Ethan is worried that without me bringing in a steady paycheck, I'll get into a habit of thinking that money grows on trees, yada yada. So, he budgets me a set amount on a debit card to buy groceries and essential items, then whatever is left over at the end of the month is mine for fun."

Angie's eyes grow big, and I instantly regret sharing this personal finance information with her. She probably thinks Ethan is micromanaging me too much or something of the sort. At least she resists adding her opinion to the mix. Instead, she just nods her head and probably is realizing yet again how good she has it with Graham, who worships the ground she walks on and actually begs her to spend more money.

"You know if you need hel—"

I shake my head adamantly, cutting off her offer. "I got this handled. I barely have bills to pay, and I can always pick up a side job if needed. I could be in a way worse position if I had student loans or a mortgage."

"I just want you to be happy."

"I want to be happy too," I say with a half smile.

Angie leans over and gives me a hug. We met as roommates and have been best friends ever since. "I need to go. I promised Graham I would eat lunch with him."

"I need to check the mail, so I'll walk you down."

I grab my set of keys from the dish near the door and lead Angie to the elevator bank. I'm glad the maintenance worker got it fixed again. Although I do prefer the stairs for some added exercise, carrying up bags upon bags of groceries is a drag when it is out of service.

Collins is waiting for us in the lobby and waves to me with a smile. He is Graham's driver, bodyguard, friend, and groomsman, but Angie basically considers him family. "Nice seeing you, Miss Nettles."

"Same to you, Collins," I greet.

"Claire, let me know if you need anything," Angie says, waving a final goodbye and heading out the door with Collins right by her side.

Sadness washes over me as I watch my best friend leave my building. I get so lonely here waiting for Ethan to sometimes show up, depending on his work schedule or last-minute changes with who is watching Finn. Being in the real world without classes and studying taking up the majority of my brain puts me in a vulnerable state with my self-esteem. The more free time I have, the more minutes I spend in the day questioning if staying in Portland was a good idea. It's the doubt and uncertainty for the future that eats at me. I need to stop my past endeavors from haunting me, reminding me of all I left behind.

I find my apartment number on the mailboxes and pull out a stack of mail. Every piece is addressed solely to me. I shuffle through it, while making my way toward the stairwell. I squeeze in a leg workout while I climb the flights leading back to the apartment.

Out of breath and feeling the fire in my calves, I push myself through the door and head to the cupboard to get a glass to fill with water. Downing the entire thing in just a few gulps, I set the empty glass on the top rack of the dishwasher and then do a few stretches to avoid stiffness and pain later on.

I carry the non-junk mail over toward the window seat overlooking the city and plop myself down onto the fraying cushion. I spend a lot of my time in this very spot in the apartment, often thinking about what I need to do to get my life back on track. It is all about making achievable goals and sticking to the steps needed to reach them.

I break through the first envelope's seal and pull out the paper that illustrates the amount I owe in student loans. I stare at the document, seeing this for the first time. I check the name on the front of the envelope and verify that it is in fact me that it is addressed to. My parents have been paying my bills for college all along, so this must be a mistake. They agreed to fund my tuition and living costs while attending River Valley University, in addition to sending me what I refer to as "guilt money" for basically ignoring me and staying on the East Coast while I was on the West Coast. They are not big travelers, so sending money probably helped rationalize their decision to not ever visit. Plus, they had a restaurant to run. Not everyone has as much free time as I now have.

My eyes scan over the bill until I find the amount that is accumulated over time. My eyes bulge out and my lungs deflate with a gasp. There is no way I can owe $304,323.

I find the sheet that has the breakdown of cost. How did I allow myself to be so naive when it came to the actual cost of my education? Out-of-state tuition is drastically more than in-state. At slightly over $45,000 per year, I owe $180,748 just for my bachelor's degree alone. Add on my master's at a whopping $123,575, and if I follow the twenty-year payback plan, I will *only* owe roughly $57,000 back in interest.

I am going to throw up.

I shove the papers back into the envelope and lean my face against the cool glass window, looking out into the city.

If I knew I had to pay for my entire duration of college on my own, I would have waited until I had a steady job before moving forward with my master's degree. In hindsight, knowing now that no one wants to hire me, I probably wouldn't have even tried to get one in the first place. What's the point of a fancy degree, if there's no fancy job to justify it?

I grab my phone and dial my mom's number. She answers on the fifth ring, and the noise in the background is a telltale sign she is working at her restaurant in northern Virginia, just south of Washington, D.C.

"Hey Mom, it's me," I mutter into the phone. "I was calling because I got this random bill in the mail."

"I doubt it's random, Claire."

I swallow hard and clear my throat. "I thought you and Dad were going to pay for my tuition like you promised."

"Bill and I," she starts, but pauses to correct herself. "Your father and I are getting a divorce. Been working toward that for the past decade anyway. He is still angry with me over you."

Tears fill my eyes. It's not my fault my mom cheated on her spouse and conceived me. She couldn't even pass me off as Bill's, since the man she cheated on him with, during a one-night stand, was a Filipino touring America for the first time on a visitor's visa. Coming out with darker hair and slightly tanned-looking skin threw Bill for a loop, so he apparently demanded a DNA test when I was only three days old.

Nothing says, "welcome to the world, little one," like betrayal. It's as if my birth put a stain on their relationship. I made it dirty.

It is hard growing up with a dad who was in my life only as a default and the stigma I put on my own self for being a byproduct of infidelity. Being mixed race in a public school is hard enough. Being conceived from lust rather than love is another hard pill to swallow. Kids teased me and called me names. Everyone assumed I was adopted, as if that is something bad.

It is of no surprise that at this stage of the game, Bill is reneging on his offer to pay for my university. Why would he want to anyway? Mom is probably going to try to get everything she can out of the settlement.

"I'm sorry to hear that," I finally say, after the long period of silence. "Mom? You still there?" I glance down at the phone and realize that we disconnected minutes ago. Dammit. I toss my phone onto the seat bench and cry into my knees.

I must have dozed off because I wake to a kink in my neck and Ethan making his way through the door with his briefcase. I rub at my muscles to remove some of the tension, sliding off the window bench to greet him.

I stand on my tippy toes and give him a hug and kiss. "Hey baby, glad you're home. How was work?"

"Good," he says, moving his attention toward the kitchen. "Is dinner still in the oven?"

I pull back and frown over his words. I've been on a very restricted diet this week during my cleanse. "I really wish you would warn me in advance on what your expectations are of me, so I'm not blindsided."

"Should be obvious," he says dryly. "If I'm going to be carrying the weight of earning the money, then the least you could do is bear some of the household burden and make dinner."

"I do work."

He sighs heavily. "It's part-time, Claire, at a gym. You have a hobby. It's not the same thing as actually having a career and you know it."

He's right. But I really don't need another reminder. "I know," I say sadly. "I've been applying for jobs and putting my résumé out there. It's not like Portland has the opportunities like Los Angeles would have to build up my portfolio and add to my work experience."

He steps back from me and his eyes go cold. He tosses his hands into the air. "If you keep bringing up the dream job you left behind, then we are never going to be able to progress forward in this relationship. You have your mind set on feeling sorry for yourself over declining that internship and keep throwing it back in my face. Enough's enough. I'm simply asking you to do some more chores around here and tidy up the place. No need to have a hissy fit over it."

I glance around the space. It doesn't even look like anyone lives here. My townhouse belongings are shoved into the spare room and anything that wasn't in great condition got sent to the thrift shop for donation. For someone who is a day trader, I would expect more luxurious living conditions. Everything here is builder-grade basic. He doesn't even have kids' toys lying around for when Finn is scheduled to visit. Ethan just ends up taking him out to a restaurant, park, or on some other type of excursion—making some excuse that kids like high-energy activities. They are not wall starers, he tells me. I don't know much about kids, but I bet they just want attentive and loving parents. Everything else is just sauce.

I move into the kitchen and pull open the fridge. "Want me to make you—" I don't even know if we have ingredients to make anything fresh. I open up the freezer. "Some lasagna?" It is the kind served in a black tray with plastic across the top that gets removed prior to going into the oven. He obviously bought this at one time for himself because there is no way I would pollute the environment with that amount of nonbiodegradable trash.

Ethan moves up behind me and wraps his arms around my waist. "Did you blow through the grocery budget money?" He kisses my neck. His touch is sweet and in direct contrast to his patronizing tone.

I turn in his arms and look at him with confusion. "Three hundred dollars a month for food and essential items is—"

"Plenty if you ask me. Maybe start being wiser with how you decide to use it."

I hate when we do this. And it keeps happening more and more. I take a step back. "Okay," I agree, plastering a fake smile onto my lips, just to end the misery. He accepts my answer at face value and runs his eyes down my body.

"You look nice today," he says smoothly. "I much prefer these softer colors on you, but try to wear less of these wild patterns."

It's stripes, for fuck's sake. I bite my tongue and resist lashing out. I have never needed to restrain myself as much as I do around Ethan. He is very charming in public, but behind closed doors, I find myself quivering back from his watchful gaze. I hate myself for allowing a man to make me feel less than what I deserve. I know this is just a season in time though. Everyone has always told me relationships have highs and lows. We have had a ton of highs, so a low here and there is expected.

I wrap my arms around his neck and massage my fingers into his skin. He loves when I do this and instantly relaxes into my touch. "So, you have your plane ticket booked for joining us in Vegas?"

"My assistant verified the purchase this morning. I'm all set."

"I'm so excited."

"I'm looking forward to hitting up the casinos and getting out of Portland. Should be a fun trip."

"Am I allowed to get a little more spending money on the debit card to use while I'm there?" I ask. I'm in between paychecks from the gym, and with needing more professional looking clothes for interviews, my savings account is basically nothing.

He nods. "I'll add some more onto what is left from the month."

There's rarely anything left at the end of the month. "Thank you."

"How about we order some takeout and hang out under the sheets?" he suggests. "I'm going to miss you when you leave tomorrow."

"That sounds perfect, but I have a class to teach in about thirty minutes down by the river."

Ethan's face drops with disappointment. "I hate that you choose exercising over me sometimes."

"It's my job," I whisper, my voice barely audible. Or to him, a hobby.

"Yeah, yeah, I know," he says with defeat. "Go. I'll order, and if there's any left over, you can help yourself to it when you come back home."

I run off to my room to change into long gray yoga pants and a bright blue off-the-shoulder long-sleeved shirt. Working out is therapeutic for my mood, and instructing others into their zen state gives me an even bigger endorphin rush.

The sun is about to set while I unroll my yoga mat in the grassy area near the river. The lights surrounding the walking path have yet to turn on, but the area is bright enough from the neighboring park and the fact that we aren't caught in the shadow of the buildings. The one cool thing about being an instructor at the gym is that I'm able to use the facility without having to pay the hefty membership cost or fees. Exercise is my outlet. It gives me strength and helps me center my focus, even when my mind seems to be in disarray.

The first members arrive and pick a spot facing toward the water. Riverboats float downstream. Some are decorated with twinkling lights, while others have the American flag blowing in the breeze from long metal poles. It's hard to live in Portland and not appreciate the dedication to having greenery and parks. It is a very likable and livable city—much different than my own hometown on the East Coast.

I set up my portable speakers and slide my headset into place.

"Hi everyone," I say as a test. Several of my clients wave and smile. "Testing."

When all the members seem situated, I turn on the meditation music and lower myself to my mat. I'm about to start the class when out of the corner of my eye I see a man jog up to our area. It isn't until he takes up a spot in the back of our gathering and unrolls his mat that I notice who he is.

You have got to be kidding me.

I ungracefully get up and walk to the back of the class.

"What are you doing here, Nic?" I hiss, stooping down to his level.

"Shhh," he chides, giving me a dirty look. "I heard the yoga instructor is super anal about maintaining the structure of her class. One of those Type A personalities. You know, the rigid and unbendable kind? Have you met her before?"

I stare at him blankly, trying to figure out if he is for real or not. "I. Am. The. Instructor."

"Oh snap."

I turn away and look out toward the water, trying to contain my frustration. "No one says that anymore, you fool." I am starting to see that Nic likes to make me feel agitated and off-kilter.

"I feel like you have some pent-up aggression that you need to work through during this class," he comments. "If we're going to work together at this whole wedding planning thing, I need you to help foster a good working relationship. Because right now, I sense some hostility. Oh, and you are making a scene."

I narrow my eyes at him and huff out a breath. "No, you are."

"Claire Bear, is everything okay?"

I rise from my stoop and find Blake looking at me expectantly. I never even noticed that he arrived at class. Usually he texts me a heads-up, but I either missed it or he decided to attend last minute. "Yeah, everything is fine."

He eyes me with suspicion but thankfully takes his place on the lawn. Blake has known me most of our college years, plus our time working at the gym. Thus, he can sense when I'm lying—like right now.

Nic glances around at the other members, who are obviously trying hard not to stare. I can even see a few smirks, and for the life of me, I cannot figure out why anyone would be entertained by our little dramatic tiff.

"Told you so," he says with a nonchalant shrug. "I just want to feel at peace and let go of some of my mental struggles. It's hard being the cornerstone for the planning. It exhausts me."

My mouth drops. "Are you serious?"

"Hmm?"

"You heard me."

"Huh?"

"Quit baiting me!" I snap, and then quickly hush.

"Can you repeat the question?"

I prop my hands on my hips and lean over farther, my shadow covering all of his features. The lights have kicked on and the intro part of the meditation soundtrack has restarted. "How can you be exhausted when I'm the one doing all of the labor and organizing? Huh?"

Nic has the nerve to try to look innocent. "See, this is exactly what I'm talking about. All this animosity you are harboring inside is messing with us. We both need this class," he says with enthusiasm. For the past month, I have only ever noticed two emotions from Nic Hoffman—annoying or not annoying. He pretty much stays in the "annoying" category on the daily. He points to the front of the class. "So go up there and do your thing, before you start to develop an even more colorful reputation." He stretches his arms above his head and then bends his body forward so he can touch his toes. His back muscles pull beneath his shirt, and I can use my imagination to visualize the definition and strength he must be hiding underneath the fabric. "Quite frankly, your hovering is kind of hampering my moment."

I let out an exaggerated exhale and stomp to the front of the class without another word spoken. I turn up the meditation music, probably a few decibels higher than my norm, and switch to the next track.

"Good evening," I say, bowing to my students, "namaste." I sit down on my mat and crisscross my legs. I try to keep my attention on anyone but Nic, but he is the tallest person. Despite being in the back, it's like he has a spotlight on himself. "Welcome to Yoga at the River. I am your instructor, Claire Nettles. Tonight I'll be leading you through a series of breathing exercises and walking you through the flow method. As always, I try to keep this class fun and do not label any of the poses I'll introduce to you with the typical professional names." Several of my clients giggle. It is part of my trademark of keeping things fresh and making members want to return. "I hope that you find some relaxation and are able to center yourself and declutter your thoughts."

I allow the oxygen to flow in through my nose and out through my mouth in deep cleansing breaths. Once I have calmed down from the initial shock of Nic showing up, I instruct the class to follow my rhythm of breathing. "In through your nose, hold for a count of three, then release out through your mouth. This is the type of deep breathing I want you to do during every movement I will lead you through. Just listen to the music and become one with the flow."

I close my eyes and listen to the moving water from the river. "Now, let's get into our *lazy starfish* position," I instruct, modeling the movement gracefully. "From that move, you are going to get into the *I've been kneed* pose and hold it there for one minute." I roll onto my back and bring my knees up to my chest. "Just let your thoughts drift with each exhale. Let go of any tension in your neck. Relax your shoulders. If it is more natural to roll to your side, do what feels best."

I typically am not nervous while teaching a class; however, this class is so different with Nic's penetrating gaze following my every movement from the back of the group. I don't even need to look at him. I can feel his judging eyes on me anyway. When I do sneak a glance at him, he doesn't even fractionally look to be meditating. He looks charged and ready to pounce. I feel my stomach knot.

Why does he need to be so intense?

Class wraps up at the forty-five minute mark, and the members disperse. Nic lingers, along with Blake.

"I can give you a hand back to your car," Blake says, taking my mat and joining it with his. "Great class, Claire Bear. I particularly liked the *day drinking* balance activity."

I giggle. "I get such a rush teaching these types of classes. And then being in nature is just icing."

Blake turns to eye up Nic and then looks at me with a quirk to his eyebrow.

"Blake, this is Nic Hoffman, Angie's future brother-in-law. Nic, this is my friend Blake." The men shake hands, and surprisingly, the awkwardness that was present at the beginning of class has dissipated. Maybe Nic really did need this class after all. My phone vibrates, and I glance down to see that it is Ethan. He hates when I'm late, especially if he is home waiting for me to get back.

"Gotta go?" Blake asks.

"Yeah."

I follow Blake to the sidewalk and turn back to wave goodbye to Nic who seems to be interested in our departure.

"He seems nice, Claire Bear."

"I'm sure he can be," I mutter.

"What's going on between you two?"

"Nothing."

Blake stops in his tracks and glances back at Nic, while I stay fixated on my car in the distance. "Claire Bear, that tall drink of fine man meat back there ain't *nothing*."

"You're right. He is a giant pain in my ass."

4

NIC

"How certain are you?" Asher asks.

"As sure as shit," I mutter into the phone. "I'm not going back into that line of work." Despite living states away, Asher and I are best friends and have been able to stay in touch over the past few years. He is someone I can trust, vent to, and count on for healthy advice. He doesn't know how to sugarcoat things, and I appreciate his honesty when I need a sounding board. It helps to have someone in my life that doesn't just give me the default reply of what I want to hear. I can simply hire people to kiss my ass. It's not a quality I need in a friend.

"So what are you going to do with your life now that you are a free man again? Please tell me you're not going to turn into one of those loafers who installs one of those European bidets to spray water on your asshole, then hire a chef and maid to tend to your every need. You'll gain like fifty pounds and have to resort to buying women from your escort database just to get a date."

"Shit, you have a vivid imagination. Gets worse with age too."

Asher cracks up laughing. "Just admit it—you're going to get bored and lazy."

"I've been a free man for some time now," I answer smoothly. He is referring to my FBI days and not my relationship status. "You know how I hate to settle or put all my money on one number on the roulette table. I keep my options open. Might even do another start-up again."

"Must be nice living off the dividends of your investments. It's not even like you have to work," he points out. I can almost see him tapping his fingers along his jawline. It is one of the mannerisms I remember best about him that he uses when he is thinking about all the possibilities.

"Pretty sure my dick would get raw if I didn't have something else to do with my time."

Asher busts out laughing into the phone. This is what we do when we are on a call; we laugh. "There are creams for things like that," he jokes.

"I'm sure you have some to share," I tease. "Speaking of which, how is the missus?"

"I'm not sharing her."

"That much is obvious."

Asher got married to his college sweetheart a couple of years ago. I was honored to be the best man and watch them tie the knot on a beach in Malibu.

"We're expecting our first child in September."

"What? No way. Congrats, man."

So much for trying to convince him to move north to join forces with me. Asher is already planting roots in the heart of Silicon Valley—the tech capital of the United

States. His once fly-by-the-seat-of-his-pants attitude will drastically change with the introduction of a child. I don't envy him at all. After being a servant to the FBI, I much prefer being the master of my own domain.

Asher and I have been friends since college on the East Coast. We met during an entry level computer class and bonded over how elementary the topics were. It became a hobby of ours to hack into the various networks and alter discussion topics that would get broadcasted on the projector screen. Nothing like bonding over a similar interest in devious acts.

Asher knew the East Coast lacked the types of jobs he was interested in and decided to move west. I would have stayed on the Atlantic Coast and made sacrifices for Tara if it wasn't for her trying to sucker me into her web of lies.

"I'm due for a trip north to check up on you in person. You know how I have trust issues."

"Don't we all," I mutter, more to myself than to Asher.

"Make sure you aren't getting soft with your skills or your workout schedule," he teases.

"Nothing soft about me," I defend. "I've been keeping up with my routines. As for my skill set, I'm pretty sure I can still out hack you on the daily."

"Ha, you wish, man," he chuckles. "But on a serious note, if you grow bored with Portland, come down to the valley, and I'll set you up with a job."

"Thanks. But I'm happy here." My family is here and even though I am not planting new roots, I'm enjoying the consistency of the old ones. "I do need a favor though."

"You always do…"

"I need a list of contacts."

"I'm listening."

"I'm looking to hire a couple of local men but need them screened before I offer employment. Ones who aren't against breaking a little of the law and are loyal and trustworthy."

I can hear Asher's throat clear. "You in some sort of trouble? In need of a few bodyguards?"

"Nah. I can handle my own drama. This is just as a precaution."

"You sure you are set on never dating again? Seems to me, your eye is caught on someone. Perhaps she is enticing you to stay in Oregon?"

I shake my head and lean farther back in my office chair. I'm at home and enjoying the solitude of having no one to answer to but myself. "It's all in connection to Graham and his upcoming nuptials. Anyone attached to his fiancée is high risk for future blackmail or extortion. Just crossing t's and dotting i's."

"I can hook you up. I can give you a few names to check out, but one person I can personally vouch for."

I knew Asher would be able to help. It really pays to have the connections I do and still maintain clean hands when it comes to the law. Even though I've made a name for myself with the FBI, I can still get wrapped up in the legal tape and do prison time until I await trial. It is best that I stay in my lane as best I can and let others risk their freedom. It also pays to have money.

"Feel free to drop off your list in person," I razz. It has been a year or more since he has been able to come visit. I expect his life with a child to be even busier.

"I'll let you know when flights are at discounted rates.

You know how cheap I am," Asher jokes. He is completely the opposite and is a splurger by nature. He fits in perfectly in the valley.

"Come visit, and I may let you drive my new Porsche 911 Turbo S. It still has the new car smell."

"As long as it doesn't smell of cheap pussy, I'm game."

I laugh into my phone. "Chat later," I say, hitting the end button.

I drown myself in business for the next three hours. I live in a high-rise condo toward the southwestern side of the city. It is within walking distance of the Entice offices and close enough to the Willamette River for when I want to go for a scenic run. The building is on the newer end and my specific unit has been renovated to add my own security features. While I do not take up the entire floor, I have two levels and access to the private pool on the rooftop that can be reserved via a floating schedule. It serves its purpose for the amenities I need at this point in my life.

When my eyes start to blur from staring at the screen, I log off my desktop and head to my workout room to burn off some of my pent-up energy. I lace up my gloves and voice command my sound system to play my heavy metal track. Stretching my neck and bouncing on the balls of my feet, I warm up to the music. When I feel the warmth circulate through my veins, I start my rhythmic punching at the bag. It feels good to take out my aggression on something. The last thing I need is to be seated next to Claire on a two-hour flight tomorrow with this much tension coiled throughout my body.

She smells like a fucking cupcake with vanilla buttercream frosting. How can someone so fiercely sexual smell like a damn sugary confection? I pound harder into the bag and pray that I can keep my cool without completely losing my mind. I can already tell Claire is getting under my skin. No one has ever had me so tied up in knots without even trying.

I can only imagine what her outfits for Vegas will do to me when her freaking oversized shirt with her peekaboo shoulders nearly caused me to combust during the yoga class. No man my age should get turned on by a female's shoulders. Yet, here I am, thinking about Claire's sexy ones. What is wrong with me?

From how I left things with her at the cafe and then last night at the river, I know she is going to pack her sassy attitude with her when we meet up at the airport. I just hope my dick can stay settled. I don't need a force like Claire in my life. She's trouble, and I'd be wise to keep my distance.

I finish up my fight fest, clean up my supplies, and shower. As the water sprays down on me, I think about how different my life would have evolved if I wasn't privy to information gathering techniques. Where would I be right now, in this very moment in time? It is in the quiet that I allow my mind to drift to every what-if scenario. Many people perceive me to be laid-back in comparison to Graham. It is only because I internalize everything and am less quick to reveal my cards.

I cut off the water and towel dry myself off. I have exhausted myself so that my body's only option is to sleep.

I wake with an erection so hard and the image of a vanilla cupcake fairy dancing around in my head. What the actual fuck? What is this girl doing to me? I have had plenty of conquests, but no one has had me so utterly twisted like this poisonous princess. She has the power to destroy me if I can't even filter out my subconscious thoughts from being infiltrated with her beauty.

I close my eyes and tug hard at my dick, thinking of all the nasty things I want to do to her. With her. It takes me seconds to come. And even less time to feel the pangs of guilt for going against Graham's wishes to keep Angie's best friend safe.

She isn't safe. Not from me, at least. My mind is laser focused on her and there's not much I can do to stop the spiral.

As much as I know she can destroy me, I know I can have the same effect on her. Everyone I choose to touch gets tainted by my singular needs. Is it worth damaging the relationship with my soon-to-be sister-in-law just to satisfy my dick temporarily?

I never said I wasn't a selfish bastard.

I saunter into the bathroom to clean up my sticky mess. I decide to take the day off—something I haven't done in months. I throw on a pair of athletic shorts and a sleeveless T-shirt. Socks and my running shoes complete my attire.

I take the stairs down, exit through the back door of the lobby, and work my way toward the river. Portland is very peaceful in the morning. Dew is still fresh on the budding flowers. Birds chirp, cutting through the silence of the city.

I jog past the Entice office and recall the day Claire entered my doors for the first time. When she told Graham basically where to stick his ego, I should have known then that the girl was special. No one does that to Graham and gets away with it. She was such a little firecracker. Still is, although something seems to have dulled her sparkle. I'm sure dating an asshole doesn't help. I am waiting for my sources to tell me he is an even bigger one than I originally thought. My instincts rarely let me down.

I didn't think much of Claire then. To be fair, I didn't think much of anything other than bringing down the drug ring. However, once she showed up with Angie and Graham for Christmas in Hillsboro, I got to see another side to her that went beyond her wild costume ideas, her horrible spy disguises, and her quick-witted personality. Instead, I got to see how vulnerable she was.

I could read between the lines and see the glimmer of sadness in her eyes when she looked at the love Graham and Angie share. It wasn't a greedy type of jealousy for her best friend, but I could tell that it is what she wished she had with Ethan. Her boyfriend is one hell of an idiot to leave his girl alone on one of the biggest celebrated holidays of the year. Then she handed me a gift. *Me*. Granted, it was a gag gift—a unicorn selfie stick—but still. I didn't see it coming; we barely know each other. I mean, I know a ton about her, but that is only because I have double standards when it comes to breaking the law. Most of the time I have someone else gather the data, so I feel less like a stalker and more like someone who is just curious.

I ask myself all the time, what's the point? It's not like I plan to do anything more than destroy. I sure as hell don't want anything even resembling monogamy or a commitment.

I run the waterfront path, feeling the morning air whip around my body as I glide along the pavement. I pass by the area where yoga took place last night. It was definitely a last-minute decision to attend the class. I tell myself that I was just making sure Claire was safe, being as it was dark out. The particular stretch near the water where she hosts her classes has been known to have an increase of petty crime after hours.

I glance at my watch that keeps track of my pace. It feels good to be disciplined in my workout routine and goals. I cut through the park and take the footbridge over the creek, heading back toward my building.

Part of the reason I chose this building is because of the security features and my ability to donate funds to customize the options. Working in the industry, I know how easy it is to get access where access is not authorized. Hence, why I love the double door feature in the lobby, plus the twenty-four-hour camera recording capabilities.

I'm not expecting any backlash from my FBI days, but I still take every precaution necessary to protect myself and those I love.

Once I'm inside my home, I shower, shave, eat brunch, and start packing my luggage. I have all intentions of letting Claire dictate what we do while in Vegas, so I need to make sure I am prepared for a variety of activities. I'm pretty sure she has gone as far as planning bathroom breaks in her crazy itinerary. How am I supposed to even go against her when she put her whole heart and soul into the planning? I'm an asshole, yes, but I do know my boundaries of how hard to push.

Reclining on the bed, I pull up my email that has the

resort confirmation and the flight information. We need to get to the airport at two, if we want to get through security and make the five o'clock boarding time. I paid the extra fee to get priority seats and to be able to jump line. It's these minor luxuries that will make flying commercial more bearable. Graham will do anything to make Angie happy, even if that means resisting the dumping of money into a private flight.

Before closing out of my email account, I see a new one pop up onto the top of the list from Collins. I open it and see the row of attachments at the bottom, along with a short message.

As expected, Collins came through on the request. He has retrieved bank statements, credit card information, hotel receipts, and household bill copies. However, the most important thing he has acquired for me is security camera footage and real-time photographs with timestamps. Damn, Ethan Maxwell has been busy. I bet Claire has zero clue what her loving boyfriend has been hiding. What a douchebag.

I close my eyes for a few minutes as I think about the approach I need to take with the newly discovered information. Claire is way too good for that man. However, it really is not my place to get involved. It's one thing watching out for her from a safety aspect, but it's a whole other ballgame inserting myself into a situation that is already jacked up.

I open up my text app and find Graham's name.

Nic: I will meet you guys at the airport drop-off location around 2 PM.

He sends back a thumbs-up icon, letting me know we are both on the same page.

I've been to Vegas at least half a dozen times, but this trip seems so different from all of the others. For the first time in years, I am excited about something other than work.

I go back into my email and open the numerous messages Claire has sent over the past month. She is a bundle of energy squeezed into a petite body. She would send me her top twenty excursions list. Then she would second-guess herself and send me a newly revised list two hours later. A day after that, a narrowed down top ten list, followed by an addendum or two. Let's not forget her thought-out reasoning for such revisions. This went on for an entire week. Somehow in the end, she wanted me to vote on her top five favorite top ten lists. Like, what the actual fuck? Who has time to do any of this?

The best part is, I would respond to the last of a dozen email messages with a thumbs-up, but never really give her a solid answer. It was too tempting to resist and prevent myself from getting another five separate responses in return. I was having too much fun trying to fluster her.

Just reading through her email lists was exhausting. I imagined what she was doing at the time of her research. Was she snacking on veggie sticks and playing with her hair? Perhaps she was in an oversized T-shirt drinking a margarita?

Even if I had a strong opinion on anything, I'm smart enough to let her take the lead and then start vetoing everything to get the passion to bleed through her veins. Either that or ignore her entirely. I am not sure which she found more annoying. Just seeing her cute frustration at the cafe is enough to make me want to keep up with my strategy.

If it's not broke, then why try to change it?

I log out of my account and open up my tracking app to see where the red dot is located at this moment. Claire is still at home. The moron she is dating is at work. I know this because the blue dot is hovering at the office space he leases.

I finish up my last-minute packing, set my security system, and head into the waiting elevator. My airport attire consists of beige linen pants and a white button-up shirt. I roll up my sleeves while I descend toward the lobby, cuffing them slightly below my elbows. I slip on my shades and walk out onto the street where my scheduled ride is waiting.

"Where to, sir?" the driver asks, loading up my luggage into the trunk of his vehicle.

"PDX."

I settle into the backseat and snap my belt into place. My pulse quickens as I watch the scenery pass by. Upon arrival at the airport, the driver removes my bags from the trunk and I pay.

I check my phone for texts and make my way into the main terminal. There aren't many crowds, and I easily spot Graham and Angie. I roll my bags over to them, accepting a hug from my soon-to-be sister-in-law. She is wearing a long sleeveless black dress and looking light on her feet. Stress has a bad way of bringing people down. I am glad she looks more carefree.

"We just have to wait for Claire," Graham informs, smacking hands with mine in a half-shake.

I slide my hand into the side compartment of my carry-on and pull out the tickets. The process should be smooth to check in and get through security. I glance at my watch and see that Claire is already ten minutes late. I should have just sent a car for her or picked her up myself. She was still at her apartment when I left mine, so it's no surprise to me that she is running behind on time.

I hear the clicking sound of high heels hitting tile before the loud screeching girly screams of excitement start. I turn and see Claire bounding through the entryway, dressed in glitter. It has to be painted on, it is so skintight against her golden skin. Fuck me sideways. How am I going to endure a two-hour flight with a hard-on?

5

NIC

My mouth drops as the gold disco ball flutters by me to get to Angie first for a huge hug. Even with heels, Claire is so short that she has to stand on her tiptoes to embrace Graham. Me? I get a wave and a glance away. I can't tell if she hates me or is just shy. It would be best for her to water and nurture the former. That's if she is smart.

"Let's get the party started!" she announces, her bubbling energy knocking down her pink-and-white striped suitcase accidentally in the process. "I brought minis."

"Um, Claire, we can't get drunk in the airport," Angie scolds.

"We still need to get through security," I mumble, but no one must hear me. I mean, how can they, over their giddiness?

Claire throws her head back and bursts out laughing so loud I flinch. I worry her boobs are going to fall out of her top. "Not miniature bottles of alcohol. We can get those on the plane," she says while digging through her carry-on. "I brought micro penises!"

I stare in shock at the tiny penises hanging from a plastic chain. There has to be twenty of them strung together to form a necklace. Who even comes up with these types of things?

Claire drapes the gimmicky chain over Angie's neck. "You know how I am a sucker for penis paraphernalia."

"Interesting choice of words," Graham mutters, moving to stand near me. I can already tell he wants no part of this nonsense. "Hope we survive this trip."

I chuckle, watching the girls live their best life. They are causing a small scene with their high-pitched laughter. However, I think most of the staring is due to Claire's obscene outfit. I'm going to go to jail if one more asshole checks out the curve of her ass in that scrap of fabric she decided to wear. She is one bend away from flashing the entire airport.

"Boys, don't you worry," Claire says, catching Graham and my attention. "I brought you both some pussy."

I nearly choke on the saliva pooling in my mouth. She cannot be serious.

"I'm not wearing a vagina necklace," Graham says flatly.

"Same," I agree. I draw the line.

Claire rummages through her bag and whips out two boxes, one in each hand. "If the description is accurate, you both can thank me later. After you've had your fun." She winks at us. Winks!

I take the box from her hand and read the words printed across the front out loud. "Pocket pussy? A penis's playground and pleasure center…a sleeve that will get the juices flowing…"

"Only the best for you boys," Claire chirps, smacking her hands together like she just gave us the most perfect gift. "I got one hairy and one shaved. Don't fight over them."

I skeptically look at the cheesy-ass male models on the front with their weird O-faces. Is she seriously thinking this is a sex toy I would actually use? There is no way I am sliding my dick into a silicon deathtrap. No. Fucking. Way. What if it gets stuck? Just cut it out?

"I prefer the real deal," I say to her, allowing my eyes to stare a little too long.

She breaks eye contact and dances around like she just won the lottery with her choice of gift. She then digs through her bag of tricks to find a sash for Angie to wear with the label "Bride To Be" plastered across the front. And then I notice the tiny words that parallel—"Same Dick for Life."

"Are we ready to go now?" Graham asks, tucking his toy into his carry-on luggage. I gave him the hairy one because it looked scarier.

I am sure the workers running the X-ray machines will have a laugh over our contents. Surely, they have seen worse come through their lines. I just hope Vegas can handle these two nutballs. I have my hands full just dealing with the one.

We pull our belongings through the check-in line, handing over our tickets and the luggage that needs to be checked. We get through security without any issues, hop on the tram, and make our way to our gate.

I use the charging dock to top off my phone's battery and relax into the cushioned chair while I watch the girls chatter about who knows what. I sneak glances at Claire, noticing her light expression is now lined with signs of panic. I watch as she tosses items from her purse onto the empty seat beside her. She must have left something important at home.

"I can't believe I forgot my medicine. I'm going to get so sick on the plane," she says to Angie, who is helping her search through the dozen of items she must have deemed as essential enough to pack.

I get up from my seat. "I'm going to go grab a drink and use the restroom," I say to Graham, who responds with a single nod.

Little convenience shops pop up every few gates, and it is easy for me to spot the medication section to pick up what Claire needs. Nearby, I find a smoothie cafe and get four drinks, all of a different variety. I'm not picky, but I know someone who is. At the checkout, I see individual prepackaged snacks and place a few on the counter.

When I make it back to the group, Claire looks so pale that I think she'll be ill before we even take off.

I take out the tiny travel tube of Dramamine and extend my hand toward her. "Here," I bark out, my voice more gruff than usual. It does something inside of me to see her so upset. "I also got everyone drinks. They are all labeled along the side, so take your pick."

Claire looks at the medicine as if I am offering her cocaine. Maybe she is shocked that I can be human after all of the hassling I have done to her prior to this trip. She mumbles her appreciation, and if I wasn't already staring at her lips, I may have missed her message. She smiles when she sees the vegan green smoothie and instantly grabs it. I laugh on the inside that she would think anyone else would choose that one as their top pick. I basically bought it with her in mind.

"Thanks, Nic," Angie says with a warm smile, grabbing the raspberry smoothie.

"Yes, thanks, bro."

I relax into my seat and sip on the peach and mango smoothie, while watching Claire swallow two of the pills in my periphery. It doesn't take long for the color to return to her cheeks and for the tension in her back to release. She must be expecting a text because every few minutes, she checks her phone. Thin lines mar her forehead over what I can only assume is disappointment.

Priority seating is announced and we gather our bags, making our way to the corridor. I hand over my boarding pass to be scanned and then wheel my travel bag down the neon lit jet bridge.

Claire is directly in front of me, and I can't get my mind to stop wondering if she is even wearing panties under the glitter. Her legs and ass are so defined that the sky-high heels only accentuate her tone. I shake my head to get the images of bending her over and fucking her from behind out of my brain. If it wasn't for the slight dread I'm continuing to feel over having to endure the entire flight beside her, I might have those fantasies living rent-free.

Hints of warm vanilla fill my nostrils as her hair shimmies behind her. She styled it today to be poker straight. The sleek shine of her dark locks makes her look exotic but forbidden. The combination is intoxicating.

I stop suddenly and pause my daydreaming as I almost crash into her as she stops to pick up her tube of lip gloss. I curse under my breath as she stands and then tugs down the hem of her dress that has ridden seductively up her silky thighs. If she wasn't still pissed at me over the whole cafe meetup and spontaneous pop in of her yoga class, I would think she is trying to punish me and my dick with her flirting. However, the fact that she is oblivious to the effect she has on me only makes me want her more.

The first-class section is assigned with our own flight attendant and some added perks when we get in the air. The seats are leather and have extra leg room. This is the best option for a comfortable travel experience—if deciding to fly commercial. Except, there is no logical way possible to be comfortable when Claire is smelling like a cupcake factory. The smell is so strong that I want to lick her skin to see if she tastes like frosting. I want to lick a lot more of her, but I need to keep those thoughts to myself before I go up in flames.

Claire looks down at her boarding pass and then up at the marked rows. When she finds the one assigned to us, she stops and secures the handle on her carry-on.

I watch as she struggles to get her bag up in the overhead compartment, huffing under her breath at me every time I ask if she needs my help. Every inch her arms lift, her bottom hem does the same. I wipe a hand over my face. She's going to be the death of me. I am shielding her with my body from the growing line behind us.

After several tries, I lose my patience. I reach around her, take the bag from her hands, and plop it into the storage with ease. I lean my mouth down to her ear and whisper, "All you need to do is ask."

Claire looks back at me with her smoky eyes. She knows exactly how to enhance the beauty that she was born with. "Thank you."

"Take whichever seat you prefer."

She smiles and then slides into the one closest to the window. Angie does the same across the aisle, opposite us. I fish out my laptop and earbuds, setting them on my seat. I toss my bag effortlessly overhead and then get myself comfortable in my seat, allowing other people to pass through our section of the plane. I pull down my tray, set up my workstation, and try my best not to ogle Claire who cannot stop reapplying lip gloss to her already red stained lips. Are her lips really the Sahara Desert or is she just trying to make me wild? I glance over at the label and sure enough it is titled "Kiss My Cupcake."

I reach up and press my hands to the back of my neck. The smell is delicious. My dick twitches as I wonder whether or not her pussy tastes as sweet.

Claire moves closer, placing her elbow on the armrest divider. Why is she leaning toward me? Shit. I need to switch seats or something. My body stiffens as she takes her phone and reaches it across my abdomen.

"Smile you two," she calls over the aisle. "Got to capture all of your moments."

Fuck. Even with the extra space of first-class, I feel claustrophobic and too crowded with Claire up in my personal space, only adding to the tension happening at the zipper of my pants.

How long does it take to snap a picture of two

complying adults? Apparently twenty-eight seconds. I counted.

"Maybe we should get one of the four of us," Angie suggests.

I groan as she flags down the attendant assigned to our section, who seems thrilled to be asked this favor. Luckily it takes her only seventeen seconds to finish the task. We are not even in the air yet, and I already feel like I'm crashing and burning.

I look over at Claire when the sound of her breathing changes rhythm. Her eyes are shut and she is gripping the armrests with white knuckles. She stays this way during the taxiing and the entire safety protocol presentation.

I order her a ginger ale on ice when the attendant is walking back to the prep area.

"Here," I say, making her eyes flutter open. She relaxes when she sees the fizzy beverage. I open the can and pour it over the ice. "This should help settle your stomach."

"Thank you."

Normally beverage consumption needs to wait until we reach altitude; however, the perk of sitting where we are is that we have better holders for securing our belongings—drinks included.

I can tell she is confused by my behavior. I like keeping her on her toes. I close up my tray and put my laptop in the pouch behind the seat in front of me. The pilot warns of takeoff as he steers the plane down the runway. Claire clutches the can and cup so hard that she gives them little dents on the side.

I take them from her after she has a sip and place them inside the special drink holders. She goes back to gripping the armrests and closing her eyes. I can hear her soft "don't be sick" chant she says to herself on repeat.

I place my hand over hers, and she opens one eye at me to see my expression. I smile down at her and tell myself that the little bumps in her breathing have nothing to do with me—and is just her mildly hyperventilating.

"How do you not get sick on every car trip?" I ask.

"Because I'm usually in the driver's seat." She takes a few deep breaths. "Or I have the luxury of blasting myself with cool air."

I turn the vents toward her. Little wisps of hair blow astray from the sides of her head. A few tickle me, they are so long.

"Is that better?"

"Yes, thank you."

It isn't until we reach max altitude that she opens her eyes fully and searches for her drink. I release her hand and watch as her throat bulges from the gulps she takes of the ginger ale. It is tantalizing to stare at her neck. I can't look away. Images flash through my mind of what it would look like if she were to swallow something much larger. Could she handle it? I can be a good teacher.

"Care for some complimentary champagne?" the attendant asks.

We all nod and accept our flutes of bubbly that are passed to us from a wheeled cart. She also passes us each a sealed bag of a variety of snacks.

The sun is still visible and the glow from it setting is spectacular. I look out the window and admire the colors on the clouds.

"Cheers to your end of singleness!" Claire expresses,

clinking glasses with me, almost making me dump mine from the suddenness.

She stretches over me to tap her glass to Graham and Angie's glasses. If she leans over any more, I may be able to tell what color of strapless bra she has on—if she even has one on.

"How are you feeling?" Angie asks from the other side of Graham. She has to lean forward to even see us.

"Much better. I think my medicine finally kicked in," Claire says, her voice full of relief. "But it makes me so drowsy."

"You sure it's okay to drink with that stuff?" I ask. "Maybe you should eat something."

She glances down at the snack labels and examines the contents. If I wasn't already stalking her with my eyes, I may have missed the slight scrunch of her face.

"I got these too," I say, standing up and grabbing the snacks I purchased at the smoothie shop from the overhead compartment. "Help yourself to whatever you want."

Claire looks down at my selections and then back at me. I can tell I have her intrigued as to why I bought some organic vegan granola bars that are preservative-free and made with non-GMO ingredients. I have never tried them before, but based on her developing excitement, I must have struck gold.

"Thank you," she says, watching me sit back down and snap my seatbelt back into place. "Oh, I need to get my hand sanitizer." She gets up from her seat and watches as I move my hands to undo my belt. "No, I have room. Just stay put."

She shimmies sideways in front of me. I get a perfect

view of her sculpted ass, and it takes everything in me not to push her down onto me, so she can feel how fucking hot I am for her. Does she have even an ounce of a clue as to what she is doing to me? She is dressed like a flipping go-go dancer. How would I not be affected?

Once Claire is in the aisle, she barely can reach the overhead compartment without teetering on her tiptoes.

"Want help?"

"I can do it myself."

"I never implied you couldn't. But do you *want* help?" The plane jostles us with a bout of turbulence, sending Claire forward toward my lap. I catch her just in time. I steady her and stand up, unlocking the compartment with ease. I place her bag on my seat and allow her to dig through it until she finds the item that she needs. I place her contents back into the storage and secure the lock.

Once she is settled back into her seat and her seatbelt is snapped into place, she squirts some sanitizer onto her hand and offers me some, which I accept. She removes the wrapper from her bar and takes a big bite. When she finishes, I watch as she rummages through her purse that she retrieved from the floor. If she needs to slide past me one more time, I am not sure I can resist the urge to grab her luscious ass.

And then I see it. Yellow. She peels back the skin and plops the tip into her mouth.

What did I do to deserve this?

Is she some demon in disguise with one mission to destroy my self-control?

"Where did that come from?" I ask, my eyes fixated on

the soft fruit entering her mouth. I sound accusatory and crazed—even to my own ears.

She stops midbite, examines the outer peel, and then answers, "Costa Rica." Her words come out jumbled because her mouth is stuffed with banana.

I sigh deeply. "That's not what I meant."

Claire finishes chewing and swallowing. "Um, the grocery store? They were on sale and they are organic." She points to her purse when she realizes how frustrated I am over this whole random banana eating contest. I mean, it feels like a fucking contest, at which I lose if I blow my load like a teenager into my linen pants.

I shake my head at the meaningless details. I need to get my head on straight. I hit my call button on the screen directly below the overhead compartments. Within seconds, the flight attendant is at my side.

"What can I do for you, sir?"

"Can I get an Old Fashioned?" I turn over to Claire. "Want something? More champagne? Ginger ale?"

"Just some water, please. Sparkling if you have it."

"Certainly."

How long does it take to eat a freaking banana? Is she savoring it? Inventing a reverse eating contest? I swear I hear her moan. Or hum. Or—

I don't the fuck know. I just do not want to look over until she is done. Finish it, dammit. Deep throat the—

Fuck.

I shake my head over the image that I'm guilty of now creating in my own damn head.

"Hey," Angie says, getting Claire's and my attention.

She is leaning over Graham who is so smitten with her that he can't take his eyes away. "You guys want a lollipop?"

"No," I snap before Claire can answer. "We're good over here."

Graham tears his eyes from his girl only to narrow them at me. I shoot him the *don't even ask* look. I'm sure he'll pry when we're playing a game of 21 at the casino, and I'm sure I will overshare if alcohol is heavily involved. Right now, getting drunk and drowning out this scene playing in front of me seems like a legit coping mechanism.

When I think it is safe and Claire isn't stuffing phallic shaped food into her mouth, I turn to look at her. Great. She is asleep. She looks like an innocent sleeping angel—but with mini plastic penises draped around her neck. What was she thinking? This cannot be normal bachelor and bachelorette party ideas. And the pussy sleeve thing? Like I would ever slip my dick into that deathtrap. I have standards.

I pull down my tray and set up my laptop so I can check my email and get a little work done. I have never been attracted to a conventional nine-to-five job. This is probably why my previous FBI work and the cheaters service was so appealing to me.

"Up for having a chat?" Graham asks quietly from across the aisle.

I look over at him and see that Angie is resting her head in his lap and he has his fingers tangled in her hair, giving it a massage. Her soft snores let me know she is sleeping.

"What's on your mind?"

"Interested in being the head of cybersecurity at HH but

also manage and train all security staff at my other businesses?"

"You haven't been compromised again, have you?" I ask, trying to get a feel for what he wants me to do that his current men failed at accomplishing.

He confirms with a nod and then a chin tilt toward Angie, signaling that he wants her out of it. She has been through enough with her drive toward becoming an investigative journalist and nearly getting herself killed numerous times. Too many to accurately count.

"I have trust issues," he states the obvious. We both do. "What do you think?"

"I hope you can afford me," I say bluntly.

He throws his head back and laughs but quickly calms down when Angie stirs on his lap. I feel hair at my neck and look over to see Claire drifting into me. She is so exhausted from the Dramamine. I get drunk off the vanilla fragrance that is now so close to me that I know I am wearing it.

"I'll pay you whatever you want."

"I'll do it but only because I get a sick thrill at catching the bad guys."

Graham's smile reaches his eyes and he settles into his seat more comfortably than when the conversation first started. I glance back at my computer screen and send off a couple of emails I've been avoiding writing all week.

Claire's hair tickles my neck and her hand slides into my lap. I stiffen and keep my breathing even so as not to disturb her. She really does need to rest. I am writing another email when she jolts up from the seat.

"Oh no," she yells, rubbing her hands up and down the front of her dress. "I'm soaked."

"What has you so spooked?" I ask, looking at her freaking out. "Why are you jumping out of your skin?"

"Look," she says, pointing down toward the empty cup on her lap. Melting ice is collected between her closed thighs and is dripping into the crevice. Goosebumps sprout on her smooth flesh, as a chill causes her to tremble.

I grab some napkins from the back flap of the seat in front of me and help her dry up the water from the armrest and leather seat.

"What am I going to do?" she asks, mainly to herself. She won't stop talking to herself. Curse words fly out of her mouth like bullets from an automatic weapon. She looks at me with helplessness. "I can't sit here like this, soaking wet. I can't believe I did this."

Angie is up from the commotion. I turn to her. "Have any spare clothes in your carry-on? A shirt? Jacket? Anything?"

She shakes her head. "No, I never thought to bring anything other than what I am wearing now."

I look to Graham. "Same," he responds. "I got nothing."

I undo my seatbelt and start unbuttoning my white dress shirt, revealing my fitted white cotton tee underneath.

"Here," I say, handing Claire my shirt to wear. "It will probably look like a dress on you. Go into the bathroom and change."

She stares down at my offering, as the tears pooling in her eyes start to dry. "Thank you," she mouths, sliding out of our row and shimmying into the bathroom. I'm sure those spaces are not designed for outfit changes. Desperate times call for desperate measures.

When the bathroom door opens after several minutes

and Claire peeks out from behind it, my heart drops. She is gorgeous. My shirt comes midway down her thighs and covers ninety percent more of her body than the glitter bomb did. Yet, here I am seeing her at her sexiest. I look at her waist and notice that she turned the penis necklace into a belt to give her look more functionality. She kept the top two buttons undone, showing off the demi cups of her black satin bra. Her sleeves are rolled up. If I didn't know I just stripped off my shirt for her, I would think that this outfit was planned and designed this way. That's how damn good she makes it look.

There's a vulnerability to her stride as she tries not to make eye contact with anyone and just get back into her seat undetected. She glides past me, and the whiff of our joint scents makes me want to bottle it up and store it forever. I know that I will be masturbating later to the image of her wearing my clothes and not feel a damn ounce of guilt over it. I earned it.

"Thanks again," she mumbles, settling back in.

Pulling out her phone, she logs into the Wi-Fi to check her text messages, and something upsets her. I can tell by her changes in breathing. I try to get a more detailed look but come up empty-handed when she tosses her device back into her purse and pulls out the freaking lip gloss. I lean my head back and close my eyes. I must be in purgatory for all my past sins. There really is no other explanation for the torture I'm being forced to endure on this damn trip.

The flight attendant gathers up all our trash and discards of it in the galley. She then passes out individual steamed towels. I place mine around my neck and rub at the tension building. The pilot announces that we need to prepare for landing. I pack my laptop into my bag and secure the storage compartment overhead.

Claire grips the armrests like her life depends on it, but still stares out into the night sky as we descend anyway. I lean over and look out the window with her as I grow excited to get the first sighting of the lights on the strip.

"Do you see them? Do you?" she asks, bubbling over with anticipation.

"Not yet, but we will," I promise. It's like I am experiencing the city for the very first time with her. Everything seems different. Never before did I care to look at the aerial view. This is probably the first flight where I even have the window shade open to see out. Usually I just try to catch up on work or sleep—ignoring everyone around me. There is simply no ignoring Claire. She makes it utterly impossible not to watch whatever it is she does.

"There," she says, pointing and tapping the window. "There. See?" She turns back to look at me.

I know I am sporting a cheesy grin but I don't care. Seeing her this happy makes me want to keep her at this high for as long as I can. "I see," I chuckle.

"Where are we staying?"

"At the Bellagio."

"The one with the fountain show in front?"

"That's the one." Without a doubt, she did her research —or watched a lot of films set in Las Vegas. The choosing of the hotel and flight were the only two tasks she didn't try to micromanage. I can only imagine what type of spreadsheet or dream board she would have created from the possibilities, if I allowed her voting rights in the decision.

The pilot gives us a smooth landing. Within minutes we

disembark and are waiting for our luggage at baggage claim. Claire and Angie use the restroom—probably to apply the eighty-ninth application of lip gloss—while Graham and I wait for the bags to come through the conveyor belt.

"Please leave her alone," he warns sternly.

I look at him with narrowed eyes. He needs to care less about what I do in my free time.

"I mean it," he adds.

"I'm sure you do."

"What about Maxwell?"

"What about him?" I counter, unable to keep the sarcastic tone out of my voice. "He's a douche."

"She is not built to handle guys like you."

"That's for me to decide. Stay out of it."

6

CLAIRE

It is slightly after nine at night when we push open the door to the massive suite that Nic booked for us. The Bellagio is definitely one of the nicest hotels I have ever stayed at. The service is amazing and the lobby ceiling decor is breathtaking. As much as I love to have some control over this trip, I am also relieved that I had nothing to do with the choice of where to stay—mostly because I cannot afford much right now. The dilemma of balancing fun and funds is something I haven't had to experience until now. For the first time in my life, I'm in debt. Unfortunately, I do not have a solid path out of it.

"I figured you and Angie would take up the master bedroom on the east side, and we would each get a room on the west side," Nic says to Graham, who tips the hotel worker who brings up our bags on a wheeled cart.

"Works for us," he says, pushing his and Angie's belongings down to their bedroom. He smacks her ass playfully, making her jump, and then she quickly scolds him for not waiting for the door to shut.

Inside the suite, there basically is an apartment set up. There's a fully stocked bar and kitchen area, a living room, two sitting areas, and a view of the strip and fountains that is to die for. We have so much living space that I think the square footage exceeds that of the townhouse Angie and I once shared. It actually exceeds my current living arrangement too. This is massive. From the amount of windows, we are able to see two hundred seventy degrees. It is breathtaking.

Nic transports my bags to my room. He gives me the one with the better view and the bigger bed. I have no idea what has changed from the cafe until now. He seems lighter and more easygoing. Maybe getting away from Portland was good for everyone. We were all probably overdue for a trip.

"What's on the itinerary for tonight, captain?" he asks me, knowing that I planned basically every moment without his opinion or approval.

I scowl over his name for me. "Not much planned. I didn't know if our flight would be delayed, so I didn't make reservations anywhere. Maybe we can just hang out here in the room and order room service? Maybe go down to the casino and get drinks. Play a game or two?"

I can tell he is thinking about my declaration. Perhaps wondering if I will whip out a trifold board or something? It is tempting. Staying organized has helped me function these past few months since graduating.

"That sounds good."

I stare at Nic's strong jaw a few seconds, waiting for the

punchline of the joke. He is starting to scare me with his amicability, which is a direct contradiction to all of our previous encounters regarding this trip. Since arriving at the airport, he has been back to being the laid-back man that he seems to like to portray. Underneath his charm, I know there is something darker brewing. Like he has a beast living inside him that wants to burst out.

I really want to shower. Even though the sparkling water I dumped all over myself doesn't have sugar, it still left a filmy layer on my skin under my clothes. There is only so much wiping I can do in a miniature bathroom. I still feel gross.

I scurry off into my assigned room and look out at the lights of the city. I have an amazing view and am not sure how I will go back to my meager living arrangements when I get back to the apartment in Portland. When Ethan and I started dating, he routinely just stayed at my place. Angie has walked in a few times on our sessions and that basically ended our out-of-the-bedroom romps that fresh lovers usually do. But as time progressed, the shiny new feeling dulled. It is normal.

After seeing where Angie is living, I thought a prominent businessman in Portland would have a fancier place than what Ethan owns. However, his car is super nice and I guess he just prefers to funnel his money into maintaining its appeal.

I texted him three times since leaving for the airport and he did not respond to any of them—despite me being able to see that they are marked as "read." This is his typical behavior. If I'm in his sight, then I have his full attention. But as soon as I am away from it, I do not exist. We have talked—

basically argued—about it numerous times. He just tells me I'm being a needy, insecure girlfriend. He says I remind him of his ex-wife who expected him to respond right away and how they didn't last because of her demands of him. He always says it in such a way that sounds condescending and with the finely weaved implication that if I continue with my own expectations, he will cut things off.

There is not a submissive bone in my body, and yet here I am trying to figure things out with Ethan. I sacrificed so much for him by declining a prestigious internship in Los Angeles just to see where things would go with us. It would have been at a health resort fit for the celebrity clientele—something I always wished to do. My résumé would have been pimped after having that type of documented experience on it, and it would have propelled me into furthering my career without having to fight like I have to do now. However, I knew moving away would have ended things with Ethan. It would have been inevitable. But the gnawing feeling in the back of my brain keeps asking me if it was worth it. I am too afraid to answer honestly, because I fear living with a regret that I may never get over.

I unpack my luggage and set out a fresh set of clothes on the bed. Everything in this suite seems to be designed for royalty, from the upscale linens to the art on the wall. It is like I am in a modern-day palace. Nic did great picking out this venue. There is no way I could even afford one night here—especially now that my parents have ended the cash flow indefinitely. I'm dreading even bringing up my situation to Ethan. He has already scolded me about the grocery budget. Maybe he is clueless as to how little I make working at the gym. Who knows how he'll react to my newly discovered debt. My bets are on—*not well*.

I meander into the bathroom and glance around at the spaciousness. There is floor-to-ceiling tiling and a shower that could easily fit ten people inside. Maybe it has in the past. Ugh. At least there is a cleaning crew at places like these. I strip down and turn on the faucet that starts six different shower heads. Water cascades off me in every direction. I set the strength to hit me hard. Staying cramped up, even in first-class, next to a Greek statue named Nic has me super tense.

I still can't believe how clumsy I am around him. I just keep fumbling and the lack of gracefulness—which is something I take pride in—is wearing on my self-esteem.

I lather my hair with vanilla-scented shampoo that is held in a wall dispenser. I love this scent. It smells like homemade ice cream. I rinse my entire body and towel dry off.

For tonight, I do a simple blow-dry to my hair and add some styling cream. I keep my makeup low-key but still acceptable for a casual evening out. I slip on my black halter top and skintight denim jeans. Other than a thong, there is nothing else that is going to fit inside these things tonight. I pair the outfit with black sequin stilettos that add punctuation to my casual but sexy look.

When I feel like I am back to being put together, I head out into the main living space and find the gang mixing up cocktails and organizing all of the room service order that they must have called in while I was getting myself ready.

"You look smokin'," Angie says, while whistling. Her eyes take in my entire look. "Like hot dayum!"

"So do you! I love your purple dress."

I watch out of the corner of my eye as Nic adds more liquor to his glass. From the pure amber color, I predict that the only mix-in is ice.

"Dig in, ladies," Graham says, passing us each a plate. "We ordered a little bit of a lot of different dishes. Claire, the ones that are on the black plates are vegan."

I can't hold back my smile. "Thanks for being so thoughtful."

"Oh, that was Nic's doing," he adds. "But if you want to slide over to the dark side again, I got these bacon-wrapped scallops that are amazing."

"They are so cute, too," Angie says, popping one into her mouth.

"I'm not being super strict this weekend, but will pass tonight and stick to the animal-free options. Thanks though."

We fill up our plates and sit around the dining room table, munching and chatting about our itinerary for tomorrow. I am super hesitant to even suggest too many of my ideas, because Nic basically thinks we should wing everything. He planned nothing. He okayed nothing. He was a pain in the ass about everything.

"I thought, if it is okay with everyone, that maybe we could explore the strip tomorrow and just see what is here. I know you guys have been here before, but Angie and I haven't. We can even separate during the day and—"

"Let you two roam the city?" Graham asks, setting his drink down a little too hard. "Unaccompanied?"

"Well, I,"—I glance to Nic for help—"was not sure if maybe I overplanned the details."

Nic clears his throat. "I reassured Claire that whatever she dreamed up would be perfect for this trip, and that sticking to her plan would definitely take the stress off of trying to come up with ideas last minute."

Wait. Hold up. "When did you actually reassure me?" I whisper-yell. I want to wipe the smile off his face. Damn he looks smug. And hot as hell.

"I sent you an email."

"What?" I whisper. I must have missed it. "Well, then, it probably went to junk mail."

His lip curls up into a smirk. "Just accept that I'm allowing you this small victory."

I turn back to the happy couple and clap my hands together. "I have a ton of surprises in store for everyone."

"I'm so freaking excited!" Angie squeals, nearly falling out of her chair.

"You girls better pace yourselves," Graham groans. "The night is still very young."

"And the city never sleeps," I call out, feeling the looseness that the alcohol gives me. I am happy and free.

Angie giggles over nothing in particular.

I hold up my I-don't-know-what's-in-this drink and say, "To getting drunk and losing our inhibitions and driving all the single men wild! Cheers!"

"No. No," Graham blurts out, "we are not cheers-ing to that."

"Oh, yes we are!" Angie defies, clinking glasses with mine before he can stop her. "Let's go downstairs and make bad decisions."

I burst out into laughter as Graham and Nic look like they just swallowed knives. I really hope they aren't going to be killjoys to our excitement. When the two of us get together, we always create lasting memories. Tonight will surely be one to add to the list. This is our first time really hanging out as a foursome. The guys do not know what kind of fun is sure to be had.

I grab my black beaded handbag and double-check that all of my essentials are in place. I twist off the cap to my lip gloss and add a layer over my lip stain that surprisingly has lasted the hours that the label claimed it would. It is worth the exorbitant cost if it actually works.

My hair dried into a soft wave, and I push some over my shoulders. Angie leads the way out of the room, dragging me along by the elbow. The men take up the rear. The entire hotel is polished and sophisticated. Since staying here was a secret to me, I didn't get a chance to research what is available for us to experience. I think the surprise of not knowing what to expect is adding to my excitement.

"Want to take a walk through the Conservatory and Botanical Gardens before we hit up the casino?" Nic asks, hitting the call button for the elevator. We get our own set for this section of the hotel, so the wait is not long at all—despite the venue buzzing with the weekend crowd.

I turn back to look at him. "Um, are they open at this hour? Do we need a taxi?"

"They are on the same floor as the casino."

"Oh, here? *Inside* the building?"

He nods. "I'll show you."

We all enter the car and Graham selects the ground floor button.

"I love this dress," I tell Angie again, who has been looking extra stunning as of late. I know it has to do with the level of happiness that Graham makes her. I am thrilled they found each other. I pretty much am the greatest unknowing matchmaker of all time. Yes, I do take full credit for being the influencer in getting them to meet.

Angie's smile lights up her face. "Thank you. I miss trying to squeeze into your clothes. But at least we're not that far away from each other."

"Just feels weird not being a yell away."

She nods. "I agree."

The doors open and we all step out onto the polished marble floor. Despite it being night, you would never know it from the bright lights cascading down from the ceiling. The men take the lead while Angie and I hang out in the back, chatting and stopping to take a selfie or two. This whole "winging it" approach is kind of refreshing.

"You can always come over and raid my closet. I've been in an organizational mode lately. So everything is in order. I even added some more essentials to my Doomsday Bin." I narrow my eyes at her as she can't contain her giggles. I don't even know why she bothers trying to cover her mouth with her hand. I can tell just from her eyes that she thinks the whole thing is ludicrous. "You laugh, but I'm pretty positive you utilized my special heels from that bin at one moment in time."

"True story. But it's like you are preparing for an alien invasion where only the sexiest on earth survive, instead of for a flood or wildfire or viral outbreak."

"Wow, sexy alien invasion, sounds like the making of a romance book you have yet to read."

"No, I've read some," she admits.

"Of course, you have."

"Never judge an avid reader by how much alien dick they look forward to."

"Wow, you are almost making me a believer." I think about her perspective while we walk through the hotel's main floor. "I better start adding more supplies to my bin then. There's only so much preparing that you can do for an apocalypse without going completely crazy."

"Preach it."

I feel pangs of guilt for enjoying my view of Nic's ass. He changed into a pair of dark denim jeans and a black button-down shirt. He could basically wear a bed sheet and still look amazing with a built body like his. He is stacked, and I can even tell the definition in his neck muscles as his arms move from the light stroll through the hotel. He has to work hard to get that type of sculpting; none of his body is an accident.

"Claire?"

"Hmm?" I ask, looking over at Angie in confusion.

"You zoned out there for a minute. Fantasizing about striking it rich tonight?"

I was fantasizing about something, that's for sure. I swallow hard as the men chat quietly with each other. Their conversation seems intense, yet they are careful not to talk too loud. I can't even make out a word—not that my focus is on words right now.

When we get to the indoor garden, it is bigger than I ever imagined. I can't even keep a cactus alive. Or a goldfish. So seeing the grandiose horticultural display of plants being used to create art is enthralling. Strung from the glass ceiling are huge butterflies made out of various plants and flowers. Oversized hummingbirds appear to be flying through the open indoor sky. A giant bumblebee looks to take flight off an enormous flower. The designers carry the spring theme down below with running water fountains, walking bridges, and wildlife made from plants scattered about.

I stand in awe over the little footbridge and savor the smell of freshness. It must take hundreds of people to execute something to this magnitude and probably even more to maintain its beauty.

"Smile, you two," Angie announces, causing me to turn around.

I stumble a little as my heel sticks in the crevice of the wooden planks, and just as I'm about to face plant, I am caught midair and righted again. I look up into the pair of blues and mutter, "Thank you." I didn't even notice Nic beside me; I was that wrapped up in my own world. He sidesteps a foot closer and places his hand at the hollow of my back. I can barely feel his touch it is that gentle. Yet, something makes it not feel innocent at all. Maybe it is because I was just checking him out during our walk here. Maybe it is because my current relationship with my long-term boyfriend is on rocky ground. Or maybe it is because every cell in my body is alive with a curiosity so extreme that I am starting to sweat.

"What are you doing?" My voice comes out more as a hiss than my intended whisper.

"Smiling for a picture," he says through gritted teeth. He nudges his chin opposite of us, making me look at Angie who is holding up her phone expectantly.

"Oh." I quickly smile for the picture and back up a step once it's over, stumbling again over the wooden groove in the bridge. Damn. Nic steadies me, his hands on my upper arms.

"Those things are a deathtrap," he comments, looking down at my sparkling heels.

I shrug. "But they look cute."

"That they do."

"When you agree with me, it catches me off guard."

"Good. I will keep doing it," he chirps, "when you least expect it."

We hang out in the garden for a bit longer and then walk through the lineup of boutiques.

"I want to go there," Angie says, pointing at the chocolate fountain. "That is heaven on earth."

"This place I'll definitely make concessions for," I say, staring at the bakery items through the window. Everything is doused in chocolate. White, milk, dark—or a mix of all three.

Angie and I don't even wait for the guys to comment. Their opinion is completely unnecessary when we have already made up our minds. We walk into the shop and read the descriptions of all the cakes and pastry items. They even have homemade chocolate ice cream and fruits dipped in chocolate.

"Is there some type of package that has a big sampling of your best items?" Angie asks the worker, who smiles and points to a display box along the counter. "Wow, that has a bit of everything. I want that, please."

"See something that caught your eye, sweetheart?" Graham asks, wrapping his arms around her as she hands over her black credit card at the counter.

Early on in their relationship, Angie resisted Graham

pushing money on her. I think it was cute how they struggled to find a rhythm that worked for them. As stubborn as both of them are, it is rewarding to see how they each adapted and let go of their walls to find a happy middle.

"Are you going to share and play nice?" Graham asks her, kissing her neck. "Or do I need to order more for the rest of us?"

I giggle as Angie makes a face at him and glances down at the box. "I *think* I can share."

We move to a table area set up outside the shop and pull down the sides of the box. Digging in, we enjoy the impromptu dessert. Not having anything planned for tonight is working out in our favor.

We devour the entire box, and I don't think I can fit one more thing in my belly without popping a button on my fly.

"I want to eat there for breakfast," Angie says, looking back at the chocolate fountain. She's always had a thing for sweets—especially chocolate.

"They probably stay open twenty-four hours a day," Nic says.

"There is no way you are eating chocolate in the morning. You'll have a sugar crash by nine and then I'll have to deal with your cranky mood the rest of the day," Graham says, tickling her sides and making her jostle the whole table as she tries to get away.

We clean up our mess and work our way toward the casino entrance, where the main lights are dimmed but the excitement of the hotel comes to life. Slot machines fill up half the floor with various money amount levels. The sounds and lights draw attention to the eye—probably because they are predictable money makers for the casino.

A bar is set up in the center, lined with liquor bottles and mixers. Beautiful women dressed in cocktail dresses are rushing to get drinks to the patrons, earning tips and helping the casino bring in the revenue by keeping everyone happy and free to make bad financial decisions. I'm sure there is a strong correlation between tipsy players and loss of money. The drinks may be free, but the hotel still manages to stay in business.

I glance over at the table games and wonder if any have a limit or not. I haven't been to a casino of this size before. On the East Coast, every one that I visited, I was underage and was just passing through. The ones in Atlantic City are scaled much further down in comparison.

"Should we start at the slots?" I ask the group.

"If you want to lose all your money," Nic responds blandly.

"Maybe you just aren't lucky," I quip.

I feel his eyes burn into me. "I don't believe in luck."

I turn my attention to him. "What do you believe in then?"

"Statistics. Math. Playing games with some sort of skill level."

"Like poker," I suggest.

"Sure, like poker. Where I can control some of my wins and losses."

"You still need some luck."

He shakes his head. "No, not really. Even with horrible cards, you can still get an opponent to fold or make a mistake. It is all about reading people and taking risks."

"How about you give slots a chance and maybe you'll learn to have some fun again in your life?" I suggest. He is right though. I really do not have money to spare. If I want to strike it rich, I better pick games with better odds.

"How about we turn this into a little game? Let's find two neighboring machines and play ten rounds each to see who has the most earnings in the end."

"What does the winner get?" I ask, wanting to know the stakes. I can see Nic's brain churning, and I wonder what nonsense he will come up with when given no parameters.

"Winner gets to plan out what we are doing tomorrow."

"Deal," I say, knowing that I have better ideas when it comes to fun.

More importantly, however, I really want to stick it to him and shove his "I don't believe in luck" statement back in his face.

7

NIC

I watch as a bright smile forms on Claire's lips, and I vow to myself to make it last as long as possible. My thoughts race with all the things I want to do to her. With her. But yet I know she is trouble. While she possesses the one quality I look for in a woman, she is also my future sister-in-law's best friend—which makes her basically off-limits. I can piss with a lot of people, but Graham would kill me if he knew the deviance of my lustful thoughts.

Graham and Angie head over to the roulette table, while Claire is scoping out the machines that she wants us to use for the challenge. If I were here alone, I would never be caught dead at the slots. They are money whores, require zero skill, and have the worst odds of winning.

I like to win.

I cover my chuckle with a hand rubbing at my chin. She is reading the side of each machine for the probability listing, while trying to find machines on the end of rows that are not already taken.

"You know these machines are going to take all of our money if we play long enough, right? It's great revenue for the Bellagio."

"Hush. I'm working."

I continue watching her "work" and am in awe of her focus on the task.

"I have watched a ton of documentaries on the art of finding the best slot machine in the casino," she rambles, glancing around the area.

"Seems counterproductive if everyone here also watched the same documentaries," I explain, trying to keep the humor out of my tone. It is hard though.

She stops and glances up at me, propping her hands on her hips. "Now, what are the odds of that actually happening?"

"Better odds than either of us actually winning on these damn things."

"Quit kicking my pet unicorn," she snaps.

I laugh and then quickly stop at the glare she shoots me. I'm definitely pushing my luck—that I don't even believe in.

"I thought you were the laid-back brother," she huffs.

"It's just a facade."

"Apparently so." She continues mumbling to herself and analyzing the machines. "Here. I found the perfect pair."

I follow her to two twin machines in the quarter section. "You are aware that the odds get better for the player as the amount of minimum money for the machine increases, right?"

"Yes, I'm aware. But I also don't want to lose that much money."

"We *are* going to lose all our money. It's just what happens."

"You are so pessimistic. Just. Stop."

"Let's go get playing cards and get them registered so if we spend so much, we can get some comps," I suggest. The hotels here reward players who frequent the casino. Sometimes the rewards are specific for high rollers and very limited.

"How much should we put on each card?" Claire asks.

I hope she lets me pay for her playing card. Collins recently informed me that she is harboring a debt from her undergraduate and graduate degrees at River Valley U. The fact that Maxwell didn't just take care of it adds to the list of reasons why he is not the best match for her. He's one of the best day traders in the city and yet he seems to be keeping a ton of secrets over his level of wealth—and how he chooses to spend it.

"One hundred each?"

"We are just playing ten rounds, so that's like $2.50."

"I doubt we can get cards with that low of an amount. How about we add one hundred dollars to them and then have money for the duration of the trip? The cards can be used in the shops too or the cafes." I would much prefer to add at least a thousand but know if I say too much, she may not want me to cover her cost.

"I, um, I don't know if I have that much on my debit card. Is there an ATM here for me to check what I have stored?"

"The ATM is over against the wall," I say, pointing to multiple machines. "But I can cover this."

"Oh," she says, her eyes wide. "I don't see how that's fair."

I shrug. "You can pay me back later." I don't mean it, but I need her to quit worrying about money right now.

"Fine."

She pouts her bottom lip out. I want to suck on it and taste the gloss she compulsively keeps reapplying. Everything she does intrigues me, and if she keeps rattling off documentary information like she's an expert, I will give her mouth something else to keep it busy. I discreetly adjust myself in my pants at the dirty thoughts I'm conjuring up in my brain of her, on her knees, accepting me for the first time.

There is no line at the money exchange and we get our cards loaded with one hundred dollars each, registered under each of our names.

"Show me to the machines," I say, following her pert ass along for the ride. It has to take great skill to be able to walk in her skintight pants and those stilts.

"Over here, I found the perfect winning machines."

There is no way she is for real, but I am too invested to not see this through. I sit down where she instructs. I'm not used to taking the backseat to anything. However, Claire's rush of excitement over this little bit of control makes me want to see her in this position more often—or at least give her that illusion.

If we were betting something more substantial, there is no way I would use freaking slots as the game of choice. I resist giving her a hard time over her selection, even if just for fun. I want to get this over with and then move on to some more strategic games where I can get to know her better.

A waitress trying too hard at sex appeal comes over before we even put our cards into the machine to ask us what we would like to drink.

"Cosmo, please," Claire answers.

"Double malt scotch, neat."

We insert our cards and I hesitate to start playing, mainly because I want to watch her in action.

"How about you start and we see how much you end up with? Then I can go."

"Okay…"

I watch as she does her first round, coming up empty-handed on matching any fruit. She combines her next three rounds together to try to earn more, with a single pull of the lever. The machine comes to life, and I watch dumbfounded as she bursts up from her seat and dances around with her hands waving in the air like she just caught on fire.

"How much did I win? How much? It's huge, right?" She covers her hands over her eyes and is so excited she cannot look. "I did a triple bet!"

I look down at the display and cannot keep my laughter from erupting from my diaphragm. Her eyes pop open, one at a time. "A whopping $1.50. Congrats."

"What? This machine is broken. I made a triple bet."

Our drinks arrive and she downs hers so fast that the waitress is still around for her to order another one. I stuff some bills into the tip glass and take a long sip from my own.

"What do you expect from a quarter machine?"

"Definitely more than what I just earned."

She pouts her bottom lip out, does another triple bet, and makes the machine ring out again. The sound is so loud, but doesn't compete with Claire's high-pitched squeal of delight. Even though she knows it can't be much, she has hope beaming in her eyes as she looks at me, pumping her arms.

The machine finally stops and concludes that her earnings are $9.25, due to scoring points for multiple lines of matching fruits.

"I am going to beat you so badly!" she chants.

"If you keep winning, even small bets like these, you probably will," I chuckle. But seeing her this carefree makes me the real winner. She, however, is in a relationship already. So, I have to play my cards correctly if I am going to make this mutually beneficial for the both of us.

Claire finishes her ten rounds with $110.25 on her card, with a net profit of $10.25.

"Not bad," I tell her. I laugh as she dances around the machine, telling me to "suck it" and that she "so has this in the bag."

I max out the winning chances, taking up five rounds at once. I pull the lever and watch as the fruit rolls along the bars, finally stopping. The machine buzzes with a loss. I do this one more time, maxing out the bet. With the pull of the lever, the machine goes wild.

"Oh shit," she groans, watching the money rack up. "I gave you the winning machine. This is all my fault."

"I'll share my profit with you."

Her laugh goes right to my groin. I sip my drink, finishing it off.

"Whelp, you just beat me by fifty cents. I cannot believe it."

"Want to renegotiate the bet?" I ask.

"Depends what you have in mind."

"Do you know how to play poker?"

"I have watched the big tournaments on TV, but it was for Texas Hold'em. I think I know the basics."

I nod and hide a grin. I honestly have no idea what to expect from her playing skills, but I am eager to find out. "How about we try the limit tables and see who comes out ahead? We'll buy in at the same amount and whoever lasts the longest wins."

"What are we betting?"

"If you win, I'll make sure Graham does not sabotage your stripper outing."

"Ugh, you really think he is going to keep us from going?"

"Have you met the man?"

Her face scrunches up. "Good point."

"When it comes to his fiancée looking at other male bodies, I guarantee you he would put a stop to it. Or tag along and make it super awkward."

She shakes her head. "Yeah, you're right. Okay, I think that is a worthy enough bet. But what do you get out of it if I lose?"

I swallow hard. "If you lose, we go to a steakhouse during this trip and you have to try a bite of everything."

"Oh my gosh, no." She shudders over the thought. "Okay, this is pure motivation for me winning. I can't even tell you the last time I had meat. Pretty sure it was bacon and Angie reminded me how smart pigs are"—she stops and looks to be in pain—"I just can't."

I can't stop laughing around her. She is so unique and different from any other girl I have been around. She is like a fresh breeze of purified air.

On our way to the table game section of the casino, we pass by Graham and a drunk looking Angie.

"Can't keep up with the high rollers?" I ask, looking down at Angie and smiling.

"This is what free drinks do to my girl. Loses count and ends up wanting to sleep anywhere she can."

"See you guys in the morning," Claire says. "Nic is planning the entire day. I lost a—"

"Just planning where we are eating breakfast," I correct. "Everything else is all on Claire." Her eyes dart up to mine, and I just act like that was part of the original deal. When she lost the bet, I saw the color drain from her skin. There is no way I can go through with the original bet. I doubt if I win tonight, I can go through with this new one either.

Graham nods. "Have a good night. Gotta get this one to bed." Angie gives us a disoriented wave and teeters on her feet. Graham braces her and ushers her toward the main entrance.

"Playing a table game was my idea, so I can buy us both in," I reassure.

Claire opens her mouth to argue but then thinks twice and shuts it. She follows me to the roped-off section where several tables are already in progress. We find one that is about to start up and take our seats. I pay the dealer in exchange for our sets of chips. She goes over the amounts and then those in the big blind and small blind positions add their chips preemptively to the center of the table.

I am glad that Claire and I are seated opposite of each other. I really need to be able to see her eyes and mannerisms to see if she has any tells.

Cards are dealt and I look at my six and eight of clubs. Nothing to brag about for my starting hand. When it gets to my turn, I check and wait for the flop. Claire raises, forcing a few people to fold. She is the only female at the table, and I can already feel my blood pressure rising over some of the looks she is getting. She is so focused on her cards that she doesn't even notice.

I call the bet and watch as the dealer burns a card before revealing a four of hearts, a five of diamonds, and a jack of diamonds. I need a seven to complete my straight. I have no chance at a flush or a full house. I don't even have a pair. I place a small bet that knocks out the remaining players, except for Claire. She glances at her cards, swallows, and fixes a piece of hair behind her ear.

"I will raise."

Fuck.

I watch as she puts in the money for what I originally bet and adds a few more chips to the stack. Is she slow playing me and milking me out of as much money as possible?

I call and throw in the chips needed for the turn card to be revealed. The dealer burns and flips a six of diamonds. Even though I now have a pair of sixes, there are three diamond cards on the board. If Claire is holding two more diamonds, she definitely has me beat. I want to know what she has.

I check. She bets. I call. The river card is a seven of diamonds. Of course. I catch my straight, but the odds that Claire is holding another diamond—she just needs one now —is highly probable. Shit.

I bet high. Triple what my previous bets have been. Part of me wants her to call so I can see her hand and learn from her methods. The other part of me wants her to fold so I can collect this huge pot.

"Re-raise."

Is she for real? I watch as she adds more chips to the growing stack. I am so invested that it would be stupid to drop out now.

"Call," I grind out, adding the correct amount. I turn over my cards. "I have a straight."

Claire flips her cards over. "I just have two pairs," she says, showing her Jack of spades and her four of diamonds.

I shake my head at her. "You also have the winning hand with a flush."

"Huh," she says, looking at the five cards in the lineup and her two. "I guess I do. I always forget to look at the little black and red pictures."

The men at the table laugh, and I can tell they are putting her in the I-am-just-here-for-fun category. I know she's playing us all. She knew she had a flush. I can tell by the crinkle of her eye that she is acting to try to get everyone here to think she has no clue what she's doing. I know better.

And deep in the pit of my stomach, I feel proud of her. She can hold her own and stay confident.

We play a few more hands, and I regain some of my chip stack. A couple of players get eliminated early on.

Claire and I are dominating the table. She is not letting anyone push her around with their hefty bets. In fact, I am nearly positive she bluffed her way to winning a huge pot when one of the young players—probably just turned twenty-one—tried to get her to drop out before the turn.

I fold when necessary and watch Claire like a hawk even when I am out of the hand. I can pick up signals from her when she has a good hand versus when she doesn't. It is subtle though. If I wasn't already tuned in to her, I would miss a lot of the twitches and breathing pattern changes.

The waitress keeps the drinks coming. I sip on a rum and coke, checking my hand to see a pair of kings. This is my best starting hand so far. I check and hope that I do not reveal that I have something good. As usual, Claire raises pre-flop and knocks out the only two other players other than us at the table.

"Call," I grunt, adding my chips to the pot.

The dealer reveals two, two, king. I look down at my cards even though I know exactly what I have. I need to make it look like I forgot. "Check."

Claire raises and I call. The dealer reveals a jack on the turn.

I toss in a few chips, Claire re-raises.

"All in," I say, staring her straight in the eyes.

She smiles a grin so wicked that it sends a jolt to my dick. "I call."

The dealer helps us manage the chips. Claire has a slight lead. The dealer turns over Claire's cards to reveal a pair of twos. She has a fucking four-of-a-kind. I let out all of the breath I am holding. The dealer flips mine and shows my pair of kings. The only way I can win this hand is to get another king, and it might not even be possible if another player folded the last one.

I watch with bated breath as the dealer burns and reveals the river card—an ace.

"You won," the guy beside Claire says joyously, touching her on her back.

I watch as she tenses and shakes out of his hold.

"Let me buy you a drink to celebrate," he says.

I am going to hit something. He needs to freaking back away from her. I start to stand, mentally preparing myself to get into an altercation.

"They are free," she says with a scowl.

Attagirl. Let him know how lame he sounds. She gathers her chips and spends time stacking them back up. I am out, but I stay so I can watch her secure her victory at the table. As long as she keeps forcing the other two players to go all in, she will eventually be able to get lucky enough to get the cards needed to win.

And after just two rounds, she does.

I slide over to join her. "Congrats. You played very well."

She cashes out and hands me her earnings. "This money isn't mine."

I shake my head. "Yeah, it is. You won it. Plus, you get to enjoy strippers without Graham going ballistic and bum rushing the place. You might need some of the extra cash for paying off those greasy testosterone junkies."

Claire narrows her eyes over my colorful description. "I at least owe you what you paid for me to join the table. I feel really weird taking this money when it wasn't mine to start with."

"Use it for the trip. Everything costs more in a high touristy area like this. Just add it to your spending money and have fun. I want you to have it."

"I appreciate it." She pulls out her phone from her handbag and looks at the screen. She mumbles a few curse words and places the phone to her ear. "Hi." There is a long pause and I can hear the demeaning tone from the caller. "I never posted any pictures. What are you talking about? How am I responsible for what Angie does? This is her party weekend and she's excited, so she probably uploaded an album. No. Whatever. You're just looking for a scapegoat and making me one because it's convenient." There's a long pause and then I swear I hear a sniffle. "I'm sorry, Ethan, for raising my voice."

I take a few steps to the side and pull out my phone to keep myself from looking like I am listening to Ethan give Claire an earful. I log on to my fake social media account and find Angie's profile. A couple of hours ago, she posted a few pictures from our trip thus far. A group shot from the plane, a photo in the suite of her and Graham, and then the picture at the Botanical Gardens of just me and Claire. I can understand how assumptions can be made from just the single photo, but Ethan is very insecure.

Claire sighs. "I said sorry. Why won't you accept my apology?"

Why is she apologizing to the bastard? He's wrong.

"Fine, then don't add money to my debit card, Ethan. Punish me for something I have no control over. Yes, I want you to come. I don't know what else you want me to do. Beg?" Claire says into the phone. "I will chat with you—"

She looks down at the phone and then up to me. "He hung up on me."

I don't know what to say that would be fractionally appropriate. What I want to say and what I should say are two very different things. "Maybe we should head back up to the suite and get some rest. Tomorrow everything will be fresh again."

Claire nods and we head out of the casino.

8

CLAIRE

My phone buzzes again from my bag and I retrieve it, sliding the answer bar to accept the call. "Hello."

"I can't believe you hung up on me," Ethan snaps.

I close my eyes as I try to keep my temper in check. It never bodes well for me to get Ethan so irate that he threatens to break up. "I didn't hang up. You must have." He is throwing a fit over nothing.

"What did I do to ever deserve how you're treating me right now?" he asks, making me stumble back a step in the elevator.

I swear this man will always play the victim. I can hear the slur to his words and know he's drunk. When he's drinking, there's no way to rationalize with him. Plus, it is super shitty to be turning his bad mood around and blaming me. This is not my fault. I know not to expect a heartfelt apology tonight or even tomorrow. When someone never thinks they are in the wrong, then they also do not find any need to say the words "I'm sorry." But who knows, maybe he'll surprise me. This whole relationship is being held together right now by hope. Hope that we can settle our differences. Hope for a better future.

"Can we please just continue this conversation tomorrow?"

"You should be damn thankful that you have me in your life. I provide everything for you. You're living off me for free. Using me."

His words sober me up fast. I, too, have been drinking. There's only so much pushing he can do to me before I snap.

"I'm hanging up now. We can discuss this tomorrow." My words come out angry, heated. I am teetering on the brink of saying something I will regret.

I hit the red end button and stomp out of the elevator when it reaches our floor. I can feel Nic's eyes burning holes in the back of me. He has enough courtesy to keep his comments to himself. I hate when people see me cry. I usually only allow Angie that privilege. We have been through so much together that baring my soul to her was a natural occurrence when we spent years under the same roof during our college days.

Nic unlocks the door and opens it, stepping back so I can walk through. I march into my room and slam the door a little too loud, considering Graham and Angie are prob-ably in bed.

The time reads 11:52 p.m. on the clock near my bed. I strip down and put on a pair of red silk shorts and a white tank top. I brush my teeth and crawl into bed.

I toss and turn, just barely falling asleep before shaking myself awake again. I feel dehydrated and in need of a bottle of water. It is slightly after three, and I feel like I didn't even sleep. My head hurts from a dull headache starting at the base of my neck and working its way upwards.

I roll out of bed and pad across the room until I reach the door leading out to the shared living space. I avoid turning on lights as to not stimulate my brain into thinking it is morning. Making my way into the kitchen, I find the fridge and pull out a chilled bottle of water. I crack open the safety seal and take a long sip. I close the door and turn to walk back into my room when I crash into a wall of chiseled muscle.

"Shit," I slur, dumping water from my bottle down my white tank. I stare down at my top as it slowly becomes see-through. I am lacking the protection of a bra, and instantly I bring my arms up to cross over my chest to give myself a little coverage.

"Sorry, I heard a noise and came to investigate," Nic says, keeping me from falling over as I rock back and forth on my feet. He is shirtless and just wearing a fitted pair of black boxer briefs. His body is stacked. Tanned and taut. He motions to my bottle. "Sorry about the water. What are you doing up?"

"I have a headache."

He nods. "It's a good thing you are drinking some water. You probably are dehydrated."

Nic's eyes move slowly down my body, settling on my crossed arms. I am pretty sure I am just accentuating my cleavage even more, but I don't know what else to do. His smirk is subtle, and I glance away to try to keep myself calm. The air-conditioned room is making my nipples press against my arms, reminding me once again I am braless.

I step back and almost fall on my ass. Nic steadies me, yet again. When did I become incapable of walking without making a fool of myself? "I better get back to bed." I sound out of breath and my lower half tingles with a need to rub myself to release. Nic brings out a wild side to me—like an itch is building under my skin and only he can cure it. He makes me feel feminine and even more petite, just by standing next to me.

I am with Ethan. I chose Ethan. Ethan is my boyfriend. I stayed in Portland for Ethan. Ethan has been treating me like shit. Ethan is currently having a hissy fit over a picture I never even posted.

How did I even find myself in the middle of a mess I don't even think I created? But here I stand, staring at an entirely different mess in the form of a beautiful six-foot-tall Greek statue of a built man. He's a dirty fantasy come to life. And his hands... Gah, his hands are huge. I can't help but wonder if every other region of his body shares similar characteristics.

"I'm going to go for a walk if you want to join."

I look up at Nic's face. The kitchen counters are lit with lights from underneath the cabinets, which cast a warm glow on his facial features. He must be able to tell I am lost in my own thoughts. Granted, they were indecent thoughts of him, but thoughts, nonetheless.

"Now?"

"When I can't sleep, I usually hit up my home gym. But I'm not at home, and I definitely am struggling with sleep."

I nod with understanding. "Same. I have so much on my

mind. Maybe some fresh air will do me good. Do you think it's safe at this hour to be walking?"

He looks surprised by my question. Maybe he just assumes I'm reckless and stupid, like I've proven many times before in the past. "You'll be surprised just how many people will be out," he says, as if he is certain we won't be alone at three in the morning.

"Let me change into something less…" I just leave the statement hanging when I realize that there is no answer that won't sound awkward. I hurry back to my room and slip on a simple yellow tank dress over a pink bra and panty set. I pile my hair on top of my head in a high ponytail, similar to the style I would do when I was a cheerleader in high school. I liked the camaraderie I had when being on a squad but quickly learned that friendship can be superficial and competition can be deeply rooted in jealousy.

When I step out of my bedroom, Nic is all ready to go in gray cargo shorts and a black T-shirt. He opens the door and allows me to go through first. I can't tell if this is him trying to play the role of a gentleman or if he genuinely is a nice guy.

I instantly stop in the doorway and whirl my body around, propping my hands on my hips. The question bugging me in the back of my head bursts out of my mouth before I can snap it shut. "Why did you give me such a hard time prior to the trip about my itinerary?"

He doesn't answer, so I awkwardly turn and keep walking toward the elevator bank.

"Because you are cute when you're mad."

His answer is so simple and said with such sincerity that I stop in the middle of the hallway and look up at him.

"What?" It's not like I misheard him. I heard every single word. Every. Single. One.

He shrugs. "You get all agitated, and I know you were forcing yourself to keep your cool. I could see the struggle in how your breath would change or how you would tap your foot under the table."

I take a step back and then another. "So you were annoying me on purpose?"

"Sure."

"Sure?"

He shrugs and glances away for a brief moment. "The end result is the same. So, how we got here shouldn't matter."

"It's all about the journey," I scoff. "And you were trying to make the journey less desirable."

He leans over me, and I think he's going to kiss me. My breath catches in my lungs and my lips part ever so slightly. But he bypasses them and instead hits the down button for the elevator. I deflate over this silly fantasy that I shouldn't be having because, for one, I am taken. For two, Nic and I are opposites that will clash. We are two species in a zoo that would never be able to share the same habitat without us both dying. His eyes lock with mine and then move down to my lips.

"Was pretty desirable, if you ask me."

I narrow my eyes at his. Is this his way of flirting? "I have a boyfriend," I remind him.

"Who treats you like shit..."

"He's still my boyfriend."

"You keep feeding yourself those lies, Claire. But boyfriends don't degrade their partners."

"Let me guess, you're an expert?"

His jaw twitches. "No. I'm not. But anyone can see what is so obvious."

The car arrives, and I rush inside. Maybe spending optional free time with Nic is a bad idea. It's already starting off wrong. He hits the ground floor button. It takes ridiculously long to get to the bottom of the hotel. It is like the car knows that the oxygen inside it is dwindling as Nic sucks the life out of me for his own sick pleasure.

We remain silent the entire trip down. Once the doors open, we walk to the nearest exit, and the cool desert air chills my skin as I adjust. The fountains are lit and dancing to music. Every light from all the casinos and hotels is on, racking up an electric bill that I would never want to pay. I guess the city really doesn't sleep. Groups of tourists gather on the sidewalk, some a little rowdy but most are peaceful.

I stare at the Paris Hotel's Eiffel Tower attraction and hope that Ethan wants to go up it with me when he flies here for the last couple of days of the trip. It is so beautiful and romantic. We just need some happy moments to counterbalance some of the drab ones.

"The real one in France is breathtaking." Nic's voice cuts through the silence.

"I bet," I say longingly. "Never been."

"Which way do you want to explore?" he asks.

I point down toward the volcano at The Mirage Hotel. Nic lets me set the pace, as we stroll along through the city. It is an extremely walkable area, with well-designed sidewalks and crosswalks. Cars actually stop for pedestrians and police are patrolling the street in a friendly, nonconfrontational manner. It is easy to tell that the city loves and welcomes visitors—and the revenue that results.

Nic and I meander. We make comments about the different hotels and laugh over some of the street performers who are still trying to make a buck at this hour of the morning. Despite him giving me a hard time over the ideas I have come up with for this weekend, he seems to listen to me ramble on about the reservations I have made and tickets I have ordered.

"I think Angie and Graham will love what you arranged."

"I sure hope so. I feel this mounting pressure to make things special for Angie after all she's been through."

Nic slows down as we watch the volcano erupt with fire. "I get that. But you need to relax a bit and quit trying to make everything perfect. Sometimes the best moments are the unplanned ones."

I let his words marinate for a few seconds before nodding. He is right. There is a balance between having a loose plan and having one so strict that it doesn't allow for impulsive fun. I need to bring back Spontaneous Claire—or her evil counterpart Impulsive Claire. Those bitches know how to live it up.

"Can you help me not be so anxious with the parts of the day I didn't plan out?" I ask. "I have the main attractions set for each day. But I left a lot of empty space in between."

He smiles. "Sure. I can do that."

"So, you have a breakfast venue in mind?"

"Yes."

"How fancy do I have to dress?"

"Pretty sure if you wear anything other than a T-shirt and shorts, you'll be overdressed."

I nod. I love chill places. "So this is a dive?"

"No tetanus shot required. It's just casual," he explains with a chuckle. "And off the strip."

"Oh fun. I was hoping to see more of the area."

We walk and chat about nonsense stuff, like *this or that* or *would you ever*? It is easy and light, except for all the pangs of guilt that stab at my strength. Maybe spending time with Nic isn't the best way to nurture my relationship with Ethan. The last thing I need is to peer on the other side of the fence to see if the grass is a different shade of green.

I chose Ethan. I need to work on that relationship if I want to have a future.

When we get back to the Bellagio, it is almost four thirty. I am exhausted. As soon as I'm in the privacy of my own bedroom, I strip off all my clothes. I down a big glass of water, use the bathroom, and crawl into bed. It feels great to lay my head on the pillow and drift off.

The muffled sounds coming from the suite cause me to stir. I glance at the clock and see that it is almost nine o'clock. Shit. I must have slept in and am holding everyone up from a breakfast out. I roll out of bed and slip on a pair of cutoff jean shorts and the homemade T-shirt that Angie made me for Christmas. She recently developed a hobby of making custom prints using a heat press. Her skills have gone up with practice and her work is better than what the big box stores sell. She also sews and has supplied me with some amazing custom workout clothes that have gotten me so many compliments at the gym—and impromptu orders in case she ever opens up one of those cute online boutiques.

I brush my hair and add some styling product to it to give my natural wave a bit more dimension. I quickly dust on some makeup and add my cupcake lip gloss to my lips. It is my way of enjoying dessert without all the garbage ingredients and added calories.

When I join the gang, all eyes go to my shirt and then the laughter erupts. It says "Puts Out For Pancakes" and has a graphic of a stack of pancakes with butter and syrup in the center of the shirt.

"Angie knows me best," I say with a shrug. "I'm a total slut for a delicious pancake and a good margarita." As soon as the words pop out of my no-filter mouth, Nic's eyes grow dark, and the once serene blue color now looks to be navy. I could get lost in those deep ocean eyes. My cheeks flush, catching me off guard. Shy and conservative are two words that are usually never used to describe me. Yet, here I am blushing a shade that only looks good on tomatoes.

Angie laughs to almost tears. "Pretty sure you would get naked for a mediocre pancake and a bad margarita too."

I give her a shrug and a grin. "Truth. I've never met a margie I didn't like. Plus, it's pretty hard to mess up pancakes."

The guys laugh. I avoid making eye contact with Nic, mainly because I can feel him staring.

"Ready for breakfast?" Graham asks, kissing Angie on the forehead and tickling her sides. They look rested and my bestie is sporting the nicest glow. Being in love looks good on her. It is doing wonders for her already amazing skin.

"This is all Nic's doing," I say. "So, if it sucks, we can all blame him."

"Get ready to strip, because we are going to my favorite place called Babystacks Cafe."

"Oh, this sounds fun," Angie says, bouncing on her feet.

"Our cars were dropped off this morning and are parked in the garage," Nic explains.

"Plural?" I ask with confusion.

"Correct," he responds but doesn't choose to elaborate.

"Wear comfortable walking shoes, because I thought we could take a small hike after breakfast at Red Rock Canyon," I inform.

We make our way to the parking garage, and Nic grabs the keys from the parking attendant. He signs a few papers and has us added to the contract. The cool thing about Vegas is that a lot of parking is done underground. It keeps the strip looking less cluttered and reserved for the glitz and glam.

"Can I drive?" I ask him softly.

"What happens if it's a stick?"

I give him my side-eye. "Think I don't know my way around a stick?"

His grin grows to a full-blown smile. "I never said that."

"But the implication was there."

I follow him to the car that can only be described as highly luxurious. The man spared no expense. It's in my favorite color too—red like Dorothy's ruby slippers. I look inside and see that it's automatic and laugh when Nic tosses me the set of keys.

"I may regret this," he says under his breath.

"Wait," I say, looking for the backseat. "How are we all

going to fit?" I quickly remember he mentioned multiple cars.

"I got two. The other one is Graham's and is silver," Nic explains, tossing the other set of keys to his brother. "I wanted to have the flexibility of being able to take Graham out whenever you girls have your night out."

"What night out?" Graham asks with curiosity, stiffening up beside Angie who just continues peppering kisses all over his face in an obvious attempt to distract him.

"It's tradition that the girls get to have their fun," I say with a sigh. How does he not know this?

"We'll have our fun too," Nic suggests. He winks at me, knowing that he promised he would handle Graham if I beat him in poker. And I did. I beat everyone.

Angie looks up at a stressed Graham. "My very appropriate and super reserved bestie planned it. I have nothing to do with it."

"Way to throw me solely under the bus," I quip, but am ignored by both of them.

Graham chuckles. "There's nothing reserved about your bestie and you know it."

"Hey!" I say, waving my arms. "I'm right here!"

They all laugh. I slide into the driver's side and try to adjust my seat and steering wheel to fit my petite needs. When Nic sees me struggling, he comes to my rescue and pushes the buttons and slides my seat into place.

"How's that?" he asks, staring at my bare legs to make sure I can touch the pedals.

"We will soon find out."

My shorts have ridden up my thighs so much that the pockets have popped out of the bottom. I pull the fabric down, but only manage to gain an inch before it slides right back up my legs.

Nic gets into the passenger seat, straps in, and then closes his eyes.

"Are you that tired? You did fall asleep after the walk, right?" I ask, waiting for his eyes to open.

"No, I'm good." Slowly, his eyes open as he tilts his head in my direction. "I'm just praying for my safety."

"Oh hush"—I smack his arm—"I'm a very good driver."

"We will soon find out," he echoes my own words, making me laugh maniacally.

I start the car, kick on the A/C, and back out of the parking spot with ease.

"This baby knows how to purr," I hum, listening to the barely audible sound of the engine. "It's so quiet." I turn on the radio and loud pop music blasts through the sound system. Then it stops suddenly. I glare at Nic. "Why did you shut that off?"

"Because you need to concentrate on the road."

"But I'm not even on the road yet." We are still in the parking garage.

"Same difference," he says casually. "Plus, you almost took out three parked cars in a row."

"They were ugly."

Nic studies me and then laughs, the full belly kind of laugh.

"And I didn't almost hit them," I defend. "If I wanted to hit them, they would be hit."

"Well, then I should be thankful you weren't in the mood for a car accident today," he deadpans.

"Yup," I chirp. "Not in the mood for that type of drama in my life. Too much paperwork and too many insurance companies involved."

"Turn left when you get up the ramp. Follow the signs to the main strip and then make another left," he directs.

"So what should I expect from Babystacks? Is this going to be an orgasmic experience or do I have to fake it?" It is too hard hiding my true self, so I don't bother. My humor is usually sexual and borders on being inappropriate. However, it takes less energy to be me than it does to try to contain me.

He laughs and grabs the wheel from me, to keep me from going up over the curb—*his* muffled words, not mine. "With me, you won't ever need to fake anything."

His words coat me like warm honey. Somehow, I know he is referring to more than just pancakes. While I was joking when I asked the question, there isn't even a slight edge of humor in his tone. I shake my head to try to get the thoughts of what he would be like in bed out of my mind.

"Quit shaking your head," he says, humor laced in his tone.

"Why?"

He grabs the steering wheel again. "Because every twitch of your body makes the car jostle side to side."

"Oh, no it doesn't. You exaggerate, just like the rest of them."

"See, I'm not alone in my analysis then," he says. "The speed limit is thirty-five on this stretch. Turn left at the next major intersection. We'll follow that road for several miles."

"Okay, Mr. Law Abiding Citizen." I settle into my seat and turn onto the road running perpendicular to the strip.

There is barely any traffic. "I really want to see how fast this girl can go."

"Not here. How do you know she's not a boy?"

I think about it for a second. "No stick."

He laughs and then points out some of the places he has visited during his numerous trips here in the past.

Graham and Angie are behind us. I can see Angie's smile from the mirror. She is deliriously happy. I want to feel like that too. Or maybe they are the outliers and striving to be that level of happy is unrealistic. The last thing I need right now is to channel my energy to aim for something unachievable.

I need to figure things out in Portland with work. If I can get a job that brings me joy, maybe things with Ethan won't feel so intense. I am stressed and feeling down on myself. It doesn't help that I am now in debt and my parents are splitting. Life can get so messy sometimes.

Nic's phone buzzes and he grabs it from the cupholder, looking down at the caller ID. "Any updates?" I can hear his breathing change, and I look over with my side-eye to see if I can see any tells as to why his whole demeanor has changed.

During poker, I noticed that the direction in which he would turn his ring would change depending on his type of hand. I caught him in a few bluffs and was so excited to ultimately take him down in the end. It had been years since I played and most of the time it was online for fun—with no money involved. Last night was invigorating to dominate the table and come back with the huge win. It is refreshing not having to rely on Ethan for every little thing when it comes to finances. I value my independence, which makes not really working a huge struggle.

"Follow him. I need concrete proof. Hire more people if need be. Also, get the temp to look at my calendar and clear my schedule of meetings for when I return back to Portland. I need several days to look at the security at HH and the other properties to see what I'm dealing with before I accept Graham's offer." Nic pulls the phone from his ear and looks over at me. "It's up there on the right," Nic says softly, and then barks into the phone, "I have to go. Keep me informed."

I take the turn a little too sharp, causing Nic to lean over into my side of the car.

"Hell, woman, you're going to crash us."

"Quit being dramatic."

9

NIC

I never thought I would rejoice for being on solid ground again, after Claire nearly got us into an accident—numerous times—with her distracted driving. Or perhaps she wasn't distracted at all and is just plain horrible at it. Worst part is, she is oblivious to just how bad she is at it. I would love to meet her driver's education teacher. I make a mental note to convince her to let me drive on the way back. I may be a risk taker, but I definitely do not have a death wish.

Graham's job offer of being his head of security keeps weighing on my mind. I know I would be the best man for the job, but I also know that I lack the ability to stay committed for long. If I accept the offer, I need to be sure I can stick with it for the long haul. I know people always say not to work with family, but Graham and I have never not worked together. We are two stubborn bastards who stop at nothing to get goals completed. It is probably why we can pride ourselves on being as successful as we are.

I hold the door open for Claire and she walks through first, looking around at the ambience and artwork featuring pancakes. The hostess comments on her shirt and helps us find a booth that fits four.

"You better drive on the way back," Graham whispers to me. "You guys were making me super nervous. I thought I warned you."

"You know she's going to fight me on it," I say, as if I already lost the battle.

"Oh, I'm aware. I have the most stubborn one right—"

"What are you two talking about?" Angie asks, narrowing her eyes as she slides into the booth first.

I slide in beside Claire and breathe in her vanilla scent. It took everything in me not to lean in closer to her while she manhandled the car and smell her hair. I had to keep reminding myself that we are a horrible match. She wants a relationship that leads to a *forever*. I want a thrill that can only be *for now*.

We are on opposite ends of the spectrum.

"Wow, they have a whole vegan and gluten-free section on the menu?" Claire says in shock.

It is one of the reasons why I chose this place. I know she said she would cheat on this trip, but she already adapted last night when we went to the chocolate shop. Plus, it is easy to find places that offer variety with a little scouring of the Internet.

The waitress takes our orders.

"So, everyone is up for a hike at Red Rock Canyon?" Claire asks, pulling out a map from her purse. "I thought we could do this trail." She points to the spot on the map that shows the path in red. "It is scenic and has some cool photo opportunities."

"Sounds fun," Angie says, looking over the rest of the trails. "Where did you get the map?"

"When we all decided on Vegas for the trip, I went online to the tourist page and requested information to be sent to the apartment ahead of time. I was able to research and keep a list of things we should do while we are here. Hiking was one of my top picks."

Claire went through so much trouble to give us all a great trip. I should be ashamed for giving her such a hard time, but she is so damn sexy when she's flustered.

Our pancakes arrive, and they look amazing. I resist laughing over Claire bouncing in her seat and clapping. Why does she have to be so freaking adorable?

"Want to sample a bite of each?" I suggest, since we each ordered something different.

Everyone agrees, and I cut off bites from my cinnamon roll stack. Cream cheese icing coats each layer and the batter is spiraled to look like an actual cinnamon roll. I hold up a piece for Claire to try. She leans in, her lips encompassing the fork. As she slides her mouth from the utensil, I wonder if she knows just how intriguing I find her. It's not like I'm keeping my feelings completely to myself. She makes me want to be bold and brazen.

Her shirt is pulled taut over her breasts. I can see the outline of her bra underneath. I want to see just how much she puts out for pancakes. I want to squeeze her twin globes and paw at her ass. I don't want to be tender. I am not a gentle lover. Can she handle my desires? Can she keep up with my needs?

I am in over my head.

I can't even eat seemingly innocent pancakes without it turning sexual.

I focus on avoiding eye contact for the rest of the meal. Angie shares her red velvet stack with us that is dolloped with an ample amount of freshly made whipped cream.

Fuck. She is moaning beside me. I cannot stop looking. Her soft sounds are music to my dick.

I want to drag her in back of the restaurant and fuck her against a wall in a dark corner. I want to make her scream in ecstasy. I want to be the reason for her pleasure. Not fucking pancakes.

I rub my hand over my face.

"Nic, are you feeling okay?" Angie asks, causing the others to stare at me. "You look like you're going to be sick."

"I'm fine. I just slept poorly last night."

Graham gives me a look that says he's not buying what I'm selling. He knows me so well. Even when we spar with each other, we are each other's greatest opponent. We know how the other thinks and can predict holds before the other can make the first move. This is another reason why we work well together in business ventures. Neither of us budges, and when it comes to security, I can see the big picture and anticipate breaches before they occur.

We continue eating pancakes and chatting about nothing in particular. Graham got the s'mores stack and Claire's carrot cake ones are pretty damn delicious for being healthy. The girls excuse themselves to go to the restroom, leaving Graham and me here alone.

"Collins said he got the information on Maxwell that you wanted."

"That fucker needs to reevaluate his priorities before I start snatching away what he thinks is his," I grind out.

"You keep your head on straight, baby bro. I have a wedding coming up and my girl cannot handle any stress. She is still coping with so many things, and I don't think my heart can handle if she relapses. Do not fuck with Claire. I don't know how many times I need to warn you. I see the way you are looking at her."

"And how is that?"

"Like you are going to eat her up alive."

I want to eat her up. Spread her lips and shove my face right into her sweet pussy. Make a meal out of her. I wonder how many fingers she can take before she is trembling from the intrusion. Will her face show pleasure or be slightly grimaced from the pain?

I wipe a hand down my face and chug some water. Dammit, he's right. I cannot keep punishing myself with these images I conjure up in my head.

"I'll accept the job offer," I say, changing the subject. Regardless of the situation he has currently, I know I can make it better.

Graham's face changes moods. "Yeah? Really? You're being serious?"

"Let me have one hundred percent control over this area, and I'll do it. I don't want to answer to anyone on my protocols or decision-making. I trust my own instincts and know I can do a good job."

"You'll do great," Graham agrees. "Hence, why I asked in the first place."

"Thanks."

"I must ask, though. Are you going to keep things legal?"

"Maybe eventually," I answer. "But if you want to verify the loyalty of your current team and have me decide who stays and who goes, then I may have to rely on some of my unsavory tactics."

Since meeting Angie, Graham has gotten more legit with most of his businesses and tracking capabilities. There are always loopholes. Even though his jewelry company is marketed toward higher end buyers looking for elegant pieces, there is a huge sellers' market for people looking for hidden tracking devices.

"Fine," he agrees. "Just do not tell me about it. Do what you need to do."

I smile. I am excited to start something new. It's a thrill to not settle and become complacent. "As for Entice, I think we should dissolve the company within the year. The purpose of even starting it is now resolved. It's not bringing in the levels of revenue it used to after the big drug bust."

"I agree."

The girls return back to the table and their hair is styled in ponytails, I am guessing for the hike.

"We bought some bottled waters from the cooler so we have drinks to bring to Red Rock," Angie says, passing us each a bottle.

Graham pulls her to him and kisses her hard. "Thanks, sweetheart."

I see Claire watch them. I know she is deliriously happy for the couple, but I keep witnessing a sliver of hope in her eyes that one day she could have what they have. Pretty sure what they found is rare and unattainable. My parents found it, sure, or maybe it found them. They get more in love with each passing year. Not everyone is that fortunate.

I thought I found love once, and the lying bitch almost took me on a marital ride that would have cost me millions in an inevitable divorce. I refuse to be blindsided again. You can't get hurt if you are doing the hurting.

When the bill comes to the table, I grab it before anyone has a chance to claim it. It was my idea to come here, so the least I can do is pay for the meal.

"Thanks for breakfast, Nic," Claire's melodic voice rings in my ears.

"Glad you enjoyed it." I smile at her. I can't keep the smile off my face. I have been sporting a cheesy grin the entire trip when I'm around her. She is sweet and yet sassy. The best of both worlds, if you ask me.

When we get outside, Claire reaches into her purse for the set of keys and as soon as they hit the air, I snatch them out of her hands.

"Hey!"

"I'm driving."

"Why?" she whines. "But I like driving. You promised we could see how fast she goes."

She is pouting. Fuck. I glance away and focus my mind on the task of maintaining a level of self-preservation.

"Your driving is too predictably bad. I've seen enough."

"Oh, you have some nerve, Nic Hoffman!"

She is stomping her foot. I grow hard over her irritation. Her legs are so tan and toned, and I wonder what they would feel like wrapped around my waist as I thrust into her. I'm sure they would stabilize her if the roles were reversed, and I was giving it to her from behind. So many possibilities, and every one excites me.

I unlock the car and slide into the driver's seat, leaving her alone while she rants and rages just outside the passenger door. Then she turns to me with fire in her eyes. She marches over to my side, and I wind down the window. Yup, she is super pissed off.

"Can I help you?"

Claire props her hands on her hips, and I see the sparks sizzling from the flames in her eyes. Claire is like a fire-cracker that is ready to detonate. She is beautiful to look at, but once you light her up, you better run away fast.

"*Can I help you?*" she echoes my exact words, looking at me like going to prison will be worth it.

This is where I should run, at the very least back down. I open the car door and get out. Her face changes with excite-ment. I scoop her up so fast, she doesn't even squeal until I have her seated in the passenger side.

"You brute! I can't believe you are manhandling me right now!"

"You like it," I say, snapping her into her belt. I shut the door and mosey over to my side. I look over at her and if looks could kill...

"You are so annoying."

"Put that tongue back in your mouth," I warn. She should know better than to stick her damn tongue out at me.

I start the engine and listen to the hum.

"Or what?" she presses.

I reach across the center console, grab the back of her

head with my right hand, and kiss the protest right off her bakery-flavored lips. They are warm. Soft. Her hand steadies itself on my thigh, causing a pulse to go right to my dick. She is an angel and a devil all wrapped up in one shiny package of temptation, luring me from the light into the darkness.

A hum escapes her lips, as I do what the name of her gloss says.

I kiss the hell out of her cupcake.

My fingers tangle into her soft hair, as some falls out of her ponytail. Her lips part, and I instantly accept access. "You taste so fucking good," I murmur into her mouth.

I want to swallow her whole. Every part of her. I break the kiss and her panting fills the quiet. The only thing I can hear is her rapid breathing and the purr of the engine.

Claire wipes at her mouth and looks out her passenger side window. "What the hell was that?" she demands, sucking her bottom lip into the cage of her top teeth.

"He doesn't deserve you," I grind out, staring at the swollen curve of her lips. "Now think again when you decide it is fun to stick your tongue out at me."

Claire releases her bottom lip, pouting it out as she stews. It has a similar effect on my mood. Was she sent to earth to torture me? Make me lose all control?

"Why did you do that?" she asks, while her finger traces along the outline of her lips, directly over the place I just kissed.

"To take the edge off."

I back out of the parking spot, head out onto the main road, and follow the GPS to Red Rock Canyon. I can tell Claire is deep in thought, or perhaps she is just avoiding me.

I would like to think my lips on hers had some sort of effect. The only effect hers had for me is that now that I know what they taste like, I can't stop thinking about how I want more.

I *need* more.

"Don't kiss me again," she grinds out.

I don't make promises I can't keep.

10

CLAIRE

"What's going on with you?" Angie asks, her eyes full of concern. "You are never this quiet."

We are on top of a cliff, overlooking the desert, taking a rest. The guys are hanging out together, chatting about business. Apparently Nic is going to be working as head of security for Graham's businesses. I overheard them chatting on the hike up here and am not sure how much of what was said is common knowledge versus private. I'm not going to spread any rumors, so it really doesn't matter if what I think I heard is true or not.

Every time Nic speaks, my mind goes elsewhere. I can't stop thinking about the kiss. For something that seemed impulsive, he definitely knew what he was doing. It was all-encompassing and unapologetic. He didn't ask permission. He just took and took. While the egotistical behavior would have bothered me with any other man in the past, I can't deny the fact that my mouth now craves his taste. Maybe it is the thrill of the forbidden that has me so tied up in knots.

Maybe I have the start of a cinnamon obsession. Regardless of what it is, I need to get my head on straight.

I am with Ethan. I chose Ethan. I still choose Ethan. I don't know how to look toward a future without it including Ethan. We have invested so much time already. He is the longest relationship I've ever been able to maintain—or wanted to maintain. Maybe it is because I sacrificed something for him that would have made me happy that is motivating me to see this through. That's what love is, right? Making sacrifices for the benefit of the other partner?

Nic is a mistake I don't need to make right now. Lately, I've been good about not making them too. Nic could just be toying with my emotions anyway. I wouldn't put it past him. He seems to enjoy seeing my lows, my weaknesses.

"I'm struggling with finding a job that is satisfying," I say. "It's been weighing on my mind." It's not false news. But it also isn't what is currently nagging me either. My lack of a real job is just a small piece of my life struggles puzzle titled "Unhappiness."

Angie nods and pulls her knees up to her chest. "I have gone from working toward my journalism goal with all my might, to basically doing nothing." She turns back and gives Graham a small wave. "*He* doesn't see it that way, but I do. I feel like my talents are being wasted."

"I feel the exact same way. And I don't know how to stop dwelling on the what-ifs. I used to be a goal setter." Now my main goal is just surviving. It's a lousy feeling comparing your past accomplishments to your current status.

"I am right with you, Claire. It's not like Graham cares if I'm working or not. Actually, I think he would prefer me doing nothing, but I need something for myself. I can't lose myself entirely in a marriage. I have to do something for me."

"Yes, yes, yes." We are in the same boat. Well, kind of. My side has sprung a financial leak, and I'm about to drown in debt if I don't figure something out fast. I fear that if Ethan knew how much I owe, he would leave me. He has alluded to not wanting another dependent, and I would definitely put a dent in his bank account and possibly his credit score. Maybe I'm just too much of a liability. Is the cost of having me even worth it to him?

Angie takes a long chug from her bottled water, reminding me to do the same. She turns her body sideways to look at me. "If making money was not a worry, what would you really want to do right now?"

"It's an unrealistic question I ask myself often."

"Maybe it doesn't have to be unrealistic," she proposes.

I shrug. I'm in a slump, and it started way before the letter came in the mail with my student loan debt spelled out for me in black and white. "I have a passion for helping people with their weight loss and nutritional goals. I want to inspire others to be their best selves and live their best lives, even if I feel like I'm not living mine right now. Working at the gym only fulfills so much of my needs. Speaking of the gym, my entire workout group wants custom T-shirts like the ones you make me."

Her face lights up. "You wear them to class?"

"And to the grocery store or the park or when I'm just lounging around the apartment."

"Really?"

"Yes, of course. You make the best clothes, and I love

the sayings you add to jazz them up and make them stand out. You should open one of those online boutiques."

"Would you help me if I wanted to start a thing?"

"Depends what the thing is," I say slowly.

"I have a very vague vision of having a network specifically made for women that includes health coaching, workout videos, clothing for all body types, and even inspirational jewelry. I love to sew and create. I also love to write. I've been utilizing my blog to talk about my own struggles, and I have been flooded with comments about how I have inspired others to seek professional help or to make changes in their life. I thought I could build off of that platform. It's a pipe dream. But I think it could be both therapeutic and lucrative."

"I think it's an amazing dream. And I think I would love to be a part of the journey."

"I was hoping you would be on board. Because I need a partner and you offer so much expertise in the areas in which I am lacking guidance. And who better to start an empowering women's group than us?"

"Exactly," I agree. I can't stop smiling or thinking about all the possibilities. I have so many ideas rushing through my head that I wish I had a portable dream board, a glue stick, and some magazines to trash to get everything I am dreaming up into picture form.

"What are you ladies talking about?" Graham asks, kneeling down behind Angie and massaging her shoulders.

"I was asking Claire for her opinion on a business idea I've been tossing around in my head," she answers. "We are both unhappy either not working or doing the mundane routines, so I'm trying to see about starting an empowering women's team and utilizing our talents."

Graham kisses her neck and then smiles over at me. "Whatever you two want to do, I fully support it. I know you do not make decisions on a whim, sweetheart, and thoroughly think things through. If you need office space or starting capital, I can be a behind-the-scenes investor. Just let me know."

I should be thrilled over his offer, elated even. But it just reminds me—yet again—that Ethan doesn't support my ideas like Graham supports Angie's. Maybe Ethan will jump on board when he sees the business model or maybe it will take turning a profit. One thing I know for certain is that if I tell Ethan the idea of working with Angie without a thoroughly thought-out plan, he'll just laugh in my face at the absurdity of it. He calls me a dreamer. Is being one such a bad thing? To him, yes. He reminds me that I lack logic and think with my heart.

"Thank you, Graham," Angie says, leaning her head back to capture his lips.

"Yes, thank you."

"I have space at Hoffman Headquarters that is not being utilized and would love for you ladies to come take a look. I've been trying to get Angie to be my personal assistant for a while," he says with a chuckle. "This is almost as good." He winks an eye, making hers narrow.

"We both know that you would get no work done if I was fluttering around making you coffee and fetching papers off a printer," she teases. "Plus, I suck at taking orders from you."

Graham nods. "This is true." He whispers something in

her ear, making her blush. "When we get back to Portland, I'll show you the floors I have open for leasing that have yet to be claimed."

I look over at Nic who appears to have swallowed a scorpion. Not sure why he cares about me and Angie working together, but from the scowl on his face, he definitely has a strong opinion about it.

Too bad his opinion is irrelevant, like basically ninety percent of the things that fly out of his mouth.

I fix my sweaty ponytail and gather my almost empty water bottle from the dusty ground. "I have one more surprise stop planned. Afterwards, do you want to head back to the hotel to hit up the pool bar to cool off?"

"That sounds amazing," Angie responds.

Going back on the loop trail is much easier because it's mostly downhill. It takes half the time to reach the parking lot.

"Want to follow us?" I ask Graham and Angie.

"Sure. Sounds good," he responds.

I don't bother even asking to drive, so when Nic holds out the keys for me to take, my smile cannot be suppressed.

"Really?" I ask, just to be sure.

"I may regret this," he snickers.

I'm relieved he is back to talking to me. Or maybe it is me back to talking to him. I can't keep track. Most of the hike was a dry spell and the silent treatment was making me twitchy.

"Hopefully you'll live to talk about it."

"Funny."

I unlock the doors and slide into the low riding seat, feeling the stifling heat from the greenhouse effect. I power up the engine and rev up the A/C to the max. I readjust my settings and fling my ponytail over the back of the seat.

"I'm so freaking hot," I moan, closing my eyes and taking a moment to relax.

"Yes, you are."

My eyes fly to Nic's. At first I think I misheard him. However, the smoldering flames behind his crystal blues tell me I heard every word just as he intended. His lingering gaze heats me faster than the desert. It is like I am being cooked from within and don't have a clear path to get out of the fire.

"I can't keep doing this," I mutter.

"Doing what?"

I try to think of the right word but come up empty. "This"—I take a deep breath—"this dance."

"You think working in a building where I'm going to be head of security is going to help? You think this attraction you and I have toward each other is going to go away? If you think it will, you are fooling yourself. This"—he motions with his hand from me to him—"isn't going away, Claire. I wish it would, trust me. You. Are. Trouble."

My ears heat. "*Me*? I am trouble? What's that supposed to mean?"

"You are everything I am attracted to and yet someone I shouldn't mess around with. You are my brother's fiancée's best friend. You are basically off-limits to me. And yet—"

"I'm off-limits because I'm already taken," I correct him. *I'm taken*. I need to keep reminding myself that this toxic desire we feel for one another needs to end before we ignite something that can't be put out.

"Sure, and that." His words have a humorous edge to them.

"Don't be mad at me if Angie and I decide to take up shop at HH. Be mad at Graham for offering."

"Right now, I'm mad at a lot of people," he admits.

"Sounds counterproductive, if you ask me." I am in a snippy mood. He put me here. I blame him.

"Didn't ask you," he huffs.

"Whatevs." I turn to Nic, looking at his uncomfortable self. "It was just a kiss. A mistake. Quit extrapolating emotions out of something that was just a physical lapse in judgment. Get over it. I already did."

11

NIC

"How do you expect me to get over this thing we have growing between us? I'm entertaining suggestions."

"The only *thing* continuing to grow is distance," Claire states. "Don't mistake it as anything other than revulsion."

My hand moves to place a piece of hair that escaped her hairband behind her ear. Her breath picks up, and I can see the sweat beading on her forehead that has since cooled from the blasting air pushing out of the vents. She is affected by me. Lying to herself may keep her content for a while, but she will eventually cave and admit what I do to her.

Claire turns her attention back to the gears and places the car in reverse, pulling out of the parking lot. She exits the park following the signs and is on a stretch of road that lacks curves and drivers, other than Graham who is following steadily behind us.

"Gun it," I instruct.

I watch as her eyes light up. She pushes down on the gas

pedal without hesitation, and the engine proves it can jump speeds within seconds. We fly down the road, dust blowing in our wake.

"Stay on the damn road, Claire, or I'm taking over."

"I am," she squeals, elated to be able to drive.

If she wasn't so bad at it, I may be more inclined to ride shotgun in the future. I grab the steering wheel as she tries to avoid a freaking squirrel. But at this rate, I doubt I'll ever have the willpower to allow this reckless behavior to happen again.

"You can't be swerving for damn rodents going one hundred," I scold. "Take it down to eighty. We're going to be getting close to town. Do you know where we are going or do you need me to pop open my GPS?"

"GPS, please."

"Address?" I inquire.

"Type in cactus garden."

"Haven't we seen enough cacti?" I inquire, truly dumbfounded that we need to go look at more.

"This is different. You'll see."

She is so excited over going there that I know I'll be watching her reaction more than I'll be looking at some thorny plants.

"Take it down to fifty," I instruct. "Shit, Claire"—I grab the dashboard with both hands as the car trembles from the force—"you don't need to slam on the damn brakes, woman. Go gradual."

"That was me being gradual," she mumbles to herself.

I feel my jaw release, causing my chin to drop. She has to be the worst driver on the planet. "You want them to wreck behind us?" My phone buzzes, and I answer Graham's call.

"You need to drive," he says coldly. "What were you thinking?"

"Try telling her that. I'll handle it." I end the call and glance over at a giddy Claire who cannot seem to get the smile off her face. She is oblivious that Graham and I were talking about her. I don't want to end her happiness. I want to bring her more. "Take the off ramp," I instruct. "Easy! This is a merge lane, and you're supposed to yield."

She follows my directions, as Graham tails us from behind. When we pull up to the self-guided chocolate factory and cactus garden, the little girl inside of Claire comes out full force. She cuts the engine and hops out of the car, jumping up and down with excitement. I resist telling her she double parked.

Angie joins her in excitement, as they give each other two-handed high-fives. Never have I seen two people who love tourist traps as much as these two.

"Let's take a group photo in front of the sign," Claire expresses, pulling out her phone. She looks around the area and then pouts out her bottom lip that I want to bite. "Crud, there's no one around to take the picture."

"Here, use my selfie stick," I say. I completely forgot I have been carrying it around in my shorts pocket since this morning. On the hike, we had another hiker snap some pics for us, so there was no need to use it. During breakfast, the waitress took one. This is the first time today that we need the stick.

I reach into my pocket and pull out the unicorn stick that Claire got me for Christmas when she came to my parents' house in Hillsboro. It is rainbow-colored and has little unicorn decals all over it. The main handle is covered in fur, and it would be the perfect accessory if I were a thirteen-year-old girl. Seeing Claire's eyes smile, I know that she is channeling her inner teen girl spirit.

"You brought it?" she asks, staring as I extend it. I laugh at the shocked look on her face.

I clip on my phone and turn it to selfie-mode. I set up the Bluetooth with ease and get the device linked to take some pics.

"I take it everywhere I go," I say seriously, making her burst into laughter at the falsity of the statement. I snap the picture right in the moment, followed by several others. We then gather as a foursome around the sign, still sweaty from the hike, and pose for a few more shots.

We start at the chocolate shop first and do the self-guided tour, where we learn about the manufacturing process and how the factory operates. It's a short presentation that ends in the store side of the building, where Angie asks basically for four of everything—maybe so she can share her bounty with all of us. However, with her, there are no guarantees. She may just binge on all of it herself. Graham just goes along for the ride, not giving a second glance at what she buys or how much it costs. If she wanted the entire store, I'm pretty sure he would purchase it for her.

"You going to eat all that, sweetheart?" he asks, hugging her from behind.

She turns her head back to look up at him with her big doe eyes. "You have to earn it."

"Ew," Claire says, making a face. "Can you be any cuter?"

I am standing beside her. I swear her body heat just made the vanilla scent she bathes herself in even warmer and creamier. It reminds me of ice cream that is melting on top of a warm brownie. All of the scents from the chocolate, paired with her perfume, enhance and engage all of my senses.

I hang back in the shop while the group goes out to explore the cacti garden. It is a unique business pairing, but it obviously works for the owner to bring in tourists looking for a gimmicky attraction. I glance around at the products for sale and find a bath bomb set that includes chocolate shampoo and lotion. I didn't get Claire anything for Christmas—mainly because I was unaware that she was going to be at my parents' in advance—when she gave me the unicorn selfie stick. It has been weighing on me for months, and maybe this little gift set featuring the local chocolates will make up for being so late.

I place a few different chocolate bars onto the counter and even find some vegan varieties.

"Can you please deliver these chocolate bars to my hotel room, so they don't melt in the car? Can you get this bath set wrapped and shipped to Portland if I give you the address? I have no problem paying any fees."

"Of course, sir," the worker says, handing me a form for the delivery information.

I hand over my credit card to pay and join the gang outside on the pathway that winds through a maze of cacti. Claire is eating some chocolate-covered pretzels on a bench. She stands up to join me, looking at my empty hands.

"You were in there awhile, what were you doing?" she asks.

"Just browsing. You got melted chocolate on your cheek."

"Where?" She wipes around her lips but keeps missing the spot.

With the pad of my thumb, I brush over the smear, cleaning her face from the chocolate. I look down at the residue and swipe my tongue over it, tasting the deliciousness. "Yum."

Claire stares at my lips, but then pivots and keeps on walking. I can sense the internal struggle she is having between wanting something and knowing she shouldn't. We share the same temptation. I'm just weaker in my ability to resist.

After the walk, we get back into the cars and drive toward the strip, where the iconic Welcome to Las Vegas sign is located. I have never stopped at the sign in all of the visits I have made to the city, but Claire's excitement makes it worth it. She is an extreme tourist. It's like she is helping me to see the city through a new lens—a brighter and more vibrant one.

Graham and Angie kiss under the sign for a photo, while other onlookers cheer them on. After a dozen more varieties of pictures, we head on back to the Bellagio to change into swimsuits.

The pool is only open to guests who are staying at the hotel. Key cards must be swiped and an attendant patrols the gated area to make sure outsiders are not sneaking in. The patio area is set up with umbrellas and loungers. For midday, the pool is jamming with a growing crowd.

I watch the girls pick out an area to set our gear. I grab a stack of towels from the shelf along the wall and carry them over to the four loungers that are now ours for the afternoon.

Angie pulls off her black coverup and reveals a purple bikini that is iridescent in the sunlight.

"Oh, hell no," Graham whisper-growls. "When did you buy that scrap of a thing?"

I chuckle at his possessiveness. He has always been this way when it comes to her. From what I can tell, Angie loves to push his buttons—and does a damn fine job at it. I think it is a game to her to drive him a little crazy. He needs someone defiant in his life to keep him humble.

Claire undoes the strap on her white coverup wrap dress to reveal the same suit but in a shimmery red. Fuck me sideways. She looks like a *Playboy* model. Did she buy one size too small by accident? Her tits are going to fall out of the top of the fabric.

I am going to go to hell for every single fantasy running on loop through my head.

I swallow hard while I watch her kick off her flip-flops and take out her hair from her ponytail. She fluffs life back into her strands, and all I can look at is how her boobs bounce with each movement of her hands.

I pull my shirt off and toss it onto my lounger. My gray trunks sit low on my hips and they offer no support for my growing cock. Adrenaline courses through my veins as I watch nearly every guy in the vicinity check out the girls.

Music is filtrating through the various speakers set up on posts around the main pool area. A DJ helps get the party started by mixing songs and adding creative effects to the tracks.

"I'll go grab us drinks," I say, looking at one of three

bars to see which has the smallest line. "What does everyone want?"

"Something that will get us completely wasted," Claire suggests, swaying her hips to the rhythm of the music.

"I'll come with you," Graham says, glaring at the back of Claire's head. She's off in her own world, and Angie is about to join her. We walk toward the bar on the opposite end of the pool. "Let's get food too."

I nod. "Good idea."

I scan the chalkboard menu that has a list of foods and beverages served by the pool. It has the typical offering of burgers, salads, and wraps. I order myself a burger and get Claire a grilled vegetable wrap with a side salad. I'm not sure she is a hummus fan, but put in an order with pita bread anyway. As for drinks, I get us margaritas—one traditional lime and one peach.

The drinks are done first, and I carry them back to find Claire struggling with her sunscreen and some asshole offering to smooth it on her. Really, buddy? I thought this lame move only happened in the movies.

"I got this," I bark out.

When he sees all six feet of me, he backs away and scurries off.

"Was that necessary?" she asks, glaring up at me, until she sees the margaritas and then she softens.

"Very necessary. Which one do you want?"

"Is that peach? Oh, I love peach."

I hand her the frozen drink and place mine on the little table beside the lounger. "Give me your lotion."

She hesitates but hands me the bottle. I squeeze a little out onto my hand and warm it between my two palms. She gathers her hair over one shoulder. I massage the cream into her bare skin, reveling at the smoothness. If she has any flaws, I don't see them. To me, she is perfection.

I close the cap and hand her back her bottle.

"Thank you," she whispers.

I sip my drink and escort her over to the stairs that enter the pool. The water is the perfect temperature. Angie and Graham join us with frozen margaritas as well.

"This feels so refreshing," Angie says, sitting on Graham's lap along the edge of the pool.

Several water fountains are set up, along with a foot-bridge that you can swim under. The DJ plays some old-school music, and several beach balls are tossed throughout the pool to the patrons looking to do more than just drink.

When the waiter brings our food, we exit the pool and chow down at our loungers.

"Oh, I love hummus," Claire says, smiling at what I chose for her.

She takes a bite from her wrap and moans over how good the flavors are. I am pretty sure she'd be a slut for pancakes, margaritas, and vegetables. It is commendable how healthy she eats and her dedication to staying fit. I eat like a teenage boy but work out like a man.

We finish our food, hit up the pool some more, and drink a little too much.

When the ice melts in our fourth beverage, I decide that there is no better time than now to switch over to the other pool where the foam party is about to start.

Another DJ is hyping up the crowd as huge blowers blast foamy bubbles onto the surface of the water. Angie and Claire jump right into the pool, laughing and dancing to the music. Graham and I join them. I stay back along the edge and watch as blow-up floats are thrown into the pool for guests to have fun with. Several employees carry a huge unicorn float that has a rainbow-colored mane.

I chuckle as a drunk Claire tries to climb on board. Her struggle and pout is so cute. When she turns to find me, she is sporting the whole "help me" look. I move through the bubble bath and make my way over to her. My hands grip her slippery hips and give her a lift. She weighs about a hundred pounds wet—at least that's how weightless she feels to me. She is all muscle, yet has a soft feminine feel to her.

Claire rides the mystical blow-up animal with Angie like they just won the lottery. Hands fly through the air in a rhythm completely different from the song being broadcasted. I laugh and watch them in a rare carefree moment.

When the festivities calm down to just lingering suds, we go back to the loungers and dry off. Graham takes Angie back to the room to get cleaned up, while Claire and I lie like content starfish in the sun. It feels great to be lazy and boneless.

I lie on my back with my hands propped behind my head. Claire is on her stomach, with her head resting on her bent arms.

I know she wants to know more of the pleasure I can give her. I sense it in her energy, in how she sneaks glances at me. She is keeping our kiss from Angie. I know this because Angie wouldn't be able to hold herself back from telling me her thoughts on the matter. I haven't been around my brother's fiancée long enough to know where her loyalty lies—Team Ethan or Team Nic. I, however, without any doubt know she will forever be on Team Claire.

Every time my mind thinks of her sleazy boyfriend, I feel murderous inside. The guy has everyone fooled. Not for long. It is like I'm in a secret competition with a man who doesn't even know he is about to lose.

In the big picture, it doesn't matter though. Whatever I want with Claire is strictly temporary. It is how I generally handle women in the post-Tara era. I keep all of them at arm's length. It is safer that way—for them and for me.

Does that make me an asshole? Of course it does. Even I can admit that. But I specifically choose women who know the score. I am picky as hell and my attraction is very specific.

I have a type.

Claire has the one quality that is common among all of the women I have gone after since Tara.

She is already taken. And that fact alone makes me desire her.

12

CLAIRE

"How's Penny doing?" I ask, readjusting on the lounger. If I don't reapply sunscreen, I worry I will get burned.

Nic perks up from the question. "Good, as far as I can tell. She is allowed to visit home more often and seems to be dating." He shrugs and looks over at the pool. "Don't tell Graham though. I only know because I keep a bit more detailed tabs on her."

"I can't imagine Graham isn't doing the same," I snicker.

"Oh, he definitely is. It's just that my technical skills are way more"—he struggles for the right word—"intrusive."

That's not the response I expected. "So, you are violating her privacy?"

"I am protecting my baby sister from assholes."

"Call it what you want, but you are basically going to make her rebel against you if she finds out. Then she is going to choose someone very unsavory. Like, think biker gang and a tattoo sleeve, with a Prince Albert ring, and—"

A tremor runs through him. "What the fuck, Claire?"

"What?" I say with a shrug.

"You have a vivid imagination. And what do you know about a Prince Albert?" he asks, his eyes full of mirth.

"I once"—I pause—"never mind."

He laughs as he fills in his own blanks. Now who has an even bigger imagination?

"We better go back up before you get crispy from the sun."

"Yeah," I agree. I'm starting to fry. "I thought we would see a show tonight. I got us tickets from the hotel concierge when we arrived for the Cirque Du Soleil show here."

"Wow," he says, smiling from ear to ear. "I think that sounds fun. I've actually never been to one."

"We could hit up a restaurant on location beforehand. Maybe grab dessert after the show?"

"I'm sure Angie and Graham would be game for all of that."

"Good, because tomorrow is strippers," I inform him. I had to squeeze that into the itinerary before Ethan joins us. I do not need anyone to sabotage my vision for Angie's epic bachelorette party. I already have Graham to contend with; I don't need Ethan's input too.

"Oh boy," he mutters.

"Oh yes!" I whoop, gathering up my belongings. "I hope there are no Prince Alberts that show up."

Seeing Nic's penetrating gaze makes me burst out into laughter. "Don't have a thing for genital piercings?"

"I prefer my dicks with only one hole."

He looks at me with a blank look on his face. "Noted."

"Glad we had this little chat," I say with a giggle.

Nic is easy to talk to and even easier on the eyes. When he laughs—usually at me—a sense of weightlessness appears in the aura that he surrounds himself in. Typically he seems to go through life with an unyielding stiffness that gives me the impression that he is pissed off at the world. And who knows, maybe he is. I barely know him.

We walk side by side back into the hotel. The blast of the air conditioning chills me, and I pull my coverup tighter to my body. The elevator takes us up to the suite, and we disperse to get ready for dinner and the show. I have never been to a circus, and I know that the acrobatics in this type of show are spectacular. I'm so glad I was able to score us tickets.

After my shower, I text Angie to join me in getting ready in my room. I select a strapless silver dress that has a black lace overlay. Blake helped me pick it out on one of our many shopping excursions. That man knows how to shop.

"Holy cannoli, you look freaking hot. Someone named Ethan is a lucky man," she hollers. "You shine!"

"Thanks," I answer. "You look amazing, as always."

Angie has on a black dress that is form fitted at the top and then flares out at the waist. It flows down to her ankles where she has on silver heels. Her engagement ring and diamond necklace sparkle with every little movement she makes.

"Thank you so much for getting us tickets to see the show. You're giving me the best memories here in Vegas. I am so lucky for you to be a part of the planning and my upcoming wedding."

I give her a squeeze. She's going to make me cry if she

doesn't stop with the compliments. "It brings me pleasure to see you happy, Angie. You deserve it too."

I slip on black strappy heels that have black silk straps that wrap around my calves and tie in a bow. I curl my hair and do my eye makeup in a smoky silver shade. I help Angie with her finishing touches, and when we are finally ready, we exit my room to go look for the men.

When they see us, they get up from the sofa to greet us.

"You look amazing," Nic whispers to me, making a warmth run from my toes all the way to my cheeks, which I imagine by now are rosy red.

His words warm me from the inside out. The effect he has on me is alarming. He is dangerous to my dwindling self-control and to my future.

"So do you," I answer honestly. He does too.

Nic's black suit is tailor fitted, and his white collared shirt is crisply pressed. He has on a satiny black tie and equally shiny black shoes. He looks like a male model, fresh off the pages of a business magazine.

We exit the suite and when I teeter a few too many times on my heels, Nic grabs my elbow gently to steady me.

"Are you okay?" he asks, his tone full of concern.

I nod. "Yeah." I look up into his eyes and nearly fall down on my ass. Luckily, he grabs me just in time. "It probably wasn't the best idea to be pregaming it with Angie in my room."

"Yeah, probably not."

It is moments like these that I think Nic cares about something more than just trying to make me crash and burn. His hand on my arm is gentle yet strong. He is a walking contradiction. He seems to consistently catch me off guard.

Just when I think I have him figured out, he changes his mood again. It is giving me a bit of whiplash.

We head to the tapas restaurant and get seated immediately. I'm not positive, but I think Graham slipped the hostess some money. I can't complain because sitting down will feel much better than standing around waiting for a table in these damn heels I decided to wear. At least they look cute.

We order a bunch of different menu favorites and dig in once the food arrives. I stick with the meatless options, except when the coconut crusted shrimp bites get passed my way. They are too delicious looking to resist. We share a pitcher of sangria and chat about anything and everything.

When I excuse myself for the restroom, I find our waiter and insist on him handing me the bill, instead of putting it on the table for anyone to grab. It isn't fair that Graham and Nic are footing the bill for every activity. Surely, I can pick up a dinner here and there to contribute.

I carry the slip to the entrance and ask the hostess where I can pay. She points over to the bar, and I walk over to hand the slip and my debit card to the bartender.

He swipes the card and frowns, trying it again.

"It's not working," he says, handing it back to me. "Maybe insufficient funds?"

I frown. The bill is barely over two hundred dollars, which isn't bad for all the small plates we ordered. "I may have enough cash," I state, digging through my bag. I pull out the money I won during poker. Despite taking home the win, I don't even consider it my own money. Nic paid for me to join the table, so it is technically his.

I hear the vibration of my phone and see that Ethan is

trying to call me. I quickly hand over a wad of cash and answer it before it goes to voicemail. "Hey."

"I just got an email saying that you are trying to use the debit card at a restaurant and it got rejected. How can your meal cost more than what you have in your account? Seems ludicrous if you ask me. What are you ordering, gold-covered vegetables?"

"I haven't been paying for anything here really. I thought treating this round would be a nice gesture."

"It would be if you didn't blow through your allowance." His words are cold. He is treating me like I am some money hog.

"I asked you to add more money to my account. Things are expensive here."

"Alcohol is expensive, sure. But drinks should be free," he explains, as if I am some small child.

I decline the change from the bartender and ask him to give it to the waiter for a tip. I add some more bills from my purse to go toward it and then turn my attention back to Ethan.

"Drinks are free if you are sitting and playing casino games. During lunch and dinner, nothing is free." Why do I even need to explain this to him? Surely he has more world experience than I do to understand that visiting high touristy cities costs a lot of money.

"I did add more money. You probably just blew through it."

"Fine. Whatever, Ethan. I'll check my account and make sure I don't try to overdraw again."

"Good to see you are acknowledging your inability to be financially responsible."

"Bye, Ethan."

If he did add more money, it wasn't nearly as much as I expected. I hate being micromanaged like this. I need my own money and to regain my spending freedom back. Money doesn't grow on trees, and new businesses usually don't make a profit the first year. If I want to survive without going absolutely crazy, I may have to keep my job at the gym or find a second job to make ends meet. Asking Ethan for more money isn't going to cut it. He pretty much has made that clear numerous times.

I make my way back to the table.

"Ready to go to the show?" I ask.

"Still waiting for the bill," Nic says, looking around the restaurant for our waiter.

"I took care of it," I say meekly.

"Thank you, Claire," Graham says with a smile. "You didn't have to do that."

"Yes, thank you," Angie echoes.

Nic, however, is looking at me with an emotion that I cannot decipher. Is he mad? Disappointed? Frustrated? I ignore his mood change and pull out our tickets for the show from my handbag, passing them out one by one.

We walk to the theater reserved for the show.

"You didn't need to spend your poker winnings," Nic says softly, as our tickets get scanned in line. We follow the usher down the long aisle toward our seats. "I could have paid for dinner."

I frown. "It makes me feel better to not be a taker."

"No one thinks that. Planning the trip takes time and effort. Both of those things do not have price tags attached.

So, me footing the bills while we are here is the least I can do."

"I appreciate the gesture, but—"

"It's not open for discussion or negotiation."

His words make me tremble. I can't help but find it an attractive quality that a man wants to take care of things. Sometimes it is nice not to have to think about every little detail when it comes to finances. What the hell am I going to do once I am back in Portland and the monthly loan bills come pouring in? How am I going to keep myself from slipping farther into debt?

So far, the real world sucks. No real job, no real paycheck, and an insurmountable amount of debt.

The show starts promptly on schedule, and we have wonderful seats in the center of the theater. I am awestruck by the introduction and sit back to allow my senses to be flooded with stimulation as the story unfolds.

The stage design is magnificent. The floor is constructed to open up to reveal a huge pool the performers can dive into or do water tricks. The flexibility and acrobatic skills of each member is commendable. Being a former cheerleader, I know how hard it is to maintain that level of skill and synchronization. I don't even think my body can stretch half as much as theirs can anymore. These performers are human pretzels.

Several times during the show, I catch myself gripping Nic's arm, as I watch particularly challenging moves being performed. The flips and the dives—truly amazing. I breathe the show and forget I am an audience member. It is like I am part of the performance, and it is truly a magical experience.

We exit the theater and find a gelato shop to get dessert. I choose the banana and coconut flavors in a waffle cone. It is a splurge moment.

"What did you think of the show?" I ask. I didn't realize how much tension was in my shoulders until I'm able to sit back and relax into the chair.

"Spectacular," Angie answers first. "Best show I've seen, to tell you the truth."

"I agree, it was very well done," Graham says, sneaking a bite from her cone, making her giggle when she catches him.

"The stage setup was remarkable," Nic adds.

"Yeah, I love how it opened and closed," I agree. "The behind-the-scenes workers should have come out at the end and taken a bow. It would have to take dozens to coordinate all the set changes and timing of when to open and close the pool."

After our ice cream, we discuss what we would like to do for the rest of the night and settle on a walk. The guys run up to the room to change into something more comfortable, while Angie and I meander through the main floor while we wait for them to come back.

There are more people packed on the sidewalks in comparison to the walk Nic and I did at three in the morning. It's overwhelming to try to move through the crowd to get to where we want to go. People bump into us. I get pushed to the side, and Nic is constantly grabbing my waist to steady me from falling. He keeps his hand on my lower back as he guides me through the sea of people, shielding me with his body from anyone who gets too close.

His protective nature must run in the family. Graham is

guarding Angie in a similar way. She is tucked close to his side, and his muscles are pulled tight under his loose-fitting jeans and T-shirt. Nic is wearing a similar outfit but fills out the fabric more due to his extra body mass. I swear the man knows how to wear denim like none other. I hope he appreciates how lucky he is to be able to build a body structure like he has. Some men can lift and lift without gaining any of the ripple or definition that the Hoffman brothers seem to be able to achieve.

It is only ten, and a lot of the hotels come to life with outdoor shows—trying to entice visitors to come spend money inside their casinos—which is exactly what we do. It is easy to get sucked in to the glitz and the glam.

We are on hour number I-don't-know of casino-hopping and free-drinking. I am pretty incoher—

"You okay?" Nic asks, fixing my wavy hair framing my face. "You look pale."

We are at Caesar's Palace. "I's loss you money."

"It's okay, baby, I have more."

"No, nopes, nada no."

"What?" he asks, helping me to stand. He keeps leaning. Or maybe I'm leaning. Or maybe I'm the one helping him to stand.

"No calls me baby. I am not anyone's baby." He smiles down at me. Despite him being foggy, he is so hot. Like hot smoke. Smokin' hot fog. Oh, I don't know, but I likeyyy.

"You think I'm hot, angel?"

I shake my head over his question, biting my lower lip.

Why are his words perfectly formed and mine sound like they got tossed into a blender? Life continues to be unfair.

"Get outs of my mind," I say.

"I'm simply stating your words back to you," Nic says plainly.

"Stop."

He holds his hands up in defense, but continues to do that weird stare thing with his eyes. "Stop what?"

I think about the question. "Making me want you."

"I *do* want you, Claire."

"Well, make it stop. And quit trying to take me."

"You keep pouting and being cute, I'm going to take you."

"Nopes. This is all your fault, not mine."

I pull away from his hold and plop my butt down on the slot machine stool.

A waitress dressed in a tight red mini dress stops at us and asks, "Can I get you guys some drinks?"

"No."

"Yeshhh," I say at a louder volume.

"No," Nic says sternly. "We're good."

She walks away. I use his body to stand up, my hands roaming all over his abs and pecs. His body is so meaty and delicious looking, like a juicy chicken nugget. Yum. Wait… I don't even like chicken. Yuck. I giggle over my thoughts.

His eyes shine at me, trying to figure out what I find so funny. It just makes me laugh harder. And harder. Snorts escape my nose, causing me to double over at the waist.

"I'm going to start getting a complex when one of the few times you voluntarily touch me, you laugh," he points out, helping me to stand upright. It's a challenge even for him, because I basically feel like my legs turned into pool noodles. His eyes dance with humor, when I'm finally able to get a good look at him again.

Tears drip out of my eyes from all of the laughter. And then my stomach starts to rumble and twist. Sweat beads on my forehead and I know I'm going to—

I dart away from Nic and rush to the nearest restroom. I burst through the door and into the nearest stall. I double over as horrible cramps overtake my body. Hands gather my hair just in time as the first wave hits—like a Mack truck that just lost its brakes. I lurch into the porcelain bowl. A hand wraps around my waist to keep me stable, all while my hair stays out of my angry stream of bad decisions.

Nic's soothing voice coats my insides, as the second wave hits with equal force.

My stomach heaves every sinful drop of liquid from my body. I vow to never drink this much again. I feel like death. I moan at the realization that Nic saw me at a low point. It's not like I'm openly trying to impress anyone, but I still like to preserve the image I work so hard at maintaining.

"You okay there?"

"Hmm mmm."

"Able to walk?"

I nod. I can't bring myself to look back until I am certain my stomach is settled. "Why d'ju follow me?"

"I knew you were in trouble when you ran for the men's room without a second glance."

"Oh." I didn't even notice. "Thanks for holdin' my hair," I say, turning around and offering a weak smile. I feel nasty.

I rip off a wad of toilet paper and wipe my mouth. Yuck. I hate throwing up.

Several men walk in and see Nic standing in the open door. His body is so massive that he dwarfs me in the confined space of the stall. The onlookers watch me wiping my face off. I get a few winks and nods. Ew. No. I guess being in the men's room with a guy who looks like a male model gives people a certain first impression of me. Oh well.

I push around Nic and move over to the sink area to clean up. Other than the condom dispenser on the wall, the place is very luxurious.

We exit, and I take a rest on the chairs that are arranged between the two bathroom entrances, trying to get my head in working order.

"I think I'm going to walk back to the hotel. Can you let Graham and Angie know?"

"I'm walking back with you. Graham and Angie left an hour ago. Before we head back, we better first go grab some juice so you don't dehydrate. Maybe some carbs too?"

I nod. I am surprisingly hungry after this fiasco. "Why did you let me drink so many free drinks?"

"Let you?" He reaches for my hand and tugs me up toward him. "When you have your mind set on something, there's no stopping you."

"One of my strengths," I respond with a half laugh.

"If you call being a stubborn lightweight a strength, then yeah. Sure."

I narrow my eyes at his sarcasm. "I'm not a lightweight. I can drink most people under the table," I defend.

"And then throw it all up thirty minutes later."

"Ugh, well, that was not part of the plan."

"Never is."

"Sorry you had to witness my demise," I say sheepishly.

"No need to be embarrassed. I'm just disappointed you didn't follow through with the lap dance you promised me. Luckily for me, I got you to agree to a raincheck."

"I didn't," I gasp, my mouth wide open.

He bursts out laughing, and I know now that he's just messing with me.

"You're horrible."

"You're sexy."

13

NIC

I am shocked at my own self-control when it comes to Claire. I've never had to work hard for any woman in my life, but there is something about this particular girl that makes it worth it. I'm not a romantic guy by nature. Yet, Claire is making it easy to want to pay for things and take care of her. No matter how many times I tell myself she is off-limits or not the type of girl who can handle my level of intensity, I am drawn to her.

It's her smart mouth and her quick wit that keep me laughing. It's her tight ass and perfect twin rack that keeps my dick in a semi-hard state whenever I'm around her. She is the perfect combination of sassy, sweet, and smart.

"I'm ready to make some more bad choices tonight," she says, making my thoughts halt.

I don't know how to handle her words. She has been a walking sex ad since she came out of her bedroom today dressed like a temptress sent to destroy my self-control.

There is only so much I can take, and right now she is pushing every single button I have.

"How so?" I ask for clarification. I know I'm staring at her. I can't stop myself.

She points to the gourmet pretzel stand and the frozen lemonade picture. "I want that."

I swallow at her innocence. Here she stands with the sexiest dress I've ever seen but is bouncing on her feet over the excitement of a soft pretzel. How can I even deny her anything when she looks this freaking cute? In this very moment in time, I want to give her the world, but also protect her from all the struggles the world inevitably offers.

"Pick out whatever options you want. My treat," I tell her.

"Oh wow, so there are four vegan options. This is like the jackpot of all soft pretzel shops. I feel like I just won the lottery."

And being a witness to her happiness, so do I.

Graham has loosely discussed with me the idea of adding some restaurants to Hoffman Headquarters to keep employees from having to leave the building when the weather gets rough—or simply to have an easy option for when days are busy. I didn't have a strong opinion when he brought it up, but now I want to make sure that there are vegan and gluten-free options for those who have specific dietary needs. I told him to offer the space up to vendors to create pop-up shops on a weekly trial basis and see which few bring in the most revenue—offering leases to the highest profit makers. This will keep employees content but also show real data to the vendors.

Claire gets us the sampler to share and we decide to

carry it outside to eat at the fountains directly bordering Caesar's Palace. This entire trip has been so fun and my cheeks hurt from laughing, especially when I am around Claire. I am dreading the mood change that will surely happen when Maxwell shows up late tomorrow night. My information retrieving skills have made it easy to get his flight number, arrival time, and the amount of money he added to Claire's debit card.

He is such a bastard to keep her under his thumb with the lure of an allowance. For someone who is raking in the money with day trading, he is finding a way to spread it out among multiple accounts to give the illusion that he is just mildly successful. How can she not see through this manipulation and dishonesty? Claire does not carry herself as being someone easily fooled. Maybe Ethan is just that charming, because someone as stunning as she is cannot be that desperate.

I would love to wrap up my hands and take a hit at him in the ring. Sparring is a way to release aggression that I accumulate if I don't find another outlet to channel my anger. Messing up his pretty face a little would definitely help me release some endorphins.

The sound of the water fountains soothes my growing temper. Anytime I think about Claire with the bastard, I catch myself getting violently mad. For someone who used to pride himself on an even temper, my fluctuating moods lately have been volatile at best. I want to smash something. I want to scream. I want to grab this girl—who is moaning over a freaking soft pretzel—and see if those same mewling sounds will be produced if I lick her clit.

Even when Tara was at the forefront of my life, I never

had this much emotional conflict when it came to the relationship. We were attracted to each other; she was pretty enough. I built a vision for our future over the idealistic notion that she would stay faithful to me before we said, "I do."

At the time I wanted forever. I wanted the single-family home, the white picket fence, and the starter pet to test out our parenting skills. But Tara cheating on me broke something inside of me that will never be healed. In the process, all the things I thought I wanted were directly dependent on experiencing them with her. When Tara got out of the picture, so did all the other things I wanted for the future.

I no longer want forever. I don't need more house to take care of, and I definitely do not want to procreate. I have gotten a taste of luxury and what power can buy. No amount of money will ever take away the responsibility of what a wife and kids bring. I am perfectly content avoiding that scenario for the rest of my life.

"You need to eat," the pretzel-lover says, holding up a piece for me to bite.

I can tell she is still a bit tipsy because she misses my open mouth and presses the doughy treat into the side of my cheek. I turn my face, as she shoves the pretzel onto my tongue, almost causing me to choke.

"Sorry," she says sheepishly.

Her pout is so cute and innocent. It contradicts the sex appeal she has going on with her strappy heels and too short dress. It is strapless, and I could easily shove my hand or face into her cleavage. I have thought about it long enough. I spent all one hundred eighteen minutes of the show thinking about it. I should be crowned a saint for being able to sit next to her during the performance as she wiggled on her seat in excitement. The bounce of her a-little-more-than-a-handful tits kept me fighting between watching them strain against the fabric of her dress and watching some people twist their bodies on stage.

I'm not sure if Claire has a thing for feeding me, but she is enjoying herself.

"Try this one," she yells with excitement, popping in a toasted almond bite before I even give her permission.

"It's really good," I say, making her smile.

She licks her fingers from where some of the crumbles stick to her skin. She washes it down with her frozen lemonade. We sit side by side on the edge of the pool while naked statues spout water from little openings.

"I'm so hot," she says, fluffing her hair.

She sure fucking is. So hot, I think she could ignite into a million flames and obliterate me. I know the desire between us is toxic, but I can't help but get pulled toward her. I'm entranced in her beauty and free spirit.

I get a whiff of vanilla, and the smell sends a signal to my cock, making it come to life. I need to step away before I show her just how badly I want her. I gather up the wrappers, take the last sip of the lemonade, and look for the nearest trash can.

The evening is warm with barely even a breeze. The air quality is definitely less fresh feeling than it is in Portland. I imagine in the heart of summer, it would feel stifling.

I hear commotion behind me, as I dispose of our snack containers.

"She's in the fountain."

"Oh, that looks refreshing."

"Can I join you, sweet thang?"

I know exactly who they are talking to before I even look. I swing my body around. Fuck. Claire is lying on her back in the fountain, kicking her feet and looking backward up at the statues. Having the time of her life.

I run over and cut through a developing wall of spectators. They are hooting and hollering and cheering her on. I want to punch some of the young punks who are asking her to remove her clothes to cool off even more.

I am about to toe off my shoes when her strapless bra comes flying through the air, landing on my shoulder. *You have got to be kidding me.* I growl and forget about my damn shoes, leaping over the side into the cool water. She sees me trudging through toward her and rolls on her stomach. Her arms flap and flail as she tries to swim away— knowing I am going to grab her and get her out. Does she really think she can out swim me in less than ten inches of water? She looks like a drunk seahorse learning to move for the first time. Maybe she is just this bad in the water. There are only a couple of feet between her and the opposite edge, yet she is not even gaining any distance. I stand over her and laugh. She rolls to her back again.

"Fun time is over," I say, reaching for her and pulling her up.

"I was just cooling off," she says, pushing her bottom lip out. I want to kiss it. Bite it. Mark her.

I bend down and grab a hold of her under her knees, hoisting her up to my chest. The top of her dress is sliding down, and I hug her closer to me to keep the assholes from ogling her. I tuck her to me and use my hands as a shield. I carry her through the water, over the cement edge of the pool, and break through the gathering crowd.

"You're my idol, sweetheart!"

"Encore!"

"Want to be my swim instructor?"

I glare at those making catcalls and saying the most asinine things. Boys can sound so stupid. I can tell that Claire is sobering up from the way she tucks her head into my neck to zone out all of the commotion.

My shoes slosh along the sidewalk as I carry her several blocks to our hotel. I don't even think she could walk in wet heels if she wanted to—at least not without spraining an ankle.

"What were you thinking?" I ask softly, walking into the Bellagio. The legs of my pants dried off a bit, but my shirt is completely soaked like a sponge from the water dripping off the drenched princess in my arms. Her hair is a mop and her makeup is smeared around her eyes.

She is so beautiful. Wild and free.

She shrugs. "I guess Spontaneous Claire wanted to make an appearance tonight. She comes out when I least expect it."

I chuckle into her hair. I can't stop myself from smelling it. Her thighs are warm again, and I want to run my hands up her legs to feel the smoothness.

"I'm thankful I got to meet her again," I say with reverence.

She tips up her head to stare into my eyes. "I'm sure you'll see more of her. Let's just hope the tattoo shops have curfews before she does something super reckless," she jokes. "I've always wanted to get something cute done."

"Oh yeah?"

"Yup."

"Anything in particular?"

She hums as she thinks. "I love sunflowers. Maybe one of those."

I walk into the waiting elevator and we travel up to our floor. When I push open the door to the suite, Graham and Angie look up from the movie they are watching to see me holding a drenched Claire.

"Oh, no. Are you okay, Claire? Did you fall? You are soaked," Angie says, assessing us.

"I voluntarily went for a swim," Claire answers. "I was so hot and well, it looked refreshing. That was after I threw up in the bathroom at the casino. I am a mess tonight."

"We all had a little too much fun tonight and indulged in the liquor," Graham says, standing up from the couch. "Make sure you stay hydrated."

"You sound just like your brother," Claire mutters.

I set Claire down and help her out of her heels by untying the ribbon that is wrapped around each calf muscle. How she even wore these damn devices boggles my mind.

"I'm glad you didn't get hurt," Angie says, coming over to hand Claire a blanket to wrap herself in. Now that we are in the building, the air conditioning is chilling our wet bodies, reminding us that we need to change.

"All of your kindness is making me feel even more embarrassed. I think the free drinks got to me. I was having so much fun trying new ones out that I wouldn't have before. Sorry if I crashed the night."

"It was a great night," Angie says, hugging her best friend. "You planned the perfect trip for us, and I'm glad you unwound and jumped into the fountain." She giggles. "As much alcohol as I had tonight, I would probably have joined you."

Claire's face turns serious. "There's always tomorrow."

14

CLAIRE

I rarely ever feel rested the morning after I make bad decisions. Last night was a record-breaker, and I have a detailed memory of the encounters to make hanging out with the gang even more cringe-worthy. I roll over and glance at my phone to see that it is only six. I feel oddly awake despite not getting much quality sleep.

The only thing that counters my bad decisions is making a few good ones. That usually means getting my butt out of bed at the first sign of dawn, tossing on some fun workout clothes, and hitting the pavement.

I decide that minimal clothes are best for a run through the dryness that is Las Vegas. I wear a neon green pair of spandex booty shorts and a matching sports bra that has a zipper down the cleavage and a razor back. I twist my hair high up on my head and sneak out into the main living space, trying not to wake anyone.

I tiptoe into the kitchen to fuel up on water. When I turn around, I smack into Nic who seems to keep doing this.

"What the hell?" I yell a little too hard, considering Graham and Angie are still sleeping.

I watch stupidly as Nic removes his workout shirt, revealing his hard pecs and ridges and—

Wait.

"Why are you removing your shirt?"

"You just dumped water on me this time," he says casually, showing me the huge growing spot on his gray cotton shirt.

"Oh. Sorry." I am a walking disaster. Oblivious. It is like my brain shuts off when I'm around him—even when I'm unaware that he is near.

"Where are you headed?" he asks, taking the glass from my hand and drinking the rest.

"You're welcome," I say sarcastically, which just adds more fuel to his already growing grin.

Seeing him put his lips directly on the spot that I just vacated sends a chill up my spine. These silly, mundane gestures are what I find the hottest. Watching him play poker the other night was almost my undoing. Him spinning chips in between his knuckles... Made me wonder the whole time what else he could do with those long fingers.

Nic clears his throat drawing attention to himself. I look up into his expectant eyes and inwardly groan.

"Did you ask something?"

His grin reaches his eyes. At least he doesn't get pissed off at my inattentiveness. "Where are you headed? And do you want some company?"

"I wanted to go for a run and detox after my overindulgence last night. Thought I would hit up the strip before people crowd it. Can you keep up?"

"You set the pace, and I'll rise to the challenge."

"You gonna go put a shirt on?" I ask, as he starts walking toward the door.

"What's the point? You'll probably just dump something on it anyway," he teases, making me laugh.

"Fair enough." I fill up one more glass of water and down it, just to make sure I compensate for the lack of humidity.

We meander through the hotel, warming up in the halls and stretching in the elevator. I have my distance tracker attached to my upper arm, and I double-check the laces on my running shoes. I have a film of sweat on my body before we even step outside. I think it has less to do with the warm-up and everything to do with the shirtless man who keeps giving me reasons to look at him.

The hotels in Vegas are so massive that running past one could take several minutes. I start off in a low jog and work my way up to a pace that is challenging but manageable for a longer distance. When I first got into running, I often made the mistake of starting out too fast. It took practice and adapting my technique to learn what worked best for me.

Nic easily can keep up. I thought he would struggle more because of his height and body structure. He is built, and sometimes the more muscle mass makes it harder to do high-impact cardio. Not for him. He is graceful and coordinated.

"Are you a runner?" I ask, keeping my eyes focused in front of me so I don't fall on my face.

"I run a couple of times a week outside. I have a home

gym and use that often. But there is only so much equipment can do for a body."

He is so right. Treadmills and stair climbers are great. However, physically moving your body in fresh air does so much for the mind and spirit. I am addicted to the rush I get when I am in a workout class or running on a new path—like the one we are taking today.

"I agree with you. I feel so much better when I am able to move freely."

I never thought hanging out with Nic would be this easy. He is becoming my friend in a short amount of time, and I am enjoying his company. While different from his brother in many ways, the Hoffman men still have a code they seem to live by. They take care of those they love, whether it be physically, emotionally, or financially. Angie has it so good and she deserves that. I know she and Graham will be the same power couple in marriage that they were while dating. Penny, however, may never be able to find independence if she gets the chance to move back to Portland and continue dating. Being the baby sister to two overbearing brothers has got to be challenging.

"What's on the agenda today?" Nic asks, wiping his face with his arm.

"I have tonight planned with Angie for our girls' night. Other than that, I didn't plan much for today."

"Good," Nic responds. "I have something in mind."

"Oh yeah? You going to share it with me?"

"Nope."

I glare over at him. "What do I have to wear?"

"Preferably more than you wore last night."

Oh, not this. "What was wrong with my outfit last night?" I frown. "I thought it looked good."

"You looked stunning. That's the problem. Every man in the entire hotel was trying to eye fuck you. And I had to keep myself from punching their faces in."

"Why do you care?" I ask. "I'm not your responsibility." I'm not Ethan's either, apparently. He is keeping me at arm's length when it comes to accepting me further into his life. Things were easy when I was still a student. Now, everything is different. Maybe this trip will turn a new page for us. I brought some surprise sexy lingerie just in case.

"As long as you are friends with Angie, then you are someone important to the happiness of my family. Graham and I protect who is important to us."

"Maybe I don't need any protection. Maybe I am stronger than you think and can fight my own battles."

"I'm sure all of that is true," he explains, "but it's not like I can turn it on and off."

We loop around and make our way back to the Bellagio, without talking much. Nic might think all eyes were on me last night, but this morning every female on the strip has eyes for only him. I saw how they watched his body move. He is powerful, yet graceful. Hard and rigid. And all—

Shit.

He's not mine. He's not anybody's.

When we get back inside our room, I shower and work through my meditation soundtrack of inspirational thoughts that I have saved on my phone. It helps ground me and acts as a mental vision board for how I want to push through my obstacles that keep me from experiencing my true happiness.

I meander back into the bedroom and see that there is a small bag resting by the closed door leading out to the suite. I open the bag and find a tiny tube of Dramamine, a vegan granola bar, and a bottle of Just Fruit. I turn over the note card and read Nic's elegant script.

Today's adventure might make your stomach do some flips, so take two pills and enjoy the light snack. -Nic

Just when I think my thoughts were cleansed through my meditation, I am back to everything being jumbled again. I follow Nic's orders and swallow two pills. We must be doing something that will cause me to throw up.

I change into a rainbow-colored sun dress with butter-flies all over it. I slip on a pair of pink sandals and secure my hair in a loose side braid. Angie joins me as I do my makeup, looking super cute in denim short overalls.

"Hey you," she greets.

"Hey yourself. How did you sleep?"

A blush reaches her cheeks as she looks away. "Really well."

I chuckle at her unintended reveal. I wiggle my eyebrows, making the pink turn to red. "I bet."

"Marrying that man is going to be the best decision I ever make. To think that he'll be bound to me for life could be a little daunting, but I know we'll always have adventures and never get bored with one another."

I want that. How could anyone not want that for their

future? "I am so happy for you. I can only wish I find what you have."

Her brows furrow. "Things seem to be progressing with Ethan. You definitely have been dating him longer than your other conquests."

"This is true." As for progressing, however, I wouldn't call it an easy journey. We seem stagnant. Everything is a struggle right now. "I usually burn through men much faster. This has to be a sign he's a keeper."

Angie helps me wipe up water that I splashed onto the vanity unknowingly, looking at me in the mirror while we talk. "Any idea what we are doing today?"

"I have no clue. Nic and I didn't correspond on this. Your guess is as good as mine." I am excited to find out what he has planned. Maybe he can take some initiative after all. The more we hang out, the more he surprises me. I lumped him into a category early on, and he is breaking down the walls of the box each minute I get to know him more.

We finish up and head out to join the men who are having a heated conversation. As soon as our presence is made known, they change their demeanor.

"Ready to go?" Graham asks, hugging his fiancée to him.

"Everything okay?" I ask, looking at Nic.

"Yeah, of course," he lies.

"You are a horrible liar," I whisper, as I watch him lock up the room. Angie and Graham go off ahead toward the elevator, and I linger back with Nic.

His eyes lighten with humor. "How can you tell?" he asks.

I stare into his baby blues. "Your eyes give it all away."

"I better wear sunglasses during the next round of poker, then."

"Pretty sure I'd still see through your attempt."

His eyes move down my body. I instantly feel vulnerable under his watchful gaze. Despite being able to decipher when he is lying, I am unable to read his other thoughts. Does he approve of me? Disapprove? Does my outfit meet his "more fabric" request? Maybe he doesn't even have an opinion about me. More importantly, why do I care so damn much?

I rarely care about anyone's approval. I have always done things my way. On my terms. Yet, here I stand at the doorway to our suite and feeling judged by his penetrable appraisal.

His fingers meet my chin, lifting it gently to meet his eyes. "Quit doubting yourself."

"Hmm?"

"You look amazing no matter what you wear. I was just enjoying the view."

"Oh." My eyes look away, at the artwork on the wall. He releases his hold on my chin.

"Hey," he says drawing back my attention. "Don't be shy."

I'm usually not. Never, really. Yet, here I am standing before him, and I can't seem to understand why he challenges me and shakes up my confidence at the same time.

"You have to realize what effect you have on men. You can't be that oblivious."

"I'm sure a handful find me attractive. I work hard at it, though," I say, looking up at him. "Doesn't come easy."

He swallows hard and rubs his hands over the back of his neck. "You have caused quite the stir at Entice, you know? You've created bidding wars." His sigh is heavy. "At least early on when you were not with Maxwell. I've had numerous recent requests for your company. You must have made a lasting impression at a mixer or something."

"Wait. Back up. Bidding wars? Why was I not privy to this information? Wouldn't I be able to see who was fighting over me?"

"Whoever bids the highest shows up on the employee end. So, you would have the choice to either accept or reject."

"Interesting. Had no idea. I was just using the agency for fun and restocking my petty cash fund. How would anyone know to request me if my profile is suspended?"

"Repeat customers. Word of mouth?"

I nod. I miss the easy money for going out and having fun. Ethan was a paying customer in the beginning, but when it became "more" we stopped the money transaction. It just felt weird. Dirty.

I think about my relationship with Ethan. He basically is still doing money transactions with me but under the umbrella heading of "allowance" and for much less than what I would be earning if I was still employed at Entice.

"I guess once I can no longer be on leave, I will have to officially resign." Right now everything in my contract is paused.

"Why are you even a ghost in the database?"

"Insurance purposes. The chance of locking in a referral bonus. I don't know. Ethan thought it was the logical next step."

Nic does a firm nod. It is almost mechanical. "We better go find Graham and Angie before they wonder where we are. Did you take your medicine I left you?"

"Yes, and thank you. I hate getting sick, and I despise throwing up."

We make our way down the elevator and find Angie and Graham in a cute boutique on the main floor.

"Sorry we took so long. Got wrapped up in solidifying plans," I fib. I can feel Nic's eyes on the side of my head. He needs to find something else more interesting than watching my reactions all the time. It is making me super self-conscious.

"No worries, we were just browsing," Angie says, clapping her hands once. "I'm so excited for today, and I don't even know what we're doing."

"You're about to find out," Nic says, pointing toward the exit. "Our ride is here to take us to our *other* ride."

I look out the glass doors and see a black stretch limo at the curb. We walk out and are greeted by our driver, who is a middle-aged man dressed impeccably in a solid black suit. The backseat is spacious, and we could easily fit more people comfortably if we wanted. Orange juice is poured into glasses and topped with champagne to create mimosas —except for mine.

Pouting my lips, I feel Nic's body lean into me. "It's not good to mix medication and alcohol."

"Fine," I grumble, accepting the pastry he keeps pushing into my lap. I take a bite of it and force my lips to smile.

"Cheers to Graham and Angie," I toast, clinking glasses with everyone.

"Cheers," everyone says in unison.

15

NIC

It takes fifteen minutes to pull into the parking lot at Elite Sky Tours.

"Are we skydiving?" Claire asks excitedly, looking at the icons on the sign.

She is fearless. Brave.

"Ha, maybe another time, sure. I'd be game, but today I thought we would all go on a helicopter tour of Vegas and the Grand Canyon."

Angie smiles ear to ear. "I've never been on a helicopter before."

"Me either," Claire adds. She can't stop looking out the window at the choppers lined up beside small planes and gliders.

I love seeing her excitement. It is obvious that she enjoys surprises, whereas I prefer predictability.

The driver pulls us up to the front of the building. We exit and meet our tour guide.

"Welcome to Elite Sky Tours. My name is Norman, and

it's my pleasure to pilot and guide your tour today. I've been flying for twenty-three years and haven't died yet."

Angie and Claire look at each other and then laugh when the guide's poker face breaks into the biggest smile. We move into the building, enjoy bottled water, and get settled in front of a large screen.

"It is mandatory at EST to have all future victims watch a safety video so that during crashes my ears are spared from screaming. Oh, and for insurance claim purposes."

We laugh over the cheesy humor and relax into the cushioned seats while he starts the projector to play the required video.

I lean over and whisper into Claire's ear, catching her off guard. "You scared?"

She turns her attention to me. "I'm less worried about something bad happening to the aircraft in the sky and more concerned about throwing up from motion sickness."

I see the fear in her eyes and it bothers me. Maybe this was a mistake to book, and instantly I am having second guesses.

"In the past, has the medicine not worked?"

She nods and gives me a weak smile. As much as she is excited to do something thrilling, she's realistic to know her limits.

"It'll be fine. Quit focusing on what could go wrong. The medicine should've kicked in by now."

I pat her leg in a friendly gesture. Well, that was my initial intention at least. Every innocent touch turns sexual in my mind. It is like one glance at her exposed skin makes my fantasies turn dark and blaze like a wildfire that I cannot control. I feel like I am some depraved perv. I stand up and leave the group during the bathroom break to go in search of the gift shop that I saw advertised on the website.

I place a chilled can of ginger ale, ginger snap cookies, and the little pressure bands that get worn on the wrists down on the counter. I pay and join back with the group. When I hand over the bag of supplies to Claire, she looks inside with confusion until it dawns on her that I am again preemptively trying to keep her healthy and calm.

"Wow, thank you," she whispers, taking out the bands and trying to put them on in the correct spot, all while paying attention to the conversations around her and fumbling with the direction insert from the package.

"Here, give them to me. I can help."

Claire holds out her slender wrists, and I examine the thin bones to find the sensitive spot between the correct two. I adjust the hard plastic ball that is attached to the inside of the stretchy bands and turn her wrists back over. Her clear nail polish makes her look sophisticated with the manicured white tips. My eyes move up to hers, and it is like we are the only two people in the entire room.

"Thank you," she mouths.

I can see the shine on her lips from where her lip gloss is smeared. She is softer today. Classy. I am starting to learn that Claire has many different sides, and each mood is represented by how she outwardly presents herself.

I am never one to exercise self-inflicted restraint when it comes to women. Despite finding Claire irresistibly attractive, it is the fact that she is attached to Ethan that makes me want her even more. If she gives in to me, then I can easily lump her into the same category as Tara. Men don't marry Taras. They fuck around with Taras. And since I have zero intention of ever getting married and settling down, then I will have fun fucking my way through a list of women who also have difficulty committing to one man. It is the perfect way to get my rocks off but not end up in an awkward situation where one party becomes too attached.

I elect Claire as the perfect candidate for my bed. I am basically doing her a favor taking her away from the bastard she is dating. He doesn't deserve her. I can provide for her better—in the short-term—than he can. The asshole gives her a freaking allowance that doesn't even compare to minimum wage. Who does that? Maybe meeting her as an escort skewed his definition of what a girlfriend actually means. Or maybe Claire is just as delusional to think that he sees her as anything other than inferior.

When it's time to go outside, we pass by a display case of memorabilia left by visiting celebrities. Everyone then moves to the helicopter that we will be using for our tour. The guide's coworker snaps a ridiculous amount of pictures outside the aircraft. Apparently, I unknowingly got signed up for a photography package when I called Graham's personal assistant, Kylie, and asked her to book this excursion. I told her to "make it special" and "check all the boxes." When I take over as head of security at HH, I will need to hire my own assistant to handle these types of matters.

"And now each couple," the photographer announces, catching me off guard. She says the phrase more like a probing question.

I am on the verge of forgoing this whole part of the package. However, Angie and Claire are having so much fun contorting their bodies into different positions just for the sake of having a fun picture to remember today. I don't have it in me to take away something that is bringing them joy. I also have Claire's leg flexibility burned into my brain for fantasy purposes. She has to have played sports or have done some type of dance lessons in her past. She is so bendable that I want to test her limits even more when I plow into her. Her ankles would look spectacular draped over my shoulders.

I have no idea what the photographer captured. I am not paying her any attention, despite hearing the girls snicker over her having eyes for me.

After finishing up the couple of pictures, the guide instructs us to enter the aircraft and strap into our seats. We follow through with the directives and load into the helicopter's back section, while the guide and the photographer sit up front.

Norman puts on his headset and starts up the blades. "I hope you all had a chance to buy some parachutes in our fabulous gift shop. And hopefully not the ones from the clearance section. Those ones are failures."

We all chuckle. He definitely is making this tour extra fun by his personality alone.

The guide gets us into the air and talks through his mic about the land and water below. He points out the different lakes and attractions. We chat in the back and I relax into my seat, draping my arm over the back of Claire's. While the view from up above is breathtaking, I find Claire's reaction to even the smallest things is what really captures my attention.

We fly along the Grand Canyon and see the beauty of the rock layers basking in the heat of the morning sun. The

North Rim appears to be holding onto its last remnants of snow, before spring melts it away. Every time I visit this wonder, I am in awe.

I glance over at Claire who is speechless. For the past twenty minutes, the only sounds coming from her mouth have been soft oohs and aahs. She is glued to her window, with her fingers digging into the seam. On occasion, she'll turn back to me or to Angie and smile, but overall, she is enjoying the peaceful view.

The guide shares some history of the canyon before looping around and taking us back to the city.

"What did you think?" I ask the group, while we exit and place our feet back onto solid ground.

"Loved it," Angie answers first.

"You did well planning this," Claire agrees. "I didn't even know this was an option to go all the way to the canyon."

I nod and smack hands with Graham's outstretched one.

"So, I thought we could visit a winery and have lunch at their restaurant," I suggest.

Claire looks at me with curiosity. "In the desert?"

"Yup. It's pretty unique."

"Let's do it," she chants.

Angie's smile beams. "Sounds amazing. Wine is my love language."

Graham looks at her with mirth in his eyes. "I thought" —he bends to whisper something in her ear—"was your love language."

Angie blushes and then smacks his arm, mouthing, "Stop." We all laugh over their exchange.

I pull out my phone to text the limo driver that we are

ready to move on to our next destination. Within seconds, he pulls up to the front of the building and helps the girls into the backseat.

The Desert Rose Winery is a half hour away but worth the drive. It is smack dab in the middle of the dusty plain and offers the only greenery seen for miles. I have no idea how anyone is able to grow grapes in this type of climate, but I am excited to try out the harvest.

"Mr. Hoffman," the hostess greets, "it is our utmost pleasure to meet you and your guests."

"Thank you," I respond with a nod.

She is pretty enough and from her eyes directed at me, I can see that she feels the same attraction. I feel Claire moving closer to me without even looking down at her. It is her scent that gives her away. She smells like a fresh baked vanilla cupcake, and her little spark of jealousy makes me smile. I wonder if she has sprouted any claws.

The hostess glances away and when her eyes slide back to mine, she appears to be back into her professional mode. "Follow me, please."

The tour options did not appeal to me when I had Kylie first call to set up a reservation, so I negotiated with the owner myself to set up a table at their on-location restaurant so we could partake in watching the head chef make a twelve-course meal of mini favorites. In addition, we will later learn about wine making and be able to make our own blend for testing and bottling.

"This is our very own Chef Mason Brunson," the hostess introduces, her hand sweeping out toward the man in all white. "He will be taking over your tour of the kitchen, as well as teaching you about the process of making our restaurant's favorites."

"Hi folks, I'm Mason. I've been in the restaurant biz for about twelve years and my claim to fame is that I was the personal chef for Gemma Valco."

"The two-time gold medalist gymnast?" Claire asks, her eyes as wide as saucers.

Mason's eyes light up. "The one and only."

"She's from NoVa," Claire adds. "Just a town over from me. But I was too young to remember her Olympic wins."

"After she retired, I was fresh out of culinary school and looking for work. What are the chances of setting my résumé on fire with her name attached to it? It was a dream job," Mason reminisces.

"I bet," Graham says with a chuckle. "Everyone has to start somewhere."

Mason pushes open a door marked for employees only and steps back to grant us access. "Follow me and I'll show you my office."

When we enter the air-controlled room, we are surrounded by stainless steel. Every surface and device seems to shine. Several workers are shimmying pans and stirring sauces. The aroma alone makes my stomach growl.

"Are there any dietary restrictions in the group?" he asks politely.

When Claire doesn't speak up, I lean in closer to whisper in her ear. "Want me to pretend I hate beef?"

She looks up at me and grins. "I'm going to cheat today. This food is going to be too good to pass up."

I swallow over her words. Something about the word

cheat makes me flinch. That's what I want her to do, right? Cheat. Yet, when the word touches her lips, a sadness washes over me. It stabs at my heart. I never really cared before. I would plow through life and women at the same rate.

"I'm sure Mason can adapt any recipe. It's not any trouble to have options," I reassure her. I want to support her personal goals, and I want her to be comfortable with whatever those may be. Her perseverance is one of the things that draws me to her. She already has an asshole boyfriend dulling her sparkle, so the last thing she needs is to stress about something as simple as food.

Claire shakes her head. "It's fine. Really. Thank you, though."

Her hand brushes against my arm, making my grin turn into a full-blown smile. She is not one to voluntarily touch me. Even though the contact is innocent, my cock stirs over just the simplicity of a single touch.

Mason guides us to the other side of the kitchen, pointing out features as he goes. "Go ahead and take a seat at the table," he directs, pointing to a metal island with cushioned chairs arranged around it.

It is U-shaped and allows for Mason to take up the hollowed-out section for his cooking demonstration. We all watch as he washes his hands and has his sous-chef keep us company while he gathers all of the ingredients he needs to make our lunch memorable.

The hostess returns with four long-stem glasses and uncorks twelve bottles of wine from a cart, lining up each along the other end of the table.

"The owners opened Desert Rose approximately forty years ago when they saw a need for a winery in an area of the United States that many would think would be an impractical location," she explains. "But they had a dream and a vision of success. Despite what many would think, grapes can grow even in the driest of climates—with some extra nurturing, of course."

"Wow," Angie exhales. She mutters something that I cannot make out to Claire, causing her to chuckle.

"The first wine is going to be paired with Chef Brunson's baby portobello mushroom cap appetizer that he is preparing now."

The hostess gives us a smile, allowing her eyes to linger on me for a few seconds longer, then passing the torch completely to Mason. We sit and watch the chef meander about the kitchen working his magic, anticipating the first bite of what he is preparing.

The chef is adding commentary where he finds necessary, while whipping up dishes for the oven and stove in record speed. He plates up the stuffed portobellos and pours us each a sample of the wine that pairs well with the creations. He does this twelve times, ending with a decadent chocolate mousse layered cake that is served with a sparkling Moscato.

"I've never made my tummy this happy before," Claire moans, rubbing her hands over her stomach.

"Hey now, I get some credit, right?" Mason asks, chuckling at her.

I can't tell if the chef is being friendly with Claire or if he is actually trying to flirt. I want to stake some claim to her, but I keep my actions platonic because of the company we are in. Plus, the last thing I need right now is to make a scene—and for what reason? I am not trying to win Claire over so she will date me. I don't date. I destroy.

"Everything was delicious," I comment, "especially the filet mignon with the blue cheese reduction." I try my best to wrap this up and get on with the next activity.

Claire finishes her last sip of wine and places the napkin from her lap back up onto the table. "I loved the chilled asparagus soup."

"I am shocked at how good a vegetable can taste," Angie agrees. "But the dessert was the showstopper."

Graham kisses her on her neck, making her smile.

We spend the next two hours exploring the vineyards and learning about winemaking. The trip ends with a bottling activity where we design our own blend in a makeshift laboratory. It is gimmicky but still fun.

"Thank you for planning these fun activities," Claire says, smiling up at me. "I may be a tadsy bit drunk."

She holds up her two fingers to try to show a small amount, but ends up just merging them together. Her eyes are starting to get bloodshot, and I gently intercept the glass that she is trying to bring to her mouth before it spills all over her outfit.

"We better switch this out for grape juice," I tease.

She wiggles her eyes at me. "With some alcohol added."

I laugh over her carefree spirit. I love her like this. Unfiltered. Happy.

16

CLAIRE

"Not going to happen," Graham says bluntly. He paces along the space in front of the couches, intertwining his fingers behind his neck.

"It kind of *is* gonna happen." I stand my ground. I am used to not backing down. "We are doing this, Graham. With or without your approval. You can control the wedding and the honeymoon and the stock markets. But this? This is all mine. So start getting your head wrapped around the idea of some strippers and equip your soon-to-be-wifey with a wad of cash. Because this is her last chance to change her mind, do a size comparison analysis, and enjoy some male attention that isn't sourced from you."

Since coming back to the hotel, I have sobered up and am ready to endure the fit Graham is throwing over the whole stripper night thing I have planned. We have had our fair share of arguments over the course of their relationship; however, this is our first one since they have been engaged.

Just when I think he couldn't get any more intense, he takes it up a notch and surprises me.

"You girls get wild when you go out and start throwing back drinks."

"True."

"See?" he huffs. "Even you agree!"

I shrug. "People don't hang with me because I make good choices. They want to be near me because I make the bad ones." I mean it as a joke, but by the growl roaring from Graham's mouth, I think it's safe to say he didn't take it as one. I get up from the sofa, but keep my temper in check and avoid reacting to his ludicrous behavior. Instead, I utilize my get-out-of-jail-free card, which I earned during Texas Hold'em. "Where's Nic?"

"What does Nic have to do with this?"

"I need him to knock some sense into you," I growl.

"He's around."

Dammit. Nic promised me he would take care of this. It was part of the bargain. So, where the hell is he?

"Graham?" Angie intercepts, peeking out from their bedroom door. "I need help with something."

He turns back to her and narrows his eyes. "What's wrong?"

"I cannot get the tie in the back of this—"

She opens the door farther to reveal a sexy scrap of pastel pink lingerie. Oh, she's good. Her hair is tousled with a fresh blow-dried look. I inhale and my breath whistles through my teeth.

Graham saunters toward his soon-to-be wife, but turns his head back to snarl, "This isn't over."

I give him a glare and a snarky thumbs-up. This interlude should buy me some more time to double-check my reservation at the club. I plop down on the sofa, pull out my phone, and find Nic's name on the list. I type out a message.

> **Claire: Where are you? You were supposed to help me with Graham and then you ditched me and he is angry and trying to sabotage all of my efforts and I promised Angie strippers and if I don't see some naked peen tonight, you are going to have to deal with me!**

> **Nic: How about some naked penis now? Will that work?**

> **Claire: Hell no, that's not going to cut it.**

> **Nic: Ouch. I don't want you to cut my dick.**

> **Claire: What? No. I didn't say that. Ugh. Where are you?**

> **Nic: Want to go to the casino and play some blackjack with me?**

I look at the top name on the text chain to verify I am talking to the correct person. At least one of us has sobered up. Nothing is making sense.

> **Claire: I only plan to lose money tonight by stuffing bills down hot men's pants. You promised you would help me make this mission a success for Angie. No backing down now.**

Nic: I got it handled

Claire: Really? Because Graham is here ready to start a brawl with me!

Nic: He'll cool off. Just chill.

Claire: I'm trying.

And then Nic does something I wasn't actually expecting him to follow through on. He sends me a dick pic. Is he for real? I stare down at the image of a naked penis. There is no way in hell this is his. He leaves out his face, but my mind can't help but wonder if this erect cock belongs to him.

No matter how many times I want to turn away or close my app, my eyes are drawn to the tanned figure on my screen. Fingers are wrapped at the base and I see the ring that Nic always wears. This is definitely his penis. I swallow hard at the realization and instantly feel my mouth water. I shouldn't be allowing myself to get turned on. It must be because I have gone days without any type of stimulation—even manual.

I smile down at my phone as another text pops up on my screen.

Nic: You look pretty when you smile.

My body whips around as the door to Nic's bedroom opens and he exits slowly with a stark white towel wrapped around his waist. He vigorously rubs a second towel over his head and hair. Every movement causes his muscles to ripple. He is so stacked that I wonder what it would feel like to have him hover over me while—

Fuck. I need to stop this.

"Like what you see?" he asks, eyeing me with an edge of humor in his sexualized comment.

"I—"

He smirks and lifts his eyebrows. "I like you speechless."

I raise myself up from the couch. "You—"

He chuckles. "Almost as much as I like you frustrated."

I turn to the main entrance of the suite. "I thought you were at the casino or something."

"I rested and took a shower."

"And sent me a dick pic," I snicker.

He nods, taking in my choice of lounge outfit. Ugh. Why do I feel like everything I do is met with his watchful eye. I am wearing a two-sizes-too-big black cotton T-shirt that exposes my right shoulder. The words "Look But Don't Touch" are across the front in white lettering. I paired it with red booty shorts that get lost underneath the hem of the tee. So, it basically looks like I am pantsless.

I had no time to change into anything else when Graham started bellowing through the suite about tonight's itinerary. I'm sure he will continue his tirade after his late afternoon romp with Angie. There's no way she'll be able to keep him preoccupied long enough for us to sneak out of here and attend the Meltin' Men show at the Starlight Club.

Every time I look up at Nic, I see the image of his penis burned into my permanent memory bank. "I'm in desperate need of help tonight. You promised."

Nic nods. "I got it handled. Just trust me."

His laid-back nature makes me want to scream. He only brings it out when he wants to appease me. The manipulation alone makes me want to smack the smirk right off his face. Twice.

I shift my weight from foot to foot. "You better be able to handle your brother."

"I can handle him," he says, taking a step closer, "and *you*."

"I don't need to be handled."

"You just think you don't," Nic chirps. "Trust me, you'll love the handling that will go down."

Why do I get the impression that his casual flirting is more than just flirting? He says things with such confidence that it makes a chill run up my spine. He's probably just a player. Men as good-looking as Nic Hoffman have to know their way around the female anatomy or are a complete failure at doing the sex. There's no gray area. He either has had a ton of practice and was able to perfect his foreplay skills or he is a lazy lover and knows that just looking good is enough for some women to be fulfilled.

I shake my head over my internal ramble. Why am I even thinking about this? Why do I care?

"I must be taking up a lot of real estate," Nic says, tapping lightly on my head, "in that brain of yours."

He is so close that I can smell the soap he used. It is different than mine. He smells like a man. A delicious one. I miss that smell. I probably just miss Ethan. *Ethan.* He should be arriving late tonight.

"I, um, need to make a phone call," I say, running into my room. "Take care of your brother. I'm not being pushed around by his overbearing ways." I sit down on the bed and plug my phone into the charging cable, so I can multitask but still get a full battery.

I pull open the text app and find Ethan's name toward the bottom of the list. We haven't been the best at communicating during the past couple of days. I hate when we are at a low. At least it makes the highs even more exciting.

Sometimes I think back to how we met and wonder if relationships can be built on foundations made of money. I can't help but wonder if I started dating Ethan because of convenience. He wanted to even out the playing field when his estranged wife, Deena, started dating someone else. It grew into something more with us. I love Ethan. And every time I think about Nic as other than a friend, I am damaging our relationship.

No one deserves that.

I type out my message and hit send.

Claire: Hey! Hope you are all packed up and ready for a fun couple of days.

Ethan: It is going to feel so good to hit up that casino and get away from here. Work has not gone well for me this week.

Claire: Oh no. Want me to call and we can talk about it?

Ethan: About to step into the shower.

Claire: Love you.

Claire: Have a safe trip.

Claire: Excited to see you.

Enjoy your shower. The conversation ends, as usual, with me sending him multiple texts and him not responding to them. Ethan and I have rarely been apart distance wise. He does travel a lot for work but other than that we are usually in the same city. Maybe we are just awkward texters. Maybe since he is arriving in less than twelve hours there is no reason to get into details about our days or anything of value. We can just talk face-to-face.

I don't even know what a rough week of work looks like for him. Does that mean he lost money? Maybe he is stressed over trends in the stock market? Didn't pick up any new clients?

Who knows.

I flop down onto the bed and text Angie.

Claire: Come to my room when you're done doing the sex.

Angie: Cummmmming right over.

Claire: Bahhahahha cheeseball

It doesn't take long for Angie to sneak into my room with her clothes draped over her shoulder and her makeup bag in hand.

"Hey you," she says, tossing her stuff on the upholstered chair and bouncing down onto my bed.

"Nice glow."

"It's sweat. Never going to get tired of that man and his capabilities."

I giggle over Angie's openness when it comes to sex. Half a year ago, I felt like she could barely utter the word without turning tomato red. Everyone deserves to be comfortable in their own skin.

"So I have a surprise for you."

"Claire, I've experienced your surprises before and they usually end—"

"With lasting memories," I fill in the blanks. "Obvi."

"With needing to be rescued."

"Nope. None of that." I swoosh my hands like wipers in front of my face.

Angie rubs her forehead. "None of what?"

"None of that negativity. There's no room in our schedule for that tonight. We are going to have the most epic night ever, and I'm pretty sure the Meltin' Men lineup tonight will hit up all of your unfulfilled fantasies."

She rolls onto her stomach and props her hands under her chin. "And how do you know this? Because I feel pretty fulfilled right now," she answers dreamily.

"I have seen the type of smut books you like to read. Basically porn for your mind, if you ask me," I say with a shrug. "So think of this show," I say dramatically, "correction—*experience*—as porn for your eyes." My eyes narrow at Angie who is busting a gut on my bed. "Why are you laughing?"

"So it is basically porn."

"No. I always keep it classy. This is 3D porn."

"Claire…"

"It is going to be so fun. And my surprise is going to make you go crazy."

"And probably cause Graham a heart attack."

"How's he going to find out?" I huff. "It's not like we will be video chatting through the night."

"He is Graham *fucking* Hoffman. He always finds out. I thought the man couldn't get any more possessive of me, but then I said *yes* to his proposal and it has triggered him into trying to shelter me away from all men. Says he doesn't trust his own species."

"So this will be a great therapy tool."

"Hah," she exhales. "Sure. We'll call it that."

"We need to leave in about two hours for dinner, so let's start getting ourselves primped."

"I'm still impressed that Graham is letting us do this."

"He doesn't have a choice."

17

NIC

"You're going to have to let up on your need to keep Angie from seeing some naked-ass men dancing around to some raunchy music while covered in baby oil tonight."

"And why is that?" Graham snaps.

"Because you're going to cause her to resent you. Let them have this memory," I persuade. I promised Claire I would get my brother to back down, and I plan to do just that. A deal is a deal.

Graham's eyes narrow on mine, his hand wiping at the scruff at his jaw, as he reclines farther into the seat he has taken in his room. "You're getting soft."

I kick my feet out in front of me, crossing them at the ankle. I am sitting opposite of him in a twin chair. "What the hell is that supposed to mean?"

"Can't remember the last time you've been this senti-mental. Rattling off things about making *memories*. What happened to my jaded brother?" He smirks, as I narrow my eyes at him. "I don't mean it as an insult. It's good to see you care about some cause other than something work related."

"If Angie and Claire start working together at HH, then what they do will turn into work," I predict. In my attempt to change the subject away from myself and my apparent *softness*, I am essentially only causing Graham more anxiety. "You do want me to handle all things security? Which means keeping a close eye on them, right? Or am I completely off base?"

Graham's sigh is audible even though we are yards apart. "Yeah, that is exactly what I want. You can utilize Collins in any way, but you are in charge." He runs his hands through his hair. "I cannot do my normal job if I'm worried about them in any way. So I will definitely need tabs kept. You can be discreet?"

"Always am."

"I trust very few people. My circle is getting even smaller with the recent breaches, so your willingness to take over as head of security will put me at ease while I navigate a weeklong honeymoon and Angie potentially launching a new career."

I give a single nod. I'm not exactly sure how I'll be able to function in a top-notch corporate security job while Claire is prancing around the building in who knows what. That girl can wear anything, and I swear it will make my cock twitch with need. If I have other men watching security footage of her, I know they will be distracted. Everyone in the entire building knows Angela McFee belongs to Graham, and if they value their life and their career, they keep everything regarding her strictly business. But Claire? I don't need a bunch of testosterone-infused jackasses getting turned on just because she bent over to fix her shoe. That is the kind of reaction men have to women like Claire. I know this as fact because I am one of those jackasses I just described. Claire is hot and fiery and free-spirited. A freaking breath of fresh air, if you ask me.

But I have zero claim over her.

She does what she wants, when she wants. The inability to gain control over a woman who cannot be tamed excites me and drives me wild with pent-up frustration.

I move to the minibar and make two glasses of Jack and Coke over ice.

"Those two get themselves into trouble literally every time they go out," Graham comments, running a hand down the side of his face. "And there's only so much discretion I can use at a place like that. Clothed men do not blend in well at stripper joints catering to women and their"—he pauses as he thinks of the right word—"needs."

I nod, passing him a drink. "This is true."

"You sure you have a tracker on them?"

"I have planted several," I say, pulling up my app on my phone that shows the GPS location of where Claire and Angie are positioned. "It is easier, of course, to have more eyes on your woman since she already knows your obsession, and I have less guilt to deal with by sneaking around. Regardless, I'll know where they are at all times. So, relax."

Graham huffs out, "Yeah, we may know where they are but there's no way of knowing if they are behaving."

I snicker. "Have you heard of something called *trust*?"

"Smartass. I can't wait until you are in the same position and asking me to keep an eye on your love."

"That's where you're wrong, bro. I'm never going to fall in love."

Graham takes a sip of his drink, tapping his fingers along the side of the glass. "We'll see."

The dots are color coded and show the location of the girls in the Bellagio. The only issue that we have not been able to work out is knowing which floor they are on. I know they are across the room, tucked away inside Claire's closed doors. But if there was a true emergency, I would not be able to locate them easily if they were a floor below or above. The Bellagio has thirty-six floors.

Graham knows the limitation to the current devices. They are worldly issues. I don't need to remind him. I just need him to relax his reins and have a chill guys' night with me. I promised Claire she would get her Meltin' Men show. As much as I don't want her putting herself at risk by going out without one of us, I know she needs this to get the whole Vegas experience and fulfill her duties as maid of honor. I want her to leave this city knowing she conquered all the items on her list.

As much as Claire's unpredictability causes me stress, I love that she has a zest for life that I rarely see anymore. Girls these days are glued to their phones, addicted to selfies, and lack the emotional layers that add depth. Fuck. Maybe there is something wrong with me. I used to prefer the shallow girls I just described. The ones who easily spread their legs for me to enter freely. The ones who didn't need me to call them the next morning, because I was just one of many they also rotated through.

"I'm ready for a night out. I could use a mind cleanse. You game?" I ask Graham.

"What did you have in mind?"

"I have a few places in mind, actually. Let me go check on the girls and see what time they are leaving. Everything is flexible for us. We don't have a schedule to follow."

"You sure we can't force them to stay?"

"Yeah, bro, I'm sure. It'll all be fine. I have a couple of associates watching out for them and paid off the bouncer to keep his eyes out for them."

Graham nods. "That does relax me a bit more. They have a driver lined up?"

"I'll make sure it is one that I run through the background checker first or hand select myself," I reassure.

"Sounds good. Thanks."

"Yup," I say, exiting the master suite and walking across the common area to Claire's room.

I give a series of knocks and wait for permission to enter. Angie opens the door just a tad, and I can see she is dressed in red glitter. I swallow hard and try not to look. She is like another sister to me. I know for a fact that Graham is not going to approve of this—

Outfit?

I look through the crack in the door and see Claire dressed in only a black strapless bra and a black lace thong walking into the bathroom. I must let out a breath different than the rest, because Angie quickly turns back and pushes me out of the room, following me.

"We're still getting ready. What's up?"

The image of Claire's lush ass cheeks, accentuated only by a scrap of lace, floods my mind. I have no space up there left for anything else except that vision of her. I want to pull her cheeks apart, rip off the thong, and bury my face in that pussy of hers.

I need to clear my head. I need to take a step back and reevaluate my desire for her. She is going to drive me crazy. I am not some teenager, and yet I stand here trying to think of anything but her so my hard-on can soften.

"Nic?"

I look at Angie's probing gaze. "Hmmm?"

"Why are you impeding on our time to get ourselves glammed up?"

"I need you to accept a driver of my choosing." I am coming off harsh and soften my tone for her midsentence. Angie has been through a lot, and I don't need to prove I am an asshole for the sake of her listening to me. She doesn't deserve that. "I also need you to keep your phone on and check it periodically. Please, if anything goes wrong or if anything seems off, you call me or Graham. Do not accept drinks from anyone other than the bartender or waitstaff. Do not leave—"

The door opens again and Claire slips out. Her hands are on her slender hips and I can tell she knows exactly why I am here, so why should I even try to hide it? She is dressed like a seductress in black and red. Straps wrap around her shoulders and neck, making her seem like she is in sexy bondage. Her hair is down, and the wavy locks make me want to wrap them around my hand and tug her closer to me. I want to devour this little sexy vixen. I want to push her against the door, lift her legs around my waist, and pump into her with pent-up need.

"You cannot dictate and micromanage the entire night,

Nic. We'll be fine," she reassures. "And I'm bringing weapons."

"Weapons?" I scoff. "What the hell, Claire?"

She prances back into the room, leaving the door wide open for me to see her rummaging around on the bed for her handbag. Every bend of her body exposes more flesh of her legs. She is petite but has curves in all the right places.

"Here," she says proudly, waving two small black tubes in the air. "Found them!"

Lipstick? I move into the room to get a closer look. "Pepper spray?"

"The extra fire kind. It'll be like getting a habanero juice smoothie to the eyes. It's supposed to shoot farther and be more potent," she explains, pride bursting from her.

"Surprised those passed through airport security," I mutter, taking a tube from her hand to examine the contents.

"I did my research and made sure they were in the checked luggage and met the liquid ounce requirement."

"But you missed that these will not pass the security protocols for the Starlight Club."

Her eyes dart to mine. "Really? They won't even let me bring these in my bag?"

I shake my head. "You'll most likely get them confiscated at the door when you pass through the metal detectors and the x-ray machine. They upped the security there recently and outlawed all personal protection devices." I know this because as soon as I found out that they were going to see a stripper show, I did my own research. The owner seems legit enough. It wasn't hard to infiltrate the club's security features to see what level of protection they use to keep their customers and employees safe. As far as nightclubs go, everything checked out, and there are no documented incidents reported there in the past couple of years.

"Welp, then I guess I will just have to use my own self-defense skills I've been working on during some of my gym sessions."

I close my eyes as I take in the words she is feeding me. "If you feel unsafe at any time, you call me. Okay? Or go straight to the bouncer. No trying to be a hero."

"Nic," Angie interjects, putting her hand on my elbow. "We'll be fine. It is entirely possible for us to have a drama-free night. We aren't in Portland. I have not been targeted since graduating from college. All of that craziness is behind us."

I smile at her and nod. She's right. Graham is just making me extra paranoid. Plus, I do trust that Angie and Claire have each other's backs. They are very loyal to each other and that is admirable.

When I was trying to make a life for myself on the East Coast, I made friends and had fun going out. However, many of my friendships were tied to Tara's friendships. So, when Tara and I split, so did my interest in maintaining our mutual connections with people. I wanted a clean break. Asher is one of the few friends I have that I still associate with from college. However, I never was a person who needed a lot of people to surround me. Just a handful is enough.

"We'll be ready to leave for dinner in twenty minutes. If you want someone other than Butch with the fake ID, smoker's breath, and criminal record to drive us around, you better step to it," Claire says, turning and walking back into her room. Her hand waves up into the air in a reverse goodbye gesture.

I can't hide my grin over her snark. She is something else. If she were mine, I would smack her ass just for the way she talks to me. Pretty sure we would both enjoy it.

It is her I-don't-give-a-shit-what-you-think attitude that she pairs with her I-just-want-to-make-those-I-care-about-happy mission that I find the most intriguing. It is fucking with my head how she can be so sweet and sassy all at once. Only Claire can pull off both of those things and make it look sexy.

"Don't fuck with my best friend's emotions."

Angie's blunt words sober me up from my daze. My eyes study hers for any ounce of leeway. None. She gives me none. Worst part is, she is one hundred percent correct. I need to stay away from Claire. Muddying the waters with her will make the wedding awkward and all future family occasions even worse. Angie is not one to mess with either. And pissing off my brother is the last thing I need.

"Message received."

18

CLAIRE

I'm glad we just ate a ridiculously delicious dinner prior to arriving at the Starlight Club, because the only items on the menu here are eye candy and liquor.

Even the bouncer is dressed to impress with just a bowtie and booty shorts that look to be made for the pool scene.

"So, part of your surprise is starting now," I say, passing the man at the back door to the club two backstage passes.

"What are those?" Angie asks, pronouncing each syllable slowly and eyeing me with apprehension.

"I thought it would be fun to get to see the guys get warmed up before the performance, so I paid a little extra." It was actually a lot extra. But I think it will be worth it. "We could only attend tonight anyway because of a lottery system. So, it is basically fate that we are here."

"Wow. This is going to be so much fun," Angie cheers.

I knew she would approve. We have fun doing anything

—which I appreciate—but I wanted to do something extra tonight for her celebration. We get a wristband and are granted access to a workout room full of nearly naked, muscles for miles, men. If there is a shortage of baby oil in this country, I know who is hoarding it. Holy fuck.

"Damn," Angie exhales, her eyes as wide as dinner plates. "I approve of this extra entree. Yum."

My eyes take in the scene of at least forty men doing pull-ups, pushups, stretches, and practicing dance moves on a wall to wall exercise mat. Every different type of fantasy should be represented in this room by the eclectic variety of man meat. Long hair, short hair, curly hair. Dark and light. Face scruff or clean-shaven. Tall, short, thin, beastly. Tats and piercings, oh my.

"I'm going to pee my pants if that guy across the room looks over at me one more time," I mumble, causing Angie to look at me and giggle. "It's like he is stalking me with his eyes. Not complaining, but he is making me wish I wore better panties. Something with better absorbency."

"I may have put on similar stupid panties too."

One tall drink of water walks over to us. "Ladies, right this way." He points over to a lounge area set up with comfy chairs and our own personal waiter. "Sit, drink, and enjoy our warm-up."

Angie and I follow the directive and relax into the chairs while sipping on mojitos. The guys periodically interact with us by sauntering over and getting so close I can make out the tribal script on some of the tats. We aren't the only ladies who purchased backstage passes, but the VIP areas are separated strategically to give the impression of exclusivity. When I shout out that Angie is partaking in her bachelorette party, we basically get lap dances. I'm just glad I stuffed my handbag with wads of cash. These gyrating hips that are inches from my face deserve to be rewarded.

"Well, this is definitely helping to set the mood for the real show," I laugh. "Not sure it can get better than this, though."

When it is time to go out to the main arena area, the waiter ushers us to our seats that are surprisingly really good. In fact, the setup is designed to look like a spider, so every group of seats seems to be decent and near a leg of the stage.

As we each order another drink, Angie leans over, taps my arm, and smiles at me. "Thanks for setting this up. I am having so much fun."

"I am having a blast, and I love celebrating you."

She gives me a hug and it feels so good to have a friend like her in my life. We are family. I always secretly wished for a sibling growing up. It would have been nice to have someone else to talk to and not feel so alone. Growing up in a house that lacked love was damaging to my view on how I perceived myself. But as a little girl, when that is all you are used to, you convince yourself that the rest of the world is living the same way.

"Hey," Angie says, looking into my eyes. "You okay?"

I plaster a smile onto my face. "Yeah, why?"

"Just seemed like you went somewhere else for a moment."

I did. But I am back and ready to forget. "Just fantasizing about the men."

"Me too." She giggles.

The estrogen levels in the room are building as the lights dim, the music starts, and the host makes his way on stage. "Hello ladies! I hope you all are ready for a wild, a spectacular, and a high-energy performance of Meltin' Men! There are several of you here tonight celebrating some special events, so get ready for some surprises, some excitement, and some stripping! Join me in welcoming to our stage, the delicious men."

The crowd goes wild with whistles and hollering while all of the men gather on stage. It is like an army made of sexy soldiers. One by one they make their way onto the stage. Some come down from cords from the ceiling, some pop up onto the stage through hidden passageways, and others use gymnastic moves to make their grand entrance.

"Yes!" I scream, as several men start dancing to the music.

The stage clears, leaving just about ten performers, each using a closed umbrella as a prop. Who would have thought something so innocent could turn so sexy. They spread their legs, hold the umbrellas like canes, and dance around them. It is as if they are dancing just for me. Eye contact is made. Pulse rates are on the rise.

"Shit, this is hot," Angie groans, waving her hands in the air, unable to contain her excitement.

It is what the female energy in the room brings. We are all in this together. Uniting to enjoy the basics of the male body. It is so fun to do something just for us. To not have to think about anything other than enjoying ourselves and letting go of the inhibitions that hold us back from being our true, sexual selves.

The umbrellas all open in unison and then the stage

turns into a rain storm. Water falls from the ceiling, soaking just the men on stage. The music turns raunchier and the crowd is on their feet.

I polish off my amaretto sour and sway my hips to the music. I forget about everything except for keeping the rhythm with my movements and watching the scene unfold in front of my eyes. There are two stages that jut out near us, sandwiching us between a group of men doing belly rolls on the floor and several gyrating their groins against chairs.

"We have some future brides in the house!" the MC announces over the sound system. "Let's welcome a few to the stage for a Meltin' Men personal greeting."

Angie jerks when her name is called, hesitating to go up on stage.

"You have to go," I insist. "See, there are two others. You won't be by yourself." I push her forward, and she gets plopped up onto the stage by one of the performers that jumped off into the crowd. "Yes, Angie!"

I snap a few pictures of her and take a short video as she gets an epic lap dance by four men that rotate through. I am so into paying attention to Angie that when I sit down, I land on top of one of the show men.

"Oh, hot damn," I gasp, looking back to see a chiseled jaw and gelled hair. "Sorry." I get up and the man behind me shadows me. We grind together and dance to the song. It is fun and freeing.

I am so involved in having a good time that I completely miss Angie coming back off stage and joining me. She pulls out some high bills and starts stuffing them into the spandex shorts of my dancer, cheering us on. Then he holds his finger up to signal to wait, takes two steps back, and then rips off his shorts to expose his tiny black thong. Bills go flying, and I can barely think over Angie's excited screams and giggles.

Sweat coats my skin as we find ourselves surrounded by our own strip show of about five men. Sexual moves are simulated and one man hoists me up, spinning me around midair. I glance over and Angie is cheering me on from her perch on one of the performer's backs, waving one arm in the air like she is riding a stallion.

"This is wild!" I scream over the music.

Angie yells something back but it is incoherent. All I can hear is her laughter and squeals of shock. When the song ends, the men wink and crawl back onto the stage, slinking back behind the curtain until another group of dancers enter.

Intermission consists of a low-key side show and an opportunity to refuel our drinks from the bar area in the back of the arena. While Angie uses the restroom, I check my phone messages and see that Nic has been trying to get ahold of me. Seven text messages and three missed calls. Ouch.

I hit the call back button and wait until he picks up.

"Hey, what's—"

"You need to keep your fucking phone on, or I'm coming there to get you both," he snaps.

"It's ladies only. No men allowed," I huff.

"Claire…" There's a hidden warning to his tone.

"I'm sorry. We are a bit distracted here, if you know what I mean."

"I cannot hold Graham back from crashing your penis party if—"

"Penis party?" I ask, laughing so hard I snort. "You make it sound like a surprise orgy. But hey, I could go for an orgy right now with as hot as this show is. They are all greased up and man meat is flying and—"

"Claire! Focus," he snarls. "I don't need any details about what poison you are witnessing. Just make sure you keep your phones on. Or I'll pay off the head bouncer to kick you guys out."

"You're bluffing."

"Try me," he threatens. "His name is Oscar."

"Fine."

"Fine."

"You drive me nuts, Nic Hoffman."

"Just do as you're told."

"You aren't my keeper," I hiss.

"I am tonight."

"Whatevs."

I end the call when Angie returns with fresh drinks, garnished with penis-shaped ice cubes.

"Sorry it took so long," she apologizes. "I had to call Graham. He was losing his mind and was on the verge of dragging me out of here."

I shrug. "We were a bit distracted."

"Tell me about it. I tried to convince him that this show is only going to make me horny and want to jump his bones when we get back tonight."

"And to think that all these years I thought you were the conservative one."

Angie giggles and gulps her drink.

The performance wraps up with more aerial stunts and more men baring their goods for an audience of sex-crazed females. Angie and I stumble out of our seats and make our way to the exit when the show concludes with each man taking a bow. I am pumped up on adrenaline and alcohol.

"Want to go dancing?" I ask, pulling Angie with me toward the line of people leaving the club.

"I think probably yeah."

We squeeze out of a side door meant only for employees, entirely bypassing the exiting crowd. The warm air feels surprisingly good after the continuous blast of air conditioning from the Starlight Club.

It doesn't take us long to find our way back onto the strip. Despite being able to see the Bellagio in the distance, walking there would be a huge feat—due to the amount of weaving between the crowds of people that would need to occur.

I turn to Angie and teeter on my high heels. "Want to walk and see if we see anything fun that stands out? Surely there's a place to dance around here."

She points down the block where a sign advertises dancing in bright pink colors. "Let's go there."

It takes a few minutes to walk to Cammy's, which is a bar and dance club just off the strip. With a minimal cover charge and a stamp to our hand, we are granted access.

"Good spontaneous choice," I compliment, watching the entire venue come to life with dance music.

"Let's hydrate with tequila and get out there," Angie insists, bouncing on her heels.

When we hit up the dance floor, we are limber and ready to move. The DJ mixes up songs and adds his own musical elements, setting the mood. Angie and I sway to the music and let go of our inhibitions.

"My fiancé wouldn't like you touching me like that."

I turn to Angie and see this drunk guy dancing behind her, his hand splayed over her stomach. She wiggles free but is joined by two of his buddies, one joining their threesome and the other moving over to me. They seem to be doing more than just alcohol. Their eyes are a bit glassy and their pupils are dilated.

"No," I state bluntly, glaring daggers at him.

"Stop," Angie says, pushing away from the main guy. He moves back to her, whispering something into her ear. I can see her flinch and my blood boils.

"She said 'stop,'" I snap. I get the guy that is shadowing me to move away. When the two on Angie do not budge, I shove the closest guy into his buddy, making them stagger backwards. "C'mon, let's go find somewhere else to dance."

We only make it a few feet when hands grip my waist, tugging me backwards. I barrel around and smack the asshole's face who thinks he has the right to touch me. My hand stings as I take in the shock on his features, quivering from my own anger.

"Don't fucking touch me!" I scream, not even worrying if I'm causing a scene.

But a scene is exactly what I cause. The three men, who were once just extra flirty, turn on us. I tug on Angie's arm, pulling her to me, while the group surrounds us. The fear creeps in, and I reach for my phone to call Nic. His number is barely dialed when the main guy snatches it from my hand and disconnects the call.

I look around for a bouncer, but the club is so packed

that even if I scream, no one would be able to distinguish the sound above the current noise level. We are on our own.

"Not sure why you two find the need to be disrespectful," the stockier one bites out. "We are just looking for some fun tonight."

"Not with us," Angie snaps. "Just keep on moving and quit stalking us."

"Let's all play nice," the average height guy suggests.

I pull Angie and start to run, only to get pulled to hard muscles again. I struggle and feel the dampness on my cheek from a pair of lips. Ew. I squirm and kick and thrash, trying to get free. I wish I had my tubes of pepper spray because these assholes surely deserve a habanero spa treatment to the eyes. How is no one noticing this commotion?

"Let her go!" a gruff voice calls out in an unwavering tone.

I know that voice...

Nic. He is here. I try to turn my face, but am blocked by the guy holding me hostage.

"Are you brain dead? Let her go."

The arms around me get torn away, and I stumble into a group of drunk dancers, falling to the ground.

"Claire! Claire!" Angie calls out.

I look up and get a kick to the face as body parts start flying over my head. A few innocent bystanders fall down, one landing on top of me. I think I'm going to get buried by the chaos, when strong hands pick me up out of the rubble of limbs.

"Wrap your arms around my neck," Nic instructs.

I do as I'm told and tuck my body to his, while he gets

me out of the building safely, joining Angie and Graham in the dry outside air.

"Than—"

"Don't you talk," he interrupts. "I don't want to hear a single word from you right now."

I frown over his disappointment.

"Bu—"

"No," he snaps. "Not a fucking word."

19

NIC

I am not an angry person. I pride myself on having an even temper. I can control my actions.

Except for tonight.

Tonight, I am about to explode.

Claire promised me she would be safe. I promised Graham they would be safe. I fucking hate breaking promises. This is why I rarely make any.

I want to scream at the trembling woman in my arms. She feels so small compared to my larger frame. I want to shake her and remind her of how horrible tonight could have gone if I didn't come rescue them.

My eyes connect with Graham's and I know he is relieved to have Angie back at his side, tucked into the safety he offers. As soon as I watched the girls go off course on my tracking app, I checked in with their driver who verified that the performance was over and that the crowd was exiting the venue. I should have known that they would get distracted or want to explore more of the city. All night, I wanted to crash their fun, but I resisted. I knew this was their girls' night to relax and enjoy some naked men. So, despite my better judgment, I told Graham they would be safe without a bodyguard. Nope. Not safe at all.

I let out a sigh. When I saw Claire's frail body lying on the dance floor, I wanted to murder someone. She brings out all of my protective instincts—when it comes to the opposite sex—that I thought were dormant since Tara.

"You all had your fun for the night. Let's get back," Graham breaks the silence.

"Are you hurt?" I ask Claire, placing her on her feet and looking her over.

She bites her bottom lip and shakes her head. I know she is a strong woman. I also know that she got kicked in the head.

My eyes narrow on hers. "You sure?"

Just a nod. That's all I get.

"You'll need to ice your cheek when we get back." I take a deep breath, trying to lessen my anger.

"I'm sorry," Angie whispers to Claire, who looks devastated that her friend got hurt.

Claire fights back the tears that pool in her eyes. Shit. I can't do tears.

Graham leads us to the idling SUV and helps the girls into the backseat. I join them, sitting so close to Claire that I can smell her vanilla fragrance.

"Are you mad at me?" she asks, looking up at me with eyes full of sorrow.

"No."

"No?"

"I was. But I calmed myself down." I watch as the

driver pulls away from the curb and takes us back to the main strip. "You should've let me know where you were going. I know why you wanted to extend your night out. I get it. But you should have let one of us know."

"How did you find us?"

"Instincts," I half lie. "I knew what time the show ended, and when your driver informed me that you both were missing, we investigated."

It is midnight, and the exhaustion in Claire's eyes is evident. Her breathing has calmed down by the time we pull up to the front entrance of the Bellagio. I help her and Angie out of the backseat and join Graham.

I know my brother was stressed out while we raced to get to Cammy's. If anything worse would have happened to the girls, he would have gone ballistic. I have seen him in action. I know his limits. They rival my own.

Once inside the suite, we disperse and go into our designated rooms. Before Graham shuts his door, he looks back at me and motions for his phone, signaling to me that I should wait for his text.

Remembering that Claire needs ice, I find some in the freezer, package it inside a plastic bag, and tie it off.

I knock twice on her door, hearing her sniffles from the other side. She opens the door, and I swear she looks more fragile than I've ever seen her. Smaller. More petite. Gone is the fierce girl who went to war over seeing some men gyrate to raunchy music. Replacing her is the defeated girl who looks like she is going to cry again.

"I brought you some ice for your cheek," I say, eyeing the minor redness that is breaking through her otherwise clear complexion. I hate seeing her in pain, and I know she is harboring the emotional kind right now.

"Thanks," she says, accepting the bag.

"Claire?"

"Hmm?"

"I'm not mad at you."

Her big brown eyes find mine. But she can't do anything more than nod.

When I get to my room, I kick off my shoes and lie down on the bed. What a night. I pull my phone out and see the notification for Graham's message pop up across the screen.

Graham: One of my current heads of security, Eugene, informed me that there was a break-in at HH. This keeps happening. The only reason the guy didn't get in fully is because the night security guards changed up their routine to compensate for one calling off last minute due to illness.

Nic: Point of entry?

Graham: Back door

Nic: Anything broken?

Graham: Two interior windows. Managed to get through the first entry with a key card. Probably a stolen one.

Nic: I want all main floor windows changed over to shatterproof. I also want motion detectors installed and the magnetic strips on the keycards aren't good enough. I plan to re-key everyone's cards with something less able to be replicated. Install sound warnings if glass breaks. Sirens to deter any unauthorized guests. I want to revamp everything and install all of the equipment myself so I can ensure it is done correctly. Set up more firewalls and secure devices with multiple passwords.

Graham: This is why I am thankful you are on board.

Nic: Safe to assume Angie is not to know about this?

Graham: Correct. I want my girl to be stress free but this all needs to be handled prior to her coming to work in the building.

Nic: Have one of your workers who is in the video control room send me the footage and I will run it through my software to see if anything pops up. I predict it is a dead end, but I like to check off all the boxes.

Graham: Sounds good

Nic: I also need the names of every single employee you have at HH. Cleaners and messengers. All. I want a full list.

Graham: Done

Nic: How willing is your current head of security going to be to hand over the title?

Graham: I actually have two heads who work together since HH is massive and could use the extra protections and guidance.

Nic: Makes sense

Graham: Eugene and Dan were about to finish up a six-month trial basis as head, after working their way up the ladder for years. They know the score. I'm sure both will accept whatever I decide. Do you plan on keeping or firing them?

Nic: I haven't decided what I want to do yet. I have very high standards and expectations, so if both can keep up, then maybe keeping them will be valuable assets under my guidance.

I shower, change into a pair of black lounge pants, and start thinking about everything I need to do to get Hoffman Headquarters secured. Trespassers piss me off. No one in their right mind would randomly pick HH to try to break into. This is targeted. If anyone will be able to figure out who is gunning for Graham's property, it will be me. It is a welcome challenge to prevent assholes from breaking in physically or virtually. In order to be thorough, I have to think like a criminal. Good thing is, I have been on the opposite side of the law a few times. Let's classify those instances under the title of research.

I hear a series of hushed voices outside my room, drawing my attention to the door. It is Claire. I move closer to try to hear what the commotion is about. I already can tell that there are tears in her eyes, just from the tone of her voice.

"You're drunk, Ethan," she hisses.

I can tell she is not impressed. He arrived in Las Vegas around 10:53 p.m. according to the notification I set on my phone and checked in to a room a few floors below us. For the past two hours, he has been hitting up the casino. Pretty sure he cares more about the possibility of furthering his wealth than actually caring about his beloved girlfriend.

"Please, you're hurting me."

I count to ten and resist breaking through the door to get to her. I do not need to get involved in their drama. Claire can take care of herself. She doesn't need me interfering in her domestic disputes.

I go back and lie on the bed, trying to clear my thoughts of how freaking sexy she looked leaving tonight for a night out on the town. How she settled for Maxwell is mind-boggling. She is the polar opposite of his ex-wife—in appearance and in personality, so it seems. I never met her. But just looking at the file I have gathered seems to give that impression.

"You look like a whore," his snarly voice breaks through my thoughts.

"Just because you're drinking doesn't give you the right to treat me this way," Claire yells back.

My phone buzzes with an incoming text.

Graham: What the hell is going on out there?

Nic: Maxwell arrived and got himself intoxicated. Arguing with Claire.

Graham: Angie is going to burst out of this room if I don't keep her contained. You know how she is always on Team Claire.

I smile at Angie's loyalty to her best friend. I am not surprised. I move closer to the door and decide to see the situation for myself. The suspense is wearing me thin.

I open the door and see Claire—still dressed like a naughty minx—with her balled-up fists resting against her slender hips.

"I'm not going with you when you are this out of it," she declares.

"You are going to my room," he demands, gripping her upper arm so tightly, I can see the tension in her shoulder blades.

"Claire, go to your room and stay there," I direct, causing her body to whip around and stare at me—and as a result, detach herself from her asshole boyfriend.

"What—"

"Just do it. I'll make sure Ethan gets to his room safely. You guys can hash this out in the morning. We can all go out for breakfast."

Even just the idea of getting pancakes again makes her scurry off into her room, leaving Maxwell to deal with me one-on-one.

"Was that necessary?" he asks, anger evident in his tone.

"Yes."

"She's mine to boss around."

I shrug, not even surprised he sees her that way. What does surprise me is how Claire refuses to see the fucker for what he is—a narcissistic, chauvinistic liar. "Sure. But this trip is for my brother and his fiancée. You're the outsider. So play by our rules or go the fuck home."

"Fine," he snaps. He looks like he wants to say more but at least has the common sense to keep his mouth shut. I'm not in any type of mood right now to control myself. I'm still bubbling with anger from the way he grabbed her arm.

"Go to your room and sober up. Just know that just because you two are dating doesn't give you the right to treat her like shit. I won't stand for it."

"Why do you care?"

I grin. "Because I don't get off on women crying, like you do."

His expression goes cold and he stumbles over to the door. I help him into the hall by pushing him along. It may even be a tad bit aggressive on my part, but without any witnesses, maybe it didn't even happen.

It is just like taking out the trash, except that even after he leaves, the situation still stinks.

20

CLAIRE

It feels good to wake up and actually feel rested. I reach for my phone and see that Ethan has tried to call and text me every fifteen minutes for the past two hours. I glance at the time and see it is almost ten in the morning. So much for going out for breakfast; might as well call it brunch now.

I hobble into the shower, feeling sore from falling down last night. I remember everything, despite having too much to drink. It was a night full of memories, from the Meltin' Men fun, to the impromptu trip to the dance club, to the Hoffman brothers coming to rescue us. Nic was not happy with me. At least he resisted from yelling his feelings at me on the way back to the hotel.

Then the Ethan drama ensued. He didn't even let me know he landed in Vegas and obviously got on an earlier flight than originally planned. I feel so disconnected when it comes to him. I really need the next couple of days to be about building us back up to the happiness level we were soaring at when we first started dating. Things were easy then.

I finish washing myself and towel dry off. I can hear loud talking coming from the shared area of the suite and can almost predict it involves Ethan. This entire trip has been so peaceful, with us all getting along. And then he arrives. Shakes up the entire dynamic.

I throw on a robe and pad out into the living room to see what the plan is, prior to picking out an outfit to wear.

Ethan spots me first, and the look on his face tells me that he one hundred percent disapproves of my decision to enter without actual clothes. He saunters over to me, stopping his conversation in the middle, and pushes me back into my room.

"Put something on, please. You're embarrassing me."

"I, um," I start, hesitating as I analyze why he's so irritated right now. We should be hugging and kissing and catching up on lost time while we were separated. Instead, here we stand, miserable yet again. "I just need to know the plan so I can dress accordingly."

"This isn't time for a fashion show, Claire. We have been waiting on you to get out of bed so we can go eat. I'm hungry. I suggested going without you but that was not received well."

I swallow. Why is he so cold? What have I done to deserve this treatment? I nod. "I'll hurry and just toss on something casual."

"I'll see you out here then."

I move over to the clothes I hung up in the closet and select a simple aqua-blue cotton dress. I pair it with seashell flip-flops and a coordinating necklace. I half crown braid my hair and let the rest loose. I don't even bother to blow-dry it because as soon as we are outside, the dampness will be gone. I have gotten used to dressing in a hurry from all the times I have used the gym's restroom to make myself presentable. It helps to stay organized—which is not naturally my strong point. I definitely have been working at keeping my belongings in order since graduating from college. Having extra time on my hands makes it easier to self-reflect and work on my flaws.

When I get out of the room, Angie is sitting on Graham's lap on the couch, Nic is pacing in the kitchen, and Ethan is looking angry near the main door. I walk over to him and wrap my arms around his waist, drawing him closer to me.

"I'm glad you got here safely," I whisper. "When do you have to meet with some business associates?"

"In a few hours."

I nod. I turn my attention to Angie and Graham. "Did I ruin breakfast?" I ask softly.

"Of course not," Angie answers. "I slept in nearly as long as you did. I was so exhausted after seeing the—"

"Filthy-ass dancers?" Graham chimes in, tickling her sides.

Angie's face lights up with humor. "Pretty sure their asses were smooth and clean, but I might have been too far away to see accurately."

"Rigggghht," Graham snickers.

I look over at Nic, who seems to be avoiding eye contact with me. I frown as I wonder why he's upset with me. It's the theme for the day, and I haven't even been up for an hour.

Okay, no more of these glum faces. I clap my hands together and force my lips to smile. "How about we hit up the brunch buffet right here at the Bellagio?"

Ethan raises his nose. "A buffet? Really, Claire?"

I sigh. "It's tradition to hit up at least one Vegas buffet according to all the message board posts I read prior to planning the trip," I defend.

"Sounds wonderful," Angie says, getting up from Graham and pulling on his arms to get him to rise with her. She moves over to me and gives me the biggest hug. It says everything she is feeling, without a word spoken. I know she wants to say something but is in tune enough to the current mood of the room to know it is not her place.

"Thank you," I whisper in her ear. "I needed that."

"Do we need reservations?" Graham asks politely. "If so, I can call down now."

"I don't think so," I respond. "If it's a bust, we can go elsewhere. Was just trying to keep things easy."

We all leave the room, Nic taking up the rear. I can feel his eyes on the back of me, while I link arms with Ethan and walk beside him to the elevators. He is stiff at my side. I sigh and whisper to him. "I know you are irritated with me over something or another, but please, let's just put it behind us and enjoy the day."

"Fine."

Lovely. I break my hold on him and walk into the elevator first. Everyone else shuffles in. Nic smacks the number on the board, and I swear I hear him growl every time the car stops to add on a person or two from each floor on the descent—which has been a rare occurrence on this side of the hotel. At a snail's pace we finally make it to the main floor.

As I expected, the Grand Buffet at the Bellagio is award winning. It's not your $5.99 special at Earl's Country Buffet, just five miles from Reagan National Airport. This is top notch and a place that even foodies go to indulge in the eclectic cuisine. I glance around the food serving areas, taking in the scene. It really is a masterpiece of art for the eyes.

Ethan's arm is slung around me as his gaze sweeps through the room—territorially pissing himself all over me. This is what he does in public. It is his pattern of behavior. I let him, despite every cell in my body screaming for me to run and not look back. He treats me like a trophy on a good day and an outdated car on a bad one. Most people see me as the outgoing, never lacking for a word, girl of confidence. But it is in moments like these that my throat dehydrates and my spine loses one more bone of support. I feel trapped in a relationship I have given up everything for, just to see where things may lead. Maybe it is my naive optimism that allows me to hold onto this—

Hope?

Illusion?

I think that if I stick around long enough and see this through, I might get everything I have ever wanted—a happy ending.

We get seated right away at a table for five, and instantly I grow tense finding myself situated between Nic on my left and Ethan on my right. I don't feel like a rose. I feel like a naive little girl, putting herself in the middle of two men who are so different that it is even hard to find just one similarity.

Ethan leans over and kisses my hair. "Good choice, babe, this place looks amazing."

I should smile over his compliment. I should be happy he is starting to make an effort at being content today. However, I can tell by the tic in his jaw that he is just going through the motions. Playing nicey-nice in public. He is surviving the morning, so he can skip off to a business meeting and enjoy the things he wants to do—without me.

"Glad you approve." I bite my tongue from saying more. He often tells me I am *too much*. To tone it down a couple of notches. He is right. I get myself excited and expressive and animated.

"What can I get everyone to drink?" the blonde waitress asks the group.

Graham motions for Angie to answer first.

"A cappuccino and a pineapple mimosa please," she says politely, handing over the leather-bound beverage menu.

Graham orders the same.

When I start to give my order, at the direction of the waitress, Ethan interrupts with, "black coffee," before I can even finish my answer. I dip my gaze into my lap. I need to stop being so sensitive. I need to stop comparing my relationship with Ethan to that of the power couple seated across from me. There is no touching Graham and Angie. So why even try to aim for something that is unreachable?

"Go ahead, Claire," Nic says softly, brushing his hand lightly against mine that is resting on my knee under the table.

I look up into his eyes. He looks like he is holding back from saying something. I frown. I can't hide my emotions well. When my own words get stuck in my throat from the ball of stress lodged inside, I curl my lips under my teeth to fight back the tears.

"Herbal tea, surprise me," Nic says to the waitress. "Two mimosas and…"—he looks at me and winks, instantly making me relax—"two organic waters."

My lips pop out from their restraints, and I huff out a few laughs. "Organic waters?" I ask.

"I am very health conscious," he responds, his eyes twinkling with light-heartedness.

Nic's silly humor is welcome right now. It is a lifeline that I hold on to as I navigate the muddy waters of keeping Ethan content but also not losing myself entirely over to the world he wants to live in.

Ethan's throat clears, drawing everyone's attention to him. "So, Nic, how's work at the agency going? I've been hearing there is a decrease in revenue in the past six months. But what do I know? I found my woman right here, so I'm not up to date with the inventory at this time."

At this time? What does he even mean?

From my periphery, I see Nic's shoulders tense up. He is not an Ethan fan—that much is obvious.

"It's going better than your daytime gig," he says with confidence.

"I'm racking up new clients left and right," Ethan offers.

"How do you know I'm not doing the same?"

I inwardly groan.

Not another pissing contest.

I'm tempted to ask them both to whip out their dicks and

just get it over with. I mean, I do know now what Nic's looks like in 2D. The sizing-each-other-up drama can be done at another time.

"I stopped paying attention ever since Claire stopped being the agency's community booty."

My eyes dart to Ethan who looks to be proud of himself of his clever joke. Ugh. This entire situation just sucks. I motion for Angie to get up with me. I am in a crisis and need a change of scenery.

"What is going on?" she asks, as we make our way to the food area.

I take a clean plate and start filling it with fresh fruit and some of the vegan options. It is nice that everything is clearly labeled. There is something here for everybody.

"Ethan arrived here with a chip on his shoulder. He's in a mood," I express. "I won't let him ruin our fun. Promise."

"Don't worry about me," she says softly. "I just want you to be okay. It is you who is suffering. And I think you've been trying to hide a lot from me. Probably think I'll get stressed out or something equally false. I'm here for you, Claire. I'm always on your side. Always. You deserve happiness and if it isn't with Ethan, I need you to know that it'll all be okay."

I smile sadly at her kind words. She gets me. "You're the greatest friend I've ever had."

"I feel the exact same way about you, Claire."

I wonder how my childhood would have been different if Angie had entered my life earlier. Everyone needs a friend like her in their life. She is that amazing. I know that I would not have gotten through college if I didn't have her by my side, cheering me on and teaching me lessons about life. She'll never be able to understand how much she saved me.

I glance back at our table and see that it is empty, except for the centerpiece and a variety of drinks. I need things to smooth out and go back to being easy. This undefined tension that is building with me and Ethan is going to come to a boiling point eventually and explode. I cross my fingers that it is not going to happen during this Vegas trip. We need to get back on familiar soil if we are going to hash this out.

Once my plate is full, I return to the table with Angie and we start eating. The men join us soon after, with Graham and Nic talking among themselves before sitting down.

Nic takes up his spot beside me, passing me the tea, a mimosa, and water. I knew he ordered for us, but wasn't expecting three beverages.

"Thank you," I mouth, my words getting stuck in my throat from the emotion. It feels weird to be cared for by the man who isn't my boyfriend, but it also feels weird not to be cared for by a man who *is* my boyfriend.

I slide in closer to Ethan and try to get things back on track. "Ohh, what did you get?" I ask, pointing to some type of stuffed pastry. "Can I take a bite?"

"It is a buffet, Claire. Go get yourself one to try. Food is unlimited."

I slide back into my chair and close my mouth. My appetite is dwindling, and I have barely taken many bites of my own selections. I take a big gulp of my mimosa, while praying I can survive this brunch without crying.

"I can see you have given up working on your image."

My eyes whip over to Ethan's. "What is that supposed to mean?"

"Drinking before noon," he points out, gesturing toward my orange juice and champagne.

"I'm not even near your son. And when I am, I try my best to be a good role model."

"Pretty sure that's a lost cause," Ethan says in a joking tone.

He must really think he is funny. No one at the table laughs. I am too embarrassed to even look up.

"Claire?" Angie's voice cuts through the awkward silence. "Want to help me find the restroom?"

I know what she's doing. She heard the exchange. She probably also saw my reaction.

"Hey you," she says, pulling me to the side, when we get to the sitting area outside the restroom. "What the hell is going on with you and Ethan? This is more than a chip on his shoulder. He is treating you so badly."

"Yeah, I agree. I just don't know what his problem is."

"What else aren't you telling me?"

I take a deep breath. My head falls into my hands, as I cover up my face. "Nic kissed me," I blurt out, not even thinking about the stress I could cause Angie with this revelation.

"Took him long enough."

My head jerks up. "Wasn't expecting you to say that."

Angie shrugs. "I sensed the tension between you two."

I sigh. "This trip is supposed to be about you—not all of my baggage."

"Claire, don't you realize that you being happy makes me happy?"

I give my friend a hug, mainly because I am in desperate need of comfort before I break down from my life falling apart. That's the problem with me, though. I tend to build foundations for a future on unstable ground. Maybe this whole time, what I thought I wanted out of my relationship with Ethan isn't what he wanted at all.

But I am invested. More invested in him than I ever have been with anyone else.

"But what happens if I don't know what will make me happy?" I ask, my voice quivering.

"You'll first have to figure out if being with Ethan is what you want."

"I just wish he didn't have some stick up his ass. He is angry with me, and getting him to vocalize his points without degrading me in public is the biggest challenge."

"You don't deserve how he is treating you. No one does."

"That I can agree on."

"So, tell me. How did Nic make you feel?"

"What do you mean?"

"What were your first thoughts running through your brain after the kiss ended?"

I think about the question and answer as honestly as I can. "My first thought was 'damn, he knows how to kiss.' Then when it ended, I was sad it was so short. And once reality set in, I felt a crushing guilt. Like someone placed a boulder on my chest."

"Why guilt?"

"I'm with Ethan. I choose Ethan. I stayed back in Portland for Ethan."

Angie nods. "I knew something was up. Do you think Ethan knows? Do you plan on telling him?"

"I made a minor misjudgment and have to deal with my own conscience. It doesn't benefit Ethan to have that in his head. I mean, Nic kissed *me*. But I doubt Ethan will care who did what if he ever found out."

"I wish he would get his head out of his ass long enough to realize he is hurting you right now. What's his deal?"

I frown. "I really don't know. I think some alone time may be in order so we can reacquaint ourselves with each other."

Angie's face changes, and I know she doesn't buy it but is polite enough not to say anything in disagreement. I am sure she feels in a tough place between saying too much and not saying enough. Truth of the matter is, I need to handle this on my own.

When we return to the table, the men seem to be harboring some tension and animosity toward one another. No one wants to break the silence by initiating conversation, and the stress of not knowing how to act in this setting is wearing on me. Do I make small talk or just stay quiet? I choose the latter and focus on trying to eat enough food to keep myself from getting sick off the mimosa.

Ethan pats my leg and gives it a little squeeze underneath the table. He leans his face closer to mine and whispers, "You letting yourself go?"

I turn my attention to him and look at him with confusion. "Letting what go?" Because right now, the only thing I feel like I'm letting go is my ability to say what I really feel. What happened to Unfiltered Claire? I fear I am losing all sense of the woman I once was. There was me before Ethan, and now me with Ethan. I thought he would make me a better woman. I thought that being with someone sophisticated would help me to be more refined. Polished. He's a father. He's an established businessman.

He's an egotistical asshole.

Ethan shrugs and points to the food on my plate with his empty fork. "Seems a bit excessive, don't you think? You trying to make yourself get fat?"

His words are loud enough for the entire table to hear, but they are too nice to act like they heard the exchange. Tears well in my eyes. I'm no longer hungry. I toss my fork onto the plate and slide my chair out. I make my way back to the restroom area and this time actually go inside.

As much as I struggle with how I see myself, I know for certain that the core of who I am is good. I look at myself in the mirror. Damn Ethan for thinking that what is on the outside trumps who I am on the inside. Why is he trying to hurt me and make me doubt myself?

I use the toilet, wash my hands, and take a few deep breaths before exiting. I turn the corner and feel a gentle touch on my elbow. Pivoting, I stare into the sad blue eyes of Nic. They catch me off guard.

"Hey," I say, looking down at my shoes as I rock on them.

His fingers tilt my chin up so I can look at him. "You are freaking beautiful. Don't let anyone make you feel otherwise. That bastard is playing a dangerous game and is about to swallow his teeth if he thinks he can get away with mistreating you in front of me. He is insecure of just how attractive you are to others."

"What? That doesn't even make sense. If he thinks I am

attractive to others, then he would be treating me like gold to keep me."

Nic shakes his head, acting like he is in on some secret. Whatever he thinks he knows, he doesn't. He is just cocky enough to act like he does.

"There's only so far you can push me before I crack. I can't keep doing this, Claire."

He is using the same statement I used on him just a couple of days ago. "Doing what?"

"Pretending."

I pull back from his touch. "You are confusing me, Nic. What are you talking about?"

"Pretending that I don't want to spread you out and slide my entire tongue into your sweet pussy. Pretending I don't want to rip your clothes off and sink into you so deeply that the only man on your mind is me. Pretending that I don't go to sleep every night fantasizing about the sounds you will make when I have you writhing around underneath me in ecstasy."

I shake my head. "You are delusional. You might be pretending, Nic. But I am certain that I choose Ethan."

"Why is that, Claire? Huh? What does he have to offer?"

"A future," I say flatly. I don't want to be having this conversation right now. I turn to walk away. Nic is not helping matters. If anything, he is just adding to my confusion and Ethan's temper.

"You keep romanticizing someone who is hurting you," Nic calls out. "And when you finally come to terms that you made a bad choice by staying with him, I just hope you are recognizable and not some shattered version of yourself."

My feet glue themselves to the floor as his words shudder through me. What is his problem? I spin around so fast and raise my hands to push at his chest, pressing them against his body. "You act like you are some relationship expert," I huff out. "When you really know nothing. Stay out of it."

His eyes flare and twitch. Maybe I said too much. Maybe I am too harsh. But I am tired of fighting and always coming out the loser. I turn around and stomp back to the table. The meal is over. I can't eat anything without feeling like I could throw up.

"I'm going to go back to the suite," I say roughly, causing everyone to rise up from their seats. I am so on edge. Being around both Nic and Ethan is causing a turmoil inside me that I have no way of settling easily.

"I'll go back with you," Angie openly volunteers. "I could use the company."

I smile through my tears at my best friend who is so pure at heart. As soon as we are away from the men, I break down and cry. "I'm sorry," I sniffle. "This trip was supposed to be fun and carefree. And somehow I managed to ruin it all."

"Claire, you can't be responsible for how other people act. You can only control your own reaction. Let's do something fun and relaxing. What do you say?"

"I say that sounds perfect."

21

NIC

"I'm going to punch Ethan's face in if he thinks he can interrupt this trip just to prove to everyone how big of an asshole he is," I grumble to Graham. He best be glad I restrained myself in front of the girls. I'm itching for a fight. The douchebag deserves one too.

Graham and I are having a drink at the hotel bar and left the girls in the suite for a pampering session. Graham arranged for them to have an in-room spa session, while watching chick flicks and snacking on whatever it is that girls snack on. Claire barely ate anything at brunch, and who could blame her for the way her asshole boyfriend kept passive-aggressively putting her down. For someone who should be thrilled to see her after days apart, he sure didn't act like it.

What a limp dick.

Maxwell wasn't too fond of the idea of Claire not coming back to his room midday, but this trip isn't about him and his sensitivity. This trip isn't even about me, which is the reason why his face isn't bashed in. However, he can only push me so far before I snap. Sharing a table with him at brunch and not hitting him should award me a trophy. But now I am all out of patience.

Seeing Claire with tears about to overflow from her eyes and the bastard who kept causing her unnecessary pain was enough to make my temper flare. Who does he think he is? He's no Casanova. That much, I am certain.

But that is how abusers are. And Ethan is one hundred percent that. He will degrade his woman so badly that she feels indebted to him. Slowly and methodically, he'll break her down until the person she once was doesn't exist anymore. It is brainwashing at its finest, and another reason why women don't leave relationships. They don't believe there is anything better for them.

Problem is, he is pulling his shit in front of witnesses— ones who have no problem getting their knuckles bloody.

Graham shakes his glass, rattling the ice cubes against the sides. "Just relax. Things have a way of working themselves out. I need to ask, though. Why do you care?"

I shrug. "Claire is technically my employee still, and it is hard to not have sympathy for her when she is attaching herself to someone like him. What does she see in that man? She can do so much better."

"She is stubborn like Angie, you know. The more you push them to see the light, the more they will attach themselves to danger. It's a curse." He gestures to me with his glass. "Trust me on this."

My brother is right. I need to care less and quit interfering. Problem is—and I will never admit this to him—I am infatuated with his fiancée's best friend. Taking her will be the easy part. Making her not hate me afterwards will be the hard part.

I keep telling myself I'd be doing her a favor—to get her away from the bastard. But I have to play the game well, so we both know the score.

"Up for some Hold'em? I need to clear my mind and refocus it on something productive."

Graham's eyes perk up. We are very competitive; always have been. It goes back to our wrestling days when we thrived on competition and got a thrill over defeating an opponent. "Limit or no limit?"

"No limit."

"Sounds good. Let me text Angie first to let her know where I'll be if she needs me."

We make our way to the casino and get granted private access to the no-limit rooms, which have their own private bank teller and waitstaff. It is an exclusive area meant for the high rollers who usually spend so much that their future rooms get comped just as a perk to hopefully return to the tables. It's not like the casino is suffering. They get a decent rake from every game played.

As expected, there's a wait for a new table to form with a dealer. The minimum number of players must be present in order for a game to officially start. I enjoy a drink and lounge with Graham in the cushioned chairs, which are an upgrade from those out on the main floor. If we'd thought further ahead, we may have been able to join the waitlist for a tournament and buy in at the designated amount. However, for an impromptu game like the one we are about to start, we have no room to be picky.

"Can I join the table?"

I don't even need to look to know that the man's voice belongs to Ethan Maxwell. I inwardly groan, refusing to even acknowledge him. He may not be the most intuitive guy, but surely I made myself clear after brunch when I told him not to fuck this trip up for Angie and Graham. The bastard had the nerve to look shocked at my statement.

I sip my drink and avoid eye contact with him, while I think about the pros of him being at our table. Maybe handing him his ass will provide me with an ounce of satisfaction. Am I being immature? Sure. Is it warranted? I'd like to believe so.

I turn around and lift my chin once to Ethan. "Join."

"Hope you brought your bank accounts," he answers snidely.

"Hope yours is as big as your ego," I mutter, mainly to myself, but if he hears it'll be a bonus.

Within minutes, the table is complete and the dealer is handing out chips based on the buy-ins. Most people stick to around $10,000. With eight players, most of whom I have never played with before, I slow play my first hand of a jack-ten off suit. When the flop doesn't help, I have no solid choice but to fold at the first line of bets. It isn't until the fourth hand that I hit my flush on the turn and send two other players into going all in pre-river. I have the ace of clubs which should be enough to lock in my win.

The dealer burns a card and then flips the last one up onto the table. As predicted, I win a huge pot—probably the biggest thus far.

"Good hand," Graham says, nodding in my direction.

I was able to secure the second highest chip lead, knock out the first player, and cripple a second. Feeling confident,

I bluff on the next hand, taking the lead. Knowing that Ethan will be gunning for me, I play conservatively for the next few rounds, letting Graham take the lead. He bullies out the two underdogs.

When the dealer announces that it is time for a break, I use the restroom and order another drink. When I return to the table, Graham is making small talk with the dealer, who has been in this line of work for the past thirty years.

It is the sound of Claire's voice behind me that makes me whip around to verify her existence. The person guarding the door allows her entry and she walks over to Ethan, rubbing his shoulders. He shrugs out of her touch, turning to glare at her.

"Quit distracting me."

"I'm sorry." Her words come out so soft that if it wasn't for being able to read her lips, I wouldn't even know that she spoke.

"What are you doing here?" he asks suddenly. "This is a guys' game."

It is true that there are only guys playing right now. But there is no rule about gender. In fact, I have seen Claire play before and she has way better skill than the asshole who is disrespecting her.

She whispers something to Ethan, who dismisses her with a wave of his hand. How cold can he be? And why is she hanging around for this level of abuse? She is fucking gorgeous and shouldn't be this desperate.

I want to growl. He is causing a scene and it is embarrassing that she is being put down in front of everyone—for the second time today. I glance over to Graham, who gets up from his seat and makes his way over to Claire. I watch the interchange and the frown form on her lips. Her hand goes up to say stop, while Graham pulls out some bills from his wallet.

When he returns to the table, I turn to him and ask, "What was that about?"

"Poor girl wanted to order some room service and her debit card bounced. Is he giving her a fucking allowance?"

"Yeah," I snarl.

"She was probably too embarrassed to ask Angie to pay, which is crazy. Angie has full access to our joint account and would have no issue picking up the tab."

I nod. This chauvinistic display of power from Ethan is becoming a problem. Unfortunately, I'm not the white knight who can execute a rescue. I'm not the good guy in all of this.

With anger coursing through my veins, I muscle through the men at the table, barely making a mistake to take me off the path to victory. After the casino's cut for their facilitation services, I win a little over $72,000—before taxes.

Graham smacks hands with me. "I let you win."

"Right," I snicker.

"I'm going to head up to the room," he says. "I promised Angie I would take her up on the Eiffel Tower once it got dark enough."

I nod and head over to the money exchange area. There are several papers I need to sign to verify that taxes will be removed from my earnings. It's the downside of playing in a public place, like the Bellagio. When I go to turn around and make my way out of the high stakes room, Ethan is waiting for me.

"I would like the opportunity to win my money back," he says bluntly.

"I bet you would."

"I'm serious."

I stop midstep. "How would you like to try?"

He thinks about it for a second, rubbing a hand over the back of his neck. "Want to come to my room and we can play a private game of Hold'em?"

"Why not just do that here?" I ask, skeptical at what he's getting at. What is he wanting from me that he cannot get from a public table game? I don't trust him. Not even sure if I would trust the deck in play.

"Stakes aren't high enough here. I didn't play my best at a table for eight. Let me have another chance to prove myself."

"Okay…"

"We can buy a deck of cards right here in the gift shop if that makes you feel better."

I nod. "It would."

"Let me just make sure Claire is occupied. Might have to throw some cash at her to make her stay busy. That girl salivates over money and will probably be spending it all at the mall."

I resist calling him a sexist. I resist punching in his face. I will call this progress. He is acting like we are part of some Boys' Club that may have existed decades ago, during a time when women were barely scratching at the surface of equality. Times have changed. He doesn't even have an excuse to act the way he does.

Claire is a freaking goddess, and Ethan is just a toad.

"Figure it out," I direct, "and I'll meet you in your room with a fresh deck."

He nods and makes his way out of the casino. It doesn't take but five minutes to grab some things at the gift shop. I even got a few items delivered directly to my suite. Spending more time with Ethan does not sound like a good use of my time here in Vegas, but I have to see this through so I can discover what his version of "high stakes" entails. I'd be lying if I said I wasn't intrigued. Surely I can turn the tables and make this beneficial for myself and not have it turn into a complete waste of time.

When I get up to his room, it is a downgrade from the suite I booked—despite still being nice. It is a larger room than the typical one bedroom ones and actually has a table area with chairs.

"When are you going to inform me about what you really want?" I ask directly. No point being secretive, now that we have some privacy.

Ethan huffs out an exhale and takes a seat across from me at the table. I shuffle the cards as his eyes bore into mine.

"You have a habit of getting exclusive luxury cars before they even hit the general market. How is that so?"

I shrug. He's right. I do manage to get ahead on the waitlist before cars are even imported. It helps when I know people and have a growing list of those who owe me favors.

"Anyway," he continues, "I have my eyes on the next model of Porsche coming out that is going to be very diffi-cult to get based on the amount of cars being made and the demand for owning luxury. However, I would love to own your current model."

My eyes narrow on his. "So if you win, you want me to give you my car?" Why he would want something used is mind-boggling to me. "Why not just wait until you can score a newer version for yourself?"

"Because taking something that is yours would make me feel accomplished."

"Your confidence is that low?" I ask, a smirk marring my expressionless face.

"You already took my money down at the tables. Publicly, I might add. Now I want something in return that is worth more to me than just money."

"And if you lose?" I counter.

"I'm sure you'll make your demands worthwhile," he grins.

I think about my winning prize. I don't need money. I don't need material goods. What I desire doesn't have a price. I rub my hands together and then lean back into my chair.

"I want to watch."

His confusion is evident on his face. "Watch what?"

"Watch you fuck Claire."

22

CLAIRE

I should be happy to have eight hundred dollars in cash to spend on myself. I haven't had this kind of money up front since the last time my parents sent me some in the mail for school supplies and general expenses. Those days are over. This behavior from Ethan is new though. He also was the most affectionate toward me since he arrived here late last night. Yet, here I stand in the middle of the Forum Shops at Caesars with actual money to spend, feeling alone and neglected.

Maybe it's guilt. The nagging thought in the back of my head is telling me to pocket the money and put it toward my own debt. As amazing as new spring sandals would feel right now, I need to be responsible toward my future. I walk around and shop with my eyes, taking in the fashions. Portland is a fun city, but some of these styles would make anyone stand out—and not for good reasons. I am naturally bold, but some of these are too wild, even for me.

I enjoy an organic strawberry smoothie near the

aquarium attraction and check my texts for messages. Angie and Graham asked me to join them at the Paris Hotel, but I didn't want to interrupt their special date night. Asking Nic to join me—while Ethan does whatever it is he is doing—now seems inappropriate. Why would my boyfriend not want to spend time with me?

When my feet hurt and my willpower is dwindling, I decide the best way to save money is to remove the temptation. I walk toward the exit and make my way into the cooling evening air. I check my phone again and see that it is almost ten o'clock. The lights on the strip are spectacular at night. It still stops me in my tracks no matter how many evenings I have enjoyed them.

At a slow pace, I get back to the Bellagio in twenty minutes, feeling a little sweaty and ready for a shower. The spa day with Angie was so relaxing that I do not want to negate the benefits of the massage and facial by letting my pores get dirty.

Earlier today, Ethan sent a worker up to my room to pack and deliver my belongings into his room. That's what it feels like too. *His* room. At least he wants to stay together. Based on the way he has treated me thus far, I wasn't exactly sure he would.

I knock on the door and then quickly remember that I have my own key. I put in the card, wait for the green lights, and then pull open the door.

Ethan and Nic are chatting at the table, poker chips scattered about the surface.

"What's going on?" I ask.

"Come here, babe," Ethan directs, opening his arms for me to move into them.

I look into his eyes for a hint as to why his mood has drastically changed. "Did you win?" I ask directly.

"In a way, yes?" he chuckles, glancing at Nic—who seems to lack any real emotion.

Nic's eyes follow my every move. It unnerves me. I bring Ethan's drink up to my lips and some dribbles out of my mouth to my chin. I quickly grab the dampened cocktail napkin that is wrapped around the base of the glass and wipe at the mess on my face. I glance over to Nic again. He is still watching me. Staring. He looks at me with such laser precision—as if I am the most interesting girl on the planet. He is getting under my skin and he knows it. Likes it, even. Damn him.

"I'd like to shower," I say softly, rocking on my feet.

Ethan nods, placing a hand over my ass. "Go shower then." He cranes his neck to reach my ear. "Put on something sexy when you get dressed. I saw some things in your luggage."

I want to snap at him for going through my things. I want to shake out of the possessive hold he has on me in front of Nic. However, this new passion of his is a welcome change from his previous behavior since he arrived. I scurry off and dig through my luggage, tucking what I need under my arm to be out of sight. I make my way into the bathroom, locking the door and double checking that it is in fact secured.

I decide on a long shower to give the men time to finish up whatever it is they are doing. I also want to look good for Ethan. We haven't had sex in some time and tonight may be exactly what we need to get things back on track. I'm not suggesting that sex fixes issues in relationships, but it sure helps with the morale. Right now, we can use any boost we can get.

I shave again, despite doing it recently. I wash my body in my favorite vanilla scrub. Typically, I would not blow out my hair this late at night, but tonight is special. I am hopeful. Plus, I want Ethan to remember all the things he likes about me. My long hair is one of those things.

I dust on a little makeup and curl my eyelashes. Two light coats of mascara make them pop. My outfit is completely black see-through lace, with straps and ties all over my ass and breast areas. I got it at a boutique shop online and love the originality of having an outfit that I was able to custom order and design myself. It wasn't cheap. I would like to think it will be worth it.

I open the door a crack and listen for talking. Nothing.

"Ethan?"

"Yeah, babe? You all ready?"

"I think so." I walk out into the bedroom and find Ethan sitting shirtless on the bed. He just has on a pair of gray boxer briefs. His eyes follow me, and I smile at his satisfied expression.

"You look sexy."

He motions for me to come closer. I listen. "You do too. I missed you."

"Been thinking how good it will feel to have your lips wrapped around me."

I'm not a huge fan of oral sex—mainly because it is rarely reciprocated. It is foreplay for the guy and if he ejaculates too soon, it is all over. If he is too much on edge, then he wants sex to finish it off. So, I am usually left disappointed. But tonight, I will do what Ethan desires. Anything is better than the rut we have been living in. I'd rather dig myself out of it than sink in deeper.

I bend at the waist, place my hands on his thighs, and gracefully make my way to my knees. I can see the satisfaction in his eyes over my ample cleavage and the way my boobs are on display—only for him. He lifts up from the bed, only to discard his boxers, baring himself to me.

I take a few practice breaths through my nose and adjust my weight so I am more comfortable. Ethan pumps his dick a couple times with his palm, staring down at me with anticipation. He grips the back of my head with his free hand and pushes me onto him with one fluid motion. I gasp for air as he slips down my throat, not really giving me much warning or time to prepare. He is needy and wanton.

I grab the sheets of the bed, to anchor myself from falling over, twisting them between my fingers.

When I don't think he is going to let me up to catch my breath, tears fill my eyes. I push at his thighs, releasing him from my mouth.

"Sorry, babe. Been too long," he says.

Not even a real apology. Not even a look of shock.

I wipe the spit from my mouth and watch as he glances to the corner of the room, behind me. I snap my body around, looking to where his attention is now drawn. I blink hard and stumble back on my feet as I take in the sight.

Nic is sitting in the armchair, one hand on his clothed crotch, the other on a glass of whiskey. I can smell it from where I am kneeling.

"What are you doing here?" I ask him. I turn back to Ethan, covering my hands over the front of me to shield both of their gazes from my indecency. I sit my barely covered ass farther onto my feet to conceal as much as I can. "What the fuck is he doing here, Ethan?" I glare at him while he hesitates. "Answer me!"

Nic clears his throat from his side of the room. "Tell her, Ethan."

"Tell me, Ethan!"

I am about to stand up and lock myself inside the bathroom, when he finally speaks. "We were playing some poker, and I lost. Barely lost. One of the things that was requested was that Nic watch us have sex."

"Watch. Us? What the fuck, Ethan! You agreed to that?"

"I wasn't planning to lose again to him," Ethan snaps at me, as if this is somehow my fault. "It's not like you're some type of angelic virgin, so quit being such a fucking prude. Plus, we were going to have sex anyway. This doesn't really change anything."

I glance back at Nic and glare. "Come up with something else, a counter bet. How I became some part of the negotiations seems very unethical when I don't even have a fucking say!"

"No."

"No? I don't have to do anything!"

Nic swirls his drink, the clinking of the ice making my anxiety flare. "Then either pay me cash or wire the money over. Your choice, Maxwell."

I turn to Ethan. "How much if I don't follow through?"

"Give us a minute," Ethan says to Nic.

I watch as Nic lifts himself up from the chair and walks to the main door. Once he is out of the room, I get up from the floor, wrap a robe around my body, and sit down on the end of the bed.

"I can't believe you did this," I mumble. "You have some nerve to involve me in your little business transactions without my consent. What is wrong with you?"

"Oh, you act all prim and proper when it suits you. Don't fucking tell me you have been modest your whole life. It is simply having sex with your boyfriend. Quit making this into more than what it is."

"How much will you have to pay?"

"Quarter of a million."

"Are you drunk?" I snap. "Lost your ever-loving mind?"

"Neither. For one, I wasn't expecting to lose. Second, I thought you would be fine with this. He just wants to watch. Not join in. Not take pictures or video. Just watch. Also, he's not a stranger."

"That makes it worse!" I yell.

"Whatever. You always make things bigger deals than they need to be. I'm really not in the mood for your drama."

He is so casual about all of this that I want to scream. I want to hit him. I put my head in my hands and just focus on breathing. Steady breaths. In. Out. When I marginally calm down, I look over at him and ask, "Why? Why does he want to watch?"

He shrugs. "Probably gets off on the whole voyeurism thing."

Ew. Ew. Ew!

I cannot believe I am in the middle of all of this mess. This trip has drastically taken a turn for the worse since Ethan has arrived. Nothing will ever be the same again.

"I don't know if I can do it," I admit. "You know"—I pause—"perform."

"Just lie there. I got so fucking hard after the amazing blow job you gave me, I won't last long in your snatch."

His words should turn me on. But they make me dry up. I want to close in on myself. It is like I want to build a shell around me to protect my body and heart from any more pain. I should run. I should get up and just walk right out and let him deal with the aftermath of breaking a bet with Nic Hoffman. This was not my plan I set into motion. I am simply part of a predicament I never asked to be in. But instead, I find my head nodding. Agreeing.

He hops up from the bed and kisses my forehead. "You're the best, babe."

I don't feel the best. I feel used. Like my body was auctioned off for the viewing pleasure of someone else. I feel disgusted and disrespected.

"Let's get this over with."

23

NIC

I don't go through life thinking I'm not an asshole. I know I'm one.

But if anything puts a spotlight on the cracks in Claire and Ethan's crumbling relationship, it will be this one moment in time.

I watch from my chair as Claire gets herself situated on the bed. Ethan strips down to nothing, and I try to zone him out from my view. I only focus on the sexual goddess who has my heart wrapped up in knots. Her hair is splayed out over the white pillow, her lacy top still highlighting and accentuating the swell of her breasts. She is perfection.

But even though my conscience knows why I'm doing this, I still struggle with the impact it will have on her life.

Ethan doesn't deserve her. And he probably never did.

I know the fucker has been emotionally abusing her for months. He probably didn't start out that way, using his charm to elevate her to feeling like they had some future together. But I know better.

People confuse my laid-back attitude for someone who doesn't care. But I fucking care.

I care about getting Claire away from someone who nitpicks what she eats, puts her down in public settings, and crushes whatever hope she has that men aren't all assholes.

But I'm not so stupid that I don't see the irony. Sure, I want her. I've been wanting her ever since I saw her untamed excitement over dressing up in costumes for holidays and random occasions. I've been wanting her ever since she came prancing into the cafe with her multicolored pens and her top ten lists. I've been wanting her from afar up until this trip.

But then Ethan showed up. And everything changed.

Is changing…

Will change forever.

Ethan kneels his weight on the bed, taking his place between her thighs. I expect him to warm her up, get her ready. But the selfish bastard just rips the crotch of her lingerie apart so he has access to her pussy. I bet he thinks his power move is sexy to women, and it may be if he followed it up with something beneficial.

When I finally take her, she will know what it means to be devoured. I rub my cock through the fabric of my pants as I think about how good her pussy will taste on my tongue. I *will* have her. This little intermission is all part of my greater plan.

When I first made the bet, I half expected Ethan to counter. However, without any hesitation, he agreed to the terms—not even asking Claire for her consent. This is the type of man he is.

Am I any better? I like to think so. I sure as hell would

have given her pleasure first before stuffing my dick down her throat. Even if she can take it, why deliberately make her suffer just for the sake of building up your own ego? I wanted to rip her away from him when I saw the tears form in her eyes. She can do so much better. I can only hope that this whole bet will help her see that.

I'm still shocked she agreed to this. What hold does this man have on her that she is willing to go against that voice in her head that must be screaming at her to stop?

That's the bigger problem. Claire has her mind so brainwashed that the only way to heal from the damage it has already endured is to put it through the detox cycle. Maybe this bet will help it along. Be the kill switch that will finally help Claire see the kind of man she is trying to attach herself to…

Ethan looks back at me and grins, completely ruining my fantasy of witnessing Claire. I let all emotion drain from my expression. I don't expect this to last long with the stamina that Ethan seems to lack, so I fix my eyes on Claire —who refuses to keep her own open.

"Open your eyes," Ethan demands. "I want to see you while I thrust inside you."

I cringe as I listen to his words, knowing that my presence here is probably fueling the need to look macho— anything to build up his ego while pushing hers down.

Ethan pushes forward, ignoring Claire's cringe as she struggles to accommodate him. I can't tell if it is from his size or the fact that she is probably dry from not having any touch meant for her. What a lazy lover her asshole boyfriend is. He pulls out, spits all over his hand, and rubs himself with the lubrication.

What a prick.

"I can't," Claire says, pushing at his shoulders.

"I'll be quick," Ethan promises. "C'mon babe. You already agreed."

"I just..." Her eyes are round and pleading. "I don't know if I can."

"Just try. Ignore him. It's just us here."

"Okay," she answers hesitantly, and then bites the inside of her cheek, hollowing it out. She stares at Ethan with a dullness to her eyes as he gets back to business. It is almost like she is seeing him for the first time. Or seeing through him. I can't tell which.

That's the plan, right? To get her to remove the fog from her eyes and see that man for what he is?

But I should have done it another way. Because seeing her this uncomfortable is killing me. And the clawing feeling scraping against my throat is now making it clear that this is a horrible idea.

I did this.

He pumps a few times inside her, looks to be in pain, and then grinds out, "Cum with me, babe," through his teeth. He doesn't even wait for her to get close. Instead, he groans, earning a look of disgust from Claire, whose spine is poker straight as she stares blankly up at a spot on the ceiling from the mattress.

"It hurts, Ethan."

"Get off her," I say, standing up to physically remove his body from on top of her.

But Claire does it first. She shoves at him so hard, he slides out and rolls to his side. She pulls her knees up to her chest and lashes out.

"Claire, are you—"

"I'm done here. You both go to hell." Her eyes are menacing and the tears pouring out will never cleanse her of the nastiness that is Ethan Maxwell.

"I love coming together," Ethan says breathlessly. He is so clueless. I watch as he wipes his limp dick onto the sheets of the bed, cleaning himself on the fabric. A tinge of pink is present and my throat closes up thinking that he caused Claire physical pain.

I don't wait to be physically kicked out. Instead, I place my empty glass on the table and walk out of their room, slamming the door. When I get to the hall, I run a hand down my face and lean my back against the hallway wall.

"Fuck," I say under my breath. "What did I just do?"

I can't go back to the suite without running into Graham or Angie and risking them knowing something is up with me. My brother has a way of reading me and right now, I know I cannot hide my expression until I decompress from what I just witnessed.

If I learned anything, it is that Claire one hundred percent doesn't belong with Ethan Maxwell. Problem is, I don't think she belongs with me either from what I just set into motion. Granted, I only want temporary—a way to fuck her out of my system—just to clear my brain of her.

I stay leaning against the wall as I try to make sense of what just happened.

Did I witness something that is a normal act between them? Or was Ethan simply showing off—in his weird and demented power move?

I head down to the bar. I don't expect alcohol to fix my mood, but at least it will help numb my mind. I call Tyler while I wait for the bartender to fix my drink. After background checking all of Asher's list of contacts he sent me, Tyler is by far the most qualified to be my information gatherer. He is discreet, thorough, and persistent. Plus, Asher has interacted with him personally on some work and that level of recommendation is invaluable.

"Any more information?" I ask him.

"Yeah, I'll email it to you. You have to see this," he goads.

"Better be worthwhile." We have only chatted a few times and instantly I can tell that his pride motivates him to excel. I don't mind his confidence, if he can follow through like he has been.

"Oh, it is. That's why you owe me a bonus." He is one of those guys who can get away with a relaxed attitude on the job, because he is that good and isn't doing this at all for the money.

I can sense the smile in his voice. "A proactive one?"

"That's the best kind."

I roll my eyes and take the first sip of my bourbon, ending the call. The smoothness coats my throat as it slides down. The subtle hints of vanilla make me think of one woman and one woman only.

I sit in silence, thinking about how Claire got herself involved with a man like Maxwell. I guess I started this whole thing in motion by accepting the applications for him and Claire for the agency. At the time, I had no idea that she was connected with someone Graham would later fall in love with. She was a member of Entice months before Angie walked into my office, looking innocent and pure. I guess opposites attract, because Graham sure isn't either of those things.

I check my email and open the links that Tyler sent. As promised, he delivered. I scan through the list of residences that Ethan owns. The apartment that he and Claire share is the least luxurious—a downgrade from his other two properties. Shit. I knew he was hiding money from her and was keeping control over her by offering her a meager allowance, but this is pretty messed up. Tyler has been keeping tabs loosely on his whereabouts and confirms Ethan spends much of his time at a residence that probably is unknown to Claire.

Is he living a double life? Back with his ex-wife? Or just waiting for someone better than his current girlfriend to come along?

I take another sip and play with the little cocktail napkin, spinning my gold ring on my finger. The more I learn about Ethan Maxwell, the more I realize that he is a top-notch abuser. He may have fooled Graham and me in the beginning, but I am done putting on blinders where he is concerned. He probably saw something in Claire that gave him the impression that he could control her, thus making it easy for him to get away with his abusive nature. He probably gets off on making her feel vulnerable.

Sometimes it is the women who appear the strongest who are hurting the most inside. To the world, they can accomplish anything with their confidence and fire. However, deep inside, they are suffering from the shitty hand of cards they were dealt.

I didn't rescue Claire from her abusive boyfriend back

in their hotel room. No, I just set her up to be abused by him more.

Fuck.

And by simply creating a setting for her to see what the asshole is capable of doing, I ultimately helped facilitate her pain. Sure, maybe now she will finally leave him—with a clean break—but was it worth it?

Women like Claire need a reason to justify leaving. There. There's her reason. Surely him accepting a bet with me where she is involved will be enough for her to finally see the light.

But I'm no saint either. I stopped being a hero when Tara fucked with my sense of security. Unfortunately, all the women after her suffer the consequences of her betrayal.

When you grow up with a mother who is the epitome of perfect and a baby sister who can do no wrong, it is easy to disillusion yourself into believing that all women are created equal. It is easy to think only men cheat. That only men use their sexual prowess to get what they want. But then came Tara. And she shattered the lenses in the rose-colored glasses I chose to wear our entire relationship.

I want Claire to be Tara. I want her to stray away from one bastard, just to join the bed of another. I want no strings. I want no commitment. I want one hundred percent pleasure.

I am not so fucked up that I don't realize how fucked up my selection process is of choosing women to entertain my bed. I simply have no clue on how to stop the comfort cycle that life's circumstances have put me in.

Maybe I wasn't dealt a bad hand in this life…

Maybe I just played the cards I did have all wrong.

I look across the bar and see the sad eyes of the woman I just left. It is her resilience and fiery personality that draws me to her, and yet, the only person I see right now is someone who looks defeated.

I try to turn away from her pain before she catches sight of me, but I can't. Everything inside me wants to absolve myself from any responsibility—pinning her hollowed expression on the bastard she is dating. And yet, I know that I had my part in making her be this broken.

Finding her name in my text app, I type out a message.

Nic: I never thought he would accept the bet. You can hate me. I won't blame you.

Claire doesn't even have the sense to look up from the bar, yet from the little dots dancing across my screen, I know she is about to respond.

Claire: I do hate you. But I still consented. So this is on me. And I have to live with that knowledge.

Her words cause my heart to ache, despite me egging them on. To say I feel remorse is an understatement. I have to live with the knowledge that I put her in this predicament. And the weight of that is nearly excruciating.

The only thing keeping me afloat is knowing that getting Claire away from Ethan will be the best thing for her.

Nic: This wasn't your fault, Claire.

Claire: Yes it was.

Nic: Even now. Even after all of this... You are still protecting that bastard?

Claire: I drove Ethan to even wanting to accept the stupid bet, because ever since he arrived, he probably felt threatened by you. Him seeing a picture of us while here didn't help. He probably thinks I'm cheating on him based on how you keep interfering. This was probably his way of making sure you knew that we were together. He probably thought accepting your terms would strengthen our relationship by getting you to leave us alone.

Is she for real right now? How in the world does she manage to take responsibility for everyone else's poor decisions? My hand tightens on my glass, and I worry that I might shatter it in my hands. An anger circulates through me as I once again bear witness to the hold that emotional abuse has on its victims.

But Claire did get something right. Regardless of how we got to this moment in time, there is no part of me that doesn't want her. She has been haunting my thoughts for weeks, and no matter how hard I try to find an alternate obsession, I can't shake her from my system. There is no escaping Claire. Not until I can have her—just once.

Nic: Claire, you can't see what is so obviously apparent.

Claire: But you can?

Nic: Absolutely.

Claire: Want a prize?

Nic: No. I just want you.

Claire: Well, lucky for me, that will never happen.

Nic: I hate me too.

My admittance stops the conversation, but from the way her fingers rotate her phone over and over again in her hand, I know I have agitated her. Let my self-hatred for bringing her pain be my apology. Because I am sorry.

I am sorry for how I was unable to come up with a better alternative on getting her to see the light. I am sorry for wanting what I can't have—what I *shouldn't* have—and knowing that I won't stop until I do. I am sorry for being weak from the power she has over me.

Maybe if I get Claire in my bed, I can move on and stop acting like a deranged madman. And maybe if I showed her how good it can be with someone who would worship her— in every way—then she would be able to break the cycle of choosing the wrong men. The ones who would only use her for their own pleasure, completely ignoring what would satisfy her in return.

It is twisted to want her just because I know she will stray. It is my main qualification on how I choose bed buddies. It is messed up that I can justify her leaving Maxwell, because he continues to prove to be an evil man. It is even more demented that I get turned on by the thought of having my slice of cake, but not being coerced into buying the entire bakery.

My toxic desire for her is causing every nerve ending in my body to inflame with the possibility of proving to her that her body was made to be explored—with her pleasure in mind.

Call me jaded. Call me a prick. Neither are false.

My eyes narrow in on Claire as she plays with her cocktail napkin. She is on the opposite end of the bar that is shaped like a square. However, I have a clear view of her.

My phone buzzes with a text notification. I open the app and see Claire's name highlighted at the top of the list.

She finally noticed my presence.

Claire: This isn't a dog and pony show. Quit staring at me.

Nic: Last time I checked, it's a free country.

Claire: Last time I checked, you're still an asshole.

My hand moves from my tumbler to my face. I wipe at my facial hair that has grown from a missed shave. My phone buzzes again.

Claire: Quit laughing at me.

Nic: Quit being so damn cute over there.

Claire: ?

Nic: You know the effect you have over me. So you flaunt it.

I must have struck a nerve because she flips her phone over, turns in her seat to look in the opposite direction of me, and misses her mouth a little when she sucks out the last of her beverage over the rim of her glass.

I motion for the bartender, handing over a few hundred dollar bills.

"What can I do for you, sir?"

"See the woman behind you with the red sleeveless dress? She needs a pitcher of margaritas. And if you can contact room service and get them to deliver her mini pancakes right here, that would be great."

"Consider it done."

I sip on my second bourbon and enjoy the solitude of my own thoughts. Saying that Claire is a distraction is an understatement. She is consuming every aspect of my current moment in life. Surely, this will all come to an end soon. I just need to get the itch scratched and then get bored.

The pitcher of margaritas arrives in front of Claire first. She traces a finger down the handle, turning it to look at the dew. A fresh glass arrives and she nods to the bartender, who offers to pour her one. I watch as they converse and growl as the bartender causes her to blush. Oh, hell no.

I saunter over to the free stool beside her and fill it up. Claire is licking the salt from the glass's rim, seeming to enjoy the contrast from the sweetness of the liquid.

She turns to glare at me, but it doesn't last long—as a smirk mars her stern expression.

"You are welcome to enjoy a drink from the pitcher I

ordered for myself," I say, nodding toward the tall glass container.

"This is yours?"

"Yup."

"Oh."

"Don't worry, I share." I am referencing the pitcher of margaritas but the implication is there.

"I hate sharing," she says bluntly. "Why did you move seats anyway?"

"Wanted to see what you were up to."

"Ha. I see you are confusing stalking for curiosity."

"I'm just waiting for the day that you wake up and stop lying to yourself. You are bored, Claire. And you are doubting the choices you made for a man who is not worth it. Probably hating yourself for missed opportunities. For trying to build a life on a fictional foundation with a man who doesn't fucking deserve you."

"Stop."

"I see how he treats you."

"And you think you can treat me better, is that it?"

"I would ruin you," I answer honestly.

"Wow, way to sell yourself, buddy."

"And maybe that is part of the appeal."

Claire swallows and goes back to looking at the pitcher of margaritas. I am getting to her, chiseling slowly at the wall she has built around her.

Why is she here and not tearing into Ethan with her anger? Why is she not crying and having a yelling match at me? Is she in shock or is she trying to figure out a way to get Ethan back in her good graces?

Maybe what I did tonight isn't going to be their end.

Maybe it will just serve as a catalyst to Ethan sticking his claws even deeper into her freedom. He will chisel away at everything that makes Claire unique, until the only thing left of her will be exactly what he created for himself.

And still, he will be unsatisfied.

"I have only one regret from tonight," I say simply, feeling bold.

"Oh, is that right, Nic Hoffman?" she sneers. "And what is that?"

"Not offering Maxwell a million to take your asshole."

"You are so sick," she lashes back.

And then I feel it. The sting from the force of her hand. The sound echoes in my ears, as the pain radiates from my cheekbone up to my eye. I don't even flinch. I revel in it actually—because I fucking deserve her rage. I need her to be angry. Anger gets the ball moving. And right now, she has a boulder to move in the shape of Ethan Maxwell. I'm over her being complacent in this life she has accepted, probably feeling there is no way out of the rut she found herself in. But there is. And if I have to lead her to the exit, so be it.

The shocked look on Claire's face has me smirking. She probably didn't think she had it in herself to finally serve to me what I obviously deserved. But at least she reacted appropriately. She scares me when she loses her fire.

I wipe the bourbon from my lips and upgrade my smirk to a full-on smile.

"Quit looking so smug or I'll hit you again."

"Good."

"Good? Why is it good?" she demands.

"Because at least you are exhibiting some type of

emotion. Plus, I deserve it. Hit me again if it helps you move forward. I promise not to enjoy it so much this round."

"I hate you."

"So you've said. But you probably hate yourself more," I counter, and by the twitch of her eye, I realize I am correct. I tip my glass in her direction. "And that there is the problem. Out of all the people to be pissed off at, you are missing the point entirely."

Spinning on her seat, she takes a sip from her glass. "The only thing I'm missing is the peace and quiet I had prior to you plopping your ass down here to make my life even worse."

There she is. Welcome back, Feisty Claire. "I'm going to have such fun ruining you for all other men." My words come out flirty, and it is because I'm grasping at anything to get Claire to wake up. Anyone would be better for her than the man who is probably sleeping comfortably upstairs without a care in the world as to where his girlfriend is right now.

"Who says you will ever get a chance to have me?"

"Oh, Claire, I already possess your thoughts. Your body will wake up and follow suit next."

"You are delusional."

I can't help but allow my lips to lift up at the corners. "Every time you close your eyes at night and lie beside that man, you will think of me. Think of what I can give you. I don't need to touch you to prove to you that I can do better. But be warned, I'm very demanding in bed."

"We can't date. Ever."

"I never said anything about some courtship, Claire."

"Good. Glad we're on the same page." Her words are sarcastic and matter-of-fact.

"But just for curiosity's sake, why am I undatable? Is it because I have a brain? Your ultimate deal breaker."

She makes a face at me, sticking out her tongue. If she knows what's good for her, she will put it back in her mouth before I do something about her sass.

"Because you are filthy rich," she says simply.

"And...?"

"And men like you are lazy."

"Is that so?"

"Yup. You rich men aren't used to needing to be good in bed. You just flock to the smell of pussy and once you get your fix, you peace out."

"Did the margaritas finally kick in?" I ask, in awe of Claire's fiery personality that seems to flare when I least expect it.

"No, but my common sense sure did."

I move my finger up to touch her red stained lips. "I would have loved to see how far you could swallow me by the red ring you would leave on my dick. You will look so beautiful looking up at me with your mouth stuffed full."

"It's amazing how reluctant I am based on your flowery description. I must be the only lame person not jumping to be first in line," she responds sarcastically with a roll of her eyes. It's her coping mechanism and way to deflect away from how she is really feeling.

"One taste of what I can offer you and you will be begging for more."

"Is this what overconfidence looks like?"

"Trust me, I will lick you from hole to hole until you

will be writhing with an orgasm so intense that you will need me inside you to lessen the force from it. You will never have to fake it with me, and I will know if you dare to try. I will be anything but lazy when I finally have you. My body is made to worship yours."

My thoughts are interrupted by the waiter bringing Claire her obscene tray of pancakes. I am glad, though, because all the talk on what I would do to her was getting me hot and bothered.

"Do you ever get tired of overstepping?" she asks me, looking at the food.

I shrug. "Not really."

"Of course not."

24

CLAIRE

"Consider it an offering of peace," Nic says softly, nodding toward the food.

He gives me a boyish shrug that only makes him look innocent. He's not though. There's nothing about him that isn't dark and dangerous. He just hides it all behind a sexy smirk or a nice gesture. But this man is lethal.

When the plate of miniature pancakes arrived, my heart dropped. Strawberries, blueberries, syrup, whipped cream, and chocolate sauce are arranged around a pile of fluffy pancakes. It is a feast for my eyes, and I can't resist. I dig right in. I indulge.

I am tipsy but not enough to ignore that the man who is seated beside me is fucking with my head. Between the margaritas and the pancakes, he is trying to wear me down.

"Seems like you keep finding yourself in the middle of an unwanted threesome tonight," I point out, motioning between me and my food.

Nic huffs out a laugh. "Yeah, this seems really unfair to me too."

"Oh yeah, you are totally the victim."

"In a way, I am."

I shake my head at him. "You are crazy. At least you don't have to live with regret like I do," I say solemnly.

"Dump him, Claire. It's an easy concept."

"Leave me alone."

I would be better off if Nic wasn't so damn attractive. He has to know his appeal to women. Probably exploits it and uses it to his advantage. Probably can melt the panties off of even the coldest pussies. I could easily ignore him if he wasn't so good-looking. The way his lips curl up on the ends with his half-smile-half-laugh *thing* he does, I can't decide on whether I want to hit him again or grind against him just to see what it would feel like.

I'm either tipsy or have completely lost my mind.

I still have Ethan's cum leaking out of me, and I'm toying with the idea of being with Nic—the man who put me in this predicament. Ethan used me. He is *still* using me. I have been at this bar for over an hour, and he has yet to text me or call me. Nothing. I don't even know where I am going to sleep tonight. I am physically drained of caring about much right now.

I want to continue to be furious with Nic. But that would be misdirected. My current mental state is in such disarray that I don't know whether or not to be embarrassed or ashamed or angry around a man who has seen me practically naked and in a vulnerable position that should have been intimate and loving with the person that I want to build a future with.

Yet, every time I think about returning to the room where Ethan probably is passed out, it all seems wrong. Everything about the whole situation is wrong.

I keep my focus on my plate of food. It comforts me in the perfect superficial way. Nic clears his throat as I continue to ignore him. He then resorts to tapping his metal ring against the side of his glass, making the most annoying clink-clink sounds.

Clink.

Clink.

Clinnnk.

Clink-clink-clink.

I stop midbite and turn my seat so I can look Nic square in the face.

"Why?" I demand.

"Why what?"

"Why did you make Ethan accept a bet that involved me fucking my own boyfriend? Are you really into that type of watching thing? You're a real sicko for involving me in your fetishes."

"I didn't make Ethan do anything," Nic says matter-of-factly. He props his chin on the palm of his hand as he stares more than just at me—he stares inside me. Like he can see a part of me that I usually keep hidden from others. "I presented him with an offer. He easily accepted. Granted, I was still shocked. If you were mine, I would have never shared you with anyone—not even just their eyes. So if you want to be mad at anyone, be mad at him."

"I am mostly mad at myself," I say solemnly.

"And why is that, Claire?"

"Because I could easily have left you both in the hotel

room to have your own jerk-off fest. Instead, I participated."
And that is something I have to come to terms with. Why
did I allow myself to be that vulnerable when I could easily
have said "no." Was it because I was scared of the arbitrary
consequences of my refusal that would have been brought to
Ethan's life? "What would he have gotten if he won?"

"My car."

I can feel my jaw lose control and drop. "Your car," I
repeat.

"Yes."

"So, you would have just handed it over just like that?"

"I would have signed over the title and gone about it in a
legal way, yes. That's how bets work. Someone wins.
Someone loses."

"So why does my boyfriend"—*who is an asshole*—
"choose something that is tangible, that he can easily take
from you? But you, Nic, choose something that is what"—I
toss a hand toward him—"a memory?"

"An *experience*," he interjects.

"Seems like an imbalance of prizes, don't you think?"

"On the contrary, I gained something even better than a
memory or a fleeting visual," he comments, finishing the
last few drops of the amber-colored liquid.

"And what did you gain?" I inquire. We are talking in
circles. I can't tell if I am getting dizzy from the alcohol or
Nic's lack of adequate conversational skills.

His large hand engulfs mine. "You're a very intelligent
woman, Claire. Think about it. I basically shot bullet holes
into the foundation of your relationship, exposing your
boyfriend's true colors."

I remove his hand from mine. I need to think clearly.

The margies and pancakes are making everything worse. He knows my weaknesses. He is capitalizing on every single one of them. "For what gain?"

He shrugs. "I have my selfish reasons."

I huff out an exhale and shove the plate of adorable pancakes away. I already ate a dozen, so there's no reason to self-destruct any more than I did up in Ethan's room. I make eye contact with Nic. It is a mistake. His amused expression is making me crazy.

His hand massages the stubble on his chin.

"Aim higher and maybe you'll actually be able to wipe that smirk from your stupid face."

"You want me, don't you?"

I open my mouth. Then quickly shut it. If I deny too quickly, he'll think I'm lying. If I delay my answer, he'll think my answer is what he is assuming in the first place. Shit.

"Good to know, Claire. Good to know."

"What? I never confirmed that," I snap, my tone a little too aggressive.

"You pretty much did."

He must find this whole situation funny because he can't stop laughing. When he finally stops, he does the weird, hooded thing with his eyes. The thing that makes my stomach do little flips, causing the butterflies to roll around. Sometimes I wonder if he is imagining me without clothes on. I'd be lying if I said those thoughts of him never crossed my fantasies at night. Hell, who am I fooling? I have those fantasies all hours of the day.

Nic basically saw me at my most vulnerable—having

sex. What is left to see? Yeah, I had clothes on, technically. But he got to see me in a position that was meant to be private.

"Come back to the suite," he whispers, drawing my eyes to his.

"No."

"Why not?"

"Because I'm not making two mistakes in one night's time."

"I would be the best mistake you could make." The words slide out of his mouth like sin. I have never been this tempted before, this drawn to someone. He is dark and dangerous, and those things just make me want him more.

His smile lets me know he knows it too.

"The pathway to hell is paved with men like you."

"Not denying that."

"I should hate you for what you put me through up in the room."

"But you don't?"

"Oh, I do. I just hate myself more."

I clean up my area, tossing my napkin to the side of my plate. When the bartender informs me that everything I ate and drank is paid for, I get up from my seat. I don't even bother to thank Nic. It is the least he could do for putting me in such a horrible predicament.

"If things fall through with Ethan, it is on you."

I watch him tap his fingers on the polished surface of the bar. "If things fall through with Ethan, it is because he is a douche. I never twisted his arm. Never threatened him. Hell, it wasn't even my idea to go back to his room to play a higher stakes game. I simply stated my terms and he jumped on them to accept. You are expendable to him. An object. So when you go back to your mundane life, with your boring boyfriend, I hope that you constantly wonder if you are wasting away a chance at something better."

"Better being *you*?" I say with more anger than I initially anticipated.

"Better being anyone but him. Your standards are so low that anyone would be able to reach the bar you have set. Raise it up a little. Make us men work for it."

"You keep talking around the fact that you brought this whole mess to fruition. You did, Nic Hoffman!" I snap.

"Maxwell wanted to raise the stakes, Claire. He knows the consequences to gambling. There's only one winner."

"You made it impossible for him not to follow through," I grind out.

"Forever defending a man who should be doing that for you instead. No, instead he pawned you off and followed through by not taking the counteroffer."

"A quarter million? How would you expect him to pay that? Money doesn't grow on trees!"

"It does for him."

My eyes snap up to his. "And how do you know that?"

"He's lying to you. Been doing it from the start."

"Lying about what?"

"About just how much Ethan Maxwell is worth."

I have heard enough of his nonsense. I slide off the bar stool and take a step closer to Nic. Leaning into his body, I look straight into his eyes. I want to say something snarky. I want to say something smart. But instead, I clear my throat, grab the watered-down pitcher of margaritas, and empty the contents right onto the crotch of his pants.

"Maybe that will cool you off." I watch as realization hits his face as I'm sure the temperature of his body is lowering. Good. "And whatever delusions are spinning around inside your head about getting into my pants? Erase them. Because that will never happen."

With a newfound confidence, I throw back my hair and do what I should have done from the beginning of this train wreck. I walk away.

Heading out of the bar, I wave to the bartender and take a few deep breaths. When I am in Nic's proximity, I can't think. It's like my brain stops working.

I need to get back up to the room I'm supposed to share with Ethan. I don't feel comfortable going back to the suite until I can get my emotions in check. I don't need Angie feeling bad about anything this trip. She always bears the weight of everyone she cares about on her shoulders. I'll be damned if my bad decisions trickle into her celebration.

The most I have even used the bed in Ethan's room since he booked it has been the little bit of time I was lying there in lingerie while Nic watched from the corner. I feel dirty. There is just no point hanging around Nic and listening to his negativity. He hasn't even been around Ethan for twenty-four hours and already everything is jacked up.

I hit the call button for the elevator, tapping my foot to the music being played through the sound system. When the doors open, several groups of people exit, allowing me to enter the empty car. I push the button for the floor I need and wait for the doors to close. Just as they start to move, a hand pops through, stopping them.

I look over and see Nic. The wet stain on the front half of his pants is undeniable. He can't even cover it up if he tries. Walking into the car, he takes one glance at the number panel, then continues to move closer to me.

Once the elevator doors close, the air seems thicker. It is like the ten by ten car is way too confining for the two of us. Hell, his body alone takes up the majority of the space. His shirt is pulled tight against the defined muscles of his chest. He stands with confidence, towering over my small frame. It feels like I could suffocate.

My words stop in my throat and can't escape. I have nothing to say to him.

"Silent treatment?" he asks, moving infinitesimally closer to me with each floor we pass. "Challenge accepted."

I push my spine into the posterior wall, pressing myself flat against the smooth surface. My eyes close as I try to ignore how amazing he smells. How he makes me feel so desired. So wanted. He makes me feel like a woman.

I feel his breath on my lips without even having to look. He is leaning down, shadowing me. Waiting for me to open my eyes and accept him.

"Stop," I mouth.

"Stop what?"

"Stop making me want you."

"I'm not going to touch you until you beg me for it."

"Why are you doing this to me?" I whisper. "Find a hobby. Take up a trade. Enroll in an online class. Do something—*anything*—with your spare time. But leave me alone."

His low chuckle causes me to stir. I fidget against the wall. Even the smallest movement causes me to brush up against him. It is like static electricity. We may be just sizzling now, but I can already foresee combustion later. Someone like Nic Hoffman could cause irreparable damage to someone like me. He plays by a different set of rules. Unfair and underhanded.

When I hear the ding indicating that the car has come to a stop, my eyes snap open. I come face-to-face with the man who has singlehandedly caused what I thought was a solid relationship to turn to dust. I push past him and walk out into the hallway. When I feel him hovering in my wake, I turn so fast that it makes my own head spin.

"Why are you following me?" I demand.

He looks at me innocently. "This is my floor."

Oh. Fuck. I look at the room numbers and see that I missed my own floor. I stomp past him, smack the call button for the elevator and wait impatiently for it to arrive again. I swear this man who can't seem to remove the smirk off his face makes my brain turn to mush. I am completely incompetent when he is within a five-yard radius of me.

When the car arrives again, I get inside and select the correct floor. Staring at Nic from a distance as the doors shut, I raise my middle finger as a salute to him.

My keycard easily opens up Ethan's room when I make my way there.

"You could knock!" he snaps out.

My steps halt, tears welling up in my eyes. "I am staying here too." *Or so I thought.* My voice is shaky with emotion. "Why are you being so cold to me? What did I do?"

"You embarrassed me."

"I embarrassed *you*? Are you even for real right now, Ethan? What the hell is happening to you?" I take a deep breath. "To us."

He paces around the room, as I toss my handbag a little too hard onto the bed. It bounces and falls to the floor. "You just laid there while I made love to you. No affection."

"Made love to me?" I dart for him, shoving him hard. "Are you kidding me?"

"No, you bitch!" His hands grab at me, and I guess I deserve it since I touched him first. My body wilts from the force of his hold.

"You are hurting me. Stop. Please stop." His cold eyes make me freeze. *Please don't hit me. Please.* "You promised it wouldn't happen again."

Tossing me away, he straightens his spine. I stumble back into the bed, feeling my back scrape against the nightstand before landing on the mattress. "I'm not even in the joking mood right now with you. What a fucking disgrace to treat me so cold while I was trying to warm you up. You didn't even try!" Ethan's hands slice through the air in fury. "It was like having sex with a corpse."

"Fuck you."

His body flies toward me, landing on top of me. I kick with all my might, not getting him to budge in the slightest. His fingers tangle into my hair, jerking my face to look at his. "Fucking would have been refreshing. No, you just lay there, just like you are now. It was humiliating."

"Get off of me!" This time he does. I pull myself up, wrapping my hands around my knees. "If you call what you did to me love, then you have issues that I cannot fix. You have treated me badly ever since I graduated from college and then you—"

"Oh, this again?" he snaps. "Blah, blah, blah, blah, blah." His hands make a snapping gesture, imitating how he thinks I talk.

"Just stop, please," I say quietly.

"Poor Claire, gave up her dream internship. Poor Claire. Always poor Claire."

"You are such a bastard," I snarl, as tears pour out of my eyes.

"It was an internship, Claire. Quit acting like you got some bigwig job. You would have been a temp. Expendable and replaceable. But, no, you keep fantasizing and bringing up this long-lost dream that Evil Ethan kept you from," he mocks, changing his voice to sound feminine and whiny.

He takes a step closer, getting into my face. I quiver back on the bed from the fear that he may hit me. He hasn't done it in a long time, but his anger is so palpable that it wouldn't surprise me if he doesn't make this once again physical. He is so close that I can smell the stale whiskey on his breath. It burns my eyes.

My head throbs from the overindulging I did at the bar. Before I say anything more that I may regret, I crawl off the bed and walk into the bathroom to change into a set of comfy pajamas. I just need to bide my time. Ethan will pass out soon. He always does. I splash some cold water on my face and brush my teeth.

I shuffle back into the bedroom, pull back the covers, and crash from the emotional exhaustion I endured the entire day. Maybe if I go to sleep, I'll wake up and all of this will be just a bad dream.

I've learned that when things get this heated, it is best to deescalate Ethan's anger as best I can—usually by removing myself from the argument.

We can hash this out again tomorrow if need be. But for now, I have no fight left inside me.

"Good night," I mutter, before allowing sleep to overtake me.

25

CLAIRE

I wake with Ethan kissing my neck. It feels weird. Like a stranger is lying beside me. Nic already suggested that I do not know Ethan as well as I thought. And the way my back feels from hitting the nightstand and how sore my arms are, I realize it is true.

It's as if someone came along and poured ink onto a beautiful love story—one that wasn't finished being written yet. I went from having what I thought was a fairy tale to quickly having it turn into a dark nightmare.

Has the person I thought I was going to be with forever been the villain all along?

But let's not leave out Nic Hoffman from this equation. He orchestrated this plummet in Ethan's and my relationship. He best be glad I didn't do more to him than just dousing his crotch with perfectly good margaritas. Sure, he didn't twist anyone's arm yesterday, but his mouth still uttered my name and involved me in his pissing contest.

It is Ethan's slimy tongue trailing up my throat that

makes me want to hurl. "I have to use the bathroom," I mumble, rolling out of bed. I just need to get my head on straight before we can be intimate again. Last night broke me. The mockery and intimidation did me in. Just the way he grabbed me and shoved me was too aggressive for my liking. It's hard to ignore all that went down.

But people make mistakes. And if he is truly sorry, then maybe—just maybe—we can move forward and heal from all of this drama.

"Up for some shower sex?" he calls out from the other side of the door. "I have a business meeting this morning but have time if we make it quick."

I groan. How can he be so clueless to know that the only thing that will fix us right now is an honest conversation? And therapy. Lots of therapy. "I think we are going to hit up a few of the casinos we missed seeing and then will head over to the airport. Should I expect to just meet you there?"

"Oh, I thought I told you…"

I open the door and stare at Ethan. "Tell me what?"

"I'm staying an extra night. I'll just meet you at the apartment when I get back into Portland."

"Oh." I thought the plane trip back would be a good way for us to focus on having a conversation about our relationship. Evaluate what we each want and how we can move forward. "You didn't tell me." My words come out a bit clipped.

"Don't need your permission either. It's not like you are paying for the ticket."

"Thanks for making me feel bad, once again, about making less money than you," I snip back. I start to shut the door, but Ethan puts his hand up to stop it from closing.

"Less money? Claire, you are barely making any money."

"Why does everything have to be about money?" I ask. "We are in a relationship. It's not a business transaction." As soon as the words leave my mouth, I am reminded of the way we met. We started out with a money exchange. Everything about it *was* business. Maybe we haven't transitioned mentally from him being a customer to being an actual boyfriend.

He sighs. "Your mom warned me about this."

My breath catches in my throat. "What? When did you talk to my mom, Ethan? What are you talking about?"

"She called me a few months back to chat. Was informing me that she couldn't pay for all of your student loans. That you were an adult and would have to handle these little blips in the radar of life on your own. Part of growing up and being responsible."

I cross my arms at my chest. He is so patronizing. "So why call you?"

"Probably to give me the common courtesy of knowing that if we were to commit further, I would be taking on a lot of your debt. It's not like you were ever honest with me."

"That's not fair," I say softly. "I just found out days ago that she was going back on her word to help me with my college loans. Up until receiving a letter in the mail, I had my finances figured out."

This is all starting to make sense. I thought Ethan's tune changed with me because of turning down a dream job in Los Angeles. Instead, he has grown cold and stingy with money ever since my mom told him I was basically walking around with a hefty debt. If he was looking for a way out of this relationship, this would be a good excuse for him to walk away.

"Who doesn't even inquire if bills are even being paid? You were just coasting through life without a care. Irresponsible, if you ask me."

"I didn't ask you." My words come out as a whisper, and I retract my shoulders when I hear his growl.

"What was that?"

"Nothing."

"I have a son to raise. I don't need two kids. One is enough, trust me. I also don't need someone to suck up all of his future funds. I have a lot of discerning to do to make sure that my next series of choices are financially worth it." His eyes rake down my body, then go back up to my face. "If you're worth it."

Damn. I've heard enough. I am nothing more to him than an expense.

"What? No argument?" he asks, following me into the bedroom, while I throw on a fresh set of clothes and start packing up my bags. I don't want to stay here a minute longer than what is absolutely necessary.

"What's there to say, Ethan? I'm always going to be the weaker link in the relationship if you only look at money as a way of measuring value. That's what this is about, right? Money?"

"If you are hiding this debt from me, then what other kind of money issues are you hiding from me? You just expect me to bail you out of trouble. I'm not your dad. I'm your lover."

"Right now, you are neither."

I pull up the handle on my luggage and wheel it toward

the bathroom. I just throw every item that is mine into the side compartment, not even caring if things get broken or damaged. Everything is a jumbled mess, and it is a great symbolism for what my life is like at this moment.

I am lacking order.

I am lacking structure.

And I am lacking the foundation I once thought I was building.

"You know what, Ethan?" I ask, turning back to look at his expressionless face. "You found out months before I did that my parents never intended to go through with their agreement to pay my tuition for my undergraduate and graduate degrees. Yet, you never told me. Why is that?"

"Would it have really changed anything, Claire? Would you have all of a sudden started looking for a legit job?"

I feel my nose flaring. My pulse is racing. "You are something else…"

"Maybe they were right in denying you the funds. It's not like you are even using your degrees right now. To them, it's probably a waste of money. I mean, hindsight is 20-20 after all."

"You've been trying to hurt me this entire trip, and for the life of me, I can't figure out why."

"Oh, quit being so flipping sensitive. The poor Claire story gets old after a while."

His words cut into me. He is deliberately doing everything he can to get me to break. And for what purpose? Sure, he is concerned about the debt I bring into the relationship and has his son's future to preserve. However, the way he is shitting all over the months we have been together —as if I am nothing to him—is the most devastating part for me. We have a past. I thought we were building a pathway to a future.

Only words of an apology will fix this mess and by the look on Ethan's face, I'll have to wait until his lips learn how to move again. I'm not even sure if he has the skill set to be able to say, "I'm sorry," and actually mean it. It's not like I have heard those words pop out of his mouth before.

"You aren't the man I thought I knew."

"And you aren't the woman you portrayed yourself to be either."

My eyes find his. "And how did I portray myself, Ethan?"

"As an easy lay. But there is nothing easy about fucking you. I have to work hard for it, and I am starting to see it isn't even worth it."

My bottom lip quivers, and I bite at it to keep it still. "I'm so done with this. I'm tired of walking on eggshells around you, trying to avoid your temper. Abuse is *never* okay. I am done accepting how you treat me. Done."

I toss the keycard on the bed and wave at him without even looking to see if he is watching. I need out of here. Fast.

I grab my belongings and exit into the hallway as quickly as I can. I lean my back against the wall and look up at the ceiling, silently wishing for a clear path out of this mess. My hand grips my luggage handle so tightly that I feel my knuckles pop.

Breathe, Claire. Just breathe.

The sound of glass breaking shakes my core, as I envision Ethan tossing the lamp or shattering a mirror. I wipe at a solo tear escaping down my cheek. I'm so sick and tired of crying over this man.

I count to ten and start to make the path to the elevator, when a hand encompasses mine on my luggage handle, startling me.

"I got it," Nic says.

"No, I got it," I say, tugging my bag away from his hand. My fingers strangle the handle with the tension and anger bubbling through me.

"*Please*. Let me." He gently releases my fingers one by one, until I am just standing helplessly beside him.

"Why are you here?" Even I can hear the tears trapped between each of my spoken words. My voice is breathy and shaky. Like if it breaks, so will I.

"Everyone has checked out already and is waiting in the limo for the tour. I thought you needed a hand."

I sigh. "I just need some fresh air before I—"

Lose it?

Crumble?

Throw up?

Nic nods and escorts me to the elevators, but before we get there, his eyes settle on my arms. Dammit. What was I thinking not wearing a sweater? It's not like that wouldn't draw any unwanted attention either to my already shitty situation. No one wears sweaters in Vegas.

Pulling away, Nic stomps back toward the room.

"Nic, no! What are you doing?"

"What I should have done last night."

Forgoing my luggage, I run to catch up with Nic— putting myself between the door and him. "Don't do this," I beg.

"Move out of the way, Claire."

His voice is eerily calm. Like he is methodically planning out his next moves. And the stress of the situation pulls me down, straight to the floor. Nic follows me down, pulling me into a hug, which oddly feels good. I welcome it. Anything is better than the physical or emotional pain.

"Don't cry. Please." Now it is his turn to beg. "I will destroy that fucker for touching you. You know that, right? I will pay him back whether it be now or later."

I feel like my heart is breaking, and it isn't until Nic has me cradled against his chest and moving back down toward the elevators that I realize a potential disaster is diverted.

"I'm sorry," I whimper, as he manages to get my luggage into the empty car, hit the button for the lobby, and still keep me in his arms.

"You don't have a thing to be sorry for, Claire. And if you apologize again for something that clearly isn't your fault, I may drop you off with Angie and Graham and go back up and murder the bastard. He should have never touched you with force, and there is no limit of hate I have for myself by not making you stay in the suite last night where you would have been safe."

"I want to walk," I say softly when the doors are about to open on the main floor.

Granting my wish, Nic places me on my feet, steadying me with a hand to the small of my back.

My part of checking out is done. Ethan has my key, and if he loses the security deposit from damaging the room that is entirely on him. The previous suite was already taken care of with Nic. My only responsibility is to walk out.

Nic has the sense to not ask me a hundred questions. He

knows something is very wrong with me. It has to be written all over my face. But instead, we just walk. I welcome the quiet. It is the calmest I have felt since waking up to unwanted lips seeking me out. How can a man think it is okay to just take without ever giving anything back?

I am angry with myself for being hurt. Being hurt is a choice sometimes. I allowed my heart to open up, and I allowed someone inside to cause it damage. This is my fault.

But is it? The more I think over the whole situation that keeps fluttering through my head like a series of pictures from a slideshow, the more I realize that sure, I stayed to have sex with Ethan. But I sure as hell didn't do anything to bring on the emotional abuse that probably started long before Vegas. I just put blinders on and made excuses for him. His methods were just sneakier in how he would deliver his nonphysical blows.

The way he critiques what I eat. How I decide to wear my clothes. The way I talk. No wonder I started to second-guess how I interacted with him. Deep down, I was always scared of his reaction.

Ethan thinks I'm not a responsible person, basing that solely off of my finances. Well, he's not responsible either in how he handles his temper. I can't keep going to bat for someone who isn't willing to do the same for me.

When we get outside, Nic sighs. I look up at him as he runs a hand through his short brown hair and looks visibly stressed. He opens his mouth several times to talk, but seems to second-guess himself and quickly shuts it.

My eyes droop, and I look at the people walking by us on the sidewalk. I arrived here a different person than how

I'm leaving. It is not in the good, metaphoric way either. I feel beaten down and battered by the rude entry into adulthood. I have no one to rely on but myself, and that is a lonely, sobering realization.

"Did that asshole hurt you worse than what I can see?"

I glance up at Nic as a few tears spill out of my eyes. I angrily wipe them away.

"Isn't it obvious?"

"Physically?" he snarls.

"No." What Ethan did was worse than getting shoved or pressed into the mattress. Anything else physical wouldn't have messed up my view of myself. Instead, he methodically attacked me for who I am as a person. If he would have just beat me up, I definitely wouldn't feel like I'm in this sort of limbo as I'm feeling right now, wondering if intensive therapy can fix what is broken. I would have just left.

I hate crying in front of others but have no way of shutting it off.

Nic manages to look genuinely sad. I didn't even think he had that emotion in his limited rolodex of feelings. He usually only expresses his top two—mad or not mad.

And I know he is livid with Ethan Maxwell.

"Don't let him ruin the ending of this trip. We had a good time. Let's enjoy the last few hours. Forget about the selfish bastard. He doesn't deserve someone pure like you."

Tears continue to fall, the trails evaporating fast in the dry heat. No one has ever referred to me as *pure* before. I almost want to snicker. I am not naive enough to believe that his words are true. Many people seem to think they know more about my sex life than I do, assuming I spread my legs for anyone interested.

"Hey," Nic says, tilting up my chin. "Things have a way of working themselves out. You'll see."

When did he become an optimist? And how much of Nic Hoffman do I not yet know? If he is anything like his older brother, I am in for a lot of surprises.

I wipe my tears away, take a few deep breaths, square my shoulders, and start the trek to the waiting limo. Nic places my belongings into the back compartment, then helps me with the door, as I slide in to join the others.

I snap on my seatbelt and smile over at Angie and Graham. "I'm so excited to see some of the other casinos."

Despite my voice being bubbly and my expression being of joy, I can already tell that Angie knows it is a facade. Luckily for me, she is kind enough to let me hide behind the lies and the bruises on my arms while I recover from the past twenty-four hours of trauma.

The driver merges onto the busy street and takes us to the Wynn. The hotel is a beautiful architecturally attractive structure. I can't help but stare at the smooth curve of the design and wonder how much it cost to construct.

The driver drops us off at the front, and we make our way into the lobby. Graham and Nic walk up ahead, talking quietly to themselves, as Angie and I take up the rear and do the same.

Angie holds my hand for comfort, looking at me with concern. "I don't need to bombard you with questions right now, but just let me ask one. Are you okay?"

"I will be. Things with me and Ethan are less than stellar. He has been treating me like a burden instead of like a girlfriend."

"I am so sorry," she says, pulling me closer for a hug. She is careful where she places her pressure, and I know she knows that I've been manhandled.

Her embrace is welcomed and so needed. I squeeze her tighter and say a silent thank you that the guys seem to be deliberately ignoring us so we can have this moment.

"I'm just scared," I stutter.

"Scared of what?"

"The unknown…"

"Oh, Claire, you are so strong. Whatever gets thrown your way, you will handle it. You always do. And you never have to do anything alone. I'm here for you. Always. Nothing will change that."

"Thanks for being such a good friend. I really didn't want to have this hiccup ruin the trip."

"Nothing is ruined, Claire. I'm having a fabulous time, and I just hope that you can silence your mind to enjoy these last moments here."

I nod. She's so right. "I can do that."

We enter the conservatory. Like at the Bellagio, the display is breathtaking. I marvel at how the intricate designs and arrangements of live plants make the space feel enchanted. Otherworldly. Meandering through the earthy village has a calming effect on me. I am instantly at peace.

When you grow up with a mom who is too busy for you and a dad who isn't really your dad, it is easy to miss the developmental milestones that help with the formation of self-worth. Even though I outwardly express confidence and am an extrovert to most onlookers, I have an underdeveloped—dare I say damaged—sense of self.

I lack the ability to set boundaries and often let myself get walked on by others. Yeah, I am bold and a bit wild. But when it comes to those close to me, I often rely on their approval and how they treat me as my way of knowing if I am worthy of love.

The world may view me as a strong, independent woman by how I dress and how I act. However, deep down, I am just looking for acceptance. And when I don't get it, I close in on myself and internalize the negativity as something that is flawed inside of me.

Nic flutters back, switching places with Angie, while we walk. I should be pissed at him more than what I am. Furious, even. But he is right in the fact that while he offered a scenario, it was Ethan that ultimately accepted it. At this moment, I wish I could hate Ethan more than I hate myself for going through with it. I let my boyfriend put me in a situation that I could easily have walked out of but chose to stay. It is that fact that lets me know that I have a lot of soul searching to do and a new vision board may be born from the character development I hope to do.

If I fear change, I fear growth.

26

NIC

The adrenaline running through me right now is causing my feet to walk faster into the Bellagio. I don't have much time until I need to be back at the airport where the others are shopping before the flight, but I refuse to leave the state of Nevada until Ethan Maxwell hears me out. And if I have to speak with my fists, so be it.

Seeing Claire looking so vulnerable and bruised this morning was my undoing, and it put a direct target on her bastard boyfriend's back. She may not be able to fight back. But I will.

And I'll enjoy every fucking second of it.

I know he's here in the building because I have a tracker on him and eyes on his schedule. If all of my information aligned, he should be back in his room, which is an added bonus for privacy.

When I make it to his floor, I find the housekeeper a few rooms down.

"Excuse me," I say politely, pulling out a handful of

one-hundred-dollar bills. "Can you please open my door? I forgot my key."

The woman nods, following me to the room that I predict will need some extra cleanup when I'm through. So, I hand over a few more bills—just in case.

She grants me access, and I quickly shut and deadbolt the door behind me.

"I have the do not disturb sign up," Ethan bellows.

"Good for you," I say, my voice dripping with sarcasm. "Too bad I don't give a fuck."

He rounds the corner, undoing the tie around his neck. "Oh, I wasn't expecting you. Are you here to ask me to play some poker? An invitation to do more than just watch?"

My fingers tighten into fists, as my eyes rake over his face. He's too smug. "You touch Claire again, and I'll end you."

Ethan tries to make himself taller, as if his height somehow would intimidate me. "Oh, is she spreading lies like she spreads her legs? She's gotten to you, has she?" He licks his lips. "Hope you don't mind sloppy sec—"

My fist connects with his mouth first, splattering blood onto the white sheets of the bed. Ethan groans, stumbling backwards, probably shocked I was able to execute the blow so fast. "Want to make this fun and keep talking?"

He wipes his face with the sleeve of his shirt, staring down at the wet crimson stain spreading on the fabric. And then he makes the biggest mistake of all—he comes after me. I dart to the side to avoid his blow, switching places with Ethan.

"You can have her. She isn't worth my time. Little slut."

This time I hit below his eye, connecting with the side

of his nose. Blood spurts out, but this time all over the front of his shirt. "You just don't learn, do you? But let me make this clear. You cause any more pain to Claire Nettles and you're a dead man."

"Give me the damn bag," I snap, watching Claire struggle to get it into the overhead compartment. When will she learn? We have been through this before on the flight out of Portland. And I'm literally less than twelve inches from her. She can probably feel my warm breath on her neck if she can pause long enough to shut off her pride. "Are you allergic to asking for help?"

"Mind your own business, bubs."

She hoists it over her head, thrashing it against the bottom frame. The bag slips out of her hand, falling behind her, and nearly knocking me in the head. I catch it just in time and pop it into the confined space with ease. Now why was that so fucking hard? She murmurs a weak thank you and scurries into her place near the window, tossing her purse below her feet on the floor.

The seating arrangement on the return flight is almost identical to how we were situated when we arrived. The only differences are that Claire is wearing more clothes, has less of a genuine smile, and is lacking the penis jewelry. I'm not complaining—just making an observation. While waiting in the airport, she must have slipped into the bathroom and changed into a long gray maxi dress. It looks new so I imagine it was one of her purchases. Similarly, I did a little shopping myself, but at the Bellagio.

Figured that showing up covered in Ethan's blood wasn't socially acceptable. I'm sure there's some unwritten dress code and all. I wouldn't know. I rarely ever fly commercial.

Claire's dress goes all the way to her ankles and covers twice as much skin as I was used to seeing the entire trip. She looks amazing. Elastic, situated just under her breasts, helps accentuate all of her assets. I may even prefer this relaxed look over her dolled-up outfits. It's a toss-up, really. She would steal my focus even if she decided to wear a generic trash bag.

"It must be really hard, huh?" I ask, snapping myself into my seat in preparation for takeoff.

"What?" she asks, looking at me seriously.

"Looking as good as you do in any outfit you wear."

She swallows hard and looks away. I see the color reach her cheeks, and it just further verifies that I am getting to her. Wearing her down little by little.

I kept Ethan alive because I knew she would have frowned upon it. But it wouldn't have been hard to pay off the housekeeper. I'm sure people go missing in Vegas all the time.

"If you think I'm going to drop my panties for any boy who comes along that says something nice to me, then you are very much mistaken." Her eyes linger on mine, as a smirk appears on her lips. "Because I'm not wearing any today."

Hot damn. I swallow hard as her words penetrate my brain. "No panties, eh?"

Her eyes look out the window, at the workers moving about on the ground. "Got you thinking, didn't I?"

"Not sure if you know the difference between what a boy can do and what a man can do for you."

She looks over at me and shrugs. "I'm starting to learn that I don't even need a man. That's what they make battery operated toys for."

I chuckle and watch as she digs in her purse, wondering if she is going to whip out a show-and-tell item for added emphasis. Instead, she pulls out a bag full of dicks. Cookies, that is. Each is individually wrapped and detailed to be so realistic that there is even pubic hair penciled in around the balls. Written across the shaft are the words—*Nuts about Angie and Graham.*

"Where in the heck did you get those?"

"I ordered them from a local bakery and had them delivered to the hotel. Here, have a dick," she says, passing me one.

"It'll definitely be my first," I mumble, removing the cookie from its packaging.

She stares at me while I take a bite out of the tip. There cannot be anything sexy about this scenario. However, the anticipation in Claire's eyes, paired with the little giggles that escape her throat, is making me reevaluate.

"Well…" Her voice trails off. "How was the taste of your first dick?"

I wipe a crumb off my lips. "Better than expected."

Claire beams with a genuine smile, not one of those fake ones she put on most of the morning. Maybe being away from the bastard has brightened up her mood. It sure has mine. Oh, and taking a few swings to his face. That always has a positive effect on me.

Leaning over, Claire hands two cookies to Graham, who

looks shocked when he sees the shape. Her vanilla smell coats the inside of my nostrils, and I breathe in the scent of her hair. She lingers in my personal space before sitting back in her seat. I have never met someone more oblivious to the appeal they have on men. She watches with a smile as we eat our cookies, snapping a few silly pics just for added embarrassment.

"Those better not make it on the Internet."

"The Internet is a big, big place. You'll never find out."

I stare blankly at her while she smiles like the Cheshire cat. What she doesn't know is that I will find out. I always do.

"Aren't you going to have one?" Angie asks, calling over the aisle to Claire.

"No. I'm doing a new nutrition challenge. Starts today."

I can tell Angie wants to ask more questions but must know this is not the best time to do so. These two have a secret dialogue with just their eyes. On numerous occasions in the past, Angie would lose her mind over how Graham and I would communicate with just a look. She's right. It's infuriating.

"What can be more challenging than avoiding bacon?" I ask, trying to keep the topic lighthearted but still get information.

Her eyes catch my knuckles, and I turn them to avoid her gaze. "What happened to your hand?"

I shrug. "It walked into a wall."

Claire's not buying it, and I don't expect her to. Luckily she gets distracted by the flight attendant who announces the safety protocols in case there is an emergency on board. The pilot taxis us to the runway, and after our belts are checked and the attendants are safely seated, we are soaring through the air.

"Did you remember to take your Dramamine?" I ask, patting Claire on the arm. Her eyes are focused out the window, and she looks less pale than she has on the times I've seen her sick.

"Yeah. In the airport," she confirms. "You seemed to disappear once we got there."

I nod, although she is not looking my way. She is in awe of how we pass through a series of clouds. I look over her and see that the ground below is no longer visible. The shine from the sun beams through the window, nearly blinding us with its intensity.

I can tell that Claire has a lot on her mind, although she seems to be doing well with the whole "avoidance approach." I know she is mad at me. Thinks I somehow helped to end her and Ethan's relationship. Maybe I did. I am selfish like that. However, the way he treated her—even when people were watching—was appalling. She should be thrilled with me—and dare I say *thankful*—that I helped to facilitate his true colors showing.

Champagne is served, which Claire declines. Snacks are offered, which she also declines. I am not sure what food challenge she is currently doing, but I hope she is doing it safely and not to lose weight. She is perfectly shaped, and I would hate for her to lose some of her luscious curves.

"Just give Angie mine, please," she tells the attendant. "She finds these little packages so cute. Then she'll have enough to make a trail mix."

It's true. Angie does appreciate the small things in life. Which is odd that she is about to marry one of the most lucrative businessmen on the West Coast. Graham can give her the world and oftentimes, she just wants some new fabric or some sheets of vinyl for her clothing designs. Or in this instance—portion-controlled airplane snacks.

I watch as Claire's breathing changes and her fingers start playing with the fabric of her dress along her thighs. She crosses and uncrosses her ankles, looking from her lap to the window repetitively.

"Just ask."

Her eyes snap to mine. "What?"

"Something obviously is tying you up in knots. Just ask me what you want to know."

I can tell she is annoyed with me for being able to read her so easily. Even though she is wickedly good at Texas Hold'em, she is unable to completely conceal her emotions around me.

"Why did you allude to Ethan having more money than he is letting on?"

"Because it is appalling how he is treating you like a gold digger and micromanaging your debit card, all while he is making millions each year—even when the stock exchange is rocky. He's good at what he does, Claire. Respected as a trader amongst peers." But he will always be branded as an asshole in my eyes. There's no going back from that once I saw his true colors.

"You wouldn't know that by our less-than-stellar apartment," she huffs. "Pretty sure when I moved in, it was a downgrade from the townhouse that Angie and I shared throughout college."

I leave out a growl. He's playing her, and she is so naive

to notice it. "He's lying to you. The place you are staying in is not even his permanent residence."

She turns in her seat so fast that she nearly knocks over my glass of champagne. "What? What are you talking about? He is staying there with me. We live together."

I can see the wheels turning in her head as she soaks up all of the information I am telling her. I didn't want to ruin her trip by sharing what Tyler found out with just some extra digging. Although, it turned out to be rocky regardless for other reasons.

"He has three places he owns. You are living in the least expensive one. It's not even his primary location. He has a vacation home in Malibu and a single-family home on the outskirts of Portland. Probably doesn't even get his mail delivered where you are staying. Ever notice why there's probably no kid toys lying around? No bills addressed to him coming through the mail?"

"He always says that he gets his mail delivered at his downtown office. And he doesn't want to spoil Finn with materialistic items, so when it's his turn to watch him, they always go out on an adventure."

"Or play at his main residence," I counter. "According to my sources, there's a huge playground set up in the back-yard, an in-ground pool, and a sandbox."

"Fuck," she whispers under her breath. "You sure?"

"I wouldn't be telling you all of this on a theory. Yes, I'm sure."

"He repeatedly tells me he has business meetings weekly in Seattle and instead of making the commute, he stays a couple of nights there." She shakes her head and runs her hand through her hair, pushing strands from her forehead. She looks pale, as if a migraine is building. "I bet he isn't even going there."

"I'm not sure. I'm only telling you what I know. Concrete evidence."

"Why? Why do you even care if I know or not?"

"Because he is an evil bastard who is emotionally and physically abusing you."

Her mouth seals shut, and she goes back to looking out the window. "He was just really angry with me over the whole bet."

"No matter what, abuse is wrong."

The flight home seems to go by faster this time around. The flight attendant gathers trash, while the pilot instructs everyone to remain seated and to prepare for landing. The sun is about to set, painting the sky with golden hues. Claire pulls out her phone and snaps a few pictures to capture the moment. Her fingers are trembling so much that I worry she will drop her device. I can tell she is about to break and is fighting so hard to keep herself from falling apart.

I would be lying if I said it wasn't affecting me too. How could it not? I am no white knight. But I do have a heart. After all, I was raised by a saint of a mother. Deep down, I know how to treat a lady. Problem is, life has jaded me enough to know that love doesn't last—so why bother? I would rather invest my energy into work and not build a future on an illusion or concept that is constructed for fairy tales.

The pilot lands the plane smoothly. It only takes ten minutes for us to taxi to the bridge and unload. Claire doesn't fight me with her luggage and from the exhaustion in her eyes, I know it's because she has mentally checked out.

Once we pick up our belongings at baggage claim, we make our way outside to the SUV that Collins has idling at the curb. He drives us to Claire's place first, which is in downtown Portland, but is not in a building that I would classify as luxurious by any terms.

"I'll walk you up and help you with your things," I state.

"I'm fine," she murmurs, hugging Angie and saying her goodbyes.

"It wasn't an offer. This is what I'm doing."

She doesn't even argue. I see defeat in her eyes, and the sparkle that once was there has dulled. The apartment building is supposed to only allow residents access, but the keycard reader on the main entrance is broken. The cameras situated to look out onto the streets are obviously decoys and look to be dated at least by a few years. There are no security guards that I can tell, and definitely no check-in desk with a live employee to monitor movement.

I will bet that Claire's actual apartment is lacking a personal system as well. How is she even able to stay here and feel safe?

I must be murmuring my distaste as we walk to the elevator, because Claire stops to ask me what I said. I just wave her off and hope that Graham catches on to this lack of safety and makes some changes for her, since his fiancée spends a decent amount of time here. I am shocked that Collins hasn't had a fit. I'm on the verge of one myself.

I can tell Claire doesn't want to be here. Ethan isn't planning to return until tomorrow morning, so at least she doesn't have to worry about him right now. Yet, it still feels weird to just drop her off in this dump. It's like she doesn't belong. She deserves so much better.

When she pushes the door open to the stairs, I look at her with confusion.

"Elevator is broken."

"Why isn't there a sign on it, then?" I ask, looking for where it might have fallen down. I don't even see sticky residue from where tape may have been stuck.

She just shrugs.

I have no problem taking the stairs and often do just to get a little cardio in or work my calves. However, having a nonworking elevator in a huge apartment complex seems frustrating. Claire doesn't seem to mind, so I don't make a big deal about it.

She directs me to her door, and then digs in her bag for what I assume are her keys. Getting frustrated, she flops down to her knees and empties out the contents onto the fraying carpet.

"Here, stand up," I say, trying to pull her up.

"No, I need to find my keys," she says, resisting my help. "Maybe I have them in my carry-on."

I watch as she piles her purse contents back inside, and then crawls over to her tiny piece of luggage. She tries three zipper compartments until she finally finds her key buried in the bottom.

Claire gets up from the dirty floor—blatantly rejecting my offered hand for help—and unlocks the door with ease.

Impossible woman.

"No deadbolt?" I ask. I am dumbfounded.

"When the door was replaced, I guess Ethan never bothered to tell the contractor that one was needed."

"Why was it needing to be replaced?"

"I honestly don't know. I hadn't moved in yet. I've only been here officially since January."

I resist my snarl. Who the hell moves his girlfriend into an apartment that has little to no security features and a broken elevator? I don't want to walk away and leave her here. It's not safe.

"Anyway," she says softly, turning on a lamp, "thanks for walking me up."

"My pleasure." I wheel her luggage inside, setting it against the side wall. Even the paint is a bit chipped. "You sure you're okay?"

"I'm fine. Really."

I pull myself away from Claire's place, forcing myself to walk down the hall. I pull my phone out of my pocket and make a call.

"I need you to watch Claire's place. There's nothing stopping anyone from breaking in. Keep tabs and report to me every three hours. If you see something suspicious, call for backup, and notify me immediately."

"Consider it done."

"Thanks, Tyler."

"But I must ask, are you okay? I know whatever happens in Vegas…"

My fingers rub at the tension forming between my eyes. I wasn't expecting Tyler to get all emo, but here we are. "I'm fine." It's easier than telling him that I'm in over my fucking head with Claire. It's better than telling him that his job title is essentially…professional stalker.

"Ouch. That's the most feminine thing you've said thus

far to me. Next thing, you'll be calling me to analyze menstrual cups."

"What?" Is he for real?

"Never mind."

"Just do your damn job, you prick."

"Go enjoy a tropical seltzer and some reality TV. You need to unwind some."

I pull the phone away from my ear, end the call, and shake my head. Tyler better the hell deliver what I need or he can learn to accept being fired. Problem is, I need him in my life more than he'll ever need me. He is my enabler.

My fingers scroll through my texts, as I jog down the stairs. When I find Asher's name, I shoot him a message.

Nic: Your guy Tyler better not let me down.

Asher: He won't. Just don't scare him off with your asshole tendencies. Or at least give him a heads-up when you go into grumpy mode.

Nic: You've always been annoying.

Asher: And you've always been set in your ways.

Thoughts of Claire catching on to me keeping tabs on her cross my mind. If I get caught, good. I may need her to continue hating me. Hating me invalidates her feelings that could develop with time. The last thing I need is for her to think there is a chance for an *us*.

27

CLAIRE

The fading memory of Nic standing in my apartment haunts me as the loneliness starts to close in on me. He stood perfectly, encased in the light glow of the lamp, a beautiful diamond against the dirty backdrop of my life. And just like every man who walks into my life, he is now gone.

A ball forms in the pit of my stomach as I walk around my apartment, looking at how I have been living for the past few months. It is like purgatory. This place was never permanent. It has always been a holding cell until Ethan decides whether I'm worth taking the chance on. And based off his Vegas behavior, I'm not certain I even want that chance anymore.

We never picked out furniture together or looked at art galleries for pieces we both enjoyed. There were no milestones hit, like buying a king-sized bed or inviting friends over for a housewarming celebration. No real holidays took place here. I barely have any memories in this apartment, and those that I do have are all laced with sexual escapades.

This is a fuck pad.

This is not a home.

I walk from empty room to empty room. There are no pictures of us hung in frames. Ethan actually scolded me once for trying to hammer something into the drywall and make a hole. Curtains are not even hung on the windows. There are just the normal commercial shades. Some of my townhouse belongings are pushed into a corner. I'd never really seen the point of unpacking them. How was I so blind for so long to not see what I can easily see now?

I feel sick inside. Ethan did not degrade me. I degraded myself. I was the one who kept my standards low, as Nic said. Why would Ethan want to rise to a bar that I never wanted to push up? I made it easy for him to use me as a sex object and not see me as a human. Sure, I set myself up for failure by dating someone from the Entice database with the hope of having *more*. But as soon as the first red flag was thrown, I should have listened and reevaluated the situation, instead of spending months in a loveless relationship with a gaslighting narcissist.

I settled for less because it was available. It is as if I knew Ethan was wrong for me all along but was trying to get him to love me anyway. And for what? A boost in my self-confidence? To think that if I landed someone like Ethan Maxwell, that somehow I would believe that I am worthy of the attention. We outgrew each other, when in reality we should have been trying to find ways to grow together.

The knock at my door pulls me from my thoughts, and I wonder if it is Blake. He often stops by unannounced, and I always welcome it—especially the days I'm here by myself.

I pull open the door, finding Angie staring at me.

"Hey you," she says, rocking on her feet.

"Hey," I say, tears filling up my eyes at just the sight of her. I'm a mess. It hasn't even been five minutes since I've said goodbye to her. "Did I forget something?" I look at her hands and see they are empty.

"Come back with me and Graham to our place. It just doesn't feel right dropping you off here. I have a bad feeling and would love to sleep comfortably."

"Oh, I don't know."

"Please. I need to detox from my Vegas trip and could use a fun workout class in the morning. We can discuss our future business plans and come up with a timeline and a goal sheet. We can even make a vision board."

Her eyes dance because she knows she has me with the vision board. It's my weakness. The thought of finding the perfect magazine clippings that express my goals is invigorating.

"Oh," she says going on, "and we can tease Graham by pretending we will be hiring young male models. We can cut out some hotties and glue them to the board just for fun, then make bets on how long it takes for him to notice."

I laugh over the last part. She must be starving for girl interaction if she is willing to deliberately agitate her beast.

"Let me just throw some things in a bag. Most of my luggage stuff is dirty."

"Take your time."

Waking up in the guest room at Angie and Graham's penthouse seems vastly different from how I have woken up at my apartment. The room is decorated with modern art, and the linens are of a thread count that must be triple what I have slept on at my own place.

I'll be the first one to admit that I have spent the past five years living without a care in the world when it came to finances. I would order the most expensive organic produce, from the freshest, most reputable suppliers. I would shop at the boutiques that ensured that what I bought wasn't also bought by a dozen other people. I would get my hair blown out by a professional. Now that right there is the epitome of entitlement. Who cannot blow-dry their own hair?

Some may say I am spoiled. But when you look at how neglectful and disengaged my parents are, it is obvious to see that the money that was sent to me was for the guilt. So, yeah, I spent it on trying to make myself feel better about my own life, when all I really want is to be loved. I basically was born with the silver spoon in my mouth—but with no one to actually help feed me with it. I had to learn to tend to my basic needs, while my parents went about their own lives.

One glance outside the curtains and it is obvious that the sun has barely risen. The fog on the ground gives the city an enchanted look. I really do prefer the West Coast over the East Coast. Maybe it was just the overcrowded feeling I got living in northern Virginia that turned me off. Plus, people just seem nicer here.

I walk over to the dresser where the start of Angie's and my vision board rests. We spent hours last night obsessing over what we wanted to accomplish. Between cutting out ideas, having an authentic conversation about each other's talents and strengths, and then working out a list of needs, I fell asleep dreaming of hope. It's that feeling of possibility that gets me excited and recharges my soul.

I quietly make my way out of the room, down the hall, and into the kitchen. The guest room is on the main floor, so the chance of waking up Angie and Graham who are on the floor above is minimal. When my life is out of control—like it currently is—I often use a structured diet to help focus my energy. Problem is, I am not in my own place, and since we just came back from an extended weekend trip, I doubt the fridge is stocked with fresh produce.

I inwardly scold myself when I hear the soft footsteps coming down the stairs. I turn and see Angie dressed in workout gear. She is not a morning person, so this is definitely showing a level of commitment from her. But then again, since she started therapy a few months ago, I've noticed a different level of discipline from her.

"We have a delivery of groceries coming this morning. I placed it last night before bed. How did you sleep?"

"Better than expected."

"Good," she says with a smile. "Any chance you just want to go for a walk?"

"That sounds good, actually. Let me get dressed."

I skip back to my room and toss on a pair of leggings and a loose long-sleeved shirt. I don't have many options, since I only packed for one night's adventure.

Despite Ethan ignoring three of my texts, I'm going to have to figure out things with him one way or another. We are technically cohabitating, although, according to Nic he doesn't need the place we share at all. Sooner or later, I'm going to need to come face-to-face with the problems we are having, instead of just trying to avoid them altogether. Change can only happen through honesty.

When Angie and I set a steady pace, I take a few deep breaths and give her the summary of what's going on—minus the parts where Nic got involved and the lost bet.

"So, things with Ethan and me got very ugly in Vegas," I start in general terms. "Actually, let me backtrack."

"Okay…"

"Turning down the Los Angeles internship changed everything for me. It was my way of committing to Ethan and seeing where our relationship would go. And it wasn't even a week after the decision that everything went down-hill. It was a gradual thing, and at first I just assumed his mood was work related. We used to spend time together, went on dates, and I felt connected to him. But when I said 'no' to my dream job, he got weird. I made that decision for him, and he went from being affectionate to making me feel needy."

"Do you think he felt the pressure when you stayed back? Maybe he expected the whole relationship to be short-term and you declining the internship somehow made it harder for him to end the relationship without looking like a jerk?"

"We are adults. If he wanted to end things, he could end things."

Angie shrugs. "Sure. But he is all about appearances."

"And money," I chime in. I fix my hair into a ponytail as I think over the whole relationship. "Maybe he thought he could do whatever he wanted and because I seemed finan-cially set with my parents sending me money, he wouldn't have to spend any on me. He is petty like that. It was easy for him to get what he wanted sexually from me, while never thinking he had to commit, and then still be able to do whatever he wanted with *his* money because I had my own."

"I mean, all of that is possible. It's hard to know what goes on inside the minds of an abuser. Some people put women down because it makes them feel bigger. It sucks and all. Therapy has taught me that I cannot control how other people react. I can only control how I respond to it."

"I'm so relieved you are finding comfort in therapy. But I'm not so sure it can be the miracle that saves my relationship."

Angie nods, agreeing. "So you thought going away to Vegas would help you both recharge and refocus your attention on each other?"

"That was the hope. But as I'm sure you noticed, it did the exact opposite. Ethan was more focused on being in the casino than with me. When he was with me, he was condescending."

"Claire, it took everything in me not to speak up to him the morning we went to the brunch buffet. But I promised Graham that I would let you figure things out for yourself and not add to your stress by sharing my thoughts at the time."

I nod. "I do appreciate you always respecting me and what you think I would need in the moment. I'm sure it was hard to keep quiet. I know if the roles were reversed, I would have failed. You know how easily my filter breaks."

She laughs. "I do."

We pass by a park and take the paved walking trail

through the center of it. Blossoms are forming on the trees and the smell of spring is in the air.

"Ethan has three residences—two I had no idea about."

"Wow, really?" she asks, looking over at me.

"I think he put me up in a rundown fuck pad and has been using his business meetings in Seattle as an excuse to not have to spend much time there."

"Damn."

"And every time I attempt to text him, he just ignores me."

"What are you going to do?"

"I think he is arriving back in Portland in the next couple of hours. Unless he got his flight changed." Knowing him, it is a possibility. I was completely unaware of his landing time when we were in Vegas and he arrived. "Maybe we can sit down and have an adult conversation, instead of just yelling at each other."

"Good luck. If you need anything, don't hesitate to ask me. The guest room is always open."

I frown over her offer. It's not fair to be living your best life and then have to deal with a third wheel. Graham and she are only getting married to make it legal. They are basically joined forever already and living daily like newlyweds. The last thing they need is some depressed downer to be moping around their place, watering down their happiness.

"Thanks, I do appreciate it."

"I know you do, Claire. I'm always here for you."

I slow down the pace to give her a half hug. We circle around and head over to the penthouse. I pack up my belongings and decide that I better wait at the apartment

VICTORIA DAWSON

in case Ethan decides to show up. He can't avoid me
forever.

When I arrive at the building, I take note again of all of the
security features that are lacking. Having Nic in this space
last night just emphasized that this is not a safe place to live.
I take the stairs. It's not like there is an alternative, so lucky
me, I love stairs.

Despite Angie's guest shower looking amazing, I forgot
to pack a lot of my toiletries, so taking a shower here is the
first thing on my mind. I use my key to enter and push open
the door to find the place completely empty. Everything is
gone.

Shit. Was I robbed?

I glance around the living room and kitchen and the
bedroom. Nothing. Everything's gone.

I walk into the bathroom and not even the partial bar of
soap was spared. It is like every memory of me being here
has been wiped clean. I wrestle for my phone in the bottom
of my bag and find Ethan's number.

**Claire: Either we got robbed or all of our things just
vanished out of the apartment…**

I am still in shock. Surely something was left behind.
Should I call the police? Try to find the landlord's phone
number on the bulletin board downstairs? I was just here
last night. Whatever happened was done within twelve
hours.

I walk out of the apartment and double-check that I got the correct room number and not an empty unit waiting for tenants. Nope. This is it.

My phone buzzes with an incoming text from Ethan. He must be done ignoring me. I pop open the app in a hurry and read his response.

Ethan: Storage Plus, unit 17, office on the corner has your key to release your belongings, 24 hour access

Claire: You packed my stuff up and shipped it away?

Ethan: I paid someone to

Claire: Why!

Ethan: I'm done with you taking and taking and taking. The apartment's lease was not renewed. Do not go back there. Drop off your key immediately in the box in the lobby or owe me a month's rent, plus the extended service penalty fee.

I must be having a seizure or a nightmare or am completely losing my mind. What else could explain this sudden shift? I am homeless.

I can't go back to Angie's. I can't stomach the thought of poisoning her mind with the toxicity that keeps oozing out of every aspect of my life. She will take one look at me and know I am shattered. With the wedding day approaching, she needs to focus on love.

I switch over to Blake and send him a text.

Claire: Hey. I hate to do this. But can I crash on your couch until I find a place to stay?

Blake: Only if you watch trash TV with me and tell me your woes during commercial breaks.

Claire: You sell a hard bargain.

Blake: You know my hetero roomie has the hots for you, right? In case you are in the market for a man-child.

Claire: How can he when we never met?

Blake: Your caller ID pic on my phone must have made a lasting impression on his libido.

Claire: I thought you said you could turn him.

Blake: Wow. Harsh, much?

Claire: Sorry

Blake: Should I get the vodka ready? I smell a breakup and it sure stinks. I just hope you didn't go as far as bleaching your asshole for that asshole.

As much as Blake and I like to joke around, it is me going through the motions. I am pissed off. Angry. Devastated. Sad. Disappointed. I am all the things rolled up into an impulsive ball of fire. Ethan better watch himself—I am that furious.

Claire: Doing a modified cleanse so don't worry about me. And yeah, Ethan is turning out to be a stranger.

Blake: Sorry, Claire Bear.

Claire: It's ok. It will be ok. :(

Blake: I know I am biased, but no one will be good enough for you.

Blake's loft is in the Pearl District, just a few blocks from the water. It is in a church that got converted and reno- vated into several loft apartments. For someone as eclectic as Blake is, this suits him. The artsy graffiti on the brick wall outside the building adds color, along with the trays of exotic plants outside of all the street-facing windows.

I jog up the three flights of stairs and am greeted by his newly dyed rainbow mohawk. Blake is leaning against the frame of his opened front door, waiting for me.

"I saw you pull up," he says, opening his arms for me to walk into them. "Come tell the Beefcake all about it."

I huff out a laugh. It is usually me who refers to him by that nickname, not the other way around. "Thanks for letting me crash. I will need to do laundry, since I don't feel like driving to the other side of town to pick up the rest of my things from some storage unit."

"Here," he says, ushering me inside his place. "I made

you a delicious glass of ice water since you are being all froufrou about some cleanse thingie."

I giggle through the tears that are freely falling down my cheeks. I am tired of crying. I am also equally tired of trying not to cry. I often wonder why I resist it so much. I usually feel better after a big ugly meltdown. However, I have my doubts that a flood of tears will make me less regretful of wasting my time with Ethan Maxwell.

I just want to get everything back to my equilibrium state, and the one thing I can control easily in my life is what goes in my mouth. So, ice water it is. I take a big gulp from the glass that Blake forces into my hands.

"Cheers," he says, clinking his with mine. He, too, is drinking a clear fluid, but I would bet it is not water.

"Where's the roomie?"

"Probably swiping for potential fuck buddies. I swear if I see one more pink taco on accident,"—he shudders, adding air quotes around the word *accident*—"I'm going to counterattack with a full-blown sausage party. I am petty like that. And I will take pictures of his reaction and make it look like he is the host."

I burst out laughing and flop down on the couch that is about as comfortable as a futon. The pressure of my body weight makes the springs boing with a tinny sound. The cushions are infused with the faint smell of nacho cheese-flavored Doritos, and just the thought of Henry bringing his conquests home to sit on them makes me want to vomit.

"How in the world did you even get paired with someone like that on the Roommate Finder app?"

Blake sinks farther back into the cushion and sighs. "I've been a victim of roommate fraud."

"Say what? Is that a thing?"

"It most certainly is a *thing*."

"Please explain."

Blake turns toward me and makes an exaggerated gesture with his hands to his heart. "Never in a million years did I ever think I would be duped this badly."

"I'm losing you here."

"His name is Henry."

I look over at Blake with confusion. "Umm, is that supposed to mean something? I know what his name is. You shared that already."

"What is the first thing you think of when you think of all the guys in the world named Henry?" he asks, rambling on with his hands flying through the air passionately over a subject so menial.

This is exactly what I need though—a distraction. I must not answer fast enough because fingers snap three times in my face, and a glare from Blake is directed at me.

"Umm…"

"Let me tell you what you think of," he goes on, making it hard to hide my smirk. "His name sounds wholesome, doesn't it? It's freaking *Henry*. Just hearing it, you'd think of a slightly immature sandy-brown-haired boy that has a golden retriever or—" He stops midsentence to hold up a finger in an ah-ha moment. "Maybe one of those doodle dogs with the curly hair. Am I right?"

"Sure."

"Well, he may be the only Henry on the planet that has a devious, single-minded, pink taco addiction who doesn't know the definition of *tact*. It is a game to him. How many ladies can he bag in a night, that is the—"

"You did not just say 'bag.'"

He nods vigorously. "I did. I've been picking up my best lingo off that Urban Dictionary site."

"Never again," I say firmly. "Never again."

"Oh and while we are on this disgusting topic, one more fun fact." He makes an exasperated face.

I brace myself for the reveal. "What is it?"

"He has a monster footlong dong."

"Is that part relevant to the story?"

"It most certainly is." Blake holds up his drink into the air. "Hail to the Henrys of this world for being thrown into the box labeled 'Underdog' unfairly, just to prove us all wrong at the end of the day."

I lift my drink into the air. "Hail to the Henrys."

28

CLAIRE

I wake from the futon-esque couch feeling like it has aged me five years in just one night. My bones hurt and my muscles ache. My stomach feels like I did a hundred full crunches, and not the half-ass kind that my peers would get away with doing during my years of high school gym class fitness tests. No, these are the intense ones I would often do during cheering practice. I hated them then, and I avoid doing them at all costs now.

I slept like shit, but it was mainly from the street noise and the rain—that would have otherwise calmed me. The entire building must lack insulation. It felt like trucks were roaring through the living room every chance I would doze off to sleep. Then the flickering streetlight that Blake describes as "charming" was also buzzing and on a few occasions hissing.

I hoist myself up, and my once sweet-smelling hair is riddled with a dehydrated cheese stench. There is nothing I want more than a shower and a fresh set of clothes. Problem is, the washer isn't quite working, so I have no other choice but to take a trip to the storage unit.

Blake has left for an early morning shift at the gym before he goes to his second job at the Boys Town store, where he is in charge of all of the clothing displays. It is his dream job to be able to create and rearrange the mannequins to model the outfits that the designer line puts out, catering specifically to guys who like to look polished but edgy with fashion.

I walk barefoot across the shiny hardwood floors and use his bathroom that is located just outside his room. The shower is tiny but at least the water is warm. It feels good on my sore back. I massage my neck and groan at the pull that I feel on my upper arm muscles. Today is going to be a physically rough day in the state I am in.

It feels counterproductive to put on worn clothes after being freshly washed. But it is what it is. I keep telling myself that this is all temporary, but the thought of having to find a new place to live is wearing on my brain. I'm definitely going to need a roommate—or five. How can I afford much of anything?

If only I can get on my feet by raking in some easy money. Then I will be able to put a deposit down and two months' worth of rent. It is while I am staring out at the street below that I get an idea. How about I activate my Entice account and go on a few dates with some rich businessmen like I used to and get paid for it? The minimum is two hundred dollars an hour, and I am familiar with the protocols prior to meeting Ethan—who basically ended my agency job by taking me completely off the market.

That's it. That is my short-term solution. I can work

around my gym hours and still be able to manage my daytime hours while figuring things out with Angie. Eager to get the ball rolling again, I log into my Entice account and hit the button to activate my profile. Everything is stored in the database, so the only thing I need to do is wait and either accept or reject potential dates.

Feeling a bit perkier, I grab my purse and car keys and head out of the loft, locking the doorknob before shutting it. I am on a mission to reclaim a piece of my life back, and I don't even need a vision board to help funnel my energy. I am that intrinsically motivated to have a chance at a fresh start.

When I arrive at Storage Plus, I am not surprised that the conditions of the units look to be less than adequate. It is a revelation to discover just how cheap Ethan is.

The guy working the office space is practically smoking indoors. Every time he grunts out a one-syllable word, it is followed by a puff of cloudy fumes that must be stored up in his lungs. Who even does this nasty habit anymore? It isn't like he is trying to hide it by the two spares situated behind his ear. I feel dirty just from the way his fingers graze mine when he hands me my key. Sleazeball.

Unit 17 is on the far end of the quad and is sandwiched between two other units that appear to have doors with gunshot holes. My door has rust splotches across the metal surface and a dented frame. The protective weather strip is frayed, leaving an ample gap. I will not be surprised if there is a snake or mouse inside. This is not one of those prestigious climate-controlled businesses. The only thing that is controlled here is probably the amount of illegal substances that comes in and out. But then again, what do I know? This is just me, people watching and being slightly judgmental.

I use my key to open the door, and when I look at my pile of belongings, it is sobering to see just how little of the space they take up. I no longer own furniture. The items I did own from the college townhouse were sold or given to local charities. Ethan convinced me that he had everything that I needed. Maybe being a narcissist means getting someone to rely on you, just to gain that level of control over that person.

I step into the concrete box and look at the cracks marring the rough surface of the slab. Huddled in a corner, collecting the water drippings from the leaky roof, are my clothes. They are stuffed in black trash bags and not even tied to keep them away from the elements leaking through the cracks in the ceiling. Fuck. What is wrong with him? Ethan didn't hire professionals to pack and move my belongings from his apartment. No, he basically handed some dude a twenty and a six-pack and said, "go move this shit."

Bent in a repurposed delivery box, I find my rewards chart that I use to help keep my eating and workout routine monitored. It is a dopamine rush for me to add a star next to each goal I conquer in a day's time. Ethan often alluded to the whole concept being childish, but his opinion no longer matters. I regret that there was a time in my life that I allowed it to take precedence.

I pull up on the first trash bag, trying to get a good enough grip to lift it toward the opened door. I make it about halfway, when the plastic pulls and shreds, emptying out the contents of the bag onto the nasty floor. My clothes and shoes spill out into the collecting puddle of water gathering in the dip in the concrete. Dammit.

I bend and scoop up as much as I can fit in my arms and carry them to the car. My outfit just gets dirtier from the muddy water that soaks into the fabric. Yuck. I go back into the unit to grab more loose items and find a perfectly wrapped gift box, addressed to me, tucked underneath a pile of dresses.

I examine the wrapping paper and bow, knowing that it was done by a professional. I have never seen a more beautiful box. I tear through the paper and discover that the gift is a set of bath products all with a chocolate scent. Lotions, bath bombs, and shower gel. I notice the little emblem as coming from the cactus garden and chocolate shop in Las Vegas. Nic Hoffman sent this to me. I don't need a little card to verify that it was him. I just know.

Tears bite at my eyes as I am overcome by the reality of my situation. I wish I could identify the paramount emotion burning in my heart. However, I feel like a mixed bag of them all. Maybe this trip to the storage dumpster is exactly what I need to move on. Maybe how Ethan is basically shitting all over our relationship is the cleanest breakup I've ever had. There is no coming back from this. No amount of therapy will ever erase these defining memories from my brain.

Whatever Ethan Maxwell needs, I am certainly not the woman to give it to him. I hope I never see that man again.

In roughly eighteen minutes, I have all of my meager belongings packed up in the trunk of my candy-apple-red

Nissan Maxima. I really hope I do not have to trade her in for something more practical. She has done me well ever since I moved out here to Portland from the East Coast. If I have to go without a car, I will go nuts. I shudder at the thought of waiting in the rain for the city bus to arrive late.

Get your head on straight, Claire. Calm down.

I turn in the key at the main office and do not even look the attendant in the eye as I wave an insincere goodbye. My phone buzzes to life as I plug it into the charger so I can access the GPS on my screen. Every city seems to have a "wrong side of the tracks" section and with all these years living in Portland, I finally found it.

When I get back in familiar territory, I park at the lot near the city park and walk down to the river. I sit on an empty bench and check through a series of alerts from Entice. Wow, that was fast. I barely even activated my profile, and I already have a surge of potential dates. I will call this fate.

Now, I just need to find an affordable apartment that won't break the bank. I doubt Blake's apartment is in need of estrogen, especially if this Henry character is as he describes. Blake can be a bit overdramatic sometimes, so it's hard to take his words at face value. Regardless, my days on the uncomfortable sofa are limited. I do not want to overstay my welcome, mainly because I never know when I may need that type of favor again.

I scan through the list of dates, some overlapping and causing what I hope would be a minor bidding war. This is good. Increased hourly rates are in my favor. I don't even bother worrying about who I am accepting or not. Everyone is vetted with background checks done regularly. I just upload everything to my calendar, and because I no longer have much of a social life at the moment, I know I am free.

To decompress everything that has happened today, I decide to take a walk along the path by the water. The fresh air always helps me to refocus and center myself.

My brisk walk turns into a slow jog. Once I get my breathing under control, I turn the jog into a run. My feet hit the pavement and my hair blows in the breeze. My arms chug along, and I feel rejuvenated from the ability to move my body freely. That is what exercise does for me. It recharges me and makes me feel alive.

When my body is physically exhausted, I slump into my car and make my way to the free clinic a couple of blocks away. If I'm going to be active at Entice with the sole purpose of making easy money, then I better follow the protocol and update my test results.

When I get back to Blake's place, I am confronted with a partially nude Henry meandering about the kitchen. At least that's who I assume it is. Who else would be making a skillet of pancakes for dinner, wearing a low-cut pair of boxer briefs?

He smells of stale nacho cheese, and it makes me want to vomit. He must take my look of disgust as approval, because his eyes flame with possibility.

Blake was right. This Henry definitely doesn't look like the golden retriever type. He doesn't have sandy-brown hair and isn't anything I would describe as wholesome. He has a man's body but a teenager's sex drive.

"Shit," he mutters, running his hands through his hair. "Did I drunk text you? You look-"

Familiar? He has seen my picture on Blake's phone. I

narrow my eyes at him but play along. "Here for the booty call. Hope your dick can stay up this time. You have quite the reputation forming."

"Fuck," he hisses. "Did Stella—" He pauses, waving the spatula in the air. "No, Stacy…yeah, Stacy. Did she talk shit about me? Lies. It's all lies."

"She said the surgery was supposed to fix the issue." I make a point to move my eyes down to his crotch and look at it as if I am trying to solve the most complex math problem. "But maybe the doctor messed up."

"Hot damn, she's a crazy bitch." He sighs and runs a hand through his hair in exasperation. "I never had surgery. She's just mad that—"

I can't contain my laughter as it bursts out of me. It is refreshing to laugh this hard again. Today has been such a mess that this is exactly what I need.

Henry steps closer and takes a better look at me. I try to only breathe through my mouth. It is like he is dusted in powdered cheese. Maybe it is oozing out of his pores when he sweats. I think I just threw up a little in my mouth. Gross.

"Wait a minute," he says, looking me up and down. "You are Blake's best friend, Claire. My future booty call girl."

"Well, that is never going to happen."

"*Never* just makes me work harder," he counters.

I start to turn around and take my place on the sofa, when Henry pulls my attention back to him with the clearing of his throat.

"Blake told me you were looking for a place to stay. For your information, my bed sleeps two."

I suck both of my lips into my mouth, before saying, "Thanks for the…" How do I even respond to this?

"I was one hundred percent offering."

"I'm not a good fit."

His eyes twinkle. "To be determined."

He makes me want to take a shower. I am starting to smell like fake cheese.

29

NIC

I've been pissed off from the moment Claire decided to activate her Entice account. As expected from a pretty girl like herself, she is causing quite the war over potential dates. Some clients have even resorted to private messaging me to try to sway the decision.

I want to break something. Smash someone. Think about anything other than Claire sitting and enjoying dinner with some rich asshole, whose only motivation in engaging in small talk is getting her into bed. Sure, Entice is a legitimate escort service that specializes in high-end dates and the elite status of catering to a plethora of personality traits. But off the books, many women engage in counteroffers that typically involve sexual favors. Angie was not one of those women, not that I would ever think of my future sister-in-law in that type of scenario. My brother will take an ice pick to my brain if I do. As for Claire, I'm really not too sure. She kept a low profile during her active status days and when she met Maxwell, her random dating came to a halt. However, Claire is struggling financially, and when someone gets desperate, there's no telling how far they will go.

It has only been a couple of days since we returned from Vegas, and I have the fiery dark-haired beauty on my brain. I can't stop thinking about her. It doesn't help that I have seen her in a bikini. I have seen her in lingerie. I have seen her after I've kissed the hell out of her lips. It is too much for my fantasies to endure. It is like having a meal entirely made up of appetizers, when all you really want is the main course.

Claire is naively optimistic on a good day, and her bright personality is strong enough to attract most men. However, she is equal parts sweet and sexy. That combination alone is lethal on my senses. I want her like I have never wanted anyone else. Just the thought of her entertaining some man for the simple price of money makes my blood boil. She is playing with fire and doesn't even realize how badly she could get burned.

I can provide for her. I can give her everything she needs...

Except real stability.

And no matter how much my conscience is telling me to run to her and force her to accept help, I know that I already blurred too many lines. For someone to be with me, they really need to know the score.

I run a hand down my face as I lean back in my office chair at Hoffman Headquarters. I should be installing all updated cameras and security features right now. I should be familiarizing myself with every employee's profile and doing my own thorough background checks. I just cannot stop thinking about what I really want with Claire, because even if I get her, I'm not quite sure our goals align. In fact, I'm nearly positive they do not.

I am not a forever type of person. I am not even into anything that remotely resembles a relationship. Everything that I partake in when it comes to the opposite sex is temporary. The women all know that, so it's not like I bait and switch things to suit my needs. The ones that hold my attention all fit the same mold, so it should be no shock to them when I fade out of their lives as fast as I enter.

My phone buzzes and I check the caller ID to see that it is Penny.

"Hey sis," I greet.

"Hi."

"To what do I owe this pleasure?" I ask, trying to keep the hesitation out of my voice.

"I was hoping you can convince Mom and Dad to let me do an early release from the center."

I swallow hard and play with my ring, rotating it around and around. "Oh yeah?"

"I just would like to start living again. Plus, Graham and Angie are getting married soon."

"You being officially released or not isn't going to affect your attendance at the wedding, Pen."

"Yeah, yeah, I know. But, I want to be able to reach my own milestones too. Everyone here says I am doing great. I've hit all my goals. I will be enrolling in a maintenance counseling program no matter where I move. I have done all the right steps."

"Have you talked with Graham about this?" I ask, already knowing the answer.

"No. You know how crazy he gets when it comes to control. If it isn't his idea, then it isn't the right idea."

I chuckle over her exasperation. "Okay, fine. I'll look into it and verify with your doctors that things are going well. If I can put the seed into Mom and Dad's ears, I will do my best."

"That's all I ask," she says, relief flooding through her words.

"I just don't want to be responsible for any relapses or downslides."

"I get that I'm always going to be the baby in the family, but you both need to dial down the overprotective-brother roles that you have spent years perfecting."

I smirk over Penny's feistiness. She is getting back to her old self and there is no better feeling than watching someone you love prosper again.

"Enough about me," Penny says, "I want to know who the lucky lady is."

"What? What are you talking about? I…" I pause as she erupts into a fit of giggles. "Penny—"

"You basically confirmed my suspicions with just the way you reacted right there. You know that, right? Denial, denial, denial."

"There's nobody."

"Angie sent me pics from the Vegas trip, and I saw the chemistry ooze from those photos."

"Whatever, little sis." It is obvious that Penny is refer-ring to me and Claire—and not Angie and Graham. The last thing I need is her concocting some love story in her head and sharing it with Mom, who will then start planning out a future wedding. Ever since Graham has decided to settle down, she is on some love-and-marriage kick. She is even claiming she missed her calling as a wedding planner. "If these types of made-up scenarios keep you entertained while you are in Seattle, then have at it. Create whatever you want in that little head of yours to keep from being bored."

"You know Mom would approve, right?"

I huff out a breath. "I don't need Mom's approval."

"Umm, yeah you do. Have you met the lady? She can get super crazy over her boys and their love interests."

"She can get super crazy over you, too," I add.

"Yeah, but we all know how I'm the sensible one. Plus, she already treats you differently because she always feared you developing that Middle Child Syndrome."

I laugh. "Developing what?"

"Google it."

"Bye Penny."

"Bye Nic."

I shut off my phone and plug it into the charging cable. It takes everything in me to resist popping open the tracker app and seeing where Claire is located at this very moment. I am becoming obsessed. Even Penny is starting to notice. With a mile long to-do list, I need a clear head if I'm going to make executive decisions about the security protocols here at HH and close the gaps that trespassers seem to be finding in the building's armor.

I move over to the conference table that I just had assembled and unroll the building's blueprints. Graham is not a stupid man. He already has so many features installed. However, the one thing he is lacking is having someone who he can trust without a doubt managing the systems. Enter me.

I spend the next hour making notes, documenting my test results, and constructing a list of employees who may be moved from a permanent position here to a trial-basis one. As far as I'm concerned, no one's job is safe. Everyone is expendable.

The sound of a knock on the door jolts me from my deep thoughts.

"Who is it?" I ask, rolling up the prints and tucking them safely inside my locked cabinet.

"It's Dan King, sir. May I come in? I am part of the security division here."

He is actually more than just a *part* of the division. He and Eugene are the backbone—at least on paper. They both have been vying for the lead position during their six-month trial basis. Prior to trying to move up in rank, both men have had years of stellar performance at HH.

When all of my documents are secured, I grant entrance and am surprised to find that Dan looks way younger than his employee profile says for his age. Must be good genes.

"What can I do for you?"

He clears his throat and stands tall. "I know that it is not official yet, but Mr. Hoffman has already informed me of the change in leadership. I just wanted to formally introduce myself and ask if I can do anything to secure my new position from being just a trial-basis position to a more permanent one."

I study Dan's expression and demeanor to try to get a feel for this man. I'm not sure of whether or not to commend him for taking initiative or be wary of the timing. It is after the normal work shift hours, and I'm sure he has done as much research as he can on me, but not nearly as much as I have done on him. Our paths have crossed a few times when I would frequent the building, but we were never introduced and he was not on my radar to care. Dan's credentials rival my own, so I am definitely interested in seeing his performance. However, no matter how you slice it, he is basically destined for a demotion instead of a promotion. Me taking the lead position is a done deal.

"What is your take on the latest security breach?" I ask, turning my attention to the wall of windows overlooking the city. My new office is one that has never been utilized before, so at least I am not kicking anyone out of their space. With record speed, contractors were able to execute all of my requests and customizations. I am one picky bastard. Not even I will deny that fact.

I watch as Dan swallows and shifts his weight onto his less dominant foot. "I think that Mr. Hoffman has the right to be concerned, and that tightening up on safety procedures will be beneficial. I was actually on a scheduled day off when it happened, and Eugene was taking over the write-up and follow-up."

"How do you think we should go about tightening security?" I ask. If Dan feels like he is on an interview, he pretty much is on one. Every meeting with a security staff member is giving me insight on what is happening here at HH. I need to know what the current system is lacking in order for me to provide some valuable upgrades.

"For one, there's not enough hired staff members during the off-hours shifts. Second, there are too many 'essential' employees"—he makes quotes around the word *essential*—

"who are privy to details that I wouldn't consider to be need-to-know."

I nod. I've had similar thoughts. Graham can only manage so many departments in his building without slowly losing control over each one and making costly mistakes when it comes to preventing problems before they arise.

My phone alerts me of a missed call. I finish up with Dan and wait until he is completely gone before checking my messages. Shit. The reason has to be urgent if Tyler is giving me a call. I redial his number.

"It's Hoffman."

"I'm outside Miss Nettles's loft and her date just arrived."

I tilt my head back and groan. "Thanks for letting me know. Anything else to add?"

"Oh, most definitely, but I'd rather not say."

"Why the hell not?"

"I plead the fifth."

I toss both hands up, almost losing the grip I have on my cell phone. "Fucking-A, Tyler. This isn't an interrogation— just tell me what I'm paying you for."

He sighs. "Asher did warn me about your mood swings," he says in a singsongy voice. "Is this one of them?"

"Asher is a piece of shit. I swear you both want me to go ballistic. Just spit it out before I come over and smack some sense into you."

"Okay, okay. Based on the reservations made, it appears that Claire and her date will be dining at El Pastel in the Parkhouse Plaza."

"Not surprised. It's one of the top restaurants in town."

"One more thing."

"Let's hear it."

"Maxwell also has reservations there tonight."

"On my way."

"Oh, snap. Are we going to end up in jail tonight?"

"It's a strong possibility."

"Dayum."

30

CLAIRE

"You look like the best purchase I have made so far," my date says, leaning in to give me a peck on the lips. There is a compliment mixed into his awkward comment—at least I think there is. He sure seems pleased with himself. This is how some men are from the agency. When they "buy" you, they think they have certain unspoken privileges when it comes to you. It never used to bother me before but right now it does.

I take his offered hand, as he guides me from the sidewalk outside Blake's loft and into the passenger side of his Aston Martin. It's a nice car. Freshly waxed and still has the new car smell that I really do not enjoy. It makes me nervous, actually. Like I'm going to smudge up the window or put fingerprints where they don't belong.

While I have never been on a date with this guy before, I have been on a dozen or more dates with guys like him. They like to flaunt their wealth and utilize the database for arm candy. With my sparkling red knee-length dress and matching heels, I hope I look the part. Having a steady flow of money will help me budget paying off my loans and being able to figure out what I can afford for rent—at least until Angie and I can figure out our pipe dream.

My date isn't the best conversationalist, which really isn't that surprising. He also isn't averse to one-sided discussions where he rattles on and on about how cool his car is and how he didn't just stick with the base model features that are built-in to all Aston Martins. No, he is an "upgrade kind of man." His words, not mine. I use my time to polish up on my acting skills and practice showing fake interest, but in the end I just stare out the window as he takes me deeper into the city.

My phone vibrates in my handbag, and I resist looking at it. I play with my identity bracelet, and it feels weird to be wearing it again after so many months I was on hiatus from the agency. I can't help but wonder if Nic notices that I am back to being active. I shouldn't care, but yet I'm curious to know his thoughts on the matter. Is he shocked? Happy that his business is still going strong? Or indifferent to the entire thing?

We pull up to the Parkhouse Plaza, one of the high-rise buildings in the downtown area. The building is an iconic structure of Portland and often featured in movies taking place in the city. The top ten floors are reserved for luxury condominiums—definitely not the type that would fit my budget.

It feels weird being here. This was where Ethan took me on our very first date when he introduced me to his ex-wife at a symphony being held here. He wanted to even the score with her fresh date, and I guess I played the part well enough because he kept me along for an extended ride.

My date helps me out of the car, hands over his keys to the valet, and ushers me toward the entrance where a formally dressed doorman greets us with a smile, a nod of his chin, and a "good evening."

"Thought we could eat at El Pastel," he suggests. "The chefs here are some of the best in the world."

"Sounds good," I answer. My voice sounds dry, and I could really use a drink.

He guides me through the lobby, pointing out the architecture and naming each artist for all of the wall displays. He acts like he has a personal relationship with each one of them. He is treating me like I have never been here before and has deemed himself an expert on all things Parkhouse Plaza.

I stare at the center pool that is the focal point of the entire lobby. The cylindrical column in the middle of the pool has water cascading down the sides, adding even more attention-popping elements to the already impressive display.

My date ushers me into the elevator and glances around for the listing—at least that is what I am assuming he is doing.

"It's on the eighteenth floor," I say softly.

"Excuse me?"

I clear my throat. "I said it's on the eighteenth floor."

He nods and hits the eighteen without uttering another word. He actually remains quiet until we are about to head into the restaurant.

"El Pastel is Spanish for the word *cake*. It actually has

multiple meanings but this is the one that the owner preferred. It is not a bakery though."

He says the words slowly so that even I can understand them. I want to roll my eyes. *Thanks for mansplaining that for me.* If only he asked me one thing about myself. Then he might learn that I grew up in a very diverse area of northern Virginia and am well acquainted with the basics of multiple languages. You get that way when you work at a restaurant that is in a high tourist area and just miles from Washington, D.C. But why would he care about any of this information? If it doesn't serve him, then why bother?

When I originally joined the agency, I found it thrilling to go out with multiple men in a week's time. I would dress the part and play a role. It was fun. Invigorating. Yet, here I find myself about a year later and am bored out of my mind. Maybe it is the fact that I am finally growing up or the fact that I am doing this solely for the money. I realize how demeaning this job can be for my own brain. I'm not some bimbo. I have ambitions and dreams. I just need the capital to get me on the path that will help me to succeed.

When the waiter seats us, my date goes about ordering for the two of us, winking at me, which I find super creepy and outdated. No one winks outside of emojis. It is no longer a thing. I want to inform him of his faux pas, but that would require me having added conversation. And right now, I just want this night to end.

I turn to the waiter and smile politely, adding, "Please make sure the items that are set in front of me are vegan." I already know without asking that a place this upscale is on the organic train. Most fancy restaurants in Portland seem to cater to the health conscious. It is part of the reason why I love living here so much.

"Of course."

I settle back into my seat. I haven't had much of an appetite since leaving things unsettled with Ethan in Vegas. It is hard to eat when life is so uncertain. I just do not have much drive. My couple of days of cleansing are over, and I am back to eliminating processed food from my diet and sticking with plant-based nutrients.

I would try to make small talk right now and feign interest, but he seems content telling me about every ingredient that went into the drink that is being served to me.

When our food arrives, I listen to him rattle off the descriptions, despite my plate being different due to the adaptations made for my dietary needs. I just let him think he is on target and focus on how good the food tastes. I honestly can't remember the last good meal I have eaten. It had to be in Vegas and definitely before Ethan arrived.

My stomach fills up fast, and I can barely finish half of my plate. When I turn to get my napkin that nearly falls to the floor, I notice out of the corner of my eye Ethan sitting and having dinner with a group of men. Beside him is his ex-wife. Her hand is on his wrist and her eyes are sparkling up at him. They are sparkling almost as much as her solitaire diamond ring. What the actual—

"I have to use the restroom," I say, not even waiting for a response from Mr. Know-It-All. I'm pretty sure I just interrupted his monologue on the food distribution used for the restaurant that no part of me gives a flying fuck about it. Who knows, he may not even notice I left.

As I approach Ethan's table, my heart rate quickens. I

feel lightheaded, as if I didn't eat enough. Maybe it is my blood sugar levels. Or maybe it is the fact that I just spent the last hour of my life enduring a horrible date just to earn money because he tossed me out on the street. Maybe it is because his ex-wife is sporting a diamond ring that could easily cover rent for years. Or maybe it is because I feel like every minute I spent with Ethan Maxwell has been an utter waste of time.

He never really wanted to be with me.

He just wanted a fuck puppet to enjoy and control while he waited out his time.

Deena notices me first and gasps at the sight of me before recovering with a curt smile. I might look deranged. But I am committed and can't back down now.

My emotions flow through me like a hurricane and without much warning to prepare. My pulse quickens. I am walking so fast that my hair tickles my ears, as it brushes against them.

"Ethan, hun, I thought you said you had this situation handled," Deena says, whispering loud enough for me to hear, even above the restaurant noise.

"You don't waste time," I snarl.

"Claire…" Ethan's tone is in warning.

His face has a few bruises peeking through some type of cream he has smeared on his skin, and his eye looks like it has a broken blood vessel. I wish to add to the masterpiece. "Are you wearing makeup?" I ask with a huffed out laugh.

"Shut up," he quickly says in a rush, as if I'm letting out some secret.

"You look like a clown." I giggle. "Actually, clowns have better makeup technique."

"Get out of here, Claire."

"I'm done being silenced and emotionally abused by you, you narcissist!"

"Calm the hell down," he growls, getting up from his seat at the table. "Are you following me?"

"And why would I do that, Ethan? Huh? What is it that you ever had to offer me that would make me want to crawl back to you? We are over. And I wouldn't come back to you even if you begged. The sex wasn't even worth it!"

"You need to calm down."

My finger shakes as I wave it in front of his face. "Thanks for tossing me out of the apartment and throwing my belongings in storage, you asshole. Do you get off on this type of shit, you sick fuck?"

"Maybe I should go up to our room," Deena says, starting to slide her chair back.

"Oh, you have a place here too, Ethan? How cute, you liar! What was I staying in? Your fuck pad?"

He hisses for me to stop making a scene and frowns at Deena who manages to flinch over my words. Of course he would own a luxury condo here and not even let me know.

"Found out you have a house too, you bastard."

"This is getting out of hand, Claire," he snarls into my face. He glances back to his business associates and mutters something to them. They are all dressed in formal suits and it makes me want to hit something.

"Why did you lie to me? Why did you hide all of your properties from me? And did the sheets even get a chance to cool before inviting your ex-wife in to warm them again? All those months of stringing me along, degrading me and treating me like trash, were just to win her back?" I watch as his nose twitches, and he reaches out toward me to try to silence my temper. He captures my wrists and squeezes so tightly that I wince. "I hate you."

"How could you possibly think it wasn't going to end like this? You were an—" He stops before saying "escort."

"And you are an asshole." I twist out of his grip, stumbling backwards. I turn to Deena as she rises to leave. "You can have him and his emotionally abusive behavior. Unlike you, I can walk away. I have zero ties and for that, I am thankful."

Ethan turns back to his group and gives a weak apology. It comes out more like a snicker. I see red. He is treating me like a fool. I am so tired of his shit. I reach around him for whatever glass of beverage I can get my hands on and toss it directly into his face. Liquid splashes all over his face and down his designer clothes.

When he notices that Deena got some splatters too, he snarls. "You are a childish bitch."

I throw the glass at his head, but he ducks in time for it to land on the table, clinking dishes from the force. It is childish but makes me feel good in the moment.

Why start a fire and not stay to watch it burn? I move to grab another drink and—

Arms bind around me, halting my action. I whirl around to see two men with the little Parkhouse security logos on their shirts.

"It's about time," Ethan says to the men.

"You are such a pussy!" I yell back.

"Ma'am, you are being asked to leave the premises or the Portland police will be called," one says sternly.

I raise both my middle fingers to Ethan's face but resist

spitting. I don't need to be fined right now or taken to court for assault. I can't afford legal fees nor a lawyer.

"I'll find my way out," I snap at one of the guards.

"You will be escorted out of this building," the other dictates.

As the men lift me up by my elbows to get me to move, I kick up my feet and plow them right into Ethan's crotch. "Oops, my bad." Several dishes hit the floor, and I no longer have any sympathy for anyone at the table. Anyone associating with Ethan Maxwell can't be stellar citizens. He only fraternizes with those like him.

"Word of advice, do not come back," the one security guard says into my ear. "Ever."

Tears fill my eyes as soon as my back is turned to Ethan. My shoulders tremble and my breath collects in my throat. I try to swallow. I try to breathe.

Mr. I-Drive-An-Aston-Martin catches up to me but I wave him off. I tell him the date unfortunately is over, and he can withhold my payment if he wants, as long as he doesn't give me a bad review for my profile. I can try to recoup the money later. I get into the elevator with the two guards and get ushered across the lobby's tiled surface.

When I look up at the entrance, I see Nic Hoffman lingering along the tall glass window, checking his cell phone. He notices me right as my eyes scan down his body. I stop instantly from my blatant perusing. In my defense, the man knows how to wear a pair of denims. It is like he has his own brand that is tailored just for him.

Nic moves closer to us and nods to the workers. They seem to know each other and maybe that is how his line of work is when it comes to these types of jobs. Everyone knows each other and word gets out about troublemakers.

I am the troublemaker.

The guards disperse and leave us be.

"What happened?" he asks, scanning over me. "Are you okay, Claire?"

I shrug and look past him out the window. "Minor misunderstanding." I still feel Ethan's hands on my wrists and my anger sparks again over the regret I didn't punch him in his smug face.

"Something obviously happened for you to be flanked by two of the security men. So, tell me."

I sigh. "I was on a date."

"A date?"

"From Entice."

Nic gives me a single nod but doesn't say any more on that topic. "Keep going," he encourages.

"I ran into Ethan and his ex-wife, and I may have thrown a beverage in his face."

"He would have deserved it. And more."

"I know, right? I may have also called him a pussy."

Nic stifles his laughter, which just makes me smirk. "Go on."

"I may have also caused quite a scene with my yelling." I allow my lips to form a straight line. Looking back on the situation, I actually think I was rather calm. I could have been so much worse. "And I kicked him square in the balls, making him knock some dishes onto the floor."

"I bet the restaurant didn't appreciate that," he says with a chuckle.

"Nope. So I got escorted out and asked to not come back." I sniffle and try to keep my emotions in check.

"There are plenty of other restaurants in the city that you have not made scenes at yet. I wouldn't worry about this minor altercation."

I smile over his nonchalant response. "What are you doing here? Why are you lingering in the lobby?"

"I live in the building down the street. A friend was eating dinner upstairs and saw that you were one of my employees," he says, pointing to my wrist, "based on your bracelet." His eyes narrow, and he takes my hands into his, turning them. "Did that bastard grab you? Your wrists are all red."

My nonanswer gives my answer. "I'm fine."

Nic's eyes level with mine. "I already warned him that I'd break him in half if he touches you again. The fucker has a learning problem, because I thought I made myself clear in Vegas." His thumbs soothe my sore muscles, as he gently massages the tenderness.

"I'm okay, Nic. I got my revenge when I kicked him." My response doesn't seem to calm him, but I continue trying to distract him from going up to the restaurant to make Ethan pay even more. I don't want to be left alone right now. "Then what happened with your friend?"

"He decided to give me a call to make sure I didn't need to intervene. The security staff beat me to it."

I look down at my red heels. "It was not one of my finer moments." Now that the adrenaline has worn off, I feel nauseous from the whole scene I caused. No one is going to take me seriously as a career woman if I can't maintain a positive public image. Breaking out into fits of rage in an upscale restaurant doesn't help—even if Ethan deserved everything and more.

"What do you need?"

My eyes meet Nic's with confusion. "What do you mean?"

"In this moment, right now, what do you need, Claire?"

I think about the question for a few seconds before answering honestly. "I need to hit something. I have all of this anger pent up inside me, ready to inflame. This whole Ethan situation has me about to burst from the anxiety of it all."

Nic nods and pulls me out the main entrance. "Come."

"What are you doing?"

"Giving you what you need."

31

NIC

"Where are we?" Claire asks, looking up at me.

"You'll know soon enough."

She is so freaking cute in her sparkling red dress and matching heels. Ethan is a fucking idiot to ruin whatever chance he had with her. I'm enjoying keeping her in suspense as we walk the two blocks to the destination I had in mind.

A couple of weeks ago this venue opened in a gutted-out first floor of one of the office buildings. I didn't understand the purpose of such a place until Claire looked up at me with her sad eyes, and in that moment I would have given her anything she had asked for just to remove her tears.

If Claire knew the effect she has on me, she could ruin me forever.

When she sees the neon sign above the entrance, she is bouncing on her feet over the anticipation. I grab the door for her and allow her to walk in first. The warehouse style room is lit with neon lights. Sections are set up with breakables to look like rooms in a house. There's the TV room, the bedroom, the kitchen, and the bathroom.

I pay the entrance fee, and the teenage worker hands us the handle for a wagon filled with a hammer, a baseball bat, and a metal rod.

"Sign this waiver," he slurs his words. "That way if you hurt yourself, you can't sue. You have forty-five minutes to smash anything you see with a pink X marking across the front. Please do not pick up broken glass. Last week some idiot came in here and needed a couple dozen stitches. Real bloodbath."

"Got it," I respond, glancing over at Claire to make sure she didn't pass out or anything.

She takes the handle of the wagon and examines the tools of mass destruction. "So, I get to go around and—"

"Hit shit," I finish with a smirk. "Just like you requested, right?"

"In the literal sense, yes."

"Well, then go do the damn thing," I persuade. "Show me what you got."

I step back and watch as she pulls the wagon toward the TV room where there are vases, lamps, picture frames, and a huge, outdated television set up on the stand. Everything is marked with a pink X and is considered fair game. Claire picks up the baseball bat first and takes a swing at the lamps. The sound of glass breaking echoes through the room.

"This is better than retail therapy," she mutters, then smashes the vases and frames. She saves the television for last and the shattering sound resonates in my ears.

I look at her with admiration. She is so strong, both physically and emotionally. "Feel a little bit better?"

She gives me the biggest smile. "Yeah, actually."

I follow her around and watch as she breaks items in each room. She has the most fun in the kitchen. She switches over to the metal rod and goes to work at destroying everything that she can. I grab the hammer and break through a series of glasses and coffee mugs, taking my own anger out on innocent inanimate objects.

Sweat beads on Claire's forehead, and I wipe a little off with my thumbs. I can see her pulse beating in her neck as she calms down. Her hair is damp and her entire body is glowing with the warmth from the workout.

I guide her to the exit and we step out into the cool night air. The city is alive with a few pedestrians, some street musicians, and the sound of cars passing. It is cloudy out and it looks like it could rain at any—

"Ahh," Claire yells, ducking her head as the sky opens up.

I tug her arm and run with her toward my parked car that is a block away. We are just a few yards away when she stops suddenly. Her arm slips from mine, as water beats down on our bodies. Then she does the unexpected. She dances.

Twirling and spinning, with her arms raised to the sky.

I watch her as she lives in the moment. Enjoying the wonder of dancing in the rain. Her eyes beckon me to join her. I shake my head, smirking at her, as I lean against a light post. My view is hazy as the droplets gather on my eyelashes, but all I care about is seeing the girl who is prancing in puddles just a few feet in front of me.

"Come on," she calls. "Dance with me, Nic."

"I'm enjoying the view," I say, laughing.

And that I am. She is magnificent.

Her bottom lip pouts out. And without even thinking, I'm stepping closer and closer to her. Her vibrant personality is pulling me toward her, and before I realize it, she is taking my hands, and we spin. Her head tilts back and her tongue extends as she drinks in the rain—like I drink in this moment.

I can't even remember the last time I acted childlike, and sharing this moment with her now makes me realize how much fun and excitement Claire brings to my life. She is so much more than just the physical fantasy I crave.

When the chill from the rain trembles through our bodies, we make our way to the car. We are soaked from head to toe. There's not a dry spot left on either of us. I open Claire's door and help her inside. Then I round the front and find my place behind the wheel. I glance over at her and am enchanted by her smile that can't seem to dim.

Happiness looks good on her.

Her eyes sparkle, and I can't help but wonder if she realizes what she does to me.

"Want me to drop you off at your apartment?"

Claire shakes her head no. And just like that, the smile is gone. The light that once beamed in her eyes has faded. I can't tell if she is now crying or if the rain drops are just dripping down her face. "No." Her word is barely a whisper.

I start the engine and turn on the heat. "Where to then?"

"I can't go home," she mutters. She sounds lost. Like she is somewhere else inside her head and not here with me in the car.

"Okay…"

"I just want to…" she says, pausing. "I don't even know what I want anymore. Have you ever wanted to do something reckless just to prove that you are alive?"

I nod my head. "Yeah."

"That's what I want to do. Something stupid. Something selfish."

She pulls out her vanilla cupcake lip gloss, and before she can get the cap off, I snap at her with a, "Oh hell no. Put that away."

Her eyes go large and she looks at me with an innocence that I normally would never find attractive. But on Claire? Every freaking thing she does is sexy.

"Have a thing against lip gloss?"

"That scent, yes."

"Oh, I may have another in here," she says, rummaging through her purse with only the lights from the street shining through the fogged-up windows as guidance.

I place my hand on hers to stop her and then move it up to her chin. I grip her gently and force her to look at me. "The smell of vanilla that you wear drives me wild with a need to fuck you. So put it away before I do something reckless and selfish. Because tempting me right now will not work out in your favor. I am that volatile."

Claire's lips form into a little O-shape and her soft exhales almost make it impossible for me not to get hard. She has zero clue what effect she has on me, because if she did, she may deliberately try to torment me.

Claire looks down at her purse and twists off the cap to the vanilla cupcake gloss anyway.

My breath hitches in my throat but sounds more like a

growl. Her eyes lock onto mine as she parts her lips, glides the tube across them, and then rubs her top over her bottom to smear it into full coverage.

"Maybe I want fucked," she states matter-of-factly. "Ever think of that?"

I make sure the car is in park and reach over for her. I drag her closer to me as my lips attack her gloss-covered ones. She tastes even better than she smells. "I do more than just fuck," I say, reacquainting myself with her lips. My fingers wrap around her damp hair as I pull her closer to me. I unfasten my seatbelt blindly and practically kneel up on the seat to get more of her. I want her here. Now.

"Take me, Nic. I want you."

"Dammit, Claire."

"Quit holding back."

"I'm not going to make our first time be in a freaking cramped car." We aren't teenagers, for fuck's sake.

"Well, you better figure something out, because I'm horny."

A growl escapes my lips, as I frantically try to get my brain to do more than mentally undress her. "I'm driving you back to my place."

"I'm not going to stop you."

I snap on my belt, shift to drive, and pull out of the parking spot, heading toward my place as Claire's words replay in my head. I should take her anywhere else, but yet I don't have it in me to let her go tonight. I want her warmth in my sheets. I want her smell to be on every inch of my space. The fantasy of losing myself inside her body has been a craving that I can't shake.

I help her out of her side of the car and use my key fob

to open the main door of my building and then the fob again to get through the second security entrance. Claire is fidgeting at my side, as I wave to the front desk attendant. I can hear her sighs and quickened breaths. She is nervous, yet excited.

The elevator takes us up to the top where my apartment takes up the entire floor. It is much smaller than Graham's place but still the biggest unit in the building. I unlock the door and help her inside my entryway. We both toe off our damp shoes, leaving them in a pile near the closet.

Claire looks good in my space. It feels different inviting her back here. No woman has ever been here before, since I moved back to Portland. I have made it my mission to only have relations at hourly rate hotels or the woman's place. That way I don't have to ask them to leave. I just walk myself out when I feel like it. It's cleaner that way.

I have served my needs well, but seeing Claire dripping wet on the tiled floor, with her red dress stuck to every crevice of her body, makes me want for more. I am worried that if I have her once, it won't be enough. That I am essentially submitting myself to a mind fuck that the only way out of is to make her mine.

But I know I'm not capable of being the man she deserves. Women like Claire want the clichéd life and the happily ever after. And with me, it is always the *never after*.

That has been my motto. And my choices always reflect that guarantee of not mucking up the waters. Yet, there isn't a single force outside of death that will keep me from her right now.

I couldn't walk away even if I tried.

Claire examines every inch she can see of my home, and

her opinion suddenly matters to me on what she thinks of my place.

"Understated and functional. But yet still very classy. I like it."

"Glad you approve. My floors will look amazing with your clothes on them."

She turns around and huffs out a laugh. "Oh yeah, the whole purpose for me being here," she says, sauntering over to me.

"This is one hundred percent your idea," I remind. "So you're not allowed to hate me."

Claire is hard to read when it comes to sex. What I saw of her in the hotel at the Bellagio was not a good representation for what she can offer. She was with a douchebag, and he was doing everything in his power to degrade her. No woman ever deserves how she was treated, and my role in that whole shitstorm is something I have to live with forever.

"Come," I say, leading her inside farther. The owner before me was the artist type and added several features to the rooms that were modern. When I bought it from her, I left a lot and paid for some of the abstract wall art and custom furnishings to stay.

Claire stops in front of an imaginative painting of Portland. I can tell she is deep in thought as she takes in the colors. My hands wrap around her, and I kiss her neck softly. She is trembling in her wet clothes, and I scold myself inwardly for not setting the thermostat higher to compensate.

"You are freezing," I say, just as a shiver runs through her.

She turns in my arms. "Then warm me up. I am starting to think you are all talk."

My hands move down to her ass cheeks, and I squeeze them so tight that she yelps from the shock of it. She is baiting me. She wants me to lose my control. Problem is, she doesn't know yet how scary that can be if I do.

I'm demanding and value the release sex gives. I push my partners to the brink and teeter them on the edge of too much, just to test their limits. But I always—*always*—leave them satisfied.

"Once I start," I say looking down at her, "I'm going to push you to your limits. I want you to be sure this is the path you want to continue on. You still have time to back out." *Before the big bad wolf gets you.*

Her eyes heat and she nods her approval. "I'm sure."

"Good."

I hoist her up in my arms and her body molds to mine. I carry her down the hall, into my massive master bedroom. I walk toward the fireplace and hit the remote to start the flames. I then carry her back over to the area rug, set her on her feet, and strip her down to nothing. Every article is peeled off her skin and discarded.

Her dress.

Her bra.

And then her scrap of panties.

"Your beauty is effortless. All you need to do is stand there, and my eyes are getting drunk off of your radiance."

Her bottom lip gets sucked into her mouth, as she rocks on her heels. I can see her throat move as she swallows. And then, her hands move up to shield her breasts from my view, while crossing her legs.

I take a step closer. "Don't hide from me." My words come out gruff. "Now's not the time to be shy. I'm going to ravish you. There's no part of your body my eyes won't explore."

My knee nudges her legs, parting them. With my hand, I paw at her naked crotch, making her jerk with the pleasure that just my palm can bring to her. She doesn't know what I'm capable of giving to her. I just hope she can keep up. I am not an easy lover. I am greedy.

Smack.

"Holy fuck!" Claire calls out, as her mind realizes I just slapped her pussy. Hard.

I use my whole hand to squeeze her naked flesh, feeling her juices leak out like a faucet onto my hand.

"That's it, my dirty girl. Your body always tells the truth."

I continue massaging her swollen flesh, teasing her lips with gentle strokes. She is so expressive with her sounds escaping from her parted lips. She is so responsive to every little touch I give to her. This is going to be pleasurable for both of us.

My palm delivers another slap to her sensitive core, eliciting a high-pitched yelp and a string of curse words from Claire. Like before, I soothe her ache with some light pressured circles.

Sweat beads on Claire's forehead as she anticipates another blow, but I instead kneel at her feet. She gasps as my mouth suctions on to her pussy. I lick. I bite. I push my tongue into her opening. Her knees buckle, and I catch her as she falls to the floor. I pull myself from her core to look at her, verifying that she didn't pass out.

"You okay, baby girl?"

"Mmm-hmm."

"Good. Because I'm just getting started."

I help her lie flat on the rug and spread her legs wide, bending her knees up toward the ceiling. I dive back in and use my thumbs to pull her apart, allowing my tongue to go deeper inside her. She is burning up and dripping with need. I want to smother myself and never come up for air.

I trace a finger along the path from her opening to her clit, covering the pad with wetness. Slowly, I slide it into her, feeling her walls cave in from the tightness. I twist my finger and bend my first knuckle, curling and pushing against the back of her clit from the inside.

"Ohhh," Claire moans, her upper body flying up. She tries to close her legs from the intensity.

"No. Keep them open," I instruct. "Submit to what I can give you. Just lie back and enjoy."

"Easy for you to say," she whispers, making me chuckle.

I continue fingering her, swirling it around to stretch her a bit before I slide completely out and add a second. She is dripping with her own lubrication, and the sight alone is making me delirious. I need to take my time with her. I need to give her a good experience, despite my cock telling me to end its misery.

Claire is moaning and that coupled with her tightness is almost my undoing. I am so hard that I may come in my damn pants before this ever goes to completion. I take a deep breath and focus my mind. I move my mouth to suck at her swollen clit, and that's all it takes to send her skyrocketing into orbit. Her orgasm is sudden, and the first wave crashes with the sound of Claire screaming out in pleasure. Her fingers pull at my hair, trying to grasp onto anything as she explodes into a high I doubt she has experienced before. Her back arches, and I hold her while she rides her wave.

After a minute, Claire tries to push me away, but I stay right where I am and work her to another aftershock. She writhes on the floor and squeezes her thighs against the sides of my head.

"I can't do more," she says weakly.

I pull up from her flesh just to look her in the eyes. "You can definitely do more." I smile as she shakes her head adamantly. She is freaking adorable and there's no part of her I want to tame or diminish. Getting her to come undone again will be a joy. "Don't deny me what your body obviously wants."

I go back to eating her out and milking out one more orgasm from her. I kneel up over her and chuckle over her boneless body lying comfortably on my area rug, with the flames from the fireplace casting a warm glow on her skin. She has a light layer of sweat on her face, and I smile over her satisfied look.

When Claire's eyes finally open, she has a smirk on her face. "I want more. I *need* more."

"That's my girl." Slowly her body is learning what pleasure I can give to it. I bend to kiss her nose. "Your wish is my command."

32

NIC

I know Claire's tests have come back negative. I have seen every recent health record and result she has uploaded to the Entice database at my disposal. I even know the exact type of birth control she uses, the dosage, and how long she has been on it. Not to mention, I've been keeping detailed tabs on her for weeks, so I know exactly where she has been and that she's only been with Ethan. Worst part is? I have zero guilt about acquiring the added details.

I pick her up from the floor and place her in the center of my king-sized bed. She looks pale against my black comforter. Her vulnerable side is coming out, and she tries to cover her breasts with her hands again.

"Don't hide your beauty from me. I promise to pay attention to all of your zones. No part of you will be neglected tonight."

I kneel on the bed and crawl toward her. I fix her hair against the pillow and smooth it out. She is exquisite. I kiss her forehead, her nose, and her lips. Then I move down to each of her peaks and give them the attention they deserve. I nip at them and suck one nipple into my mouth, savoring the taste of her skin. My tongue makes a wet path around and laps at the sides, making her moan deep within her throat. It is music to my dick, making me even harder and ready to break free.

I kiss down her stomach and then down one leg. I lick my tongue from her foot to her core and then back down the other leg. Claire twists and turns on the bed, making mewling sounds as I make a feast out of her. Her chanting of my name spurs me on. In this moment, I want my name to be the only one that ever leaves her lips.

"Play with yourself," I instruct, sliding off the bed to remove my clothes. She hesitates and her eyes twitch with nerves. "You heard me. Do as you're told."

Claire looks so uncertain. Just when I think she will refuse, her hand trails down over her flat stomach and between her parted thighs. She teases her clit and rubs.

"Good girl. Keep going," I encourage. "You look so fucking hot. Get yourself ready for me. Put your fingers in and stretch. You'll have a lot more to accommodate soon."

My mouth waters as I watch from the sideline as she grinds her apex against her own fingers. This is such a turn-on that I know I'm not going to last long.

My cock springs free from my boxer briefs, and I pump it a few times while watching Claire pleasure herself. I kneel on the bed, remove her fingers from her pussy, and then suck one by one until they are clean.

"You taste so good," I comment, making her blush. I enjoy the hint of pink I can create on her skin with just my words. In another time and another world, I might think she was made for me. That her body was designed for my eyes and hands to worship.

"I need you so badly," she whimpers.

"And you will have me."

When I reach for the drawer in my nightstand, Claire lets out a whimper, and for a second I think she is going to have second thoughts.

"I want to feel you inside me"—she clears her throat and a shyness I wasn't expecting from her hits her cheeks—"without any restrictions."

Saliva pools in my mouth. I want that too. But I also don't want to complicate things more than I know I already am. Going bare is a step toward an emotional connection, I don't have the ability of giving her. Yet Claire's beckoning eyes lure me into her, entrancing me with the way her lips let out a purring moan, as her eyes soak in every hard inch of my impatient cock.

"I was just tested," she says, more as a persuasion than as a clarification.

I know. I know way more about her than is ethical. "Okay."

"Okay." The simple word plays on her tongue. But it's the smirk she is sporting—one of victory—that makes me chuckle to myself.

I smile down at her and line myself up between her thighs. "You're being such a good girl."

Claire sucks in her bottom lip, and I barely hear the moan escaping her mouth. She is a fucking dream—a dirty fantasy come to life. And if it stays like this, I never want to wake up.

I place the head of my cock at her entrance and rock

my hips back and forth, just allowing an inch in with each movement forward. My slow pace is torturous for us both. I don't want to hurt her or cause her any discomfort. I know I am bigger than her ex-asshole. I don't need to rip her apart just to get my rocks off. Her pleasure is my pleasure.

"Oh Nic..."

"It's okay, baby girl. I got you."

I feel her juices seeping out, lubricating her walls to grant me easier access, and it is in this moment where I realize just how much she has a praise kink. I think she likes being my good girl. But if she only realized just how naughty and bad she really is.

"You are so fucking tight," I grimace, worrying that I'm going to cause her a tear. "Relax. I can feel you tensing up."

"I'm trying," she groans. "But you are a bit intimidating."

I reach between us and pinch her clit until I feel her inner walls release their lock. I press and rub her bundle of nerves until she is so worked up that she is thrusting her hips upward to get more of me inside her. "Yes, that's it, baby," I encourage. "Let me in." I push forth the last two inches and am balls-deep inside her warmth.

I kiss Claire's lips, tasting the faint vanilla flavor. After giving her a couple of minutes to adjust to my size, I start to move again. Out and in. I glide through her pussy, trying to get deeper. Sweat beads on my forehead, as I struggle to hold out longer.

With a sudden jerk, I pull out completely, laughing at Claire's shocked expression and whimper of disapproval.

"On your knees." I watch as she kneels upward and

shake my head. "You're not going to suck me off. Get on all fours, baby girl."

Understanding lights up on her features at my meaning. I help her get situated and comfortable. Then with hands on her hips, I slam into her from tip to root, savoring the feel of her wet heat. I find my rhythm and angle myself so I hit her G-spot, making her squeal with delight.

My eyes soak in the scene of the sexy goddess, on all fours, with her luscious ass bouncing to the force it has to endure of my slamming against it. Craning her neck, Claire looks back at me, her dark hair stuck to her forehead as she submits to the pleasure. I commit this image to memory. I never want to forget how gorgeous Claire looks at this moment.

As my balls tighten, I call out, "I'm close. Get there."

I reach around and play with her clit, while my other hand smacks her ass cheeks. That's all it takes to send her flying into ecstasy. I'm going to have so much fun testing her limits. This little tigress likes a bit of pain.

"Nic!"

"Fuck, I'm coming," I groan, thrusting one last time into her, as my cock erupts. I pant and continue a slow rhythm inside her, trying to draw out the orgasm to the longest length possible.

I soften a bit and slip out of Claire's pussy, rolling to my side and taking her with me. My cum drips out of her onto my thighs and I can't force myself to do anything about it, other than to enjoy this moment.

We lie like spoons, with her ass to my crotch. I kiss her sweet-smelling hair and wrestle with the comforter until we are under its weight. Exhausted from the cardio, I drift off into a peaceful slumber, just hoping that we reunite again in my dreams.

———

I wake to the memory of Claire and the sun peeking through my blinds. My hands move around the bed, searching for my heat source.

"Claire?" I call out, sitting up and looking around the room. Where is she?

I roll out of bed and check the attached bathroom and then the rest of the apartment. Out in the entranceway, I see that her shoes are gone. Shit. Why did she leave before I could feed her breakfast? I rub my forehead at my newfound desire to make sure she is properly fed. It's not like I ever cared before her. I have been with plenty of women after Tara and at no time did I give a shit about their wellness. They were just a pastime for me. Just a body to fulfill a basic need.

I meander back into the bedroom and see that the red dress is gone—further adding to the fact that Claire walked out on me. I never had a woman leave voluntarily after sex. This is why I always chose a location where I was able to perform my own vanishing act, without any awkwardness the morning after often brings.

Taking my phone from the pocket of my discarded pants, I open the tracker app and locate Claire. She is at the gym. It is not one of her work days, so I bet she is there getting a workout in. I know I have some adrenaline I need to work through this morning, so I really can't blame her.

I throw on some black mesh shorts but skip the shirt. I

walk into my home gym and blast some metal music, putting on my pair of boxing gloves. I'm not angry. I'm confused. Though the vigor at which I punch into my bag is the same.

Claire Nettles is under my skin. And I want more of her beneath my sheets, under the weight of my body.

She was sensational last night. How her entire body blossomed and glowed under my touch. Her responsiveness and the way she looked at me alone was enough to make me lose control. No wonder my head is so confused and a bit salty for her leaving me when I could have woken her up from her slumber with my mouth.

I take a cold shower to ease the tension growing in my lower half. When I finally start to feel the chill, I towel off and throw on my work clothes that consist of a tailored suit and white dress shirt. Working for Graham has its perks. The dress code is not one of them.

I check the tracker and find that Claire is just leaving the gym and heading toward the Pearl District that is just north of here. I watch the dot move throughout the streets and then stop at a section of town that has been re-urbanized after being abandoned for years. It is not the nicest area despite the attempt at the renovations.

I change over to the call feature and dial Tyler's number. "Hey, I need to know why she's hovering at this section of the Pearl District. Figure it out and get back to me immediately."

"Because you pay me the big bucks, I already know the answer to this."

"Then why was I not informed," I snap. I don't need Tyler's freshness. If he wasn't so damn good at his job, I would tell him where to stick his commentary. No wonder Asher recommended him. They both have shitty personalities and think they are funnier than they actually are.

"I emailed you."

"Never checked. Tell me now," I demand, my tone antsy. I sound like a drug addict waiting for the next fix. That's what this woman does to me.

"I told you about this loft that she is staying at. Seems temporary until she finds a place. Maxwell booted her out of the apartment."

"Fuck! Is he insane?" I ask, but don't expect Tyler to answer.

"Is that a real question?"

How did I neglect to see how much Claire is still suffering at the hands of Ethan? Why didn't she tell me she was homeless? No wonder she didn't want to go home last night. She didn't have a home. After what went down in Vegas, I thought maybe she would ask to stay with Graham and Angie for a couple of days while she got her things out of his place. I mean, it's not like Ethan doesn't have other places to stay. The asshole has been lying to her probably the entire time they've been together.

"Tell me more."

"Okay, I got the deets."

"The what?"

"I'm about to spill the tea."

"What? Why?" What the hell is happening? I run my hands over the back of my neck. I'm a few seconds away from exploding from the suspense.

"Never mind. Anyway, Maxwell broke his lease before renewal was up. So, Claire's camping out at Blake's place."

"Who the fuck is Blake?" His name sounds familiar, and I wonder if we met. Maybe at yoga? And just when I think I can't hate Maxwell any more than I already do, he does something else to make it worse. What did Claire ever see in him?

"Blake is one of her besties."

I groan. "Dude, you did not just say *besties*."

"Oh, you can bet your asshole I did. You probably met him, he is very eclectic in his style."

I shake my head at his terminology and struggle to even find the meaning behind his lame ass comments. "Tell me more about this Blake guy."

"Met at River Valley University. Worked at the gym close to the campus together. He is—"

"Any idea if they had relations?" I interrupt, cutting to the core of my potential issue with him.

"She has the one thing he doesn't want."

"And what is that?"

"A vagina."

I huff out a breath that sounds like a bark. "Anything else I should know?"

"Blake has a male roommate, Henry, who is extremely promiscuous. And not gay."

"Fuck."

"Can you remind me again?"

"Of what?"

"Do you like her, like her?"

"Bye, Tyler."

"Toodles."

I sigh and end the call. Is Claire going to move in with them? Maybe this isn't temporary for her at all.

It's not like she has many options with her limited savings.

What a disaster. I scold myself for not discovering this information about the lease sooner. No wonder the run-in at the restaurant was so heated between the two of them. She got booted out of the place she was trying to make a home. He better be glad I wasn't there to even the playing field.

I rub at the back of my neck. It's not even eight o'clock in the morning, and I already can tell that today is going to be a challenge to get through without losing it on somebody.

I lock up my apartment and take the elevator down to the ground floor. As I make my way to my car, more thoughts of last night drift through my head.

Claire smashing objects.

Catching raindrops on her tongue.

The glow of her skin as I pumped into her from behind.

I start the engine and drive to the corner coffee shop outside of Hoffman Headquarters to pick up a blueberry muffin and a cold brew coffee. I badge in through security and head up to Graham's floor to meet him in his office.

"Wasn't expecting you here yet," I mutter, looking at my brother sitting behind his polished desk.

When we first joined forces, I never thought he would ever be the type of businessman that he is today. However, with his money sense and skill set, I really shouldn't be surprised.

"Had to get away from all this wedding planning craziness. Angie needs the space from me, because I'm always trying to fix everything so she can stop worrying. But right now, she just needs someone who is there to listen and not swoop in and throw around money."

I nod and sit in the chair in front of his desk. "Things should basically all be planned by now. Getting close to the date and all. Right?"

"You would think. But then something will go wrong every couple of days. Anything from a miscommunication with dress alterations to a linen order not arriving when it said it would. I am about to call up the wedding planner and forbid her from relaying these types of details to her. Angie is going to crack, and this is supposed to be the happiest day of her life. Mine too."

"You could always involve Mom more," I suggest.

"She would love that. But you know how Mom is. Angie wants simple but elegant, not over-the-top and expensive."

"I'm sure things will smooth out."

"They better," he sighs. "Now, back to business. I saw your proposed plans that you faxed to me, and I have a bit of concern over your expected staff reduction projections. That's a hell of a lot of severance packages I'll be paying out, not to mention disgruntled reviews."

I nod. "I can see why it looks alarming, but in this area you want quality over quantity. Plus, the breaches in your security are hard to pinpoint if you have too many access points and rotation of staff in the high-privacy areas. It would be like having a very secure password and passing it out to three people instead of ten."

Graham leans back in his leather chair and strums his fingers on the top of his desk. "I trust you implicitly on this matter. Should we warn any of them with a notice as per the contract?"

"No," I state bluntly. "We need to avoid any internal

backlash prior to the departures. I want to do the firing all at once so there is no time to cause any damage or allow time for counterattacks in retaliation."

"It sounds like you are expecting a war."

I swallow hard and loosen the top button on my shirt. Maybe I am overreacting. Maybe I am just angry over Claire walking out on me this morning. I have not heard from her. Not a text. Not a phone call. Nothing.

"Want to watch a little experiment?" I ask, rubbing a hand over my chin.

"What did you have in mind?"

"It is a watch and see type of adventure," I explain. I dial in Tyler's number and tell him, "Now is a good time."

Graham sits up in his seat. "What's going on?"

I pop open my phone and access the security cameras from the lobby, tilting my screen over so we can both watch the display.

"How did you gain access to the live footage on your phone?"

I chuckle. "This is why you need me here, right? To seal up every crack you have in your security and give you the most current features." I point to the screen. "And this will be a good test to see how easily someone can access your building."

"What are you—"

Graham halts his words as a beautiful brunette enters the screen and starts a conversation with one of the workers. Her hands are animated and she is maintaining a smile the whole time.

"I hired an actress to pretend she is the planner for your

wedding. She just needs to drop off a portfolio on your desk."

Graham glues his eyes to the screen and watches as the woman gets granted access to the elevators, completely avoiding the metal detectors and the bag search.

"Well, I'll be damned," he utters, his facial expression turning to a grimace.

"Even I'm surprised at how easy it was. Let's see how far she can get through the building, shall we?"

Graham closes his eyes and rubs at the tension building between his eyebrows. "I hired people to worry about this kind of shit. I don't have time for it with everything else on my plate. Do what you can to fix this and any other issues. Keep me informed on the things that I really need to know. Otherwise, shield me from this type of drama."

"Already working on it."

I glance back at the live camera footage I am able to extract from the patrol room and watch as Claire walks into the lobby and gets stopped immediately by several security guards. I'm unable to get the voice overlay but can tell she is frustrated.

"Is Angie here in the building?" I ask, glancing over to Graham who looks visibly stressed.

"No, why?"

"Just wondering why Claire would be here at this time."

Graham looks at his phone and then mutters, "Well, Collins is bringing her here now as we speak. She cannot sit still and just relax." He sighs. "Wants to work her ass off. Not for the money, granted, but for a sense of purpose. Her words, not mine. She means more to me than anything I possess here on earth. I try to express her worth and value to me daily. But she's excited about this new business idea, and I love her too much to ever try to prevent her from exploring the things that may bring her joy."

I get it. I have known my brother my whole life and seeing him with Angie has been a game changer. A small part of me misses caring about someone other than myself and my immediate family. The more rational side of me realizes that it's for the best.

"So it's a done deal that she will be launching a business with Claire here at HH?" I inquire, inwardly groaning at the added stress this new venture will create for me. Just knowing Claire is a few floors away will drive me insane. Seeing her sensuous body pop up all over the security feed will further my developing obsession. How am I going to get any actual work done when I'll be constantly wondering what she is doing? Or what she is wearing underneath her work attire?

"Never met two more strong-willed women in my life. They are a pair to be reckoned with. Watch them completely pummel any competition and take this world by storm."

"No doubt." I stand up and make my way to the door.

"Keep me posted."

I turn back and nod. "Will do."

I shut the app down and head toward the elevator. Once it arrives, I hit the button for the lobby. I have a feisty little minx to deal with and brace myself for the impact.

33

CLAIRE

"I'm here to meet Angie Hoffman," I state again, this time slower. "Angela. A-N-G—"

"We know how to spell it," the guard snaps. "Very funny."

There are two flanking me. One is tall and the other is short. Both are annoying and taking this lobby job way too seriously. I'm in disbelief that something like what I'm experiencing could happen at Graham's place of work. Surely, he has better protocols in place than what I'm currently witnessing. I know I wind up on his shit list a lot, but I can guarantee he would not want me to be accosted like this. He may have a thing for control and all, but this seems highly unprofessional.

"Can you just get Graham down here to fix this?"

"Um, okay, sure," the tall guard says, looking at his coworker and laughing. "We have heard this one before, right? What's your name?"

I take a deep breath and count to five. "Claire Nettles." I

pull out my driver's license and hand it over. "See? Just like my ID states."

"Do you have a badge? Does Mr. Hoffman even know you are here?" the shorter guard asks, eyeing me with more than just suspicion. He is treating me like I'm some intruder or an enemy threat.

He and his teammate have been giving me a hard time for the past ten minutes. I reach for my phone to text Angie and immediately it gets torn from my hands. "Hey! You can't do that!"

"Just did," the tall guard states flatly, an evil glint in his eyes.

"Give it back," I snarl. I'm trying hard not to make a scene, but it is difficult keeping my cool when I'm losing all my patience on these two stooges.

"There are lockers you can utilize. No phones allowed on the premises. Only those with special privileges are permitted," the shorter one states bluntly, but examines my screen to see if I actually sent anything. They are having their fun going back and forth with their banter. "You aren't special."

I am being treated like a criminal and am shocked that Graham would find any of this interrogation appropriate. "Better figure out how you're going to remedy this situation before I get you all fired. Turns out, I'm best friends with the CEO's fiancée."

"Ironically enough, we have heard that line before as well."

I narrow my eyes at both. "How long have you both been working here?"

"Two weeks," they both say in unison.

"Going to be the shortest job of your lives," I huff. "Now. I'm going to tell you my terms." I put my hands on my hips. "Get Graham fucking Hoffman on the phone right now. He will verify who I am. Or—"

"Or what?" the short guard goads.

"Or you can take a sabbatical when I kick you both in the balls!"

A hand grips my elbow gently, pulling me back. I whirl around and swing my hand so fast before realizing what I am doing, smacking it into what feels like a concrete wall.

"Fuck!" I wail, holding my hand in pain and doubling over.

"Shit, Claire. You're going to break your hand," Nic gasps, holding me from crumbling to the floor. I peek up through my lashes and look at the semi-amused man standing over me, with redness blooming on the side of his face from where I must have hit him. Uh-oh.

Why does he have to wear a suit like he does? It is fitted and designer. I can feel the fabric on my skin and know that it cost a pretty penny. He is rugged yet classy. The combination is intoxicating on my senses.

It was hard leaving Nic this morning when he looked so cute curled up in his sheets and comforter, but I had to walk away before my heart started to get attached. It is totally my MO to jump from one failed relationship to the next. However, I am trying to regain some purpose back in my life, and with that mission comes personal sacrifice and much-needed reflection.

"How did you get in?" the taller guard asks, looking Nic over like he is a threat. "Who are you?"

"Your new boss," Nic states coldly. "You both can meet

me at the end of the day in my office. You are dismissed. Go back to your patrol until it is time to have our meeting."

I straighten up and glare at their retreating forms. What assholes!

"Are you okay?" he asks me.

I fix the hem on my pastel pink skirt and smooth out my ivory silk blouse. I usually dress more boldly than I chose to this morning but being the first day on the job, I wanted to look more subdued. Polished.

"Yeah. I had it handled."

His fingers graze over my palm. "I'm talking about the impact you made to your hand when you assaulted me."

"Oh." As the adrenaline wears off, I can feel the throbbing pain develop through my wrist. Shit. I hope I didn't injure myself to the point I can't do my lifting. Tomorrow is arms day. "I never assaulted you."

His eyes come to life with humor. "Um, you most certainly did."

"Hard to call it assault, when I'm the only one who got hurt."

I bite my bottom lip and wince as Nic turns my wrist to examine it.

"Come with me," he says, not even waiting for me to respond.

That is Nic Hoffman, though. He does whatever the hell he wants and just expects obedience. I'm not sure how he ever handled having a girlfriend in the past, but he knows his way around a woman's body well enough to give me the impression he has had many. I just assume they were all formed from the same cookie cutter. Maybe he isn't used to being around someone like me. Someone who has an opinion. Someone who likes to be independent and bold when necessary. I would like to think that I'm not just like everyone else. I've never been the girl to fit in with a crowd. I have accepted that I may just be different. And that is okay.

I walk with him to the elevator. At no point does he stop touching me in some aspect. It is friendly, at least at surface level. But when I think about all the naughty stuff we did last night in his bed, I can't help but flush from just the memory. Can we be just friendly—especially when my body craves his touch?

I clear my head from lumping myself into any category even remotely resembling a relationship status. Nic and I haven't really talked about those things before, so I'm fine keeping things casual, especially when my focus should be on launching a new career. Plus, I'm basically treating last night as a one-night stand. It was a hella good one-night stand, though, for the record. Despite it being an unplanned thing, it was by far the best sex I have ever had. Nic is an attentive lover and skilled at anticipating needs. I felt devoured. I just wonder if he was as fulfilled as I was. I didn't reciprocate oral or even give him a hand job. Hell, I didn't even get to touch him. Sheesh. I feel very much like a taker, rather than a giver.

Nic probably got his curiosity fixed and is satisfied at leaving things as friends, but are we even friends? It feels weird to even put a label on anything right now. Gah, I'm making things so complicated in my head that I'm starting to give myself a headache.

"I should inform HR that I was assaulted," Nic says, stepping aside to allow me to enter the elevator car first.

I pivot and glare up at him. When his lips lift into a smirk, I sigh and roll my eyes. "Not this again." I lean against the back wall, as he selects the floor he wants. "If I assaulted you, then you would at least have a mark."

He chuckles. "So that is your definition? No mark equates to no assault?"

I shrug. "In your case, yes. If anything, your face assaulted my hand."

He throws back his head and bursts out into laughter.

I narrow my eyes at him. "If I can't do arms tomorrow at the gym, you are going to be responsible."

"And how should I take responsibility for my unfounded actions?"

I step a foot closer and lean up to whisper in his ear. "Do that thing with your tongue." When I move back to my corner of the car, I watch as my words penetrate Nic's senses. I feel like I'm testing an unmarked boundary. I know I have some effect on him based on how I can see his Adam's apple bob and his feet shift their weight. There is something about a man of authority that gets me hot and bothered. Just seeing him in his element, handling those barbaric security guards with just a few commands, makes me want to jump his bones.

Right here. Right now.

"What thing?" he asks, feigning innocence.

Oh, he thinks he is so cute. "The *thing*."

He taps the tip of his finger to his lips. "Got to be more specific. My mouth has many talents."

"Shutting it is not one of them."

"Claire, Claire, Claire…"

His breath flutters across my face, warming me. Or

perhaps it is the way his suit continues to stretch taut across his chest with every little movement. He is a model and a caveman all wrapped up into one amazing Armani package. Maybe knowing what is waiting under that suit is what is stimulating my need right now. Or maybe it is because sometimes it is fun to play with fire.

"Never mind," I say, turning away. "I got bored." My body jostles with the sudden stop of the car. "What in the—"

Nic saunters over to me and is on his knees before I realize what is happening. He pushes up the hem of my skirt and easily tucks it into its own waistband. His hands slide up my calves, over the backs of my thighs, and then pull the fabric of my panties to the side to allow for his tongue to lick me from pussy to clit. My knees buckle and my hands reach back to the railing for support, gripping it as tightly as I can to keep myself from crashing to the floor.

"Is this the *thing*?" Nic asks, humor laced into the tone of his words. His tongue flicks back and forth over my clit, acting as a human vibrator.

"Ahhh!" I call out, moving my sore hand to Nic's head to ensure he isn't going anywhere. He is right where I want him to be. "Hell, Nic, you have a wicked tongue."

"So do you," he says, tickling my most sensitive parts.

It takes just the pressure of his thumb at my entrance and the movement of his tongue to send me on the path to an intense orgasm. I steady myself as Nic resurfaces, fixes my skirt, and then licks his lips of my cum.

"You taste like a cupcake," he says with a lopsided smile.

Nic presses the button to send the elevator moving

again. It stops on his floor and we get off. He holds my good hand and ushers me through a series of security doors, using multiple keys and even a hand scanner. Several of the staff members look at me, and I just duck my head and try my best to avoid eye contact. I'm certain that all of his newly acquired employees are making their own speculations and judgments.

Nic unlocks the door to his office. His name plate is just outside on a professional plaque. It looks fresh. He is the man in charge and something tells me he has zero fucks to give when it comes to making enemies here at Hoffman Headquarters.

He lets go of my hand and saunters over to his desk, opening the top drawer and hitting a button on a remote. The wall of TVs disappears behind a wooden panel. He then opens up a mini-fridge and pulls out a gel ice pack. He walks back, as my feet stay glued to the area at which he deserted me. It is like my shoes are made of bricks. I just stare at his work space, gaining more insight on him as to how he operates. He is a minimalist. Only needs the essentials—nothing extra.

Like his apartment, Nic values clean lines and modern elements. His personal space is put together, just like his outward image is. Calm and collected. But I know that underneath the perfectly pressed collared shirt is a man with a rugged and unquenchable sex drive. Something tells me that last night I only got a small sampling of what he has to offer, and I'd be lying to myself if I wasn't wishing I could get to experience the sequel.

When I move a certain way, I can still feel the soreness between my legs from the aerobic activity we engaged in the night before and then the little preview we just had in the elevator. I'm in a constant state of arousal around Nic, to the point where I may need to start stowing away fresh pairs of panties in my purse—especially if I want to stay dry.

Nic takes my right hand and places the ice pack on the center that took the brunt of the blow. I am shocked that I hit him like I did. In the moment, I was so enraged that I lost control of my bearings. It's not like I go around just hitting people because I get mildly offended. With the whole thing going on with Ethan, coupled with my nerves about being here today to potentially start a career, I wasn't thinking clearly.

"How does that feel?"

I look down at his much larger hands that dwarf my own, then back up to his eyes. "Good?"

He examines my bones. "At least nothing looks broken. Maybe look who the culprit is before you try taking a swing next time." There is humor in his tone.

"Might not have stopped me anyway," I snicker.

"I may have deserved it. If not this time, then definitely the next."

I laugh. "Pretty sure I was the only one who suffered from my lapse in judgment."

"This is true." His eyes get serious, as I shift my weight to my heels. "So, I believe I owe you some compensation for causing you unnecessary pain. Albeit, completely out of my control."

I nod and smile big. "Yes. Yes, you do. Time to pay up." I yelp as he hauls me to his desk, knocking documents and a fancy pen to the floor with just the swipe of his hands. "Someone's eager," I mumble.

"You have room to talk. Did you wear this skirt"—his hands grip my ass and push up the fabric—"because of the ease it allows for me to pull over your panties and slip inside you? Did you know I would be here working and you wanted to make it nearly impossible for me to actually think straight?"

"Maybe."

"Your delectable body is a punishment to my self-control."

My lips kiss and suck on the skin right above the collar of his shirt. He places me on the smooth desk top and undoes his zipper, releasing his cock from the confining fabric. He reclines into his leather chair and wheels it closer to me. Taking each heeled foot, he pulls them apart, places them on the armrests, and slides my panties over. My nerves hit a high as he stares. Just stares at me. This is different from how he was in the elevator. It is even different from how I was last night laid out on the rug in front of the fireplace. Now, he has more time to look. Better lighting. His attention makes me want to sway with insecurity.

Am I good enough?

Has he seen and experienced better?

As confident as my outward appearance is to the world, my entire life up to now has been a struggle to find my place. Maybe it is the clichéd result of not having a father figure in my life. Maybe it is from having a mother who saw me as a byproduct of her impulsivity. Regardless, the little girl in me is as damaged as I was when I first found out the truth of my origin. Some wounds will always remain. As time goes on, the scar tissue just builds and builds, giving me a calloused reminder of their depth.

Nic moves my panties back into place and presses a thumb over the growing wet spot forming. "You captivate me, Claire."

I hang on Nic's words of validation. I choose to take them at face value. I have known him long enough to understand that he doesn't just say words to say words. What he chooses to say has meaning, purpose.

With one swooping motion, he is under my skirt again and licking along the silky strip of my panties, directly over my pussy. I lean back on my hands, throw my head back, and moan. I tremble and throw myself forward, clawing at his clothed back.

Nic pulls me down onto his lap and I ungracefully adjust to the change in location.

"Lift your hips," he instructs, waiting for me to obey.

He doesn't have to ask twice. I raise my body up, while he pulls my panties to the side, and sit down on his cock. I grind my hips downwards, allowing him to enter me fully. My thighs bracket his and we become one living being.

"Hell, Claire," he huffs. "You feel so good wrapped around me."

Nic's hands guide my hips up and down in a fluid motion that gives us both what we need. After just a few lifts, we are both gasping for air as orgasms ignite through us, hitting the boiling point.

"Damn," I mutter, sliding from Nic's knees and readjusting myself.

"You left me this morning," he says casually.

"I did."

"I didn't like it."

"It wasn't personal," I counter. I find my bag lying

lopsided on the floor and walk over to retrieve it. I completely forgot I had it with me. "Angie's here. Gotta go."

Nic tucks his cock back into his boxer briefs, zips up his fly, and secures one button on his suit coat. He looks way less rumpled than I feel. So much for breaking out the ironing board this morning at Blake's. Luckily that guy likes to look good, too, so he has all of the essential items in stock to impress.

My eyes trail down Nic's towering form as he walks toward me. He pulls me to him, bites at my bottom lip, and lifts me just enough to slide back down his body—one slow inch at a time. I can feel how hard he still is through the fabric of his pants and it makes me want him all the more.

"Keep looking at me like you're doing, and you won't even leave this office today."

"Quit making it sound like a punishment."

His eyes examine mine, putting us in some sort of staring contest. Finally he breaks the silence and utters, "I'll walk you out."

34

CLAIRE

Nic does more than walk me out. He basically escorts me to the entrance of the area Graham has leased to Angie and me at HH to work on our business.

"Thanks," I mumble, feeling weird that we have said nothing to each other since leaving his office space. Maybe he is having regrets. Maybe I'm being a woman and overanalyzing every little detail.

"Hey you," Angie greets, giving me a hug. She waves behind me to Nic who retreats. "What do you think of the space?" Her smile is contagious and just seeing her excitement makes all of my doubts that this could work melt away. "I ordered a bunch of the basics and had them delivered overnight."

I glance around the huge room and am already in love with what has been done. Everything in the room is of the primary colors of red, blue, yellow, and green. Huge frames adorn the wall, just waiting for some photos or art to be placed behind the glass. A huge U-shaped table is situated with a projector screen in the opening, allowing for discussions. Lines are clean and neat. The computers are of top-notch value and the sleek monitor screens continue with the modern theme.

"I love it. Wow. Just wow," I say, clapping my hands together once. "It actually feels like we could do amazing things in this space. How in the world did you get this all put together so quickly?"

"Can you tell I am desperate for something to do with my life?" she teases. "I thought binge watching TV and online shopping would be entertaining, but I was getting bored out of my mind just waiting for Graham to come home from work."

"Oh, I get it. There's only so much stimulation I can get out of working at a gym. It gets to be so redundant after a while." I walk through the space and check out the items Angie picked out.

"When I'm motivated to do something—*anything*—with my life, I get a bit obsessed," she says defensively. "It also helps that my fiancé is the freaking owner of this building and gave me no limit on the budget when it came to the start-up aspect."

"Ha." I exhale. "That is definitely a perk."

Angie tugs my hand and pulls me to the lounge area with huge sectional sofas, all in a gorgeous blue shade. "I hope you didn't mind me going ahead and taking care of some of the setup. I know you planned so much for the Vegas trip that I thought your mind would need a break."

That's the thing with Angie—she is always so thoughtful and attuned to everyone else's feelings. She is the best kind of best friend.

I kick off my heels and put my feet up on the cushions. "I haven't been in the best of states lately, so you taking over this aspect is very much appreciated."

She grabs her iced coffee from the end table and takes a sip. Then she curls her feet under her butt. "Yeah?"

"Yup. And I wasn't my best self last night at dinner when I ran into Ethan unexpectedly. Things have been *so* not good between us and we are, without any doubt, over."

Her eyes fill with concern. "That bad?"

My teeth graze my bottom lip as I debate on whether to even share my dirty laundry. With a wedding date approaching, I don't need to weigh her down with this crazy drama.

"Claire?"

I look over at her. "Hmm?"

"No matter what is going on in my own life, I'm never too busy for you. I am here for you always. Please don't start holding back."

I nod. She is right, and I've definitely been holding back. "So, I got asked to leave the restaurant." My voice sounds so sad, even to me. It lacks the bubbly timbre that usually accompanies my words.

"Was he alone?"

I shake my head. "Nope. He was with some colleagues, I assume. And his ex-wife, Deena. He has been lying to me for months or maybe even the entire time. I think he was using the escort agency to date me as a way of getting back at her. Or a way to make her jealous. It all kind of makes sense in a way, because the first time I met him, it was to meet her and her new boyfriend." I shrug, looking off into the office space, as I think back to the defining moments in our relationship. "So, yeah, Ethan and Deena are engaged again. And he has other residences other than the ratty fuck pad apartment I was in."

"What?" she snarls. "What a bastard! He sure put up a good front when he would visit our townhouse during college."

"Most narcissists are amazing actors. He sure fooled me."

"I'm sorry, Claire. You deserve so much better."

"He made me feel so cheap in that moment. As if my feelings don't matter. He knew I liked him more than a quick thrill. But then he started gaslighting me and emotionally abusing me. And I don't understand why. What did I do to make him turn like that?" A sob breaks out of my throat and Angie holds my hand while I let out all of the tears I've been trying to keep from her.

"Claire, you listen to me. Because I want to make myself very clear." Her eyes level with mine. "There is no reason for the abuse. Because if there was an actual reason, it would just be an excuse to put the blame on you. And there isn't anything you did wrong. This is on him. And it doesn't matter whatever he tells himself just so he can sleep easy at night. Because abuse is wrong, no matter what."

Tears cascade down my cheeks, and I wipe angrily at them. I feel like I have wasted a chunk of my life working toward a future that was impossible of ever becoming a reality. I am exhausted from putting forth more effort than the guy I invested my time on. "I never want to see him again. Ever."

"Yeah?"

"Yes."

Angie leans over and wraps me up in her arms. "Good.

He doesn't deserve you, sweetie. But I have to know...what got you kicked out of the restaurant?"

"I may have thrown a drink in his face."

"Better than a fist," she snickers.

"I sneaked in a quick kick to the balls though."

"Ha, it was well deserved. He better hope our paths don't cross."

I imagine it was hard on her to keep her cool around Ethan. It would have been extremely difficult for me, if the roles were reversed. "I do appreciate you allowing me the space to figure it all out on my own."

"Claire, I am always on your side. Always. I just hope you stop sacrificing your identity for the approval of others. You don't have to change for someone to love you. You just need to find your person. The man that truly wants to be with you will accept you, flaws and all."

I allow Angie's words to marinate inside my head. She is so wise, and I often forget how similar we are when it comes to life's challenges.

Feeling empowered, I straighten up my posture and put my game face on. "So, let's get down to business and start laying the groundwork for our journey."

"I'm so flipping excited over joining forces with you that I can't shut my brain off because my ideas seem to be endless," she squeals with pent-up energy. "So, I need your expertise about coming up with an execution plan and some mock-ups for what we want to accomplish. Up for a brainstorming day?"

"Perfect. Let's each make an independent list about our ideas on what we want our women's line to focus on and maybe a name for our brand will come to light. Then we can think about the type of people we need to hire to help us get the ball rolling."

Angie and I each grab a notebook from the desk and a gel pen from the fresh pack of pens I brought for this momentous occasion. We find our own space on the sectional sofa and get to work jotting down our ideas. I pop my earbuds in and set my phone to play my playlist by my favorite artist, Punch Drunk.

Around noon, we finally get up from the sofa and laugh when we look over each other's lists. So many things align that it is refreshing to have someone who is on my same page.

"Let's go out for lunch and we can talk about some of our ideas," Angie suggests.

"Sounds great. Hopefully I won't get accosted at the security checkpoint on the way back in," I mumble.

"Oh, no. Really? That happened to you? I will talk with Graham. He has been so beyond stressed over some issues happening here. When it comes to invasions and untrustworthiness, he takes it to a whole other level of anger. He values loyalty above all else. Probably why he is so relieved to have Nic on board to handle all things privacy and security. The two Hoffman brothers are a fierce combo of testosterone."

I nod. Nic definitely wasn't happy when he found me in the lobby being interrogated by the wannabe police. If looks alone could kill, there would have been two casualties. As much as Angie talks about Nic's calm demeanor, I know that underneath lies a very calculated man. He doesn't seem to waver on his decisions, and I doubt his expectations are anything but intense.

We head out of our office and make our way to the elevator bank.

"Do you need to let Graham know you are leaving?" I ask, trying to avoid any issues for her later on.

She shakes her head. "Nope. One of my stipulations to working under his roof is that I don't have to report to him during the work day. I know he has a personal team looking out for me, but I made him promise they would be unobtrusive and would give me the illusion that I am independent."

"Wow, I bet that was a hard concession to make on both sides," I comment, entering the empty car that just arrived. I know you were dead set that the security detail was unnecessary for a long time."

Angie looks over at me. "Yeah. I totally was. But then I realized how selfish I was being in regard to Graham's need to protect those he loves. And I just gave in and accepted that it was part of being in a relationship with him. I've grown to love Collins. I mean, he is the keeper of all the secrets. So, he's basically family to me now."

I smile. I try to mentally push back the feelings I have over wanting those things too. I want a family. One that wants me as much as I want them. I fight the tears that start to develop in my eyes. I have no place for sadness in my life today. Today is about starting over and making new memories. Positive ones.

We walk past several security officers, and I resist glaring at the two who accosted me this morning. I don't return the half smile they give me, but at least I can exit the building without incident. The air is warm but the humidity is low. I love this time of the year, when everything starts to look fresh again. Trees are blossoming.

Birds are happily chirping. Winter's dreariness is officially over.

"What are you in the mood for?" Angie asks, looking down the street.

I look with her and spot Collins getting out of his vehicle. I don't even think that Angie notices. Maybe she is just immune to it all. He has sunglasses on and looks impeccably dressed. Everyone who works with Graham and Nic seems to be. I may have to up my wardrobe game if I want to look the part. What got me by for my escort work won't get me by coming into this fancy corporate building on the regular. I just need to have a steady paycheck first, and unfortunately, that is the main component that start-ups lack.

"Something lunch-y?" I suggest. "Maybe Toss Up?"

"Sure. I'm not picky."

The salad shop is just a block away and has a line of people outside the door, waiting to get in. Angie and I chat easily about our individual brainstorming session we had this morning.

"What is the one thing you want to accomplish?" I ask.

"I want our platform to empower women."

I nod. "And it will. I think we need to utilize what we are best at and market ourselves as a power couple—so to speak."

We move forward a few places in line and continue to chat.

"Are we selling a product or classes or what exactly?" she asks.

"Probably going to sell your asses," a voice behind us

booms with laughter. "Bunch of cheap whores from the database."

My body whips around to see Ethan glaring down at us, and within seconds we are surrounded by half a dozen people in nondescript clothing—some men and some women—with Collins looming in the back. I didn't even know they were bodyguards, that's how much they blended into the crowd.

"You prick," Angie sneers, and when she tries to step forward, Collins cuts through the group to intervene.

"Miss McFee and Miss Nettles, please move up in line and don't give any regard to Mr. Maxwell. He seems to have lost his logic."

Taking the hint that there might be a physical confrontation yet again in public, Ethan smirks, blows me an obnoxious kiss, and then exits the shop without a fight.

"Damn, he is ballsy," Angie whispers. "What's his deal?"

"Probably to try to ruin every good thing I have going for me."

"Well, let's not let him. The best revenge for someone who does you wrong is letting him see that you are way better off without him. And you are, Claire. You don't need his toxicity in your life. You one hundred percent deserve better."

I nod my head, trying to get back into a workable space mentally. Ethan always throws me off my game, and I can't keep allowing him to infiltrate my thoughts. "I think we should start with a product line, meant only for women. Designed by women, created for women," I answer, trying to detox my mind from all things Ethan. "I think we should have a strong social media presence, post live videos of our design creations, and anchor our products to emotions. Focus on how our products make us feel."

"I agree. Any thoughts on a title?"

When it's my turn, I order a bowl of greens and stick with all of the vegan options, doubling up on a couple of my favorite toppings. Once we pay, we find a seat outside at a table and continue our discussion while nibbling at our food.

"Empowered 4 You? Girl Power?" I ramble. "Maybe…" I chew up a bite of my food, growing frustrated over a brand name. "Oh, this is tough. I am struggling."

"How can we portray that women don't need anyone? I mean, it is great to find your person. But we can do it all without a man. How can we send that message?"

I shrug. "Being a loner… Like RSVPing as a plus none. Ha, I guess I have your wedding on my brain. And my RSVP once said 'plus one' for Ethan, and I have to change it to 'plus none.' I don't need his type of negativity in my life anyway."

"That's it!" she chants.

"What?"

"The name. *Plus None*. I think that is a great name. Shows that women don't need a date to feel valued. We need to find it within ourselves. Love from inside before you can let another person love from the outside," Angie explains. "Plus None."

"It does have a nice ring to it," I say. "Plus None. Hmm, it does sound good. Let's make sure it isn't trademarked or anything crazy like that."

"So, what should we work on first when it comes to products?"

"I love looking through magazines or seeing social media influencers and seeing an entire outfit. This is probably why I love the displays at malls. Helps me figure out what looks good with what accessories. What are your thoughts on having a detailed survey and creating weekly or monthly subscription boxes?"

Angie sits up in her chair and taps her index finger over her lips. "A complete box with jewelry, an outfit, and some makeup or skin products? Maybe even some health items? I've been working at creating clothes that have inner adjustments so they will fit if you lose or gain five pounds."

"I think having a complete box that is customizable is what will propel us into the next generation of subscription purchasing. Including the jewelry, the accessories, skincare, nail polish, plus a workable outfit... That's what busy women need. There are so many possibilities for things we can include in each box. Where do we go from here?" I ask, finishing up my salad—which I thoroughly enjoyed—and checking the time on my phone.

"Let's go back to the office and start ordering the rest of our supplies. Tomorrow, let's brainstorm a prototype for our subscription box. Let's get all of our ducks lined up and then start figuring out who we need to hire to get the production going."

"Thank you," I say softly.

Angie looks over at me confused. "For what?"

I smile sadly. "For giving me something to look forward to."

She squeezes my hands. "This is a dream come true to work with you. You are my very best friend."

I squeeze back. "Feeling's mutual."

My phone buzzes with a text notification and with one glance at my screen, my stomach is in knots.

"Everything okay?"

I nod, my attention drawn to my device, as I stare at Ethan's message.

Ethan: You owe me a few grand for my suit you ruined.

What a fucking prick! Isn't he happy with his precious ex-wife? Engaged, no less. He needs to find another hobby and stop this harassment. Besides, the man apparently has a boatload of money he kept from me the entire time we were dating. He can go buy himself another suit and leave me the hell alone.

"Okay, Claire. Obviously something is wrong."

Pulling my attention away from my phone, I put on my brave face—the one that I use as my armor. I got myself involved with Ethan in the first place, and it is my job to set him straight on my boundaries, despite being broken up. I don't need to drag Angie into this drama. If it wasn't for her security detail, she may have hit him right across the face.

"Everything is fine. Well, at least it will be."

35

NIC

I have no idea how I am expected to get any work done when my clothes still smell like a vanilla cupcake and Claire's pussy. Despite just going at it with her several hours ago, my cock is still semi-hard and wanting more. That is what she does to me. She puts me in a constant state of craving. It's like I am so thirsty and nothing I can drink will quench my thirst.

I watch the two dots on my tracker app as Angie and Claire make their way toward HH. I could have flattened Kevin and Leo when they gave Claire a hard time, but basically allowed a complete stranger to get up to Graham's office floor without being stopped. It is so utterly backward to what I would want that I can't help but think I was being pranked. Granted, I set the staff up for failure as a test, but here at HH we have a lot invested and value all things security. The men are new here, which makes them even more expendable.

I've been having my eyes in HH's doings for months

prior to joining the staff as the official head. Hacking and exploiting weaknesses is a bit of a hobby of mine. Of course, I had Graham's best interests in mind. Despite him having training in cybersecurity, my schooling was far more extensive. Plus, my brother has had a very rough year and lost a bit of his focus. Just like in our wrestling days, we thrive on competition but work best as a duo on the same team.

I log out of my computer and set an alarm to send a notification to my phone if anyone tries to log on while I am gone. I lock my office door and set the passcode. No one needs to be in my space—not even the cleaners—especially while I'm gone. I walk down the hallway and look at the desk I set up for my future personal assistant. I will be accepting applications this week for the position.

It's not like I really need someone to make me coffee or photocopy some papers. However, I need the position filled to manage employees and field phone calls while I handle more pressing matters. Plus, I am looking for someone with experience as a guard, so I can multipurpose her if I need someone to patrol female-only areas during work hours. Sure, I'll allow her title to be a PA, but I'll pay her to be more.

Graham's previous temporary heads of security were moved into other positions, obviously as a demotion. The only reason I plan on keeping Dan King on the team is to see if he will retaliate from being butt sore over the minor pay cut and the loss of a prestigious title. He knows that his new position is again temporary and has already visited me once to try to get that to become more permanent. I can't fault the man for taking the initiative. The recent breaches alone should have given him a clue that he was heading toward a demotion. He should be glad that he even has a job. One negative recommendation from Graham will blacklist him from any security job in the entire state of Oregon. Hell, maybe the entire West Coast. I hope he treads carefully knowing his days are numbered.

Dan's coworker, Eugene, who was trying to secure the head position as well, didn't make it on the list of employees sticking around. After reviewing his history and seeing that most incidents happened on his watch, it was an easy decision to let him go. I broke the news to him an hour ago and promised that his résumé would not be tarnished if he chose to resign on his own free will. A severance package will still be offered and be hefty enough to give him the time needed to secure another position elsewhere.

I ride the elevator down to the lobby and watch as Angie and Claire make their way inside from the lunch outing. I stand on the sidelines and watch as my employees greet them with a smile. Everyone knows that Angela McFee is Graham's woman and not to mess around with her in any way—if they value their life and career. However, Claire Nettles is not given that type of special treatment around here—yet. There was never really a need to brief workers until now. If Claire is going to be frequenting the building, then my staff needs to be aware that she is not someone to accost or harass. I have run every background check there is on her. I know she is safe. Thus, she deserves the same special privileges as Angie gets while here in the building.

I watch Claire's retreating form, enjoying the bounce her ass cheeks do when she is wearing her pencil stick heels. Problem is, one of the dumbass guards also is enjoying the same view. Fuck. I feel murderous inside as I watch Kevin whisper something to his coworker Leo and nod in her direction. I want to gouge their eyes out for looking at her like that. This is strike two for these asshats. The irony is not lost on me that I was just looking at Claire the same way. I know my carnal thoughts are not censored in my head, either. I have a very vivid imagination and a detailed list of fantasies I want to role-play out with her. However, I don't need my workers to be admiring anyone on the job, let alone making it into a spectator sport right in front of my face.

When the girls disappear into the elevator, I come out of the shadows and give a stern look to the two guards who look petrified at the sight of me. Good. Be scared.

Your days are numbered. Start polishing up your résumés.

I'm already getting texts from Graham that the word around here is that I am a relentless hard-ass who has an axe to grind. It's accurate. Some have even taken it upon themselves to visit his office to inquire about the change in power, which he has been quick to confirm that I am in charge of all things security. Maybe if everyone knows that I don't piss around, they will actually keep this place from being infiltrated.

My phone vibrates with an incoming call and when I see it's Tyler, I answer immediately. "It's Hoffman."

"Take a deep breath."

"What? Why?"

"It'll calm you down."

I swear he enjoys the shit he pulls with me. "Dammit, Tyler. Just tell me."

"Everything ended well. However, Maxwell confronted Angela McFee and your boo at Toss Up Café."

"My wh—" I stop midsyllable. "Never mind." Him and his crazy jargon. Some days I think I'll need a translator just to understand Tyler's point. "That fucker just doesn't learn, does he?"

"I'm kind of hoping you ask me to get frisky."

I shake my head at him, although he's not here to see. "Is that synonymous with violent?"

"Why yes. Yes it is."

"Are the girls okay?"

"Yes."

"Just keep eyes on him when you can. I don't know his motive for making the breakup so messy."

Tyler sighs. "We all want what we can't have."

When six o'clock rolls around, I wait for the last nonsecurity employee to leave the building and make my way into the conference room for a chat with my staff who are under my lead. Since learning that Maxwell continues to taunt Claire, I've been in a foul mood.

"Here at Hoffman Headquarters, I value loyalty and honesty above all else. There are going to be some changes in positions and job status over the next week. I am passing each of you an envelope that will either state your job title and newly revised description or will contain a severance check for your termination—effective immediately. I also am normalizing salaries and following a tiered scale to help with pay increases based on living costs and job experience.

Bonuses each quarter will be awarded to those who exceed the expectations and will be at the discretion of each team lead."

I scan the group for any reactions. Everyone has the decency to keep their emotions in check. I look at my notes in front of me to make sure I did not forget anything that I wanted to say, while I have everyone in one room right now.

"If you are being let go, I hired a third party team to assist in escorting you out of the building and collecting all badges and key fobs. You have one hour to gather all personal items and exit the premises. If you are considering a lawsuit for HH forgoing any written notice of this termination, the contract has a clause that entitles any employer to exercise any firing of employees, granted that a severance package is in place."

I try to keep my emotions out of my speech and try not to second-guess any of my decisions. It doesn't feel good to end careers today. However, there have been two recent near break-ins to the building and that is a huge cause for concern. It would not surprise me if there is a mole among us. The way to weed him out is to cut the majority of the staff in order to completely vet my new hires and keep a better eye on the remaining employees. I do not need a ton of mediocre workers doing the job that a few high quality ones can do.

I pass out the envelopes and watch as seals are broken to reveal the verdict letters. The room fills with white noise as I exit to leave them to gripe or celebrate without me bearing witness to it.

I head to my office to email the headhunter about finding me a qualified personal assistant who also has some security background. I up the starting salary and reiterate one more time that the person must be a female and must have prior job experience. The last thing I have time for is to hold hands while someone wets their feet in my world.

I turn on the television and connect with the lobby's exit cameras to see some disgruntled workers carrying out empty printer paper boxes of supplies. Some people may say I get off on the power, but that is false. I don't feel good about firing anyone. However, I also know that locking the security down at this building is a priority. I check all of the motion sensors and wait until everyone leaves.

Standing up from my desk, I double-check that I am logged out of all of my devices. I shut off the televisions and close them behind the moving wall with the push of a button. I then head toward the video room, with my rolling cart of boxes that I need to unpack. I have a lot of work ahead at installing all of the new video cameras, configuring them with the current operating system, and then setting up all of the security features to prevent any malicious hacking. I am taking zero chances and starting from scratch with nearly every security feature here at HH.

I order in Chinese takeout and munch on the noodle dish while I hit the fifth-hour mark. It is after midnight and while I'm exhausted, I feel relieved knowing that I am over halfway done.

A motion alert sets off an alarm from my phone, and I access the new camera at the front door to see Claire standing outside in the dark. What the hell? Why is she trying to enter HH at this hour of the early morning?

I grab the elevator down and run through the lobby

before she can walk away. I deactivate the alarm on the exterior doors and push the main one open.

"Oh hi," she says sheepishly. "Wasn't expecting you to be the one who—"

"What the hell are you doing alone on the streets? It is dangerous for a woman to walk around at this hour in Portland," I snap, pulling her inside the safety of the building. I am fuming. Does she really not understand what could happen? I inwardly scold myself for not setting a motion alert on my phone for if she moved more than a quarter of a mile past a certain time. Maybe I could have prevented her from making a stupid choice.

"I left something in the office," she says, confused. "Why are you overreacting? I don't feel like I did anything wrong."

I rub at the back of my neck. I need to calm down before I scare her. "You could have called."

"Called who? It's not like you have an operator here at HH. I thought the night guard would just let me in to grab what I need."

"Called me." *You difficult woman!*

She looks at me with confusion. "Why would I have called you, Nic? I didn't even realize you were camping out here all night."

I sigh. Maybe I'm overreacting. I have been known to have done that once, maybe twice, in my life. "I'm replacing all of the security features before the work shift starts in the morning. What did you forget that you need from your office?" It is an intrusive question, but based on the fact that she is here at HH in the wee hours of the morning, I get to be that nosy.

Claire glances away and then back up at me again. "Apartment key."

"And you just realized it now?" I snap. "Where the hell have you been if you weren't at home?"

"I don't have a home, Nic. I'm staying with a friend."

Her words hit me like a punch to the gut. I know this. I guess saying the word "home" was a slip of the tongue. Ugh. What a freaking mess. I should just pick her up and haul her butt to my place and demand she stay there, but commitment-phobes like me don't do romantic shit like that. This is real-life, not some Saturday night network cable romance movie, with a guaranteed happily ever after.

"Answer my question," I say coldly.

"I went to the gym."

I glance down at her yoga pants and quick-dry workout shirt. Her hair looks freshly washed and blow-dried. Something about this picture looks so wrong. Feels so wrong. "You're telling me that you left work at 6:07 p.m. and have spent the last seven plus hours at the gym?"

She nods, and I want to hit something.

"Unbelievable."

I need to step away from her before I lose my mind. I walk toward the elevator and hit the button for her floor, as she follows me inside.

"Sorry if I pissed you off," she says meekly.

I look at her. "I just need to wrap my head around the idea of you living at the gym."

"I'm not living there," she defends.

"Then why not go to your apartment and knock on the door to be let in?" Why is this such a hard concept?

"I was already at the gym when I realized I didn't have my keys. And it is late. I didn't want to wake anyone."

"You are neglecting your needs and that stops tonight."

Propping her hands on her hips, she glares at me. "Quit being so dramatic. You are worse than your brother."

"Prove to me otherwise," I growl, not getting distracted by her attempt at lighthearted humor. I am *not* in the mood. Thoughts of her hanging out at the gym and using the facilities for taking care of her personal hygiene just sound sad to me. Is she afraid to go back to the loft? Blake may be innocent and nonthreatening, but what about his dipshit roommate?

"Listen... I went to the gym after work and grabbed some clothes out of my locker. I think best when I am moving, so I was online shopping for the office while jogging on the treadmill. Then they were having a late-night yoga class, so I hit that up. A coworker's car broke down, so..." She stops her sentence and then taps her foot onto the floor. "What's so funny? Why are you grinning?"

I wipe a hand down my face. "It's nothing."

"It's obviously something."

"It's just that it's rare to find a girl these days who has yoga pants that actually make it to a real yoga class and aren't just worn for comfort."

Once my words penetrate Claire's ears, she bursts into a fit of giggles. "Fact," she laughs. "But these"—she points to her bottoms—"have made it to several, including the one I hosted at the river. They are very much my favorite pair and are workout whores."

I let out a laugh. "Good to know. Then what did you do?" I inquire.

"I went into the locker room and showered and changed. But then I got tired, so I took a little nap on the sofa there. It is a twenty-four-hour gym, and I have unlimited access because I teach some classes."

I listen to her ramble. It sounds innocent, but I can't shake the feeling that she was avoiding going back to Blake's loft. "How are the sleeping arrangements at your friend's place?"

"Less than stellar," she huffs out a laugh. "But I have slept in worse places. No big deal. I'm pretty sure my entire junior year of high school was spent on a blow-up mattress because my parents were too busy with the restaurant to bother thinking of anything else. Or maybe they didn't want to invest money in a real bed for me if I planned on leaving for college. Who knows with them."

I want to ask more about her childhood but resist. I need to keep the lines from being blurred. Asking personal questions about the past will just make things more complicated.

"I would have just stayed here and started my work shift early if I had appropriate clothes," she points out.

"You can't pull these long hours without it taking its toll," I comment. "Plus, you just started here. No need to set the precedent that you are a work addict."

She smirks. "Pot meet kettle."

"Touché." The elevator stops and we exit together. "I installed a new lock on your office doors and can show you how to use it."

"Thanks, but I'm pretty sure I know how to open a door," she says with a smirk. "Put it in and turn? I think I got that handled."

My teeth grind together over the sexual nature of her words. "There's more to it than just that."

"That's what they all say."

I walk her through the new entry process, handing her the new set of replacement keys. We are standing so close that I can smell her hair. It is freshly washed and smells like strawberries. I feel cheated. Not that I have anything against strawberries. It's just that I'm more of a fan of vanilla. Her stomach growls.

"You're hungry."

"My stomach will get over it."

"Claire…" Her name trails off my tongue with an added syllable.

"Nic." She does the same thing with my name.

"Go find your apartment key and let's go have dinner in my office. I have leftover Chinese."

She makes a face. "I avoid MSG."

"I only order from the place down the street that cooks everything with organic ingredients. Otherwise, I get headaches." Her eyes perk up, and I can tell she is running out of excuses. "Go get your apartment key, Claire."

"Fine." She turns on the lights and walks over to the sectional sofa. I watch as she leans over the cushions and digs her hands in between the sections, until she finds her lost key. She waves it into the air with elation. "Found it."

"Good. Now, let's go eat."

36

CLAIRE

I watch as Nic pulls out the takeout boxes from his mini-fridge and fixes me a plate with the vegetarian options. The last thing I ate was the salad for lunch with Angie and now I am starving. The sight of food alone is making me salivate, and my stomach starts to cramp with need. My mind has been so elsewhere lately that I am losing track of time and of my meals.

Ever since the café confrontation, Ethan keeps texting me threats—nearly on the hour, every hour. If he's not careful, he may find that I don't play nice. I'm not paying for his stupid suit. He knows I don't have money right now, so I imagine he's trying to torment me just for fun or set up some automatic texting system to do his bidding.

My eyes scan over all of the boxes Nic arranged. "Are you going to eat with me?"

"Do you want me to?"

I nod. "I hate eating alone."

Nic's smile is sweet, and the more time I spend around

him, the more I start to realize that he does have a good heart. He just hides it from most people's view. He treats me very differently than he treats Angie, Graham, or his employees. It's as if I get to see layers to him that are hidden beneath a strong and rugged facade he tries to keep secured in place around his exterior.

"I'm going to go to the break room and microwave this," he says, walking toward the door with two plates in hand.

"I like mine barely warm."

He nods and exits. When he returns, he places the plates down on the center of his desk. "You can sit in my leather chair. I can grab the other one."

Before I can argue, he is guiding me behind his desk to take the more comfortable seat, with the leg room. "Your office is very nice," I say looking around.

"Thank you. I have a few more items arriving next week."

My first bite of food is so delicious that it only takes a couple of minutes before I am scraping up the last bit from my plate. Nic pushes his toward me, taking my empty one in return.

"Eat."

"I, um…" It feels weird eating this many carbs in front of a man. "I shouldn't."

"You are obviously starving."

"Not sure how," I laugh, "when I just ate half a pound of noodles."

"They are good, huh?"

"The best."

"I only made a plate for myself so I could tempt you with it," he teases. "Enjoy."

Nic sits back in his chair and watches as I hesitantly fork a mouthful of food between my lips. He specifically kept meat from the plate, so maybe he was intending to give me his serving the whole time. I never get bent out of shape over calories. I just like to eat healthy and fuel my body with quality food. However, after months of dating Ethan and dealing with his snide comments about what goes in my mouth, I am in need of a little mental detoxing. Being apart has helped me to see how truly abusive he was toward me. I do deserve better.

After my last bite, I slouch down into his leather chair that smells like him and exhale. "I'm going to need to be carried out of here."

Nic chuckles and clears the plates from the desk, taking them out of the room. When he returns, I am checking my phone for the time.

"I better get going so I can at least catch a few hours of sleep prior to the work shift starting all over again," I mutter. I am one of those people who can function on less sleep. However, I am way more productive if I get my minimal five.

I gather up my bag and wave goodbye to Nic. I am a few steps down the hall when I feel his presence behind me. I turn around and look up at him with confusion. Maybe he wants to make sure I don't set off any alarms since it is after hours.

"I'll walk you out."

"Oh, okay."

I fidget at the elevator bank and accidentally press the

up button when calling for the car to arrive. I bite my bottom lip and quickly press the down arrow. Except I completely miss the button and hit the metal frame instead. An awkward laugh bubbles out of my throat. I must look like a lunatic. We stand—in complete silence—and wait. The elevator arrives and we enter it. I suck in some air, feeling like the oxygen levels change once the doors close. It is as if Nic takes up way too much space and every glance he makes in my direction is making my toes curl.

I know what he is capable of—in and out of the bedroom. He must know the effect he has on me because the grin plastered on his lips makes it appear that he is part of some inside joke.

"Quit it," I huff.

"What am I doing?" he asks. His tone sounds innocent, but I know the truth. There is not a freaking thing about Nic Hoffman that is innocent. He isn't fooling me.

"Stop looking at me."

He tips his head to the floor and chuckles.

"Stop laughing at me too," I demand.

"Am I allowed to smile? Or does that bother you too?"

"Only if you can do it without staring at me."

He starts laughing again. Dammit. He is making me go insane. He is so entertained by my bossiness that I don't know whether to smack him or join him in laughing at the spectacle that I am making of myself.

The elevator doors finally open, and I rush out ahead of Nic, brushing past him in a flurry. I need air. I need to breathe and clear my head. He jogs up beside me, hits the code on the door and pushes it open for me. As soon as the fresh air surrounds me, I feel like I can function again. Nic makes me claustrophobic without being in a super confined space. He just has that aura about him.

"Thanks for dinner and for letting me in to find my key," I say, rocking on my feet. I am acting weird, and I need to leave before I say something embarrassing—which happens to be how I operate around him.

"I'll walk you to your car."

"No."

"No?"

I shake my head adamantly. "You don't need to do that."

"I'm doing it," he states bluntly.

"No."

"Why the hell not, Claire?"

I hold my breath and close my eyes.

"Claire…"

"Because my car is still at the gym. I'm just going to walk back to the loft apartment instead."

I can see the anger in Nic's eyes and deep down I knew he would be. I turn to retreat, and as soon as I am a footstep away, his arm reaches out and grabs ahold of me, stopping me in my tracks. He is direct with his actions but not aggressive. I look down at where his hand touches my skin. It feels like he is scorching me—but in the best kind of way. That is what the man does to me. He makes me melt.

"Why is your car at the gym?"

I can tell he is struggling to remain calm. His voice is shaky, and it feels as if I'm in trouble. "I ran out of gas. And I had some of my coworkers put it in neutral and help me push it to the curb."

Nic rubs at his temples as he stares at me. Maybe he thinks I am seconds away from saying "just joking." The sad part is, I am not. It has been a week from hell, and my car needing gas is just the shit sauce on my shitty ass sandwich. I was close enough to the parking lot at the gym, so I can keep it there until I can go buy a gas can and refill it. It is not a big deal. *Please don't make this into a big deal.*

I watch as Nic types something into his phone and then reaches for my hand, which I accept without really thinking. I allow him to walk me to his car that is parked at the curb. I enter without argument, feeling defeated by the struggles of the day. He revs the engine and starts on a route that will not lead to my loft.

"You need to make a left up at the intersection," I say, leaning forward in my seat. Maybe I never gave him the address and he's confused. I mean, I'm pretty confused as well. That is what lack of sleep does to me, and ever since I was coerced to have sex with Ethan as a bet, I have not had the most restful nights. And now he's texting me without an obvious motive, other than to make my life even harder. "Why are you giving me the silent treatment?" I ask. I can tell he has some strong emotions brewing inside of him. His fingers are wrapped firmly around the steering wheel and his white knuckles are showing. When the radio comes on, he slams his hand on the button to shut it off. I watch as his breathing is more exaggerated. "Are you pissed off at me?"

"Yes."

"What? Why?" I scoff. "What did I do?"

"You are the most aggravating woman on the entire planet."

"Well, you are the most frustrating man on the entire planet."

"Walking alone on the streets at night... Never asking anyone for help when you really need it... Starving your—"

"That last statement is false."

"Well, you are at least skipping multiple meals a day. I can tell you are losing weight. And you are without a doubt pissing me the hell off."

"Tell me how you really feel," I mumble, slinking back into my seat. I feel drained of life. My clothes are fitting a bit looser, but that is usually a good thing. No one ever complains over less body fat. Why is he so moody?

It isn't until Nic is pulling into the parking garage at his building that I realize what is happening. I am too emotionally exhausted to care. Or maybe part of me is thrilled that I may actually find rest in his king-sized bed, curled up next to him. I close my eyes and press my face against the cool glass of the window. There's no stopping Nic when he is on these types of missions, so why even try?

My door opens and hands reach in to forklift me out. Nic is back to not talking to me and I prefer it that way, as opposed to him slinging snappy judgments at me. Homeboy probably never struggled a day in his life. He comes from the picture-perfect family who seem loyal and loving. We are from two separate worlds, yet the only thing I can think about is getting into his orbit.

Like magnets, I am drawn to him. But I'm pissed at him too. He has to work for it, so I might as well enjoy myself. I pull out my lip gloss and make a production out of rolling it along my lips, as we make our way toward the elevator. He should have never let me be privy to the information that I drive him nuts with this gloss. Now it is just too much fun to taunt him with it. I circle around for the third time and then rub my lips together, smoothing out the sheen evenly. Nic's growl is audible from deep in his throat. Good. *Suffer in silence, buddy.*

"You are baiting me," he comments, ushering me inside the elevator as soon as the doors open.

"And what do you think you'll catch, Nic Hoffman?" I ask. "Feelings?"

His eyes go cold and he shakes his head adamantly *no*. "Those days are over. I'm not some white knight who wants to rescue you and make you forget about every man who has done you wrong. Instead, I am the dark villain who saw an opportunity and got off on taking you from *him*."

I know who the "him" is. The *him* is Ethan Maxwell. But Nic's wrong. He does care about me. This is more than him just fulfilling a sexual kink. He thinks he is damaged somehow, and I'm reckless enough to believe that the right woman could change everything about his perception. Or at least have fun trying.

"Good," I hum. "Bad boys are always more fun."

"Is that so?" he growls.

"One hundred percent."

The elevator stops, and we exit into his apartment. I don't even bother asking why we are here. It's not like he is in the market to do anything I say right now. His body language is hard. Impenetrable.

I kick off my shoes and toss my bag beside them on the floor.

"What would you say if I told you I have a *thing* for dark villains?"

"I would say you are incredibly reckless and naive."

I click my tongue and stare at my nails. "Good thing your opinion doesn't matter to me."

I smell him before I feel him collide with me and push me back against the wall. His lips crash into mine and he takes and keeps taking. He lifts me a foot off the ground and my legs wrap around his midsection. My hands run all over his back, scratching and clawing to get him closer to me. He licks every drop of gloss off my lips and when he has his fill, he pulls back to smile wickedly at me.

"Hope you enjoyed yourself," I state sarcastically.

His cock twitches through the fabric of his suit. "Not nearly as much as you probably did. Let's take a look."

Nic keeps my ass balanced on one forearm, as he continues walking deeper into his home. I kiss at his neck, biting a little to make him squirm. Just when I think we are going to make it to his bedroom, he throws me down on the sofa and is peeling my yoga pants off my body. It is not a slow and seductive dance. No, this is primal and hurried. Like if he doesn't get more of my body, he will die a starving man.

I lift up on my elbows and watch as Nic struggles with the damn pants. His grunts of struggle are met with the sound of seams ripping.

"Hey! These are my lucky pants!"

"They are about to be your *get lucky* pants," he corrects, tearing the fabric from my body.

Nic gets up from his knees and starts tossing every article of clothing from his body. Belt, pants, boxers, suit coat, dress shirt, undershirt, and his socks are all removed. He stands naked before me and I am enthralled. My eyes cannot stop looking, so I don't even try to hide my blatant perusal of his body. His eyes smolder, and in this moment, I feel like a seductress and a princess—all wrapped up in the package of a gym logo T-shirt. That is what Nic does to me, though. He makes me feel wanted even in a ratty cotton shirt with fraying graphics. I lift it above my head, but leave on my bra and panties. They are nothing special. Just a spare set I had at the gym in my locker. Black and stretchy.

"Stand up," Nic directs, offering assistance.

His hands reach up to my breasts, weighing them between his big hands. I hope they are enough. I hope I am enough. And then slowly and methodically, he helps me remove the last bits of fabric that keep me concealed from his eyes.

Pulling me to him by my hips, Nic reaches up his fingers to tug my lip that I didn't know I was chewing out from underneath the cage of my teeth. He leans his long body down to eye level and blinks hard. His tongue slips out of his mouth and he closes in on me, licking along the exact place where I was gnawing. I no longer smell the scent of vanilla. Nic swallowed that up in the foyer. Instead, I have the intoxicating scent of citrus and wood surrounding me.

I groan loudly and start to climb up his body. His hands lift me from my ass, squeezing my plump naked flesh. I wrap my legs around his waist and rub my bare crotch against his erection. I can feel movement but am too in the moment to realize what he's doing. I claw at his hair, messing it up even more. My lips are on his neck, teasing and playing with his smooth skin.

I gasp when my bare shoulders hit the coolness of the windows, feeling my body pressed flat against the glass.

"I want you," I breathe, "so badly."

I open my eyes long enough to see Nic's hood over with desire. I want him. Like I have wanted no one else—ever. And I want him *now*.

I push the feeling into the back of my head that our newly developing relationship is just for sexual gratification. I know there is more to it. A man doesn't go out of his way to feed a woman or care for her if it is just to get his rocks off. Yet, here I am, smashed up against a glass window overlooking Portland, while Nic plasters himself to my body. There is no place I'd rather be than here, sliding down onto his cock, screaming his name.

37

NIC

I'd be lying if I said I didn't like the little arrangement I made with Claire. It's not like I planned it this way—things just happened organically. For the past two weeks, we have been fooling ourselves into thinking we aren't cohabitating together—when in fact that is exactly what we are doing. Every day at the end of the work shift, she attempts to go back to her shared loft. And then every day, she somehow ends up at my place.

I mean, I'm pretty irresistible. My words—not hers.

In fact, Claire hasn't been to the loft since I made a surprise visit and saw just how inappropriate her cheese-puff roommate Henry was being. Fucker better be glad I was having a good day. First thing I would have annihilated would have been his roaming eyes. Followed by the snipping of every one of his vocal cords. Just the way he said her name with a weird accent was enough to send me to the red zone. In my defense, the dude is the self-proclaimed King of One-Night Stands. Yeah, he even got shirts made.

Claire doesn't belong at the loft sleeping on some worn out futon, when I have a whole apartment that her body can make look better. Since we started our unofficial arrangement, we have experienced the sofa, the kitchen island, my workout room, and the elevator. Even when I think we have fucked each other to boredom, she will surprise me with a naughty text at work, that will nearly always lead to a trip to my place—and the removal of all the clothes.

She has even resorted to being creative and sending me dick appointments via text, where I have to accept or decline based on the date, time, and location. Like I would ever say *no* to her. Her appetite for sex rivals my own—and that is saying something.

Claire is the joy and excitement my life didn't realize it was lacking until she danced her way into it. I have never been with someone so sexually liberating and confident. Claire doesn't give a shit if the lights are on or off. Clothed or naked. Hairy or bare. She finds it thrilling if neighboring buildings may see her sexy silhouette in the window, as I thrust deep inside her. Just when I think she is satisfied, she will flash me the killer smile that lets me know just how hungry she is for me.

Despite me making it a mission to keep things casual, Claire's belongings are scattering across every room and into every crevice with each passing day. Her organic vegan protein powders have made the front row in my drink mix cupboard. Her hair ties are circling knobs in the bathroom. My workout room is full of her bright-colored outfits draped over equipment, from our latest romps while trying to break a sweat.

I have gotten used to leaving work at a decent hour,

instead of living there. Claire has given me a reason to focus on something other than my career. We have been running in the mornings, hitting up local coffee shops, and laughing over the hideous movies she picks out. Her taste is eclectic, and I love trying to keep up with her desires. I have even been teaching her a few wrestling moves on the mats laid out in my home gym. She is a ball of energy, and I have zero intention of trying to tame her. I welcome her spunk—in and out of the bedroom.

How we are able to keep our arrangement a secret is the most mind-boggling. Graham and Angie are just weeks away from the wedding, and their lives are consumed with honeymoon details, dress fittings, and last-minute changes to the plans. It's not like I need to hide anything from my brother, but I know he would not approve of me having this type of no-strings-attached fling with his fiancée's best friend. He already could tell I was attracted to Claire and made it clear that I was to keep it cordial.

I know how this will end. *It will end.* I just want to live in this fantasy a little longer before all ties get cut and emotions inevitably become complicated.

Claire knows the score. She has been very careful not to show me too much attention at work. We have similar desires of keeping our fling on the down low.

I doubt she knows how much I watch her on the camera footage, and I know for certain she is unaware that I track her whereabouts. Running into her throughout the building can't all be random occurrences. She is smarter than to believe it is. However, outside of HH, she probably has no idea to what extent I pay attention to her location. The tracking has become a security blanket for me, under the shield that I am doing a favor for Graham.

Maxwell has been quiet since confronting the girls at the café, and I can only hope that he learned that they are untouchable by the financial message Graham and I sent to him. He can think he is master of the stock market, but he is not master of the clients in this city. Our connections run deep, and there are numerous people who still owe us favors.

I'm sitting at the island, sipping on my first mug of coffee for the day when Claire sneaks up behind me and wraps her hands around my torso. She is warm and smells freshly washed.

"You smell delicious," I say smoothly. "Good enough to eat."

"I'm going to get used to your shower," she says, kissing my neck.

I swallow the sip of coffee and spin around so I can take a good look at her. As expected, she looks stunning. The girl can wear anything and look great, but there is something about a tailored knee-length dress that makes me wonder what is underneath. Did she select lace thigh highs today? Maybe a silk bra?

"How much more time do you need?" I ask, kissing her on the lips. They are soft. Plump.

"I just need to do my hair," she says, reaching around and grabbing a forkful of melon from my plate.

"I can make you more. I also ordered more of those muffins you like with the almond butter. Oh, and some of those overnight oats bowls."

"With the acai berries?"

"Yup." How could I forget? Claire nearly jumped for joy the first time she found the packaged bowl in my fridge. I can only imagine her reaction to a real gift. I load up a chunk of melon on my fork and offer her another bite.

Claire puts her hand up in protest. "No, I'm good. My stomach is nervous this morning."

I frown over her words. "What's going on?"

Her sigh is an obvious signal of her stress. When Claire is anxious, she tends to hold in her breath and then let it out with an audible exhale. She has done this three times already this morning, so she must have a lot on her plate today.

"Just a big day at work. It is one of those planning days that may change our direction, depending on how the discussion goes."

"Any way I can relieve some of the stress for you?"

"No," she says with another big exhale, "I just need to face this head-on. I have a fear of failure that comes out when I pressure myself to be perfect."

"Sometimes there is beauty in the imperfections of life."

She nods and smiles. "I couldn't agree more." Her mind seems to be elsewhere, and I wish I knew what she was thinking.

I smooth out her dress around her hips. "You look amazing in this shade of green. Brings out your eyes."

Claire's face lights up. "Thank you," she mouths, her words getting stuck in her throat.

I kiss her on her nose. My fingers touch her dark and silky hair. "For what it's worth, I think you should leave it down today. Just get the dampness out, so you don't get sick. It is a chilly morning."

I walk Claire into Hoffman Headquarters and bypass the security checkpoint all together. I have hired basically a new crew, eliminating every previous worker who appeared too wet behind the ears or disloyal. No matter how many chances I gave Kevin and Leo to prove themselves to me, they did not rise up to the challenge and got replaced. Their infatuation with Claire was enough to send them packing. In addition, I was harboring resentment over the lobby encounter and my opinion was forever tainted from it. Overall, I downsized the security head count by half. The fewer people who know about our operations here, the better.

I have only been here for a few weeks as the official Head of Security and already I have made a name for myself. I would like to think that I am formidable but fair. However, based on the number of jaw ticks I witness as I arrive every morning to the building, I imagine there are also a few choice words attached to my unrelenting demands.

Not one incident has occurred with Claire entering or exiting the lobby. Most days, I am rolling in with her beside me, and only those wanting to apply for unemployment would want to interfere with my morning ritual. There have been a few rare times that Claire came in after me, sleeping in after an exhausting night in my bed. Nonetheless, everything has been smooth.

"I will see you later," she says, getting on the elevator.

I want to say something more to her. To tell her that if she needs me, to text and I will be right there. I know today will be an emotionally draining day for her, but yet the words that I should say get stuck in my throat. So, instead, I just retreat into my main floor office and offer her a simple platonic wave—as if we are just friends.

I check a few of the alarm systems for breaches and find pleasure in knowing that since I have been on board, there has been nothing shady happening. I close and lock the door and make my way up to my central office, where I conduct most of my business.

Getting off the elevator, I notice Graham sitting behind the desk where my personal assistant really should be—if I ever get around to hiring one. I have narrowed down the résumés to three potential candidates but have been putting off the interviews all week.

"Wasn't expecting to find you here this morning," I say, leaning my back against the wall. "Rough night in the Kingdom of Paradise?"

Graham stares at me, as if he is analyzing the stock market. "There's something different about you."

"Probably just my new suit." I'm starting to get used to the formal attire. My prior jobs never required more than dress pants and a button-down. However, the way Claire's eyes glaze over at the sight of designer labels helps me not gripe about all of the fanciness.

"Nope. Not that," he says. "You look happy."

"Maybe it's the control that I have been craving all along."

I can tell by his eyes he doesn't believe me, but he has the decency not to push. I quite frankly have no idea what he is talking about. Sure, I am overall content. But, I wouldn't be making a big deal about it. It's not like I've been depressed or emotionally drowning prior to his psychoanalyzing session.

I start to walk into the break room to make myself a mug of coffee and feel Graham's presence at my back.

"You're doing a great job here. I knew you would."

I turn around and lean my backside against the counter, crossing my legs at my ankles. "I appreciate it." I wait to see if there is anything else he wants to discuss. It's not like he would make a special trip up here to say what he could easily do with a text.

"I need a favor."

"Okay."

"It's big."

"Good thing we are family."

"I have to go to New York City."

"When?"

"Tonight." Graham sighs in frustration. "It is a sudden trip that needs my physical presence. I have to see a few associates who are flying in from the Middle East."

"Let me guess, you have asked Angie to go with you and she refused."

"I have not asked Angie yet, but I can bet you she will say no."

I chuckle. "Yeah. I can see how aggravating it can be to be attached to someone so stubborn."

Graham rubs at the back of his neck. "Angie is so dedicated to jumpstarting Plus None that she can't see straight. Besides putting in a full shift here at the office, she then goes home and is researching and planning. Says it is fun for her." He shakes his head. "She is going to work herself into the ground if she thinks she can maintain this schedule. Learning the work-life balance is key."

I want to tell him that Claire is the same way, but he doesn't need to know how much time we've been spending together. I also want to tell him that before Angie came into his life, he had no concept of balance. Work was his life.

"So, my favor…"

"Let's hear it."

"I need you to look out for her. Collins is on a paid vacation for the week, otherwise I would ask him. You both I trust. Anyone else, I'm not so sure."

I nod. "How long will you be gone?"

"Minimum of two nights. Probably more. That okay?"

"Sounds reasonable," I mutter. "What could go wrong?"

"Ha. Everything."

"That's a bit dramatic, even for you," I say with a laugh.

Graham sighs and runs his hands through his hair. "Literally every time I leave or let my guard down, Angie gets herself in trouble—and it usually involves Claire."

"I think I can handle them," I snicker. I've been enjoying handling the one at least.

"Good, because I know I can't without losing my mind. And I predict a girls' night will be high on their to-do list."

"Okay."

"I'm going to expect you to give me a report on her every couple of hours. I can't conduct business if I'm worried about her. She is my reason to breathe."

I take a sip from my mug, savoring the smooth rich taste. "I wouldn't expect it any other way, although I'm a bit surprised it's not every thirty minutes."

Graham shakes his head at me. "The other thing I wanted to talk to you about is Penny."

My breath catches in my throat. I have not been keeping as close tabs on her progress as Graham has, so I hope she is doing well. "Okay…"

"She called me and asked if I would try to convince Dad to sign the early release papers."

"She called me about the same thing the other week too."

"Thoughts?" Graham asks, visibly stressed. We both want what is best for our baby sister—even if it means keeping her at the facility longer.

"I'd want to discuss the potential consequences with the doctors first before I would feel comfortable moving forward. I think she is really wanting out of there by your wedding date so she can start fresh again."

"Why would the date she gets released matter?"

"I have no idea. Women confuse the hell out of me."

"Ha," Graham chuckles. "Join the club."

"Maybe she met someone and wants the freedom to date."

Graham's eyes turn dark. "No."

"No?"

"Not unless I approve of him."

I laugh over Graham's overprotectiveness. "I'm sure she'll love having her two brothers screening all of her candidates. Maybe if we tell her that when she's released, we'll both chaperone her dates, then she will reconsider rushing her exit out of there."

"Who says there will be more than one candidate?"

"You know there will be. It is karma for all of the times we sabotaged her dates when she was in high school."

"You know how teenage punks are, Nic."

"Yeah, I know. I used to be one of them. I'm not saying I have regrets about protecting her. I'm just being realistic."

"She can date when she is thirty."

I burst out laughing. "Angie is going to have so much fun while you are away and she gets let off the chain."

Graham groans. "You have one job. Just keep her safe."

"I can handle it," I say confidently. "It'll be fun."

"You really have no clue what you are in store for..."

"There's only one way to find out."

38

CLAIRE

I finish up my meditation session in the room we partitioned toward the back of the office space. I feel rejuvenated and ready to start my day with a visionary planning session.

It is still just the two of us, with the new hires arriving next week to fill some much-needed positions. Until then, we are on our own to get everything lined up for the expansion.

"The first thing we need is a prototype box. Then we need to market the hell out of our lineup," Angie says, turning on the light box that is mounted to the wall.

"Let's start pinning up our ideas," I suggest. "I really like the idea of adjustable clothing." I grab a black marker and write down my thoughts onto the light box. "Were you able to create some design examples on the computer?"

"I did something better," she says, pulling out a rolling closet from the side of the room that has ten outfits hung on hangers. They are all in different styles and colors.

"Wow. Where did you have the time to prepare mock-ups?"

"I've been working so much when I get back home that I think Graham is disturbed over my dedication. I'm just happy that I found something I am passionate about again."

I nod. "I feel the exact same way. I've been working on our branding. I am thinking of some catchy sayings that we can print on the top of each box under our logo *Plus None*."

"I would love to hear them," Angie says, smiling. She is always so encouraging and understanding that it allows me to be my true authentic self without the fear of sounding stupid.

"One idea is—Unwrap, Wear, Share."

"Oh, I like that. Does share mean social media posts?"

"Yeah," I acknowledge. "Maybe we can have an easy setup for customers to post their box findings. Turn it into a contest or a raffle for their next box being free to stir up business."

"Love it."

"I also had the idea of—Custom, Cute, Controlled."

Angie smiles. "You are really good at this type of thing. And to think I almost got a job where all I did was work with words."

"Tear me. Wear me. Share me."

"Add that," Angie says, pointing up to the light box.

I walk up to the board and add my ideas. I also pin up my visions for lifestyle boxes to represent needs and help customers. Workout Warrior Box. Damsel in Distress Box. Love for Lounging Box. Boss Bitch Box. The Breakup Box.

"I love these ideas," Angie cheers, clapping her hands

together. "Best decision I have made is teaming up with my best friend."

"Thank you," I say, putting the cap back on the marker. "Oh, and what are your thoughts on eliminating numbers to tell sizes? I was thinking of assigning names to represent the size of the clothes but be more positive."

"Yes!" Angie chants, nearly knocking over her chair when she jumps up to write the idea on the light board.

Our office space is cozy, yet functional. We added more decor, sewing machines, seating areas, and a workout room. Lamps, wall art, and some fun pillows make the office feel more like a lounge area than an actual workplace. Angie and I want a place to relax but still be able to focus. Boxes have been arriving daily with supplies, and making the space our own has been the most thrilling.

"Graham has been a grumpy butt all morning. Coming in today is exactly what I needed. I love the progress we are making."

I walk over to the wardrobe rack and start looking through Angie's ideas. The clothes are made from the softest cotton blend, have custom features, and are adjustable. My fingers graze over the wrap dress. I love it. It is definitely something I would want to wear, and the fact that it is able to be adjusted makes it work for a variety of body types. Genius.

The workout gear prototypes are made from luxury fabric and appear to fit the body but still be flattering. Angie has left the heat press images and words off, allowing for customizing based on survey questions.

"I'm sorry that he is being weird," I state, "but some-times I work best when I'm in a mood."

Angie giggles. "Ain't that the truth."

"What is the timeline we are looking at?"

"Looking at the calendar, we still need to hire a few more people to get everything lined up for our soft release scheduled for after the wedding. We need a technical team to build and manage a website, the survey data, and all of the algorithms. In addition, we will need to have a factory off-site that will be handling all of the manufacturing, packing, and shipping. I think we need to hire a director of sales, marketing, and product in the next week or so."

"That's a lot," I exhale. "Do we even have the means to hire this many people and not be turning a profit?"

"Well, having a board of directors and bidding for funding for our start-up is potentially what has to happen. We will be able to get a chunk of money to handle hiring, scaling the product, and launching our idea into the world. Right now, we have a sole investor—Graham. I just want to make sure he is only offering starting capital and will fade out his cash flow once we get established and move onto the next series of funding as we progress. Last thing I want is for his money to just be wasted."

"It's your money too," I correct. "But I totally agree. I want this to work out just as much as you do."

"The headhunter will be here soon, and we can discuss with her what we need in terms of potential employees."

"Great."

"Plus, we already have a few new hires starting next week."

I nod. "Things are starting to line up."

"It's crazy, isn't it?"

"So crazy," I say, "that it has to be meant to be."

The sound of our office door opening causes us both to turn around and see the Hoffman brothers filling up the entranceway with their muscular bodies. They sure are a force to be reckoned with. Both men are equally talented and possess the qualities that can get the job done. I just hope I am not on the receiving end of their wrath. Rumors have been flying around during some elevator rides and restroom trips about the unyielding force these brothers make. I'm not surprised.

"Hey you," Angie says, running up to Graham and flinging herself into his arms. He catches her and quickly fixes the dress that spreads across her backside to keep her from being exposed.

I get up from my seat and walk over to the group, careful not to let on that I would have loved to have jumped on Nic in a similar fashion. He gives me a look that makes the panties melt from my bones.

"What brings you boys here? Checking in on us?" I tease.

Graham clears his throat and sets Angie back on her feet. "We have some matters to discuss."

His words cause a wave of anxiety to flow through me. Something is obviously agitating him. Angie has already hinted that he is in a bad mood.

I lead everyone over to the sofa area that we recently enhanced with an area rug, some fresh potted plants, and extra pillows. Everything is bright and bold.

"I just got the news that I have to head to New York City tonight," Graham states, taking a seat right beside Angie. She is practically sitting on his lap.

She frowns. "I hate being alone at night in the penthouse."

"I know, sweetheart."

"Maybe I can sleep over at Claire's?" Her eyes are sad, and she looks over at me for support.

"I—"

"That's not a good idea," Nic says, interrupting me before I can state the same thing. He is hovering along the side of the sofa, instead of actually sitting down.

I glare at him for his unnecessary two cents. Why does he care? "It's not that bad," I defend. "But in all honesty, there's not more than an uncomfortable sofa to sleep on." The usage of the word "sofa" is an embellishment. In reality, the futon-esque bed that I am forced to sleep on at Blake's loft is as comfortable as sleeping on rocks. Lumpy and lacking any real form. "And it smells like stale dehydrated cheese powder." I see Angie's eyes well up, and Graham instantly comforts her.

"Will you just come with me on the trip?" he asks, looking down at her trembling form. "We can sightsee and go to dinner when we are there." She is trying to keep herself calm but I know the struggle. "See a show?"

"You know I can't."

"I can handle things here," I try to persuade. "You are free to go."

"No. We have too much to do here, and when Graham goes away, he never knows how long he will be gone. The last time I accompanied him, two nights turned into four."

"Then I can just come and stay at your place," I say softly. "Is that okay?"

Angie looks up at Graham with hope.

"Yeah, of course. You are always welcome at our home, whether I'm there or away. You are family to us."

Nic's eyes twitch.

"Okay, great," I say, clapping my hands together. "We are due for some girl time."

"Nic's in charge of you both," Graham says, his tone hard.

My arms cross at my chest. "I don't need a keeper," I say bluntly.

"You do when you are with my fiancée," Graham counters. "You both are magnets for trouble."

"I bet you we will not have a single incident while you are gone," Angie chimes in, perking up over the idea of having me over.

Graham kisses her hair. "Don't make promises to me that you can't keep."

"It's not a promise. It is a bet."

"And we know what happened the last time you lost to me," he says smiling, making her blush.

"I really don't need a keeper, though," I say, looking over at Nic who looks like an immovable statue. If I push this, I know I'll lose.

"Too bad you don't get a choice," he says flatly.

I scrunch up my nose at him and stick out my tongue. I can see his whole demeanor change, as he shifts his weight.

I get up from the couch cushions and exit into the break room where I fix a mug of tea, adding in my monk fruit sweetener that I have come to love. I add a little slice of lemon from the fridge and squeeze it into the hot liquid.

I feel Nic's presence behind me but don't even turn

around to address him. "You are like my personal satellite, homing in on my whereabouts," I point out.

Nic chuckles. "You act like your body doesn't like the attention."

"Oh, it does." I pivot and look at Nic leaning against the door frame. He really knows how to wear a suit. My mouth waters just looking at him.

"Don't stick your tongue out at me and then walk away."

"Or what?" I ask, turning back around to stir my drink, humming to myself. I remove the tea bag and place it into the trash can. Then I continue ignoring him, taking a sip of my drink, my back turned to him.

Nic's breath is at my neck. I can feel his dick pushed up against the small of my back. His hands reach around me. He places them onto the counter, caging me in. "Or you may just find yourself impaled on my cock where someone can walk in and see."

"And this is a problem, how?"

I hear the slam of the door behind me and the lock clicking into place. Nic takes the mug out of my hands and puts it farther back on the counter, out of my reach.

"Brace yourself with your hands."

I extend my hands and lean over against the edge of the counter. My dress flips up over my waist, and Nic's gasp lets me know that he approves of my thigh highs and lace panties.

"Fuck, you are breathtaking," he compliments. "This is going to be quick and hard."

"Well, then hurry the hell up," I goad.

"You drive me wild, woman."

Holding my hips, he slinks to the floor and shoves his face into my crotch, licking me through the fabric of my panties. I can barely keep myself still, as he makes a feast out of me.

Before I'm able to orgasm, Nic stops and stands, lining himself up. He pulls over my panties and sinks into me with one sudden move. He knows I am ready. I am always in a permanent state of readiness whenever he is nearby.

He moves one hand from my ass and travels it up my side, making me squirm and thrust back against him. He gathers my hair with one hand, pulling it to allow his mouth access to my neck.

Our grunts and moans fill the small cavity of the room. Sweat beads on my forehead, as Nic completely has his way with me. I love him like this. How he completely removes the control from me, so I have no time to think. To obsess. To second-guess. It is just a feral desire coming to fruition.

"I hope my memory is embedded in your brain as I leak out of you the rest of the day," he says, reaching around me and pressing his fingers on my clit.

"Well, I hope the smell of my pussy stays on you as a reminder," I grunt out.

I toss my head back in ecstasy, my hair flying wildly in the moment. I brace myself with arms extended, shifting my hips backwards to thrash into Nic's unyielding thrusts.

"Give me it, Claire. Let go."

"Ahh…"

"Your pleasure is my pleasure," he growls out, sucking in air deeply.

As if his words are my release button, I relax my inner

walls and allow the orgasm to move through me like a hurricane.

"Nic!"

"Yes, baby girl… I'm right there with you."

I feel the flood rush through me, as Nic holds us both up from flopping onto the floor. His cock pulses inside me, filling me up with his release. I turn boneless. Nic scoops me up, kisses my ear, and places me up onto the countertop.

"When you act like a bad girl, you get fucked in break rooms."

"What happens when I act like a good girl?" I inquire, genuinely curious.

Nic's sexy smirk lets me know he likes our little flirting game. "Then you get fucked in break rooms."

"Seems to me, I always win."

He fixes my panties into place and smooths down my dress. With gentle fingers, he runs them through my hair, straightening the mess that was made in the act.

It is in these little gestures of attentiveness that I fall a little harder. A little more. Until I know that I won't be able to stop what is happening between us.

I think I am in love with Nic Hoffman.

39

NIC

Graham warned me that watching out for Angie and Claire would have its challenges. He just didn't warn me how exhausting it would be on my nerves. He was one hundred percent correct in telling me that disaster follows these two wherever they go.

It started with Claire tripping and falling on her way out of the building, nearly causing a blood bath as she opened up a previous wound she had scabbed. Then when I got both of the girls back to the penthouse, Angie started throwing up with what I assume was food poisoning. I called Graham's personal physician, Dr. Mitch Saber, to come check her out and confirm that she just needed to suck down some fluids to avoid dehydration. He prescribed her some anti-nausea pills just in case the food poisoning is really a stomach bug. There's no good way to check for viruses, so it was really just a backup plan.

Fielding calls from Graham, who is literally going insane with worry over his girl being sick and hurt while he is away, is not fun either. I have basically told him that if I'm going to take care of things here, I need to spend less time trying to take care of him too. I cannot split my focus and get the job done right.

I finally have Angie resting comfortably upstairs and not retching into the toilet. Claire is camping out on the sofa and refusing to eat. What in the world... I am going to scream if she doesn't stop acting weird.

"I can order you some takeout from the vegan place just a couple of blocks away. There is also a really good Greek place that just opened."

"Ugh, quit talking about food. My stomach feels wavy," she groans, doubling over.

"What do you mean wavy?" I ask slowly, feeling the vein in my forehead popping.

"I need fresh air. Open the window."

I stare at her in disbelief. Being at the top of the building, there are no windows that open. That is not a thing.

"I'm going to—"

Claire darts up from the couch, runs down the hallway, throws herself into the spare bathroom, and slams the door.

"Claire," I yell, trying the doorknob. Luckily, she didn't lock it.

"Ahhhh..."

I grab her hair as she retches into the porcelain bowl. She is trembling and crying, making my heart hurt from seeing her this way.

"Hey, baby, it's okay. Just let it all out."

After about four bursts, she slinks back into my arms, as I hold her on the bathroom floor.

"I knew we shouldn't have had deli food for lunch.

Probably both got sick from all of the preservatives and nitrates and carcinogens. Yuck."

"Do you feel better?" I ask, rubbing her arms and sides. She feels so small in my arms, like a delicate little flower.

"Yeah. I feel much better now."

"Less ocean wavy?"

"Much less," she giggles.

"Good."

I pick her up and carry her over to the sink. I load her toothbrush—a new one I found in the drawer—with toothpaste and hand it over to her. Her weak smile is on her lips in the reflection of the mirror.

"Thanks for taking such good care of me."

I want to tell her that it's nothing special. That I am just doing for her what I would do for a friend. That's what we are, right? Friends. I promised Graham I would look out for Claire and Angie. This is just part of my duty.

I help Claire get to the spare room, stripping off her clothes and pulling over her head an oversized sleep shirt. She refuses to unpack her little pink-and-white-striped suitcase. When asked, she just shrugs sadly and mumbles something about the stay here just being temporary. Something tells me that she is used to temporary but yearns for forever.

I turn back the comforter for her to climb inside the bed. Her body barely takes up a quarter of the mattress. She looks so small and fragile against the stark white of the sheets.

"I'm going to go get you some ginger ale and maybe something light to have on your stomach. Are you in the mood for anything else?"

"Just a drink is fine. No food, please. Just the thought of eating anything is making my stomach clench."

I nod. "Okay. Be right back."

I walk into Graham's kitchen and find the ginger ale that I had delivered when Angie first started showing signs of illness. I fill up a glass with ice and pour the soda over top, watching it fizz. I slice up some lemons from the fridge and squeeze some into the glass. This is what Mom would do for me as a child when I had a stomach bug. The citrus from the lemon always settled my stomach.

When Claire takes the first sip, she closes her eyes and moans with delight. "This tastes extra good."

I smile at her. "I'm glad. I'll let you get some rest." I turn to walk out of the room, and Claire reaches for my hand to stop me.

"Please stay with me."

I nod and remove my pants and shirt to get more comfortable. Claire moves over to make more room for me, and I climb in beside her. My body molds against hers, and she instantly relaxes to my gentle touches. I wish I could say she makes me a better man. Problem is, I can't stop thinking of ways that this is all wrong. That sticking around longer is just prolonging the inevitable.

I am not the type of man who women dream about. I am too realistic to fall for the phony promise of forever.

I can't sleep with Claire's soft body pressed up against me. My dick has been alive since her first inadvertent touch, and I've been struggling to sleep ever since. If she wasn't as sick as she was the night before, I may have woken her up with some kisses or some purposeful touches. I have seen her sexual appetite. I know she would be game.

She rolls and stretches, moving her arms above her head as she groans. Her eyes open slowly, and she turns to look at me.

"You stayed," she murmurs, sleep still present in her voice.

"You didn't give me much choice," I say with a wink.

Her eyes study mine. "You are such a good guy, Nic. Thanks for taking care of me last night. I'm glad you were here with me."

"I'm not a good guy, Claire."

"Whatevs."

I pull myself up and rest my elbow on the pillow. "I've done unthinkable things in order to get my own way."

Her eyes narrow as she allows my words to penetrate her brain. She sits up and leans back against her pillows, her hair draped over her shoulders, wavy from sleep. "Why are you trying so hard to convince me otherwise?"

"I just need you to know that I'm not the honorable man you think you see. I'm just good at concealing the truth."

"Whatever," she chirps, obviously not taking me seriously—as if she knows me better than I know myself. "If being all mysterious and emo makes you feel like more of a man, go for it. But I'm a pretty decent judge of character—Ethan aside—and what I see is someone who just needs a little validation. I'm sorry you were hurt in the past, whatever that may be, but healing takes time, and I'm available if you ever want to talk about it."

My eyes dart away from hers. She may think she knows

me, but she doesn't. I watch in silence as she meanders into the bathroom and starts the shower. I want to join her, but I also need to stop blurring the lines. She is getting too close. Her heart is getting too involved in thinking we have a chance.

I leave Claire to get ready for the day and make my way into the kitchen to fix some breakfast. Angie is coming down the stairs when I finish flipping the last pancake.

"Wow," she states, looking at the skillet.

"What?" I ask, turning around and narrowing my eyes. Why does it feel like every little thing I do today is met with a full-blown psychoanalysis?

She hums. "Oh, nothing."

"I know you have something on your mind. Might as well share it."

"It's just that Claire loves pancakes." She shrugs. "That's all. Carry on."

I know this, of course. It is probably why making them was the first thing that crossed my mind. But who doesn't love pancakes? Pretty much no one. So, making this into a big deal is not necessary.

I turn back around and plate up my creations, just in time for Claire to walk out of the spare room wearing a long lilac tank dress. I know the color well because it is Mom's favorite shade. She often sprinkles that color throughout my parents' house. Having an eye for design, it is easy for her to make everything look good.

Claire walks closer to me, and I can't help but notice how her curves are accentuated by the fit of the fabric. Even in just a simple cut dress, she looks stunning. Then again, she always looks amazing.

"Wow, you made pancakes?" she asks, standing on her tiptoes to get a better look.

"Yeah. I used almond milk." I refuse to make eye contact with either of them. Both girls keep staring at me for different reasons. Both keep hovering around me like I am part of a filming for a documentary.

Everything is weird, because they are making it that way.

Claire takes a seat at the island and accepts the plate of food I offer her.

"You guys feeling better today?" I ask, trying to change the subject off my cooking.

"Much," Angie answers first. "And I am ravished and ready to binge."

Claire just nods, taking a big bite of her pancake. I know she approves because she eagerly goes back to cut off more with the edge of her fork.

I eat standing up, allowing the girls to take up the majority of the space at the counter.

"I need a distraction while Graham's gone or I will go nuts," Angie whines. "I hate when he's away, and I can't go with him. Plus, not knowing when he'll be back is killing me. Anyway, are you up for a night out after work?"

Claire's eyes come to life. "You know I always am," she chants.

I know by tonight my nerves will be shot, and I'll be walking around like a madman. I know that they both are going to make it extremely difficult to keep them safe without getting myself arrested.

But most importantly, I hate it when my brother is right.

"Oh no, Nic looks stressed," Angie says with a frown.

I glare at my soon-to-be sister-in-law. "I'm not stressed."

"Yes, you are," Angie says with a smirk.

Claire's face turns serious, but I know it is fake from the twinkle in her eyes. "We promise to be good girls tonight and follow all of the rules."

I look up at the ceiling and let a groan escape. "I highly doubt that even you believe that."

"It's not our fault that trouble finds us," Claire defends, scraping the plate to get every morsel off. "We are innocent."

I shake my head at her, serving her another two pancakes. I'm so happy to see her back to eating. "What time should I be ready for girls' night?"

"You aren't invited," Claire says boldly.

"We both know that's not true."

40

CLAIRE

Open Mic Night at The Shack has become a ritual for Angie and me since our college days. While the venue has been able to up its security and stick with the fire code laws, the place is still a dive in comparison to the places we frequented in Vegas.

No matter how much whining Angie and I did, there was no getting out of having Nic chaperone us. Trust me, we tried. I even lowered myself into offering some very specific sexual favors as part of the negotiation process. Apparently, the wrath of Graham or the mere chance of us getting hurt while we are here weighed more to him than me offering up my ass in a cat costume—which I am glad about because I was only bluffing. I'm not sure I will ever be ready for that level of trust with a man. The ass part, not the costume. I love costumes.

As expected, the line at The Shack is obnoxiously long. My pencil stick black heels scream at me in defiance, as I teeter on them. Waiting outside in the spring is much better than the winter. However, my outfit selection is the same, regardless of the season. I have on a skimpy black dress that has a strapless corset as the top. My hair is piled high on top of my head, and I have on dangling silver earrings that almost touch my shoulders. My makeup is shimmery and bold. If I was on the street, I would probably look like a hooker.

Working long hours and obsessing over money and where to live have taken a toll on my body. I'm exhausted and stressed over the uncertainties of my future. I haven't talked to my mom since the day we discussed my tuition bills. Part of me hoped she would voluntarily call just to check in with me, but as usual, she is too wrapped up in her own life's mess to have a care about mine. It should hurt me more than it does. Maybe I'm numb to it all. Or maybe I am just unlovable.

Angie and I are close enough to the front of the line where we can finally see the bouncer. Nic is hovering behind us like a father figure, fitting into the scene as you would expect an introvert to fit in at a party. Maybe with a few drinks in me, I can start calling him Big Daddy or something equally embarrassing. I'm sure he would hate it, and that makes me like the idea even more.

Ever since we had the whole I-am-dark-and-dangerous conversation in the spare bedroom, things have been weird between us. I know it has only been twelve hours, but I can tell awkward when I feel it. It's as if Nic is having a battle inside and he is the only fighter. Yeah, he made me pancakes and that was sweet. But then when we walked into HH, he didn't even address me when I was walking away. One minute he is making out with me and then the next he is telling me he's not good for me. I thought women had this type of reputation for being wishy-washy, but Nic has everyone beat.

I look over at Angie checking her texts. "Has Graham contacted you? Everything okay with him? I wonder if—"

"Hmm?" she asks, looking at me with confusion.

I shake my head. "It's fine. I'm just excited for a night to relax."

Angie nods and then places her phone back into her handbag. "I'm sorry, Claire. My mind is elsewhere, and I need this night too. Between the wedding approaching and all of my ideas getting jumbled in my head over Plus None, I feel like some days I'm drowning in just my thoughts."

I give her hand a squeeze. "I know we aren't sharing a roof consistently, but I can always come over and hang out with you if you need girl time."

Her smile is sad. "I don't deserve you."

"Nonsense," I huff. "We were meant for each other, and you can't ever deny that."

Angie wraps me up in her arms. "I love you."

"Feeling's mutual. And there's no return policy. You're stuck with me for life."

"For that, I am thankful."

When we pay our entrance fee and get inside, the place is jam-packed, just like it always was. I haven't been here in months. Despite the safety flaws supposedly fixed, I wouldn't know at first glance by how everyone is standing shoulder to shoulder.

I try to push my way through the crowd but no one budges.

"This place sucks," Nic growls behind me.

I completely forgot he was even here tagging along, so his voice startles me and makes me jump.

"Quit being so hoity-toity," I say, scrunching up my nose. "You don't come here for the ambience, you come here for the cheap drinks and greasy food."

I grab ahold of Nic's arm and use his body like a train to push through the crowd. Everyone is smart enough to back away and make room for us. I squeeze into an opening at the bar and wave over the regular bartender like I have stock in the place.

"I need the cheapest beer you have on tap and the worst tasting whiskey that exists in this hellhole," I say. "Oh, and one of everything on the appetizer menu."

"And for you?" He eyes me with a smirk.

"A margarita, of course!" I turn to Angie and give her a look. "Make that two!" I call back.

"So you want to get me drunk and take advantage of me?" Nic asks, shadowing me from behind.

"No, I want to get you drunk so you will stop pointing your nose up like you are better than this place."

"It's unsafe here."

I turn around, placing my back against the bar. "Quit thinking about work. Just relax your shoulders and enjoy the financial freedom that cheap beer gives to people."

He throws back his head and laughs. "Well, I can't wait to take the first sip of financial freedom."

"Wait no longer," the bartender says behind us, placing four drinks down onto the bar's surface for the three of us.

There is nothing fancy about the margaritas served here, yet they are so good. Just cheap tequila and secret sugary lime mixture over ice.

Nic places some cash onto the bar and tells the bartender to keep the change.

"Thanks for the drink," I say, giving Nic a weak smile. I watch as he takes a swig from his beer and resists making a face—even though I know the struggle is real. "How does it taste?"

"Like liquified cardboard."

"Yum," Angie chimes in, giggling. "You are definitely Graham's brother." She changes her voice to be more masculine. "'I only drink craft beer.'"

I laugh over her impersonation and do one of my own in my man voice. "I only like cigar lounges with better ambience."

Angie and I are laughing so hard that we are snorting. Every time we glance at Nic, we go back to losing it. He is so stiff tonight.

Bar stools free up, and I climb up onto one awkwardly, probably flashing anyone who decides to watch. Nic and Angie sandwich me in, and we sip on our low shelf liquor. Well, Nic is done with his before I can really get comfortable on the stool. Short girl problems.

Open Mic Night features local artists and poetry readers from all around Portland. The clientele averages around the age of twenty-two, but there is a thirty-something crowd that seems to frequent the venue, probably on the prowl for young dates.

"Do you spot anyone we know?" I ask.

"No. And it's not like we graduated that long ago."

Nic clears his throat beside me, and I look over at his expression of indifference. I wish he would tell me why he is so moody lately. I also hope that sex can fix it, as it is my only superpower.

After half a drink, I cut myself off, feeling lightheaded and not my best self. I lean my body weight against the bar top and listen as the next performer is announced. When the tall drink of water makes it onto the stage, Angie and I suck in air through our teeth. At least we both can still appreciate the male form—no matter what stage we are in of life.

"Really, ladies? Are you really checking out guys here?" Nic says, looking uncomfortable.

"Oh stop," Angie scolds. "You know I'm deliriously happy with your brother. Plus, women can check people out without it being creepy like you guys all seem to make it."

"Hey, don't stereotype me," Nic says laughing. "I have feelings too."

I get the bartender to bring me a glass of ice water and guzzle it down with just a few gulps. The food arrives, and we snack on the grease-filled appetizers. As soon as the first piece hits my stomach, I feel queasy and stop before I get sick again. All of my work at cleansing toxins from my body will be for nothing if I destroy my insides with this one meal. I ask for some celery and carrots that I know they use to garnish their hot wings baskets.

Angie has moments of sadness when I glance at her, and I know she misses Graham. She once told me that when he is away, it is like her heart is only half beating. I am positive Graham feels the same way about her.

Nic tenses beside me, and I can tell he is counting down the minutes until we leave. I thought being here would feel nostalgic. Instead, I feel like I have already moved on. That being bumped into constantly and having splatters of beer spilled on me is no longer what I would call fun.

More acts make it to the stage, and the volume at which the sound system is set to is almost deafening. I feel my brain pulsating.

Angie leans into my ear. "I feel too old for this place."

I smile. "I was just thinking the same thing."

"Let's go dancing instead," she suggests.

"Where do you have in mind?"

"Some place less crowded and more our style. Incognito?"

"Sounds great."

As we are about to exit the building, my eye catches Deena in the corner of the room—with Ethan nowhere in sight. Her eyes track my movement. She looks so out of place, and I wonder if she's following me. Why else would she be here of all places?

Powering on my phone, I shoot her a text.

Claire: Quit stalking me.

It doesn't take her long to check her phone and respond with her typical snark.

Deena: Stay away from my husband.

Claire: Ex-husband.

Deena: We are engaged, you home wrecker!

Claire: You must be delusional to think I'd ever want Ethan again. He's damaged and there's not a pussy on this planet—and that's essentially all you are to him—that can fix that for him. But have fun trying. He loves having someone who he can control. I'm done. Tell your FIANCE to stop texting me.

Deena: Bitch

"What has you looking so satisfied?" Angie asks, as we get into the back of the vehicle.

Nic is his usual tense self. The man needs to loosen up a little. My little nonverbal spat with Deena is giving me a bigger pep in my step. Maybe some of my good mood will rub off on him.

"Oh, just the joy of sitting back and watching karma do her job."

Angie looks at me with suspicion. "But you're good?"

I shake my head. "Yeah. I'm great, actually."

41

CLAIRE

In his sleep, I am able to get a better look at Nic's features. His strong jawline. His five o'clock shadow. I am able to notice how he fills up over half the bed with his body. I mean, no woman ever would not find the muscular and uber-masculine man attractive. Must suck to be him.

With hesitation, I trace a finger along his cheekbone, around his lips, and then along the pulsing vein in his neck. I lean in and press my lips to his, savoring the softness.

I'm not surprised he is sound asleep. We stayed up way too late dancing and laughing. Turns out, Nic has some moves I haven't seen before, and the sway of his hips on the dance floor almost caused me to come on the spot. It became our little game to sneak seductive moves whenever Angie would use the restroom or turn her back. I hate hiding things from my best friend, but it serves no good purpose for her to know that Nic and I are together—at least not until we make our relationship status official.

While we never had *that* conversation, I know that he

isn't seeing anyone else. We spend our working hours in the same building and our off hours together. Nic may not want a label, but to me, he is very much mine. A friend doesn't rub your feet. A friend doesn't turn the massage into back-to-back orgasms either. We have been *more* for a while, and I couldn't be happier.

"Having fun?" he asks sleepily, opening one eye and then the other.

I look down at my hands that are exploring his body. "Yup."

"Glad I could meet your needs."

"And then some. Now, go back to sleep, so I can keep admiring you before you say something to ruin it all."

Stretching up on his elbows, he gives me a sexy smirk. It's the one where only the one corner of his lips lifts up, and his eyes get hooded as a result. It's the one that stops my breath and makes me wonder how someone like me got a man like him.

Girls like me end up with losers. They sure as hell do not score men like Nic Hoffman.

He is attentive. He is giving. He is a caffeinated jolt to my self-esteem.

Nic reminds me that I deserve good things, even if I don't always think I am worthy of them.

I straddle him and rub my pussy along his hard length.

"Someone's horny," he says, his voice gruff.

"Always around you."

I lift up my hips and slide down onto him. Nic flips me onto my back, remaining inside and pulling out my pleasure so fast that I am left panting from the fierceness.

"You can do more," he states, as if it is a fact. He is so

cocky and acts as if he knows my body better than myself. It is a sobering fact that this is very much a possibility.

Even when I think it's not possible, he proves me wrong. Maybe I'm a challenge to him. Maybe his ego won't accept anything but me being depleted and drained of my energy. Regardless, I just hold on for the ride and allow him to dictate my pleasure—openly and willingly.

I lie spent beside him, curling into his side as we both relax into the soft comfort of the king-sized bed.

"Claire?"

"Hmm?"

"We need to talk."

Normally I would be wary of a conversation that starts out like this. But lying naked beside him, with the proof of his arousal leaking out of me onto the sheets, I know that this talk is much needed and a way of putting our relationship into terms. We both deserve it.

"Okay," I say, lifting myself up against a backdrop of pillows. He is finally able to accept what we are. He just needed time to come to his own conclusion without any pressure. If we can admit our true feelings to each other, it will be easier to share them with our family and friends. I am tired of hiding. I want to scream to the world that Nic Hoffman is my man. Hands off, ladies. Eyes off too.

"I've been wanting to tell you this but struggled with finding the right words. So, bear with me..."

"It's okay," I say, squeezing his hand for moral support. "Just take a deep breath."

"I think I am—" He stops midsentence and looks into my eyes. It's as if he is searching for a lifeline, and I care about him too much not to throw him one.

I smile at him. I know this is tough. Neither of us expected it. "Nic, I feel the same way. I am in love with you too."

His eyes look like the light gets shut off behind them. He removes his hand from mine and sits up on the bed. His hands squeeze into the sheets, balling them into his fists, before moving them to the back of his neck.

"What did you just say?" he asks, holding his head as if my words of declaration are somehow causing him pain.

"I said that I love you," I whisper-choke.

Isn't it obvious?

We've been spending every nonworking hour together. My belongings are scattered about his apartment, as if we unofficially moved in together. He makes me breakfast on most mornings or we grab it to go on our way into work.

"No."

"No? What do you mean *no*?"

Nic rubs at the sides of his face. "This"—he motions with his hands back and forth between us—"was never supposed to get this far."

"Well it did," I state bluntly. Why is he so freaking stubborn?

He stands up from the bed and paces around the room. "Temporary, Claire. This was supposed to be temporary! It was just an interlude."

I shake my head at him, pulling the sheet up to cover my chest. I no longer feel comfortable in front of him. I no longer feel desired. And the safety net that I once saw in him is shredded apart, just like every fucking good thing I ever had in my life. "An *interlude*?"

"Yes, Claire, dammit. This was just—"

"You did *not* just describe what we have together as a fucking filler activity." My tone comes out angrier than I expect, when deep down I am devastatingly sad. Destroyed and broken. I'm as expendable to him as I was to Ethan. And even now, as my heart shatters apart into a million unrecognizable pieces, I imagine taking Nic back in this moment—if he would just say sorry.

But he doesn't say sorry. He doesn't say anything. He just fucking stands there watching me move further and further away from him emotionally, without a care.

It's almost like he likes toying with my most vulnerable insecurities, breathing life into them, and reminding me that at my core I'm unlovable. Not even my family wants me.

"I don't have relationships, Claire. I just fuck for fun."

"Glad I could be a palate cleanser for you," I state sarcastically, throwing myself out of bed to find clothes to wear. I walk over to my unpacked luggage and pull out a long-sleeved dress and slide it over my head, forgoing any undergarments. "Why are you trying to waste away what we have together? Huh?" I ask, charging toward him. I place my hands on his chest and push. "Why? How do I deserve this treatment? We have never been casual. Why are you trying to act like we were? I am your brother's fiancée's best friend, and you are basically treating me like shit. A fucking bed warmer? Really? This is really happening? What are you scared of, Nic Hoffman? And why was I tempting enough for you to want to bed in the first place? Out of all the women you could have shoved your cock into, why choose me?"

His jaw ticks over my ranting words. "I have a type, Claire."

"Oh really? And what type is that, Nic?"

"I like bad girls. Ones who stray. Ones who know the fucking score."

His words burn like a wildfire raging through my body, inflaming everything into a fiery ball that culminates and settles in the pit of my stomach. I feel disgusted and betrayed by this idea that we could be good for each other, when in reality, he is the worst type of man for me. In all of my dating history, I have never had someone hurt me as much as Nic Hoffman has hurt me in this very moment—not even Ethan.

I don't want to be his bad girl. I don't want to be his anything.

Tears well up in my eyes, and I wipe harshly to keep them from falling in front of the very man who caused them to form in the first place. I don't want to shed them. Nic doesn't deserve to see my raw emotion. He doesn't deserve any part of me.

My nose runs as my eyes refuse to stay dry. I sniffle into the sleeve of my dress, trying to force the zipper of my luggage to close. I huff and tug, trying to press down on the case at the same time I pull on the metal handle of the zipper.

Nic walks over to me to assist, and I shove him so hard to stay away from me.

"Don't you come near me!" I snap, picking up the luggage sideways and carrying it toward the door, with articles of clothing sticking out of the sides.

"I'm sorry, Claire. I never wanted—"

I turn around in the frame of the door to glare daggers at his pale form, making him stop midsentence. He has the promise of *never* written all over his face. How could I be this stupid? Everything is so obvious when I take off the rose-colored glasses and really see him for what he is. His hollowed heart doesn't need fixing—it needs destroying. And I can only hope that no woman after me ever feels the rage I have boiling inside for this weak man.

"Let me—"

"No! Not another word."

I have heard enough from his mouth. He has the nerve to look sincere. What a fraud!

"I'm sorry."

"Oh, don't do that. Don't give me the fake fucking apologies. And what do you have to be sorry for when this was probably your ultimate plan the whole time?" I watch as his face pales, and his eyes look off to the side of the room. "It was, wasn't it? You bastard!"

"Claire—"

"I hate you. I fucking hate you. I hate everything about you." But not any more than I hate myself for falling in love with a man who only was destined to break my heart.

"I know," he says solemnly.

"We are over. So even if you manage to get your egotistical head out of your ass long enough to see what you are missing out on, I will never go back to you. I have too much self-worth to degrade myself any more than you have done in this moment. I deserve better."

"I know."

"You know what the biggest side effect of sleeping with you is, Nic?" I ask, hoisting my luggage up so it doesn't fall out of my arms.

"What?"

"Regret."

My word strikes him and in the moment, it makes me happy to lash out. He gives me the last word, and I walk out into the hallway and out the door. I call for the elevator and text Angie that I need to go out for the day. I hate leaving her alone when she obviously dislikes it. But I hate being around Nic Hoffman more right now, and getting away from him trumps everything.

Damn him.

I wish I could hate him more than I hate myself right now. But deep down, I am so disappointed in myself for believing that I am enough for a man to change.

Men don't change.

They just hide their feelings until they blow up in their faces. Unfortunately, his explosive declaration hit me straight in the heart.

I keep falling into the same cycle over and over again. Maybe it's not the man who needs to change? Maybe it's me. I'm the one who is damaged and needs to be fixed.

42

CLAIRE

I'm not even inside the protection of my car when my phone buzzes to life. Leave it to Nic to want me now that I've walked away. Except, when I glance at the sender, it's not from Nic at all. The messages are from Ethan, and some are time stamped hours ago.

Ethan: I need to talk to you.

Ethan: Ignoring me will have a cost.

Ethan: CALL ME DAMMIT

Fuck him.

I open the driver's side door, fling myself inside, and toss my phone down onto the passenger seat. I hate Ethan. *I really fucking hate him.* Looking back, most of our relationship is now just a series of a bunch of regrets. He made me live in trash. He treated me like trash. He is trash.

And part of me blames Ethan for Nic becoming part of my unhappy ending.

If it wasn't for Ethan being a horrible man, then I wouldn't have allowed Nic to sneak his way into my life.

Sure, I learned lessons from both men, but those are lessons that people could go through life never learning—and still turn out fine. But instead, I carry around this mental burden of an ex-boyfriend who won't go away and a man who couldn't get me to go away fast enough.

Why do I always pick the wrong men?

I left one bad relationship just to enter into a worse one. Without a doubt, Nic is most definitely the worst out of everyone I've ever dated. Nic befriended me, seduced me, and then gave me false hope for a future. I honestly wish he would have kept up with being an asshole for the duration of all our interactions.

It's easy to hate the asshole.

It's confusing to start to like the asshole that is jaded.

I thought I could fix Nic. That somehow, I held this unseen level of power—and responsibility. But he's not my responsibility at all. He's not my anything.

Then there's Ethan. I thought I could ignore him, and that is proving not to be the case. His attention torments me and I'm tired of him preying over my shoulder—trying to taint everything in my life that he touches.

But today it stops.

Because if anything is going to change, that change has to start with me.

Opening up my search engine, I type in Ethan's full name. Why I never thought to do this prior is a mistake on me. I give people the benefit of the doubt. I'm too trusting.

And just like that, I have the address for Ethan's single-family home in the suburbs. It's the house he hid from me and never wanted me to visit. I apparently deserved the fuck pad while Deena lived it up in the mansion.

I start my engine, flick off the radio, and settle into the silence that envelops me. Allowing the GPS to dictate where I'm going, I pull out of the parking garage and onto the street.

I'm done being controlled.

Ethan Maxwell is about to get checkmated.

Like most of my ideas, this one sounded better in my head. I just can't control my curiosity over Ethan's alternate residence and have to see for myself. Ever since I learned he has been lying to me about just how much money he makes, I've been itching to get my own look at everything I missed out on while we were still together.

While the prick had me living in a rundown fuck pad, he was sneaking away to his luxurious abode—which is practically a mansion. My eyes scan the residence, with the perfectly manicured lawn and the magazine-worthy views. All the time we dated—or should I say *fucked*—he kept this pristine palace tucked away for safekeeping, careful not to allow my presence to taint its beauty.

Well, too fucking bad.

I'm here. And I'm not going anywhere until I get my words out. Ethan's been on me ever since I told him off at the Parkhouse Plaza. He started this shitstorm, so it's on him to handle my wrath. He used me, and I was naïve enough to let him. But that's all about to change.

Grabbing my phone out of the pocket of my dress, I take a selfie with my middle finger raised in front of his home and then type out my message.

Claire: You want me? Come and fucking try to get me.

Placing my device back into my pocket, I walk along the perimeter of the house. Ethan could be anywhere right now, but I'm positive he'll be standing in front of me soon enough. Then it'll be easier for me to get a punch in on his pretty face. Heaven knows he deserves it.

I find the playground in the backyard that is behind the pool. Everything is so obvious now that I know the truth. Ethan was never going to commit to me. It was never part of his ideal plan. Instead, I was strung along until he either got back with Deena or found someone better.

Sitting down on the swing, I kick my feet out to get momentum. All these months, I was a temporary fix for Ethan's sex drive. When things started fizzling out, I should have known he found another source to keep him satisfied. If there's one thing I'm sure of, it's that I'm never going back to that fucker ever again.

"I see breaking and entering will be an addition to your rap sheet."

My neck jerks toward his voice, as my stomach drops. "I entered. But it's you I'm going to break."

"You owe me money."

"I owe you nothing."

"Oh, you most definitely owe me. You have the Hoffman brothers trying to derail me."

"As usual, I have no idea what you're talking about, Ethan."

"It's low, Claire, to get them to mess with my career."

Using my feet to slow down the swing, I jump off before it fully stops. Dressed in an expensive suit, I can tell he is returning back home from something important. His foul mood is present on his face, and a part of me silently gloats over being the reason why. I hope I inconvenienced him, just as much as he's been inconveniencing me.

From being forced to move, to having to go to a damn storage facility, to getting kicked out of one of the best restaurants in town...

To say, "I'm over it," is only putting it mildly.

"What do you want from me?" I demand, taking a step closer with each spoken word. My voice is calm and steady, but the adrenaline rushing through me is anything but. It's as if I'm charged and ready to snap. I wave a hand into the air, toward all his possessions. "You have everything you could possibly want here, and yet you can't keep my memory out of your fucking head. What, Ethan? Are you going to pull the whole 'if you can't have me, no one can'? Is that what this is? And have you even told your precious Deena the truth? Because I bet she's curious as to why you are fucking her but thinking about me. You need to cut the ties and leave me to live my own life. Stop texting me. Stop trying to get my attention. Are you bored? Is that it?"

"I want to continue our arrangement."

My eyes twitch as I study his face. What is he talking

about? "You're going to need to clarify. I have no clue what you're even saying—yet again."

His eyes roam over my body, taking extra time at every curve along the journey. He's so gross. How did I not see it before?

"Be my little side chick."

"Your wh—"

"Spread your pretty legs," he says, gesturing to my crotch, "and I'll make it worth it like I've done all along."

"You are nuts. Like pathologically insane."

He takes a step closer, forcing every hair on my arms to stand in salute. "You've always had a smartass mouth on you. It's about time you learned some respect. I'll have fun silencing you with my cock shoved down your throat."

Bubbling from deep in my belly, I let out a guttural growl. "I'm done being your whore, you self-serving, delusional prick! There's not enough money in circulation on this entire planet that would ever entice me to want to go back to you."

Without thinking, my hand swings back and whips through the air. The whistling sound hits my ears before connecting with the strong jawbone of Ethan Maxwell.

Crack.

Pain sears through my entire arm, radiating from my palm all the way up to my shoulder. Fuck, that hurt.

Shock permeates my conscious thought, as disbelief fights its way to the front. Ethan deserved what I served him. There's no denying it. But I still can't believe I actually hit him.

I hit him.

Gripping my hand, I clutch it to my chest, doubling over

from the impact. My knees start to buckle, and I force my legs to stay strong. Now is definitely not the time to fold and crumble at this monster's feet.

"You little bitch," he snarls, coming out of his trance. Grabbing my hair, he drags me through the yard.

Tears flood my eyes as my fingers wrestle with his to let go. "Please stop!"

"Don't you dare start. You did this," he sneers, continuing to walk. "And you're going to pay."

"You're hurting me!"

"That's the point."

I double step to keep up, feeling like my scalp is going to get ripped off my skull if I slow the pace too much. Lifting my knee, I connect with his groin, causing Ethan to release his hold on my hair.

Spinning around, I run toward the direction of the driveway where my car is safely parked, only getting a few yards before a force hits the back of my knees. My body flies forward, and just as I brace myself for hitting the earth, I am launched upright and over Ethan's shoulder.

"Fuck you!" I scream, beating on his back. I wiggle until he can no longer hold me.

When I'm on my feet, my sore hand whips through the air again, but this time it's caught and twisted around to the back of me.

"Pay up in cash or in pussy for what you owe me, you fucking whore."

"Or what?" I stand my ground. "You going to rape me?"

"Rape would mean you don't consent. And we both know how hungry your cunt is for what I can offer it. You don't become an escort unless you love a little degradation. I get off on it too."

"Go back to your fiancée and treat her like an animal— if that's what she's into. But it stops here with me."

"You want me, Claire. Otherwise you would have picked a neutral place to meet up and not my family home. You're testing me by coming here, but I'll always come out the victor."

"I don't want anything from you!" I shove him back, but when I do, his hand cracks across my face. Tears jolt out of my eyes, and I stumble backward. When my vision clears and Ethan's smug face fills up my entire view…

I go ballistic.

Throwing myself forward, I thrust my entire body into his, causing him to fall. Straddling him, I rip his hair with one hand and pound on the side of his face with my other hand.

I hit.

And slap.

And punch.

And bite and kick and slam.

When my sweaty body is so exhausted from the fight I no longer want to be a part of, I step away from Ethan's limp body and make the trek to my car. Glancing over my shoulder, I see my ex-asshole attempting to get up. But he doesn't follow me.

And I can only hope his spirit no longer has any fight left in it as well.

It's a sobering realization that I have few people in my life to lean on in this moment. I can't call Graham. I definitely won't call Nic. And while Angie would help, it would pull her into a shitstorm she doesn't deserve to be in.

So I drive and drive.

When I get to Blake's loft, I throw my unclosed luggage onto the sofa next to Henry who is playing some murder-everything-in-sight video game. He grunts a hello and then undresses me with his eyes in between scenes. I feel like I need a shower.

Making my way into the kitchen, I retrieve an ice pack from the freezer and apply it to my swelling hand before using it on my face. If I'm going to keep taking swings at men, I should probably learn some type of fighting technique, because dammit, this hurts.

"Where's Blake?"

Henry points to his room, and I walk over and give it a couple of light knocks. He opens, gives me a once-over, and then frowns. "What's wrong? You're holding ice. Something is obviously wrong. I won't take no for an answer. You are going to tell me everything."

I walk in, flop down on his perfectly made bed, and cover my eyes with my hands. "My life is a mess."

"Again?"

"Yes, again."

"Oh no, what happened? Start from the beginning."

"I fell in love with a man who is incapable of loving me back. And the guy that I broke up with prior to that is curled up in the fetal position on his front lawn from the injuries I inflicted on him. All well deserved."

"Damn, girl. Love? There's so much to unpack here.

You really think it's love? Didn't you just meet him? And are you going to be arrested?"

"It's love," I say flatly, trying to follow Blake's train of thought. "I wish it wasn't, but it is. And it sucks. Zero out of ten, I do not recommend. And as for being arrested, I sure hope not."

"How did this happen? And so quickly?"

"Nic and I have known each other for a year. Plus, over the whole wedding planning, we've spent a ton of time together. Trust me, if I could choose who I would fall in love with, I sure as hell wouldn't have picked him."

"Oh Claire Bear, I'm sorry," he says, sitting on the edge of the bed, patting my leg. "How can I help without being your rebound?"

I laugh through my tears. Of course Blake would make me laugh at my lowest. Every time I think about the moment I told Nic that I love him and seeing his appalled reaction, I get sick to my stomach. Ugh, how could I have been so stupid? For someone who prides herself on reading people, I sure misread Nic.

"I just need to gain control of my life and make some money so I can find a place to live on my own. I'm tired of allowing life to drag me down."

"Give yourself time to grieve for a relationship that is ending, Claire. Otherwise you are just masking the pain that you feel inside and will just move laterally, instead of moving forward."

I nod. "You're right. But change starts today. Mark my words, Blake, I refuse to look back when I can move forward."

"You're going to need to grieve for the loss of this relationship, Claire Bear. So, all of this tough girl facade may work on someone else, but you don't have me fooled. Let's go watch some movie where a pet dog dies, and we can cry it out together on the couch."

"That sounds counterproductive."

"Nope. Quite the opposite. We need to detox from these bad relationships with the cleansing of tears. It will be ceremonial. Like saging yourself from the inside out. Would you prefer those highway dog rescue videos instead? I'm sure we can find a compilation clip."

"The one where another dog pulls a hit dog out of traffic?"

"That's the one. So worth it."

"Henry is there with his warm cheesy breath playing video games."

"Not for long. The dude needs to get a hobby."

Blake pulls me from the bed and pushes his door open a bit too hard, making it slam against the side wall.

"Easy!" Henry yells, jumping back farther into the sofa where I have to sleep tonight.

"Eww," Blake whines, making a face at his roommate. "What are you eating?"

"My feelings," Henry mumbles, shoving more cheese curls into his mouth. "It's been an emotional day."

"Claire and I need the couch," Blake says with authority. He's usually not this brash, but desperate times must call for desperate measures.

"Friends with benefits. Nice."

Just the way he emphasizes the word "nice" makes my skin crawl. Henry is so—

Immature?

Inappropriate?

Brazen?

All of the above.

"Up," Blake reiterates, snapping his fingers. "You've been here the entire night. Claire's back, and we're having a movie marathon day."

"Now that sounds like a fun time for a foursome. There's room on my lap for you, Claire."

I scrunch up my brow in confusion, but before I can ask what he is talking about, a tall, blonde chick walks out of the bathroom, wearing a ratty no-name band T-shirt and a cutoff denim miniskirt.

"This is Lilly," Henry says, motioning toward the stranger.

"It's Lucy," she corrects.

"Well, this is fine and dandy," Blake says, clapping his hands together, "but Claire and I have a date for two." He holds up his two fingers and wiggles them in front of Henry's face, as he dodges the obstruction to see the screen. "Only two."

"Okay, okay," Henry snickers. "I can take the hint."

"Can you?" Blake asks directly.

Henry winks at me, shuts off the video game, and walks Lucy to the door. "I'll see you when I see you." How vaguely romantic. "Off you go." He starts shutting the door as she puts her hands up to halt the movement from the hallway.

"My shoes," she pouts, sticking her bottom lip out. "I left my shoes." Her whine makes me snicker, as I watch this scene unfold with Henry taking top rank as the Master of Douches.

Henry sighs as if Lucy is the most annoying person in the world. "I put them outside in the hall. I'll call you," he says, shutting the door and locking it. He turns and leans his back against it. "*Never.*" His eyes meet ours. "I owe you both for saving me from that unnatural disaster. She is so damn needy. And I'm pretty sure the plastic surgeon messed up on her jugs-of-juice. I don't think there's supposed to be any discharge. But what do I know?"

"Eww, Henry," Blake says, covering his ears.

He turns his attention to me, ignoring his actual room-mate. "There's only so much man meat loving I can put up with. I'm putting a Do Not Disturb sign on my dick for the day." He walks over to us and plops back down on the middle cushion between us. "What are we watching?"

Blake and I groan but do not make Henry move. I prop my feet up on his legs.

"Can you take off my socks and rub my feet, Henry?"

"Anything for you, Carly."

"It's Claire."

43

NIC

I pour some more whiskey and down it with one gulp, slamming the glass tumbler onto the kitchen island. I feel sick inside over Claire leaving and wanted to run after her, scoop her into my arms, and make her stay. Except, I couldn't. I have let things get too complicated. I thought with my heart instead of my brain for too long.

I never should have gotten involved with someone so close to my family, and yet here I sit like a pathetic shell wishing she would have kicked me in the nuts, so at least I would have physical pain to mask the emotional pain I'm currently feeling.

The way her heart broke in front of me, while I told her our fling was an interlude, is something I'll never forget.

I knew how this would all end, yet nothing mentally prepared me for the magnitude of just how tragic it would be.

I feel like shit. I probably look like it too. And not a

single cell in my body cares about anything other than drowning myself in the sorrows that I created for myself.

I could have stopped Claire from leaving, and yet, I simply allowed her to walk out of my life. While she may not realize it in this moment, I did her a favor.

I'm not boyfriend material.

And leading her on to think I could be is my biggest regret.

She didn't know the score, because to her, it never was a game.

There's a knock on the door. Whoever it is must have a key to be allowed onto this floor in the first place. I stumble to the door and open it, finding Mom with her arms full of linens and wedding decor. I take the supplies from her hands and place them on the dining room table.

"Nic, I wasn't expecting to find you here." She opens her arms up for a hug and I accept. I need it more than she will ever know, and yet, I'm not the victim in this shitstorm. I'm the villain. She pulls back after a few seconds and examines my appearance. "What's wrong? You look like you haven't slept in a month." Her hand touches my forehead. "Are you ill?"

"I'm fine," I say softly.

"You are obviously lying. Don't think I haven't been noticing you avoiding me either."

I rub at my forehead as a headache starts to form. "I was meaning to call you back."

"Sure. Now where is your brother?" she asks, looking behind me and around the room.

"He's in New York. I'm keeping Angie company until he's back."

"You boys keep ignoring my calls, and I'll just spontaneously pop into the office and cause a ruckus. How does that sound?"

"Sorry, Mom," I groan. "Been busy with work."

"There's more to life than making everything into a business transaction, Nic. When are you going to go on a vacation? Take some time off? Live a little. Maybe date again?"

Before I'm able to give Mom a canned answer, Angie runs down the stairs and greets her future mother-in-law in a huge hug.

"Thank you for coming today to work out these last-minute details. You always have such an amazing eye for these types of things."

"I love that you are allowing me to be a part of this amazing celebration. Graham sure is lucky that he found you. We both know how difficult that man can be."

Angie laughs over Mom's candid descriptions. "We are both pretty lucky," Angie says softly.

"I've been trying to call Claire with no luck getting her to pick up. Is she going to join us this session?" Mom asks.

"She texted me a bit ago and said that something came up. So, I guess we are on our own."

I can't help but worry about Claire. My tracking app only provides the GPS coordinates—no details. Separating is for the best, but the feelings of wanting the best for her did not just go away. I will always want what is best for her. If only she would realize that I'm essentially protecting her from me. She was right when she said she deserved better. I'm not ever going to be the man she dreams about.

"Since Graham is gone, how about you come back to

Hillsboro with me for the night and we can work out the last few details for the wedding?"

Angie looks at me, and I can tell she is biting her tongue over my appearance. I must look pretty unkempt, because she keeps staring at my hair.

"Is that okay, Nic? It'll give you some time to not have to babysit me," she teases, but it pretty much is the truth. Graham doesn't take any chances when it comes to her welfare.

"Yeah. That sounds like a good plan."

"Good," Mom says, "now we can talk about my boys behind their back and you can fill me in on every little detail that they try to hide from me."

Angie huffs out a laugh and runs upstairs to pack a bag. Thankfully, it doesn't take her long, because I know Mom cannot resist interrogating me just to fill the silence. My head is throbbing with a headache, and I just need to shower and lie down.

Once the penthouse is empty, I drag my feet into the guest room's shower and let the cold water chill my body. I stay there with the water cascading down my shoulders until I feel numb. I dry myself off and toss on a pair of black workout pants and a gray T-shirt. I find Graham's home gym and set the weight limits on the equipment. I start the surround sound to play my favorite metal music through the speakers and push myself through the circuit. I maintain a punishing rhythm until my body cannot take any more reps.

When I'm drenched in sweat and doubling over from exhaustion, I hit the shower again. I meander back into the bedroom and flop down on the bed. When the smell of sweet vanilla fills my nostrils, I throw myself off the sheets as if they turned into fire. I rip and tug until the entire bed is stripped of all the reminders of Claire. I toss the fabric into the laundry bin and settle on top of the bare mattress, too worn out to remake the bed.

I allow sleep to win. But it is the haunting images of Claire that trap me in my nightmare.

Right before the sun sets, I crack and give Claire a call to tell her I'm sorry. I click on her number and hear the sweet sound of her voice recording stating that she is unavailable to take my call. The words I want to say get stuck in my throat, so I just click end and toss my phone on the bed.

In reality, what is there to say? It's not like I've changed my mind. I'm damaged on the inside. I want to blame Tara, but maybe it is really me. Maybe there is some part of me that allowed a woman into my life who was going to hurt me. I easily ignored some red flags early on with Tara. I painted her to be the picture of perfection in my head. I set such high expectations on what I wanted out of a relation-ship—a marriage—that maybe she was destined to fail. Cheating might have been her easy way out. It sure made me never want her again. Problem is, it is ruining me for every girl after her.

When things ended with Tara and the pain wore off, I had this overwhelming sense of relief that I dodged some kind of bullet that was heading straight for my bank account. With Claire, I don't feel like I have dodged anything. The moment she walked out of the penthouse was the moment my heart bled for what could have been.

Claire deserves better than me. And as lousy as I feel right now, I'm pretty sure anyone else could fit that role.

My phone buzzes from the bed, and I snatch it up thinking it is Claire returning my call. I look at the caller ID and see that it is Tyler, my personal henchman and information seeker. I know he's not calling to chitchat about the weather, so I brace myself for whatever news he will surely share.

"What's up?"

"Figure this is redundant information but just wanted to let you know that Claire is at the mixer event for Entice at the mansion tonight and is working the crowd."

"Fuck," I hiss. "Really? You sure?" I completely forgot that an event was even scheduled for tonight. It's not like I keep close tabs anymore on Entice happenings, since I have hired people to keep me in the loop when necessary.

"Yeah, I'm sure. There's no mistaking a woman in red with a firecracker personality."

"Fuck," I groan.

She does love to wear bold colors. And she looks radiant when she does. Anger boils inside me at her not even giving herself twelve hours to let things settle between us.

"She is going to start a war here among the men pining after her."

"Keep an eye on her until I can get there."

"Okay, but hurry or get the bail money ready. There's only so much I can do from the shadows."

"I should be there in about forty-five minutes."

I end the call and toss my head back to look at the ceiling. What the hell is she doing at a mixer event meant primarily to meet men and set up future dates? Is she trying to make me suffer or just hellbent on making a buck?

I take my third shower of the day, throw on a black suit, and take the stairs down to the parking garage. I have an energy running through me that I haven't felt all day. The mansion that is rented for the escort mixer events is in the beautiful countryside, several miles outside of the city limits of Portland. With rolling hills and the most enchanting land-scaping, it is a breathtaking venue. No wonder Angie and Graham are choosing to say their vows here.

I toss my keys to the valet and take the stairs two at a time. I nod to the doorman and make my way into the entry-way, scanning the area for Claire. I find her at the bar, surrounded by other female escorts who are having a lively chat about something.

When Claire spots me, she takes a long sip from her beverage, eyes me up and down, and flares her nostrils. She looks ready to fight, and I brace myself for whatever it is she thinks will make herself feel better.

"Oh, yay me," she mumbles, tossing back the last of her drink. "Listen up, ladies." All eyes turn to her, as if she is the kingpin of the group, about to make some grand announcement. "We have another alpha asshole in our midst."

"Claire…"

But she ignores my attempt to silence her. "Ladies, meet the one and only Nic Commitment-Phobe Hoffman. You know, our brothel-keeper. The man without emotions. The guy who hits 'em and quits 'em. The pimp with the golden dick." She claps her hands loudly, aiming them in my direc-tion as a tribute. "Take a bow, Nic. Take a bow."

My eyes twitch as I take in the scene and listen to her rattle off her word vomit for all to hear. Her face looks puffy underneath her layers of heavy makeup, and I wonder if she has been crying. "Claire…"

She ignores my warning. "He may be the boss with some calm and collected manners, but this man will fuck the panties right off your pelvis. But as soon as it comes to showing any true emotion, this bad boy only knows one— fear. But nothing lasts forever. Everything has an expiration date and mine hit its deadline." She signals for another drink, and I can already tell she has had one too many.

I grab Claire by the elbow and pull her away from the bar. I lead her to the back patio, despite her resistance and cursing.

"We need to talk," I say calmly.

"Are you here to purchase me, Nic? Give me a little test drive to warm up your dick again? I'm sure it's gotten cold."

"What? No."

"Good. Because you have a shitty refund policy!"

"Just calm down, please."

I let go of her and she whirls around, her hand stretched out to slap me. I catch it midair and hold it in place. Her face twists into a wince, and I let go of her hand. What the hell? Is she hurt?

"Fuck you, Nic Hoffman!" she fumes with rage.

"Hey now, use your good girl words."

She shoves at me. "Don't follow me."

"Don't go dating some assholes just to piss me off."

"Why do you care? I'm no longer your concern. Are you

one of those types that if *you don't want me, let's make it so no one wants me?*"

"I don't want you to get hurt," I say softly.

"Too fucking late. I'm hurt." She points a perfectly manicured finger at me. "*You* hurt me. You broke us. I will never forgive you either."

"I know." My words come out sad. And in a way, I hope she follows through on her promise. She'll be way better off if she steers clear of me.

"So stay out of my life. Let me move on the way I choose to move on."

"I'm not going to sit back and watch you fill up your calendar with a bunch of men."

"Well, you can't stop people offering." She makes a face, and I can't tell what is going on in her head. "Just like I can't."

"Oh, I *can* stop it."

"So, you are going to fire me?"

"Maybe."

Claire turns to stare out at the water in the pool. The lights are on and it looks majestic under the night sky. She tips her head back and loses herself to the stars. It wasn't that long ago she was catching raindrops on her tongue. It wasn't that long ago we were taking pictures with a unicorn selfie stick. It wasn't that long ago she was trying to swim in a Vegas fountain. It wasn't that long ago...

And yet so much has happened in between.

But there is nothing carefree about her now.

Stress mars her features, and I'm the artist who painted her world with darkness.

When Claire has had a moment to collect her thoughts,

she turns to me with fire in her eyes. "You Hoffman boys really have some nerve, don't you? You walk around the earth stomping on anyone in your way and exerting all of your weird control techniques. You're not my pimp. You don't get to choose or reject men for me."

Claire turns around and storms back into the mansion. I follow closely behind her. She walks up to a group of men, gathered around in a circle talking about the stock market.

"Sorry to interrupt," she says boldly, "but on the off chance that you find that my agency profile disappears from the website, then use this number to set up another date with me." She digs into her handbag and pulls out these little black business cards that have lips pressed into the corner. The graphic is embossed using a red, shiny ink. "Looking forward to seeing some of you in the near future."

"She's off-limits," I say with finality.

Claire glares at me and barks out, "That's not true. Ignore him."

"You proposition her, and you can expect to be exited from the agency. Your membership will be revoked."

"He's bluffing."

My eyes twitch at the scene Claire is making. I reach for her elbow and usher her out of the mansion as fast as I can with her wearing her deathtrap stilettos and grabbing appetizers off trays on the way out. She tosses a few into her mouth, in between slapping at my hand to let her go.

"Go home and calm down."

As soon as I say the word *home*, Claire's bottom lip trembles and tears burst out of her eyes. It feels like I have a self-inflicted stab wound on my heart that I keep reopening.

It takes everything in me not to hold her to me and tell her that it'll be okay. She will be okay.

I'm not good for her.

I'm not good for anyone.

Even if I was looking for something more permanent, Claire and I are not compatible. I keep hurting her indirectly and in return, I am hurting myself.

I motion for the valet to hand me her keys. "Get a driver here now to take Miss Nettles back to her place," I say purposefully.

"Of course, Mr. Hoffman," the worker says.

I turn my attention back to Claire. "I'll get your car dropped off at the loft."

She walks away from me along the cobblestone driveway, refusing to make eye contact. Against the curb, she rests her body, pulling her knees up toward her chest and wrapping her arms tightly around them.

I'm so sorry, Claire.

I broke us.

There's no one to blame but me.

When the driver pulls up and helps Claire into the backseat, she rolls down the window and sticks out both middle fingers.

I deserve her rage. I deserve everything she has to dish out to me.

And the sad part is, she has already moved on. This time without me.

Bye, Claire.

ACKNOWLEDGMENTS

I would like to acknowledge that I would not have continued along this writing journey without the support from my friends, my community, my readers (at every stage), my family, my editors, and the embrace from fellow authors who are eager to answer questions and share their knowledge. How do I say thank you, when thank you seems to be not enough?

You all have built me up instead of breaking me down. The words of encouragement... The enthusiastic cheering for me... The likes/shares/comments/saves on my posts...

Have changed my life.

When I started writing back in 2012/2013, it was during a time in my life that I didn't think I could have children. I was so alone going through my infertility journey, so I took to writing stories about love and redemption. I felt flawed. So I created my own flawed characters and my own book babies to take my mind off the utter devastation of my body failing me.

When I was finally able to get pregnant, my books took the backseat to this life I always dreamed about having. However, my characters haunted my mind. They begged to have their story told.

Thank you for giving me the confidence to share a part of my heart with you, and cherishing it while it is in your possession.